Whistling Past the Graveyard

ALSO BY SUSAN CRANDALL

Back Roads

Sleep No More

Seeing Red

Pitch Black

A Kiss in Winter

On Blue Falls Pond

Promises to Keep

Magnolia Sky

The Road Home

Whistling Past the Graveyard

Susan Crandall

Gallery Books
New York London Toronto Sydney New Delhi

Gallery Books
A Division of Simon & Schuster, Inc.
1230 Avenue of the Americas
New York, NY 10020

This book is a work of fiction. Any references to historical events, real people, or real places are used fictitiously. Other names, characters, places, and events are products of the author's imagination, and any resemblance to actual events or places or persons, living or dead, is entirely coincidental.

First Gallery Books hardcover edition June 2013

For information about special discounts for bulk purchases, please contact Simon & Schuster Special Sales at 1-866-506-1949 or *business@simonandschuster.com.*

The Simon & Schuster Speakers Bureau can bring authors to your live event. For more information or to book an event contact the Simon & Schuster Speakers Bureau at 1-866-248-3049 or visit our website at *www.simonspeakers.com.*

Designed by

Manufactured in the United States of America

10 9 8 7 6 5 4 3 2 1

Library of Congress Cataloging-in-Publication Data

ISBN 978-1-4767-0772-3
ISBN 978-1-4767-0773-0(ebook)

For my family,

Bill, Reid, Melissa, Olivia, Allison, Mark and my mother Margie.

This book was so special to me that I couldn't choose just one of you.

1

July 1963

My grandmother said she prays for me every day. Which was funny, because I'd only ever heard Mamie pray, "Dear Lord, give me strength." That sure sounded like a prayer for herself—and Mrs. Knopp in Sunday school always said our prayers should only ask for things for others. Once I made the mistake of saying that out loud to Mamie and got slapped into next Tuesday for my sassy mouth. My mouth always worked a whole lot faster than my good sense.

Don't get the wrong idea, Mamie never put me in the emergency room like Talmadge Metsker's dad did him (for sure nobody believed the stories about Talmadge being a klutz). Truth be told, Mamie didn't smack me as often as her face said she thought I needed it; so I reckon she should get credit for tolerance. I heard it often enough: I can be a trial.

I was working real hard at stopping words that were better off swallowed; just like Mamie and my third-grade teacher, Mrs. Jacobi, said I should. I got in trouble plenty at school for being mouthy, too. Most times I was provoked, but Principal Morris didn't seem to count that as an excuse. Keeping one's counsel was important for a lady in order to be an acceptable person in society. Not that Daddy and I thought I needed to become a lady, but it meant a lot to Mamie, so Daddy said I had to try.

Anyway, I'd only been about half-successful and had been on restriction twice already since school let out at the end of May. Once for sass. And the second time . . . well, I don't really count that as my fault. If it wasn't for a dang rotten board, it never woulda happened.

Out past the edge of town was a haunted house, a big, square thing with porches up- and downstairs. It had a strange room stacked on top that was made most all of windows—that's where people saw the ghost lights on foggy nights. There wasn't a lick of paint left anywhere on that house, and the shutters had lost most all their teeth. Vines grew through the broken windows on the first floor, snaking around the inside and back up the fireplace chimney. It was hundreds and hundreds of years old, from back in the days of big cotton. I'd been there plenty of times, but I'd never seen a ghost—and I wanted to see a ghost almost as much as I wanted a record player. I figured my problem was I'd always been there in the daytime. What kinda ghost would be out in broad daylight? So I got me a plan. After Mamie went to bed, I snuck out, rode my bicycle out there to see my ghost, planning to be back in bed long before she woke up. I pedaled as fast as I could and had been all sweaty and out of breath, and my legs almost too shaky to climb the front steps, by the time I got there.

I hadn't been inside that house more than a minute, not near long enough for a ghost to get interested in me, when I stepped on that rotten board. One leg shot through to the basement. I kicked and pushed and hollered, but there wasn't no getting out. It was the middle of the morning the next day when the police found me. Mamie was madder than I'd ever seen her . . . and that's saying something. I got restriction and the belt and my bicycle taken away for the rest of the summer. It'd been worth it if I'd seen my ghost. I reckon all my hollerin' and kickin' had kept it away.

I'd been off restriction for over a week. The Fourth of July parade and fireworks was coming up the next day, the best part of the whole summer—other than Daddy's visits home, which were almost as scarce as holidays. He worked down in the Gulf on an oil rig 'cause all the jobs in Cayuga Springs didn't pay as good. We had to talk with letters 'cause there wasn't a phone out there in the ocean. Sometimes he called from

Biloxi when he got a weekend off, but that was long distance and cost a lot of money so we had to talk fast, and Mamie hogged the phone telling him all sorts of stuff I know he didn't care about. I did most of the letter talking between me and Daddy; he wasn't much of a letter writer. But he liked mine and said they always made him smile, so I wrote a lot.

On July 3 I woke up with bees in my belly. As I put on my white Levi's shorts and tied my Red Ball Jets, I promised myself I wouldn't sass or do anything to make Mamie need to say a prayer. I couldn't risk missing everything—and that's what Mamie'd do, she'd ground me 'cause she knew that would hurt way more than a wallop. Mamie always knew what punishment I most dreaded. It was like she could see inside my head.

If I got in trouble now, I'd have to wait a whole nother year for fireworks.

I took extra care in making my bed just right; I even made hospital corners on the bottom sheet. I zipped my pj's into the Tinker Bell pajama bag that Daddy gave me two Christmases ago and set it just so against my pillow, nice and neat. I even picked up the dirty sock I'd dropped last night on the way to the hamper instead of kickin' it under my dresser with the others that Mamie thought the washer had eaten.

Then I stood back and tried to look at my room through Mamie's squinty, work-checking eyes.

A-okay.

I felt good as I headed down to the kitchen, sure that she wouldn't find nothing wrong with my room today.

Through the screen door I saw her hanging a load of our pink bath towels on the line that ran from the back of the house to the corner of the garage. She had two clothespins in her mouth, her lipstick making a bright red *O* around them. She had on a yellow dress and flat canvas shoes that matched. Even this early with no one but me and the squirrel in the backyard tree to see, Mamie took care about her appearance. She was always looking at magazine pictures of Jackie Kennedy and trying to fix herself up like her—Mamie even got a new haircut last year. Worryin' 'bout how I looked was one part of being a lady I wasn't looking forward to. Thank goodness I was only nine and a half and still had some time left.

With a quick glance to make sure Mamie was still busy pegging towels, I opened the bottom cabinet door and stepped on the shelf. Why she expected me to fetch the step stool all the way from the utility room every time I needed something from the top cupboard, when the shelf on the bottom worked just fine, was one of Egypt's mysteries. I got down my favorite bowl, Daddy's from when he was a kid; the picture on the bottom had faded so much you could barely see the cowboy and his lasso anymore.

I poured myself a bowl of Sugar Frosted Flakes—they're grrrrrreat!—and before I even got a spoonful to my mouth, Mamie come in the back door and said, "Good morning, Jane."

The spoon stopped halfway to my face; milk ran over the edge and dripped onto the table. "Starla," I said through pinched lips, but was careful not to look up at her 'cause she was sure to think I had on what she called my defiant face.

"We agreed yesterday to start callin' you by your middle name," Mamie said just as if it was the honest truth. "It's so much more suitable for a young lady."

We hadn't agreed. Mamie agreed. I just stopped disagreeing.

I started to say that out loud, then remembered my self-promise not to sass.

"It's high time for you to start thinking about how the world looks at you," she said. "Your name is one of the first things people know." Mamie was real concerned over what people know about us. She stood up real straight and stuck out her hand like she was going to shake hands with an invisible somebody standing beside the sink. Then in a prissy, high voice she said, "'How do you do? I'm Jane Claudelle.'" She switched back to her normal Mamie voice. "See how nice that sounds. *Starla* makes people think of a trailer park"—she flipped her hand in the air—"just sittin' there waiting for the next tornado." Mamie had a real thing against trailer parks. We weren't rich, couldn't even afford help like the LeCounts next door, but Mamie liked to make sure I remembered there was folks out there who had less than us.

Fireworks. Fireworks. Remember the fireworks.

I shoved the Frosted Flakes in my mouth to keep all the words spinning around in my head from shootin' out.

Truth be told, no matter how hard Mamie tried to make me agree, I'd never give up the only thing my momma gave me before she went away—the only thing left since Mamie burned Mr. Wiggles with the Wednesday trash the last week of third grade anyway. She said he was "too filthy for human contact." I know nine-going-on-ten was too old for stuffed animals, but it still felt wrong going to bed without him.

"Daddy likes my name," I said after I swallowed. Mamie liked everything about Daddy, so that couldn't be considered sass . . . could it?

Mamie huffed. "Porter let Lucinda have anything she wanted—and see what it got him." The way she was looking at me made me think I was what he got and he'd be a whole lot better off without me. But I was Daddy's girl; he'd be lost without me.

"Lucinda—" Mamie started.

"Lulu." The word was out of my mouth before my mind could grab ahold of it. All the sudden, I felt like I was sliding on ice, arms flailin', about to fall flat. Lulu had told me not to tell.

"What?" Mamie's head turned and her brown eyes stared at me.

I'd started it. If I clammed up now, it'd be even worse. I dunked a flake floating in the milk with my spoon, staring at it as it popped right back up. "She wants to be called Lulu," I said real quiet, not sassy at all.

"Since when?" Mamie's red lips pinched together.

"She said so in my last birthday card." My birthday cards from Lulu was private, even Daddy wouldn't let Mamie snoop in them.

"Certainly not by her own child!"

"Now that I'm gettin' so grown up, she said it'd be better for her career if people think we're sisters."

"Career my—" Mamie snapped her mouth shut like she did when she wanted to yell at me in the grocery store but couldn't because we was in public. "What will people think, you talkin' like that? You call her Mother or Momma, or I'll get out the soap." She sighed. "Lulu, dear Lord, give me strength."

I bit my tongue and slid out of my seat.

Real quick, I washed my bowl and spoon and set them in the drainer, all the while the pressure was buildin' up inside me, like it always did before I did something that got me in trouble. Lulu was gonna to be famous, that's the only reason she left me and Daddy when I was just a baby. People around here were so jealous . . . so was Mamie, that's why she always looked so sour whenever Lulu's name come up. Lulu was gonna be famous all right, and then she'd come back and get me and Daddy. We were gonna live in a big house in Nashville with horses and whatnot, and Mamie would have to stay stuck here in Cayuga Springs all by her hateful self.

Just before I went out the back screen door, I turned around and looked at Mamie. I was real proud when I kept my voice respectful. "My name is Starla. Not Jane."

Then I run out the back screen before she could say anything else. I heard it slam behind me, but kept running around the corner of the house.

I was real surprised not to hear Mamie hollerin' for me to come back.

I decided to spend some time in my fort, just to stay out of Mamie's sight so I wouldn't fall into getting in trouble. Course my fort wasn't really a fort, but a giant, waxy-leafed magnolia in our side yard. Mamie said it was almost a hundred years old. Back before I knew people weren't as old as I thought they were, I asked if she remembered when it sprouted. She'd scrunched up her face like she was gonna be mad before she laughed and told me she was only forty-two years old, too young to even be a grandmother of a six-year-old.

Anyway, the tree. The branches go clean down to the ground and there's just enough space for me to get inside. Nobody can see me. I keep Daddy's old Howdy Doody lunch box in there with stuff I don't want Mamie to stick her nosy nose into—mostly stuff that belonged to my momma and whatnot. I'd even found two pictures of her in a drawer in Daddy's room. Mamie kept everything in there just the same as it had been when Daddy'd been growing up. I wasn't even supposed to go inside, even though Daddy had told Mamie I could have his room 'cause it was bigger and he wasn't hardly ever here. Mamie had told Daddy she'd think about it, but that was a lie. When I asked her when I'd be able to change rooms, she'd looked at me with those hateful eyes she gets and said, "Never." Now I sneak in there and sleep at night sometimes, even though I never even wanted to before. What with Mamie's bedroom being downstairs, she never even knew. I was always careful not to leave clues.

I opened the lunch box and pulled out the birthday cards from Lulu—one for every year except for when I turned six; that one must have got lost in the mail.

I laid on my back and read them, tracing my finger over the big, loopy *L* in *Love you* and the little *x*'s and *o*'s that were kisses and hugs sent through the mail. I spent some time thinking about Momma—Lulu recording her songs up in Nashville, getting famous. The memory of her was worn and fuzzy on the edges, since I hadn't seen her since I was three. But I know I have the exact same color of red hair, so that's the brightest spot in the picture I kept in my head.

Back when Momma and Daddy and me all lived together, I remember liking to twist her hair around my finger while she held me on her hip. I loved the way it felt soft and slippery, like the satin edge of my blanket. Momma didn't like it though, 'cause she'd spent a long time getting it to look just right and I messed it up. I remember her and Daddy getting in a fight once when she smacked my hand away. It was all my fault, and I'd felt bad. When we all got to live together again, I'd be careful not to cause any fights. I put away the birthday cards and closed the lunch box. Then I just laid there for a spell, watching light dance with shadows and thinking about what I was gonna name my horse. By 10:32—I knew the time exactly 'cause Daddy had given me a really neat Timex with a black leather band for Christmas—it was already about a thousand degrees out. The brick street out front looked like it was wiggling from the heat. Dogs had already crawled under porches and into garages to get out of the hot sun. They would come out after sunset with cobwebs on their noses and dirt clinging to their coats like powdered sugar.

Wish I had a dog.

One like Lassie.

She'd follow me everywhere. I was thinking on how she coulda gone to get help when I fell through the floor in the haunted house when I heard *clack-clack-chhhhhh, chhhhhhh, chhhhhhh, chhhhhh, clack-chhhhhh chhhhhh-clack.* I knew who was coming, wearing the metal, clamp-on skates she'd just got for her fifth birthday—Priscilla Panichelli. I called her Prissy Pants. She wore dresses with cancan slips and patent leather shoes every ding-dong day. She wasn't even gonna have to work at changing into a lady when her time came.

I was kinda surprised she'd risk getting those shoes all scuffed; skating on our broken-up sidewalk was dangerous business—which accounted for the *clack*s. I bet her big brother, Frankie, who was in my grade and called her way worse things than Prissy Pants, had made it a dare.

I moved so I was behind the tree trunk and held real still, just in case. Besides dressing like a doll, Prissy Pants could be a real pain in the behind with her goody-two-shoes, tattletale ways.

Then I heard trouble. A bicycle was coming fast with a card clappin' against the spokes. It meant only one thing: Jimmy Sellers, turd of the century. Jimmy was gonna be a hood, anybody could see that. But Mamie, and truth be told a lot of the other old people on our street, thought he was a "nice, polite Christian boy" 'cause he was a real brownnoser, too.

Prissy Pants was like a lightning rod to Jimmy's thunderbolt. She was just too shiny and clean to not try and mess up—even though it always seemed like an accident.

As I said, I had no warm place in my own heart for Prissy Pants, but Jimmy was twelve, almost a grown-up. Him picking on her was just . . . wrong.

I held my breath and hoped that bicycle would buzz right on by.

Chhhhhh-clack-clack. Silence.

Prissy Pants must have seen Jimmy.

The card slapped the spokes just a little faster, and I thought trouble would just keep rolling down the street. I moved around the trunk and peeked out just in time to see Jimmy's bike jump the curb and head right for Priscilla.

She stood there in front of the LeCounts' house like a possum staring at a Buick.

Jimmy pedaled faster.

I jumped out of my fort, too far away to do nothin' but hold my breath.

At the very last second, he cut the handlebars and swerved around her. Priscilla jerked backward and fell flat on her flouncy heinie. One of her skates come loose from her shoe and hung from her ankle by the leather strap—she wouldn't need that skate key hanging around her neck to get that one off.

She squealed, then started a real-tears cry, not her usual just-for-that-I'm-gonna-get-you-in-trouble cry.

Jimmy swooped in a circle and come back around. He stopped his bike and looked down at her. "Gosh, looks like you'd better practice some more with them skates."

Prissy just cried louder and used her key to loosen her other skate.

I got what Daddy calls my "red rage." I was hot and cold at the same time. My nose and ears and fingertips tingled and I couldn't breathe.

I run down the block and grabbed his handlebars, jerking them to the side. Instead of making Jimmy fall down, he just let the bike go and stepped over it as it fell into the grass beside the walk.

"Go back to your tree, shitbird." Jimmy shoved my shoulder.

"Shitbird!" I swung. His nose popped.

The blood hadn't even touched his top lip when I heard Mamie yell, "Starla Jane Claudelle!"

Good-bye, fireworks.

2

I'd had trouble sleeping because of the sticky heat and thinking on all I was gonna to miss: cherry snow cones and fried okra, winning the blue ribbon in the horseshoe throw (this woulda been my fourth year in a row as champion for the ten-and-under age group), penny candy falling like rain from the parade floats, fireworks and sparklers. It was enough to get my ears burnin' all over again. Grounded on the Fourth of July, of all days. And Miss Prissy Pants hadn't even stuck around to come in on my side of the story; did nothin' but get up and bawl all the way home. And of course, Jimmy had been real convincing—I bet his nose didn't even hurt that much.

Mamie had made me walk Jimmy's bike home while he held one of our dish towels filled with ice on his nose and she fussed over him like he'd been crippled or something. She made me apologize to Mrs. Sellers (which she probably deserved 'cause she had such a horrible kid for a son) and to Jimmy (which had nearly made me barf). The whole way back to our house I got the ladies-do-and-ladies-do-not lecture, which started and ended with how embarrassed she was by my "trashy, street-gutter" behavior and always had a bit about not saying *ain't*. Hey, I didn't even want to be a lady.

After stewin' and sweatin' all night, I was tired and extra grouchy Fourth of July morning. Guess it didn't really matter; sass or not, I was still on restriction on the best day of the summer.

I walked into the kitchen, real quiet, hoping to avoid another lecture. Mamie sat at the table in her pink-and-white seersucker housecoat, her pink slippers, and a pink lace hairnet over her pink sponge curlers—I forgot to mention, Mamie liked pink best of all the colors and was real sad that my red hair kept her from buying me pink dresses. She was looking at the S&H Green Stamp catalog, drinking coffee and smoking a cigarette. Mamie loved that catalog enough to marry it. Our grocery even had double-stamp days; if we was out of bread and one of those days was in sight, we'd go breadless. Which is kinda funny, 'cause we got our toaster with Green Stamps.

Mamie looked up at me. I braced myself; if I got sassy now, who knew how long I'd be on restriction—probably till Labor Day. But she didn't start yammering about me being a lady, or being an embarrassment to her and Daddy (even though Daddy wouldn't even know to be embarrassed if Mamie didn't keep telling him stuff). She just nodded toward the fancy, new Norge refrigerator Daddy had bought for her. She'd been so proud of it that she'd made the whole bridge club come into the kitchen to look at it. A long list of chores was taped on the door. She must have been up all night thinking up stuff for me to do.

"That should keep you out of trouble today while I'm gone," Mamie said in a way that said this wasn't gonna be the end of my punishments.

I felt a hot prickle run over my skin—the red-rage prickle. I looked her right in the eye and said, "Maybe I'll just run away from home. Then you won't be embarrassed by me anymore—and you'll have to do all this stuff yourself." Like I said, I was grouchy.

I half-expected a slap, or at least another day stuck onto my grounding, but Mamie just blew out a stream of cigarette smoke and pushed herself up from the table and headed out of the kitchen. "I'll go pack your bag." Over her shoulder she said, "But remember, you can't leave until next week, after your restriction is over."

Gritting my teeth, I snatched the list off the refrigerator. It was worse than Cinderella's.

I stomped back up to my room without breakfast. Milk would have soured right in my mouth.

While Mamie went to the Fourth Festival, I was Rapunzel in the tower. I crumpled the chore list and threw it into the corner of my bedroom. I sat on the floor in front of my window with my elbows on the sill and watched as the LeCounts loaded their station wagon with a picnic basket and lawn chairs and four of the five kids piled in. Ernestine, their colored maid, stood on the porch holding Teddy, the baby, raising his chubby arm for him to wave as the family pulled away. She was probably glad to see 'em go. I liked Ernestine fine, even if she was a grouch most of the time, nippin' at me to not step on the flowers and to stay away from the cistern. I reckon she had cause to be grouchy. Them LeCount kids was the wildest and noisiest in town; and there just kept getting to be more of them all the time.

Our upstairs is hot as the hinges of Hades. Usually if I wanted to stay out of sight, I'd take to my fort. But today, I sat in my bedroom. I kinda hoped when Mamie got home late this afternoon, she'd find me passed out from heatstroke. Then she'd feel bad over ruining the one good day of the summer for me. Maybe I'd even have to be put in the hospital; that'd fix her.

I sat looking out the window and sweating for long enough that my hair started to stick to my forehead. Then I started to get ideas: What if I went to the parade? Mamie was at the park. I could go stand with the big crowd of kids on the corner near Adler's Drug Store, where you had two chances at candy when the parade turned from Magnolia Street onto Beaumont Avenue. Mamie would never know. If I came back right after the parade, I could be home before her easy. I'd hurry through enough of the chores to keep her from being too mad. If I looked tired and pitiful enough, all sweaty and weak from hunger, maybe she'd let me go to see the fireworks. Bet she wanted to see them; and I ain't allowed to stay home alone after dark.

This could work out fine. Course I'd miss getting my blue ribbon and the snow cones, but at least I'd have some of my Fourth of July.

But what if Prissy Pants or somebody from church saw me? Or worse, Mrs. Sellers, who knew I was grounded 'cause Mamie made a big deal of it in front of her.

Just then I heard Jimmy's bike coming down the street, headed toward town. He had a big, white bandage across his nose. He looked up, saw me in the window, and gave me the finger. I didn't know exactly what that meant, but I knew it was dirty.

Well, that was it. No way was I letting the turd of the century see the parade and ride back past here with his pockets full of candy while I melted into a big puddle of lady.

I slipped out the back door and down the alley, not that anyone was left in the neighborhood to tattle. Still, at each cross street, I looked careful before I stepped out in the open.

I waited behind the post office until a group of kids heading toward the parade passed by. I talked Drew Drover—he'd had a crush on me since second grade—out of his Ole Miss Rebels baseball cap and put it on over my red hair.

Ten minutes later I wiggled into the middle of the group of kids in front of Adler's Drug. The color guard had just passed, and people were puttin' their hats back on. The first float rolled by, the one with the Cotton Queen and her princesses, and a long line of floats and horses and marching bands was behind it. Candy flew like cottonwood seed.

I was a genius.

My luck held through the parade (thank you, baby Jesus). No tattletales saw me, and my pockets was bulging with candy. It'd be a whole lot easier to do my chores eating Pixy Stix and jawbreakers—after all, I hadn't eaten breakfast.

All of the kids started to head toward the park. I hung back, wishing I could go, too. Even though it'd be several more hours before Mamie got home, the park was too dangerous. Not only was she there, but Drew had taken his cap back and there would be way too many church ladies around for Mamie not to get wind that I wasn't home doing chores like I was supposed to be.

"Starla!"

I quick ducked behind the light post. I was tall and skinny, but not skinny enough to hide behind a light post. I was caught.

I peeked around the post and saw Patti Lynn Todd, my best friend in all the world, running toward me. Patti Lynn had a real family with a sister and three brothers and lived in a big house on Magnolia Street. She even had a dog.

"I been lookin' all over for you," Patti Lynn said, tugging my hand. "Come on, you're gonna to be late signin' up for the games."

"Can't. I'm grounded."

"'Cause you broke Jimmy Sellers's nose?" Patti Lynn knew me well enough not to ask why I was at the parade if I was grounded.

"How'd you know?"

"Everybody knows. Prissy Pants' brother told. Jimmy's still trying to get everyone to believe that it was Rodney Evans who done it."

I laughed. Nobody'd believe that story. Rodney Evans was the biggest hood in town, wore a ducktail and rolled-up sleeves on his T-shirt. He walked the streets in his black boots with metal taps on the heels just looking for trouble. And he usually found it. If he'd lit into Jimmy, Jimmy would have had lots worse than a broken nose.

"I'm on restriction for a whole week."

Patti Lynn smiled. "It was worth it. Maybe Jimmy's nose'll heal all crooked." She linked her arm through mine. "Come on. I'll hang out with you for a while."

"You'll miss all the games and whatnot."

She shrugged. "Don't care. It's no fun without you."

We headed to the school playground, inventing crazy stories that Jimmy would probably try to get people to believe to hide the truth that he'd been beaten by a girl.

Patti Lynn was the best best friend ever made.

Twenty minutes later, Patti Lynn and I was making daisy chains out of clover blossoms, so I didn't notice the pink-and-white Packard pull up until I heard the car door slam. Mrs. Sellers, for who knows what reason, had showed up at the playground.

Wish Mamie could see her, out here for all the world to see in red-checkered shorts—Mamie could give her the ladies do and ladies-do-not lecture.

Mrs. Sellers come flying across the pea gravel fast enough that it was shootin' out from beneath her Keds. I guess I forgot to mention that yesterday I'd discovered she was real prickly when it came to her "little boy."

"Starla Claudelle! Your grandmomma know you're here?" By then she was on me, diggin' her fingers into my arm and gritting her nice white teeth at me. All the sudden, I was sorry I'd ever felt sorry for her; she looked like a witch hiding under perfume and powder. I shoulda known a person with a son like Jimmy couldn't be too good herself.

I looked right up at her with my defiant face. "Yes, ma'am. She knows."

"Well, we'll just go and see about that." She pulled me toward her car so fast I couldn't do nothing but run along beside her.

"Bye, Starla," Patti Lynn called. "See you later."

Fat chance. I was never gonna get off restriction.

As Mrs. Sellers yanked open the passenger door, she said, "Your grandmomma is right, you're no-good, cheap trash, just like your momma."

My ears started ringing. My face got hot and prickly. "When did she say that?" Sometimes I think she hates being my mamie—once she told me it was a shame I'd even been born, so I guess she does.

Mrs. Sellers looked at me with a wrinkled forehead. "What? Well . . . every time I see her, poor woman. Now get in the car." She tried to shove me in, but I dug in.

"My momma is gonna be famous. And your son is a mean son of a bitch!" It was the worst thing I'd ever overheard my daddy call anyone; so I figured it fit Jimmy Sellers just right. I yanked my arm free.

She made to grab me again, her face looking for all the world like Jimmy's when he was gonna beat the living daylights out of someone. I gave her a shove. She fell backwards squealin' like a stuck pig, landing in the dirt.

I ran like the devil hisself was on me.

"You come back here!" The screaming made words. "You're going to reform school for sure!"

I'd done it now. I was a goner.

I ran until my lungs burned like they was filled with hot rocks. Then I walked. That's when it was hardest not to cry—when I slowed down. Mamie said I was gonna end up in jail someday, said she'd be happy if they throwed away the key. So I knew she'd be happy to turn me in if I went back home. I wasn't sure what I was gonna do, but going back wasn't on my list. I was too worked up inside to think clear and make a plan, so I just kept going and hoped something came to me.

I'd already passed the lumber mill and the city dump. I'd turned at every crossroad I'd come to, figuring a straight line was easier for the police to follow. Still, I kept my ears peeled for the sound of the sheriff's siren. I wondered how long I'd have to go to prison if they caught me. I'd seen it on *Perry Mason* you could get fifteen years for assault with batteries . . . which was lawyer talk for beating someone up.

Feeling as low as skunk's toes, I wondered if I should maybe head for Nashville. Lulu was probably my only hope; she'd hide me. Daddy would just haul me back to Cayuga Springs 'cause he was all about accepting your just desserts. Besides, it'd break his heart to see his little girl go to prison. Mamie would probably do a dance when she figured out I wasn't never coming back to be an embarrassment to her ever again.

Trouble was, I didn't know how to get to Nashville, or even what direction I was headed exactly. I always went by rights and lefts, gas stations and flagpoles, not easts and wests; which was another disappointment to Mamie. I just couldn't get those directions to stick in my head unless I was standing on my own front porch, facing the street.

I tried to think about which way my house would be facing by taking my mind backwards to town, but I lost track of the turns and was no better off than before.

The sun wasn't any help neither, sitting up there high in the sky.

Maybe I could hitchhike. Somebody old enough to drive would surely know east from west. I'd have to be careful and not to hitch a ride with anyone from Cayuga Springs though.

That's when I realized I hadn't seen a single car on the road since I'd passed the lumber mill. Everybody was picnicking, playing games and swimming, not driving from place to place.

I walked along, sun beatin' down on my head between the shady spots, getting thirstier and thirstier. The sweat stung my eyes and my feet was swollen like melons inside my shoes. I closed my eyes and for a minute I could see my crumpled body beside the road with buzzards picking at my red hair and eyeballs.

That thought made me determined not to die, no matter how happy it might make Mamie and Mrs. Sellers. So I got my mind busy on something other than my misery.

I thought about the last time I saw my momma. Mamie said I was too young to remember, but she was wrong, wrong, wrong. I remember the way the sun sparked on her red hair—it was in a ponytail. I remember she picked me up and twirled me around before she put me in the car to go to Mamie's. Momma had been wearing a round skirt that spun out like a top. I remember she sang with the radio all the way there. I remember the way she smelled when she hugged me good-bye, like oranges and maple syrup . . . she'd made us pancakes for breakfast.

I hadn't eaten a pancake since.

I wondered if, when I saw her in Nashville, her hair would still be in a ponytail. Mamie kept my hair cut in a pageboy (she did the cutting herself, so my bangs were almost always whopper-jawed). She said nobody wanted to see that much red hair, especially if it's a rat's nest, which it most always was 'cause, when Mamie brushed it, she pulled so hard my scalp felt like it was being cut with a million little knives dipped in vinegar. When I got to be a teenager, I was gonna wear a ponytail and tie it with scarves that matched my clothes, just like Momma had.

Everybody in Cayuga Springs treated my momma like a secret. But it seemed like I was the only person they wanted to keep the secret from. Sometimes when Mamie had bridge club in the summer, I'd sit below the living-room window outside and listen. The ladies had plenty to say about Momma, all right. Hateful things. Lies. They squeezed them in between their bids and trumps, like it was part of the game. That was when I'd get a good red rage going and head into the house to tell them all to shut up—course I'd be punished, but it would be worth it. But so far, I'd never once got to say it. The second they heard the squeak of the screen door they got quiet all by themselves. It saved me being punished, but just one time I wished I'd been able to tell them how un-Christian-like they were.

Even Patti Lynn's mother talked about Momma on the telephone when she thought I couldn't hear: "Oh, you know, the little girl whose mother abandoned her. . . . Yes, the one who thinks she's going to be a singer in Nashville. Can you imagine? I feel just terrible for that child."

At school, my teachers and Principal Morris was extracareful never to mention my momma. It made me feel like I'd been hatched from an egg or something on Mamie's front porch.

I used to ask Daddy about Momma, about things she liked, what was her favorite color, did she hate spaghetti sauce and chicken livers like I did? He used to answer me. Then he got so he just said, "Starla, I already told you a million times. I'm sure it's in your head somewhere, look for it." He didn't get mad exactly. But it always made him leave the room, so I stopped asking.

Momma was even getting to be a secret with Daddy; course she'd always been a secret with Mamie.

Secrets. Secrets. Secrets. They made me feel ashamed of loving my own momma; made me do it in secret.

Well, once I got to Nashville, I'd be able to love her right out loud.

I marched on, holding that thought close. Just when I thought I couldn't take another step in the heat, I heard a rattle and chug coming up behind me. I almost jumped into the ditch to hide until I was sure it wasn't somebody who'd take me back to Cayuga Springs, but was quick to change my mind. Reform school seemed better than being buzzard food.

I turned around and waited. I didn't recognize the truck. It was one of those real old ones with big fenders scooping over the front tires and a windshield in two separate pieces. It had shed most all of its paint, with a robin-egg-blue splotch the size of a dinner plate on a hood the color of an old scab.

The gears ground and the truck slowed as it passed me. A skinny colored woman peered out through the windshield. I didn't recognize her, but even if she knew me, being colored she couldn't make me go back if I didn't want to. But I reckon she could tattle.

She coasted by, then stopped a few feet ahead of me.

Pretty sure I was in the clear 'cause she was colored and I didn't know her, I went right up and stood on the running board of the passenger side. I held on to the wing vent and looked through the open window.

The colored woman smiled. I could tell she was nice.

"What you doin' out here all alone, child?" she asked in a voice that sounded like a lullaby.

"Goin' to Nashville."

She shook her head and pressed her lips together. "Nashville. Now that's a long, long way." For a minute, she looked like she was making up her mind if I was telling the truth.

Maybe I'd made a mistake. Maybe I should just take out for the woods. Too bad I was more scared of being ate than I was of the law right now. I stuck.

Finally, she nodded. "You look like you's about to fall to the heat." She picked up a mason jar off the seat. "Here." She handed it to me.

I was horrible thirsty, but I didn't take it; Mamie had made it clear: no matter even if we're about to expire from thirstiness, we don't drink after negras. That's why there was signs on the water fountains everywhere, so we'd know where we was supposed to drink.

The woman shook the jar a little and the water shot through with thirst-quenching sparkles. "It fine. Been washed and I ain't opened it since the water went in."

My tongue felt like a wadded-up sock in my mouth. I'd already broken enough rules I could never repent enough to save me. If I was going to h-e-double-hockey-sticks, I wasn't gonna go thirsty.

I reached out and took the jar. It didn't leave my lips until it was empty.

"Obliged." I wiped a dribble from my chin with the back of my wrist and handed the jar back through the window.

"You momma know where you are?"

"That's why I'm headed to Nashville. That's where my momma is." Hellfire or not, it was best to keep my lies as close to the truth as possible.

"Who 'posed to be takin' care of you?" Her brows scrunched over her eyes, just like Mamie's when she was unhappy about something but couldn't say right out.

Panic licked at my belly. If I told anything near the truth, this woman would tattle for sure—coloreds feared the law lots more than they did a redheaded white girl.

So I loaded a lie. "Nobody but my momma. She's expectin' me." Then I realized the woman probably wouldn't believe any momma would let her little girl hitchhike, so I dug deep for another. "I . . . I . . . gave my bus ticket to an old woman with a sick grandkid and no money. He was almost dead, so she needed it real bad. I can hitchhike there just fine." I tilted my head and squinted, hurrying past the lies. "You headed that way?"

That's when I heard something like a little hiccup and looked down at the floorboard of the passenger side. A baby . . . a red-faced, wrinkly white baby . . . wrapped tight in what looked like a pillowcase with crocheted lace on the edge and embroidered flowers, was inside an oval bulrush basket barely big enough to hold his tiny self.

I looked back up at the woman.

She smiled again. "That there's baby James. And I'm Eula."

"I'm Starla."

"Never heard that name afore. Starla," she said, slow and soft, then nodded. "Nice."

"You don't think it's trashy?"

Her brow wrinkled like I'd said something crazy. "Sounds like a nighttime winter sky . . . you know, when the air is sharp and the stars so bright they look like little pinpricks to heaven."

Nobody had ever made my name sound so beautiful. "That's what my momma thinks, too." My throat felt tight just thinking it might be so.

Baby James made more noises that sounded somewhere between a little squeak and a purr.

I cocked my head looking between him and Eula. "You the maid, then?" Plenty of babies were toted around by their colored maids, especially today with parents busy with older children at the Fourth of July Festival.

"Hmmm." She reached over and flipped the latch on the passenger door. A tiny gold cross sparkled at her throat; she was a good Christian woman. "I can give you a ride, if'n you want."

"All the way to Nashville?" I asked, wondering how far I had yet to go.

"Partway only. But better'n walkin' in this heat."

And ending up buzzard dinner.

I pulled open the door; its old hinges squeaked loud enough to startle the baby into crying. I climbed up on the seat and put my feet on either side of the basket.

"You mind holdin' James while I drive? He needs comfortin'."

I looked down at that baby. He reminded me of the newborn kittens the LeCounts' calico had in the holly shrubs on the side of their house last year, all pink and wrinkly. And he was oh so small. I figured I'd break him if I tried to pick him up.

"He looks okay down there to me," I said. "Maybe he'll quiet when you start drivin' again."

She looked at me with a sly smile that said I wasn't foolin' her. "Here now." She reached down and scooped him up and plunked him in my arms. I couldn't do nothin' but grab hold.

He wasn't much bigger than my pajama bag, but lots squirmier. And his squallin' was getting louder.

"Tha's right. Now jus' slide this sassy"—she picked up a pacifier from the basket—"into his mouth and give him a little jiggle."

I did, and James's squalls slid down to whimpers. Then he started sucking on that sassy and got quiet and still.

"There now," Eula said. "Better."

He was better. And me, too, now that I knew I wasn't gonna die in the ditch.

She let out the clutch and the truck jerked into motion. She smiled over at me and James, and I felt like she and I already knew each other better than just meeting.

She said, "Now ain't it a lucky thing that I found you."

3

Eula drove me lots farther than I'd hoped. I reckoned we were moving in a direction that more or less got me closer to Nashville, since Eula knew that was where I was headed. The hot air whirled around the inside of the truck, some relief from air sticky as cotton candy. James had fallen asleep and was getting real heavy for such a little thing.

The trees grew closer and closer to the road, crowding in like they wanted to take over. There was places where their branches reached right out and shook hands over our heads. Still, most of the time the sun baked us like biscuits right through the windshield.

My arm was turning numb when Eula glanced at me. "You got yo'self a real nice touch with a baby." She smiled over at me. She had a little space between her two front teeth, which were extra white against her dark skin. She looked at me like I was special.

I couldn't help the lick of pride I felt, even though it was a sin. Mamie always said the only thing I was good at was making trouble. "Never held one before."

"Well, now, you's got a gif' then." She sighed, keeping her eyes on the bleached-out pavement. "I got that gif', too. It's real special . . . 'rare as hen's teeth,' my momma used to say."

A gift, huh? Too bad Mamie'd never know. "You been a maid long?"

She nodded. "Since I was prob'ly not much older'n you."

"I'm only nine and a half!"

"Um-hmm." She sat up a little straighter and lifted her chin. "Got schoolin' up till I was eleven—the colored school only go to eighth grade anyway. Read better'n my momma ever did." She got quiet for a minute and I listened to the hum of the tires and the rough growl of the truck's engine. "I started out takin' care of the neighbor's young'uns while she worked . . . six of 'em, they was." She smiled. "Law, my hands was full, but I was happy as a fox in a henhouse. Then when my momma died, I had to get me some real work with cash pay, not just chickens and eggs. That's when I started with my first family."

"What about your daddy?" My daddy worked all the way down in the Gulf so he could put clothes on my back and food in my belly. "Didn't he take care of you?"

Her face got hard and she made a sound like she was choking. "Pap couldn't even take care of his own self. Can't recall a job lasted him more'n a month. He just too mean."

Poor Eula. My daddy hated being away from me, but he sacrificed so I could have everything I needed. He didn't get home much, but when he did, we did all kinds of fun stuff. One time he bought me my bicycle from the Western Auto and taught me how to ride—it's a blue Western Flyer, bought big so I didn't outgrow it. It was pretty dangerous at first 'cause I had to hop off the seat to put my feet on the ground when I stopped, but it fit me just right now. And me and Daddy almost always go to the drive-in movie when he's home; we get popcorn and Orange Crush. And when I was seven, he took me all the way up to Calling Panther Lake to go fishin'.

"You been workin' for the same family all these years?" I asked. Patti Lynn's maid had been with them since her parents got married; Patti Lynn and me both loved Bess to death—she made the best chocolate chip cookies in the whole of Mississippi. We liked her daughters, too; they come to help when there was lots to do, but went to school regular and didn't work like Eula had. And I couldn't even remember when Ernestine didn't work for the LeCounts.

Eula's face went soft and kinda sad. "No'um. Been several."

"You always been a maid to a family with kids?" I really wanted to put James back in his basket before my arm fell right off, but I didn't want Eula to think I didn't really have a gift 'cause it was the first one I'd ever had.

She seemed to know what I was thinking. "Go on, put him down. He stay asleep now."

That's when I realized there was no way I could put him down, 'cause my numb arm wouldn't work. "Um . . ."

"Uh-huh. I see." Eula nodded, slowed the truck, and pulled off onto the grass beside the road. I didn't recall when we'd turned off the highway with the painted center line and onto this country road with the tar bubblin' up from the sun.

She got out and walked around the truck. She was really tall . . . and I'd never seen a woman so skinny. After opening the passenger door, she reached out and took James. As she lifted him from my arms (thank you, baby Jesus), my fingers went all tingly and it felt like ants was biting all over my arm.

Eula tucked James into his basket with hands so sure and practiced I felt ashamed of my pride in my gift.

As she climbed back in the truck, she said, "We be home soon, sugar."

"But I'm goin' to Nashville."

"Well, course you are. But there ain't nobody on the roads to give you a ride today. You can come home and have supper with me and Wallace, sleep, then be on your way to Nashville t'morrow. Maybe I get Wallace to drive you partway." She nodded and smiled and I thought Wallace must be a real nice man.

'Sides, I was hungry. I'd eaten a jawbreaker already and wanted to make my candy last as long as I could. And I'd only seen one other car since I'd gotten in the truck, and it was headed the other way.

"What about James, don't you have to take him home?"

She leaned back against the seat, wrapped her hands around the steering wheel, and stared out the windshield. "I keepin' him."

"Overnight?"

She dipped her chin as she put the truck in gear and it shuddered back onto the road.

A while later, we run out of pavement and was travelin' a dirt road, kickin' up a plume of dust. We passed a long stretch of brown-watered swamp, edged with water weeds and green scum. It was full of old cypress and tree skeletons that dripped with gray moss. A bit after that, we turned off that dirt road onto a double-rutted lane that cut into the woods.

As we drove through the tangle of trees and weeds, branches made screeching noises as they scraped the rusty truck. Goose bumps shot down the back of my neck and I tried to tell myself it was just 'cause of the sound, but it really was more than that. The trees swallowed up the sunlight. With my sun-blind eyes, everything was fuzzy and gray and I couldn't see nothin' at all in the shadowy places. We'd left the real world, the world of Cayuga Springs and Mamie and Patti Lynn far behind and was in a place that felt darker—and not just 'cause of the light.

The truck made a curve in the lane. I looked over my shoulder and the square of bright that was the hole to the road was gone; there wasn't nothing but woods and gloom. I wondered if I'd made a mistake. Mamie always said I never did look before I leaped.

I told myself I should be glad to be someplace safe from the law and Mrs. Sellers—and that a woman as nice as Eula was gonna give me dinner and a place to sleep. Anyway, I didn't have much choice. I couldn't never go home again. And I couldn't walk to Nashville when I didn't know how to get there.

Sure wish I coulda said good-bye to Patti Lynn.

I'd thought about running away plenty of times. I'd even thought about asking Patti Lynn to come with me. But her momma and daddy lived together and she didn't have a grandmother who hated every cotton-pickin' thing about her. It really wouldn't be fair to ask her to give up all her good stuff just 'cause I wasn't keen on running away alone.

I always figured it'd take about a week to get ready. I'd store food in my closet a little at a time so Mamie wouldn't notice and pack up my favorite clothes and Daddy's lunch box from my fort. I'd write a long note to Daddy and Patti Lynn, who were the only two people who would miss me.

But as it turned out, leaving Cayuga Springs was an emergency, and all I had was some sticky penny candy in my shorts pockets.

The truck hit a particular bad hole and about bounced me off my seat and onto James. Lucky I grabbed the door and kept where I was; I'd crush that baby for sure.

Eula looked over at me. Instead of hollerin' at me to be careful of the baby, she laughed right out loud. "You should see your face, child . . . all eyes and eyebrows." She made a face that looked like somebody done sneaked up on her and poked her in the backside, the whites of her eyes big and round.

"I didn't look like that!"

"Yes'um, you did." She made the face again.

I laughed right along with her this time.

We were still laughing when the lane ended in front of a house. It sat up off the ground on square, brick supports. The metal roof looked rusty and the porch sagged a little. The white paint was most peeled off, but the house somehow still had a tidy look about it, like somebody didn't have money but still cared. Some chickens were scratching in the yard, and a rooster was flappin' his wings on a stump at the edge of the woods. A big ax was next to the stump, and some chopped wood was layin' on the ground around it.

The door to the house swung open and a big bear of a man, wearing gray pants with suspenders and a white shirt with short sleeves, walked out. He was nearly as tall as the doorframe . . . nearly as wide, too.

Eula stopped laughing. Her hands tightened on the steering wheel and she cleared her throat.

The man come off the porch. "I was 'ginnin' to wonder where you'd got to. Deliverin' pies don't take all day." His voice was so deep it more rumbled than talked.

The second he laid eyes on me, he stopped in his big-bear tracks. Now his eyes had that just-poked-in-the-backside look. "What you doin' with that white girl, Eula?"

Eula jumped out of the truck. "Now, Wallace, it gon' be all right. She on her way to—"

James let out a cry like I was pulling his arms off or something.

The man pushed past Eula and stuck his big head though the open passenger-side window.

"Lord in heaven, woman!" He spun around so fast, Eula jumped backward. "What was you thinkin', stealin' a baby?"

I didn't like the way he yelled at her, or the way he leaned his big body over hers. She didn't back away, but I could see the scared in her eyes. I jumped out. "She wasn't stealin'! James's family is busy with the Fourth Festival. She's takin' care of him."

He looked over his shoulder at me with dark eyes as narrow and hateful as Jimmy Sellers's. The man had little, square teeth that looked way too small for his head. "Who is you?"

"Starla Claudelle." I stood up extra tall; Mamie said you had to stand your ground with the colored.

"Wallace," Eula said, and put her hand on his giant arm.

He swung his eyes back to her. "You always was stupid, but you done lost your mind! You can't take care of yo'self for even half a minute."

"It ain't what you think—"

"You get permission to take this baby, this white girl?"

"No, but—"

He raised a hand the size of a frying pan and swung. She flinched and ducked. He didn't connect with skin and ended up only messing up her hair. The front stuck straight up now where it come loose.

I wanted to break his nose. Truth be told, I was too scared—which made me madder 'n a hornet.

He lifted his hand again, but didn't swing. "Don't you push me, woman!" His hand went from flat to a fist. He breathed real deep twice and then shouted, "Get in the house!" He looked at me. "And take them chil'ren with you!"

Eula took my arm and shoved me toward the front porch. "Go. It'll be all right, child." Then she snatched James in his basket from the truck.

I looked over my shoulder. The man had both hands on his head like he was trying to keep it from exploding. He walked in little circles, muttering, "Now you gone and done it. We dead. Dead. Dead. Dead."

Eula hurried me up the steps, across the wood porch, inside and through the house and into a tiny room in the back that was even smaller than my room at home. The floor was covered with cracked blue and gray linoleum, and the little window didn't have a curtain. There was an empty baby cradle with a knit blanket folded inside it and a rocker. I wondered where Eula's baby was, but didn't get the chance to ask.

After setting baby James's basket on the floor, she bent down, took my face in her hands, and looked in my eyes. "Listen to me, child. You gotta be real quiet while I get things straightened out with Wallace. He in a foul mood, and when that happens . . ." She didn't finish, but I could see she was most as scared as I was. "I get him to see, then we have some ham hock and green beans, maybe I make up some corn bread, too. You like corn bread?" She nodded as she spoke and I nodded right along with her. "Good then."

She turned and left the room, closing the door behind her. I heard a key turn in the old lock. I wasn't sure if it was to keep me and James in, or Wallace out.

It was all I could do to make myself breathe. I wanted to trust Eula. I really did. She was a Christian. She was kind. But that Wallace was another thing altogether. He looked like he could be worse than Mrs. Sellers, Mamie, and Jimmy Sellers all rolled into one big bundle of mean.

And what did he mean, "steal" James?

I moved real careful and put my ear to the door. Eula's footsteps sounded like she was afraid the floor might splinter right under her. Boy, did I know what that was like, being afraid just the sound of your feet moving on the floor could make someone mad at you. Patti Lynn's maid, Bess, called it "walkin' on eggshells." I reckon that's as good a way to describe it as any.

Holding my breath, I waited for the sound of the man's deep, angry voice, but all I heard was the squeak of the screen-door hinges and the sharp clap as it closed.

This wasn't at all what I'd imagined when Eula asked me to come home for supper. Eula was so nice, I thought it was gonna be like dinner at Patti Lynn's—everybody around a table, polite and nice, talking about their day, telling silly knock-knock jokes.

I decided I'd better figure out a way out of here, and fast. The window was small, but big enough me and James could get through, if I could get the bottom sash all the way up.

My stomach got all knotted when I saw the rusted-closed window latch. I worked up all the spit I could in my dry mouth, then spit on it. I waited until I counted to fifteen for the spit to do its work. Then I hit the little lever until the heel of my hand was fiery red and burned like the dickens.

The latch wouldn't budge even a hair.

4

The door rattled and I sat down real quick next to James—who'd been caterwaulin' most the entire time, like he was doing his part to cover up the sounds of me trying to get us free. I tried to look like I'd just been sitting there the whole time.

Ever since Eula had closed that door, I'd been thinking about what she'd said about James; that she was keeping him. When I'd asked if she meant overnight, she'd kinda nodded, but that wasn't the same as saying yes. Facts are facts. I'd heard it often enough when I'd tried to explain myself to Mamie. And fact was, she was keeping James—a baby Wallace said she had no claim to. The other fact was me and James was locked in tight. Was she planning on keeping me, too?

"Well, now," Eula said, as she came in, going right over and reaching for James. She had a bruise growing on the inside of her wrist, purple and angry. It hadn't been there when she'd left us. "Sounds like baby boy here is hungry." James didn't stop crying when she picked him up, but he sounded less like someone was trying to kill him. "There, now. I got some formula made up. You be fine, jus' fine."

I was just beginning to wonder if she'd forgot I was in the room when she looked at me. "You want to come out and hold him while I fill his bottle?" She acted like the whole ugliness with Wallace hadn't even happened. But that bruise said everything she wasn't.

"Um, I was just thinkin'. I don't want to be any trouble for y'all. I think I'll just keep on walkin' toward Nashville. There'll be cars out after the fireworks are over." If I could get me out of here, I could tell Lulu when I got to Nashville that there's a baby been kidnapped. Maybe she could make a nonymous call to the law like they do on TV. I sure couldn't call; they was looking for a little girl who'd attacked Mrs. Sellers. They'd be sure to put two and two together, 'cause all adults can do that.

"It be dark then!" Eula said, her eyes more worried than sneaky. "And country dark ain't like city dark, sugar. Out here there ain't gonna be no cars comin' from fireworks neither."

"I . . . I really need to keep movin', in case my momma starts to get worried." Then I added, "She's spectin' me." No colored person would risk keeping a white girl from her momma, no matter what two and two added up to.

"You ain't goin' nowhere." The bear's voice came from the doorway. How had that giant walked through the house and I hadn't heard him?

Eula jerked her head in a way that made me think she hadn't heard him neither. Right quick she turned back to me and smiled, but it wasn't right.

"That right," she said, holding that smile only a ninny would think was real, "not until tomorrow mornin', when it be safe to travel." She stood up with James, then brushed right past Wallace, who gave her the stink eye as she did. "Come on then, Starla. Let's get baby boy fed."

I was slow getting to my feet, trying to come up with another argument to get out of here. Then I realized Wallace was still standing there between me and the doorway. I jumped up and hurried past him, feeling his eyes on me the whole time.

Across from the room with the cradle was a bigger room with an iron bed and pressed curtains on the window. A picture of Jesus hung over the bed, not baby Jesus, but grown-up Jesus. I decided Eula had put it there, not Wallace.

As I walked into the kitchen, I looked through the door on my right into the living room. The dark green couch and chair were old and lumpy; lace doilies sat on the arms and the tops of the backs. There was a rug on the floor, but no TV or big radio like some old folks had. On the table next to the chair was a Bible and an old oil lamp like Patti Lynn's momma, who collected old stuff that she called "antiques," had.

In the corner was a potbellied stove with a metal chimney that went up and out of the house near the ceiling.

No TV. No radio. No switch in the little room with the cradle. It was like Little House in the Big Woods. I'd never been in a house without electricity before.

The floor behind me dipped and I knew the bear was right behind me. I hurried myself right on to stand by Eula in front of an old cook-stove with a pile of wood in a box next to it.

"Here now," she said to me. "You pull out a chair and sit down. You can hold James while I get his bottle ready."

Eula seemed to have a lot of baby stuff, bottles and whatnot, considering there wasn't a baby anywhere around.

James was crying so much his face was red as a June cherry. His little fists were tight under his chin, and every once in a while he'd kick his legs enough he nearly popped out of the crook in Eula's arm.

I put my hands behind my back and took a step away from her. "I can get his bottle ready."

Wallace made his footsteps heavy and loud as he walked into the living room.

The three chairs at the kitchen table didn't go together. Eula hooked a foot around the leg of one and pulled it out. Then she nodded for me to sit. "Don't be scared of him." I wasn't sure if she meant Wallace or James until she added, "Remember, you special. You got a gif' with little ones. Mustn't waste one of the good Lord's gif's."

I sat and she plopped James in my arms. How did how legs so scrawny kick so hard? With the pillowcase wrapped around him he looked like he was trying to win a potato-sack race. I held tight so he wouldn't kick himself right onto the floor.

Eula got a bottle ready, then turned it upside down and shook out a couple of drops onto the inside of her wrist.

"Why'd you do that?" I asked. For having a gift with babies, I sure didn't know much.

"Make sure it ain't too hot."

I was afraid Eula'd want me to feed him too; my arm was getting tired and my ears hurt from his hollerin'. Lucky for me she picked him up and sat down in the chair on the other side of the table.

Once that nipple plugged up his mouth, James finally stopped crying. Wallace was muttering and stompin' around in the living room on those big bear feet. Eula didn't pay him no attention, so maybe he was just cranky in general.

Truth be told, she didn't pay me no attention neither. She looked at baby James all dreamy, humming real low and rocking from side to side. The window was right there, open enough that I could slide right out. Wonder if she'd notice? Maybe I was making more of being locked in that room than was right. Eula had said I was leaving in the morning—and Wallace hadn't gone all crazy mad like he had when we first showed up.

I thought of Jesus over her bed.

"Do you pray, Eula?"

Her eyes left James's face for the first time since she'd picked him up. "Of course I pray, child." She looked down at James and her face looked like one of the angels in the Bible-stories book I had, all glowy and soft. "I pray, and God give me little James here."

"So you're keepin' him . . . forever?" My stomach felt sick. She had kidnapped him.

"Nobody want him but me. And the Lord, he work in mysterious ways."

I couldn't believe that a momma wouldn't want her own baby. All mommas wanted their kids. "My momma and daddy want me," I said, just to make sure she knew it wasn't all right to keep me.

She just smiled and moved James up onto her shoulder and patted his back.

"Doesn't God want you to have your own baby?" It would make more sense for God to give her a colored baby than a white one.

Now she looked really sad. "Oh, God give me babies, but God take them away. All away." Her last two words were whispered, kinda like an amen at the end of a serious prayer.

"They died?" I said it too loud, but I'd never heard of a baby dyin'.

The only people I'd ever known die—well, I reckon I didn't really know them since they died before I was even born—was my daddy's daddy in the War and my momma's momma, Ida, who Mamie said was white trash and died when momma was in junior high. Mamie kept a picture of granddaddy wearing his army uniform in the living room on top of the TV. He was a hero.

"Most all afore they was ever born," Eula said it so soft and sad that I didn't want to ask any more questions about babies.

We ate dinner, but even though James was finally quiet and asleep, it wasn't a pleasant time. Eula talked in a chattery voice, asking about school and my momma and whatnot. I kept my answers on the same street as the truth while Wallace sat there and eyed me like I was a big pile of stinky dog doo.

He wasn't eating neither, not a single bite of ham hock or corn bread. He must have had a mighty thirst though; he filled his glass with water from a big mason jar twice.

Once I had my belly full, I could finally think half-straight. Even though I couldn't understand how it was true—seeing how Jesus loved all his children—Mamie said all coloreds were less than us. I was still learning all of the rules, even though some of them didn't make a lick of sense to me. But since that was the way of things, I decided I could get myself out of this jam by just ordering Wallace to take me to Nashville, or at least to the highway.

I sucked in a deep breath and said, "Mr. Wallace." I looked at the top button on his shirt and not his eyes. It was easier to stay bossy that way. "Eula said you'll be takin' me partway to Nashville tomorrow. My momma is expectin' me, so we should leave early."

Those eyes got squinty and he grunted.

I went about my business, just like Mamie did when she'd told me something she knew I wouldn't like. I almost asked to be excused, then caught myself. I needed to keep my bossy white self the only one Wallace saw. I got up from the table.

"Where you think you're goin'?" His voice rumbled from deep in that big body. He was talking kinda peculiar, too, slow and like his tongue had gotten too fat.

I heard Eula suck in a breath. I thought of that bruise on her arm. I hoped me acting bossy didn't make Wallace mad enough to start punching.

"Takin' my plate to the sink, like I always do after supper." I took the enameled tin plate and my fork and walked over to the drain board next to the sink with the hand pump.

I took it as a good sign when he just took another big drink and didn't say anything else.

Things were gonna work out. Tomorrow I'd be on my way to Lulu. I felt bad that I was gonna have to have her call the law and report a kidnapped baby; James's momma had to want him. Poor Eula was gonna be really sad. Maybe God would let her have another baby though, a colored one, once James was back with his real momma. I decided I'd say a special prayer for her at bedtime in case it would help.

As me and Eula finished clearing the table, I stopped dead when I realized there wasn't a refrigerator to put the butter in. I about knocked myself in the head; course there wasn't a refrigerator, there wasn't any electricity.

Eula looked at me with a frown. "What you lookin' for, child?"

I just raised my eyebrows and the butter crock.

"That there be butter."

"I know!" When she busted out laughing, I knew she was workin' me. "So where am I supposed to put it?"

"Well, now that depends. Sometimes we got ice and use that icebox over there." She pointed to a wooden cabinet sitting on the floor. It had small door on top and a bigger door beneath it. "But we ain't got ice, so we use the springhouse."

I'd seen a springhouse when our class went to tour an old plantation near Natchez. I couldn't believe anybody still used one.

"Come on," Eula said.

We took the butter crock and a quart bottle of milk down the hill behind the house a little ways. Eula kept reminding me to watch my step, not to trip over roots and whatnot. I finally told her I wasn't a baby and had been in plenty of woods all by myself—which wasn't exactly true, 'cause Patti Lynn had always been with me. But Patti Lynn knew I could figure out how to walk by myself.

Sure enough there was the springhouse, but it was smaller and more rickety than the one on that plantation. This one was shoved into the creek bank. Eula opened the door. It was so dark in there I couldn't see for a minute. But it was so cool, I wanted to walk right in anyway, even if I broke my ankle stumblin' in the dark.

"Wait here." She took the butter crock from my hands and stepped inside. "Now, we best get back, else Wallace'll worry."

I nearly laughed at that one. Wallace had been sitting in his chair with his eyes shut for the past ten minutes. But he wasn't there when we got back.

As we did the dishes, Eula lit an oil lamp 'cause it was getting dark. I got a cold spot right in the middle of my stomach. Right about now everybody back home was set up to see the fireworks, their blankets and folding aluminum lawn chairs all over the golf course waiting for full dark. Right about now the sparklers would be coming out, too. I never had any, even though I asked every year, but Patti Lynn always shared hers.

Back when I was four, before I even knew Patti Lynn, some kid left a hot sparkler wire in the grass. I stepped on it and burned my foot. Mamie yelled at me 'cause I'd taken off my sandals, but then she'd gone to every blanket near ours looking for someone who had a cooler with ice. She'd pulled me onto her lap and held the ice on my foot until the last red-white-and-blue firework melted from the sky. It had almost been worth the pain and the angry blister, being able to sit like that.

As Eula scrubbed the iron skillet from the corn bread, I heard Wallace walking back and forth in the living room. Every once in a while I'd hear him say stuff like "Woman gone done it now" and "Can't see no other way."

I leaned close and whispered to Eula, "Wallace still seems pretty mad,"

She gave me one of her real smiles and winked, so I figured there was nothing to worry about. "He always mad when he in the juice. Best jus' stay outta his way."

"Juice?"

She nodded toward the mason jar still on the table. "Moonshine. Hard liquor."

"What you whisperin' about in there?" the bear called. There was a thud like he walked into something. "Gawwwwddammit!"

"Jus' 'bout the baby, Wallace," Eula said sweet as pie. "You okay?"

"Shut up!"

I looked at Eula. I couldn't imagine anybody, man or not, telling Mamie to shut up. But Eula just kept scrubbing that pan.

"That baby gonna kill us." He mumbled some, then said, "If'n you wasn't so gawwwddamn stupid, we wouldn't be in this mess. I shoulda got rid of you long time ago."

Eula leaned close and said in a voice even lower than a whisper, "He don't mean it. It the juice."

"He in the juice when he give you that bruise?" I pointed to her arm.

She sighed. "Sometimes things happen tween a husband and wife. You see when you grown—"

"I said shut up!"

Eula shrugged and we stopped talking.

Back in the room with the stuck window, she made me a pallet on the floor. She unfolded a patchwork quilt and shook it out, letting it fall onto the pallet.

"My momma made this quilt," she said, running her hand over it like she was pettin' a kitten. "From old dresses given to her by the woman she a maid for back in the day. Momma used tell stories 'bout the different scraps, describe the dress it come from, tell if it was for a special occasion or holiday." Eula stopped talking for a minute and I wondered if there was something wrong. "I don't remember none anymore," she said, real quiet and sad, like she'd lost something special.

How could scraps of old dresses that hadn't even belonged to you be special?

"In Cayuga Springs?" I asked. "You lived there with your momma?"

"No, indeed. She worked in Jackson for a right prosperous family, a judge the husband was."

"You work in Cayuga Springs now? Is that where James come from?" I was getting real curious about her, not to mention curious about who might be looking for baby James. I wanted to get away from here, from the cranky bear, but I sure didn't want anybody from Cayuga Springs to find me and haul me off to jail. I wondered if the law had already come looking for me at Mamie's house, found out I'd run off, and was putting out PPBs to other police like they do on *Dragnet*. Just the facts, ma'am. I bet Mrs. Sellers told them a lot more than that.

Then I thought, What if they send Eula to jail for kidnappin' James? I sure didn't want that.

"Best you don't know where James come from."

"You said nobody wants him."

"That right."

"But . . . all mommas want their kids."

"That so?" She lifted her chin and looked down her nose. "Then what your momma doin' up in Nashville while you been in Cayuga Springs?"

Since I couldn't tell the God's honest truth and it was getting hard to keep all of my truth stretching straight, I used one of Mamie's answers. "It's complicated and you don't need no details." There was never any arguing after Mamie said those words. I crossed my arms to say, That's that.

Eula squinted at me from the corners of her narrowed eyes. "Well, now, I bet it is. Your momma even waitin' for you? Or you done run away?"

Now she was making me mad. And I was just trying to keep her out of jail. My red rage took hold of my tongue. "How you gonna keep a white baby till he's growed up without anybody findin' out?"

"This baby left on the church steps, his momma don't want him. Nobody want him. So the good Lord give him to me."

"How do you know the good Lord didn't want the preacher to have him?"

"'Cause he put me there to see it happen—me and nobody else."

Guess I couldn't argue that, it wasn't Sunday or anything. Then a question popped in my head that should have before now. "Why would anybody leave a white baby at a colored church?"

She got stiff and looked away. "Was a white church."

"Oh, no!"

Wallace had called her stupid, but she couldn't be dumb enough to take a white baby from a white church!

She drew away a little and looked toward where James was sleeping in his basket. "I thought he was colored," she said, her voice more prickly than I'd ever heard. "It was a colored girl who I see put him there."

"Why didn't you just leave him when you saw he was white? Somebody woulda taken care of him."

"I didn't see he was white at first."

Now she was just making stuff up. "He don't look at all colored to me."

"He wrapped up tight as a caterpillar in a cocoon, face and all. They was a car comin', so I pick him up and drive off afore I seed he was white."

"Oh, Eula, you gotta take him back."

She shook her head. "Too late for that."

I considered for a bit. "Just go back tonight and leave him on that church step where you found him. Nobody will see you."

"No!" This time her head was jerky as she shook it. "No. Good Lord have a plan. Ain't for nobody—even a white girl—to question." She grabbed up a pillow and fluffed it, like that was all there was to say.

I was real mixed up about baby James. I just couldn't believe his momma truly didn't want him. Was Eula so crazy for a baby that she made that story up? But if it was true nobody wanted him, Eula would take real good care of him. How was a white baby gonna grow up in a colored house? In Sunday school they said we got to accept and be grateful for what God chooses for us. Did God want James with Eula? It was all too much to untangle in my head. Plus I had to make sure I was gonna get out of here tomorrow. So I decided to be agreeable—something Mamie said I didn't even have in me.

"Yes, ma'am," I said, real sweet. "Like you said, the Lord works in mysterious ways." Still, it seemed to me that God giving her a colored baby made more sense.

She laid the pillow on the pallet and smoothed the case. "Sorry it ain't a proper bed."

"It's okay. It's only for one night anyway," I said, real definite to remind her I was leaving in the morning.

I took off my Red Ball Jets and tucked my socks inside them.

"G'night, then." She went to the door.

Maybe I'd just take off out of here tonight and not chance it with Wallace in the morning. I didn't like the idea of walking around out there in the dark woods—what if I got turned around? What if baby James was kidnapped and I couldn't tell the police how to find this place? It might be better to take James with me, but babies were probably particular tasty to bears and whatnot.

I waited, my heart skipping fast, hoping not to hear the lock.

The door rattled a bit, then I heard the skeleton key and clunky *swick* as the lock slid home.

It wasn't a minute later when I heard them, Wallace and Eula. Rough, strained whispers muffled through the wall between the bedroom and kitchen, like talking through two cans and a string. For a while I couldn't make out anything, then Wallace's voice got a whole lot louder . . . and clearer. "Don' argue with me, woman! There ain't no other way." Eula said something quiet that sounded like it had some begging in it. "We ain't gonna talk 'bout it no more."

Eula's voice got some louder. "But, Wallace, they's jus—" Her voice cut off like it had been snatched from her mouth. I thought of that bruise on her arm and wondered if he'd just added another one. Wallace seemed like a shaker to me. I'd had plenty of arm bruises myself from Mamie jerking me so hard my mouth snapped closed.

It got quiet then. I wondered what Wallace meant. It couldn't be good if Eula had been begging like that.

I couldn't believe my biggest problem this morning had been missing the fireworks. As I looked out that stuck window at the black night, hearing tree frogs and crickets that sounded big as cats, I wished I was back in my hot, sweaty bedroom in Cayuga Springs.

5

Back when I was in second grade, I come home from school and caught Mamie stuffing something in the trash barrel back by the alley. Usually I used the front door and heard Mamie call, "Go change your clothes," even before the door closed behind me. I hated changing my clothes after school. Not so much the changing. It was more setting away shoes and putting my dress on a hanger, which was a real pain in the behind. That day I'd got a brilliant idea. If I just went straight to the backyard, I might be able to get dirty before Mamie saw me. And if I was already dirty, there wouldn't be a reason to make me change.

I walked along the side of the house, crouched low in case she was looking out the windows. It was cold so they were closed and I didn't have to worry about noise givin' me away. Once I got to the back corner of the house, I made a run for the tire swing Daddy'd hung when I was five.

That's when I saw her by the trash barrel.

Well, she looked as surprised as I was. She jumped and squeaked, grabbin' her chest like he heart was gonna leap right out. She hurried toward me and, with a hand on my shoulder, moved me toward the back door. She said I'd startled her, but she looked for all the world like she was doing something sneaky, something she didn't want me to see. It was my job to take the trash out and Mamie never did my job, even when I had tonsillitis. I got even more suspicious when she sat me down in the kitchen before I'd changed my clothes, poured my glass of milk for me, and let me have two cookies—and they were the good ones Mamie bought for bridge club that I wasn't allowed to eat.

As I ate my cookies, I got to thinking. If Mamie didn't want me to see what she'd put in the trash, I was gonna have to be crafty like a fox in finding out what it was. If she knew I was suspicious and looking, she'd just make up something I was doing wrong and send me to my room—believe me, she'd done it before. She'd send me to my room all right, and then hustle right out there and either burn the trash (which wasn't supposed to be done until the next day) or move whatever it was she'd been hiding. Either way, I'd never know.

I needed a plan.

For the rest of the afternoon I went around the house gathering up every scrap of trash I could find. There was a good stockpile underneath my bed. I took a grocery bag to my room and stuffed it with broken crayons, filled-up coloring books, two socks with holes in the toes, and wadded up Kleenexes. I even pulled out all of my gold-star papers from school; I'd been keeping them in one of my drawers so I could show Daddy when he came home to visit. All of the sudden it was more important to find out what was in that trash barrel than it was to show Daddy I could spell *bakery* and *away,* match a chicken to an egg, and tell the number of stripes on the American flag. There weren't any arithmetic papers, 'cause arithmetic gave me fits.

I blew my nose ten times, just to make more Kleenexes. Mamie heard and told me to wash my hands if I was getting sick. In the living room, I found two old church bulletins and threw them in the bag. I sure hoped Mamie was done with them.

By the time we'd finished dinner, the trash can in the kitchen was filled to the top. I picked it up and headed out the door while Mamie was busy putting bonnets on the leftovers and finding a place in the refrigerator for them.

It almost seemed too easy. I couldn't let myself be fooled; I'd been caught plenty of times when I'd thought the coast was clear.

On the path to the trash barrel, I glanced back at the closed door; no Mamie peekin' out.

I checked again when I got to the alley.

Coast clear.

Real quick, I set down the trash can and stepped up on the cinder block Mamie had put there so I could dump the trash. The barrel was half-full. At the top, there was a lot of newspaper, all loose and crumply, not folded like newspaper is supposed to be.

I had to hurry. I held my breath, hoping there wasn't any maggoty garbage in there and stuck my hands in the newspapers. Nothing squishy or squirmy got against my skin. Instead I found a brown cardboard box, a little smaller than the box Mamie had sent some cookies to Daddy in. On the outside of the box, under a long row of stamps, was my name and our address. The brown mailing tape had been slit.

Mamie had opened a box that had been sent to me! I only once got a box parcel post; it had been from Daddy on my birthday when he hadn't been able to get home.

After another look at the house to make sure Mamie wasn't stickin' her nosy nose through the crack in the curtains, I opened the flaps on the box. At first I thought it was empty, then I saw the envelope—a big manila one like Mrs. Jacobi used at school to keep flash cards in. It had my name on it, with big *x*'s and *o*'s, and I knew it was from Momma.

I felt my red rage coming on, but did like Daddy told me and took deep breaths until it passed. I couldn't let Mamie know I'd found what she'd hid.

The envelope was stiff, not bendy. The flap on it had already been torn.

I heard the rattle of the back-door knob; thank goodness that door sticks. I stuck the envelope up under my shirt and grabbed the trash can. By the time Mamie had the door open and was asking what was taking me so long, I had the trash dumped and was on my way back to the house.

She looked at me real suspicious as she opened the screen and waited for me to come in.

"I saw a raccoon and chased it off," I said before she could ask me more questions. Mamie hated raccoons in the trash. I just kept walking, afraid if I looked at her sneaky, package-opening face, my red rage would come barrelin' back. "If it's all right, Mamie," I said real sweet, "I'm gonna go take my bath now. I don't feel good."

She reached out and put a hand on my forehead. "No fever. What's ailing you?"

I had to think fast. What does Mamie hate as much as raccoons in the trash?

Me throwing up!

I grabbed my belly. "Uh-oh." I ran straight for the stairs.

"Oh," Mamie called. "Let me know if you need me."

Whenever I threw up, Mamie got all gaggy. I'd been throwing up on my own since I was three. It was just easier that way. Besides, wasn't nothing Mamie could do but stand there and hold a cold cloth on the back of my neck—and gag. I could do both of those things myself.

I went into the bathroom and locked the door. I pulled the envelope out from under my shirt and stood there just staring at it, at the way Momma made a big loopy *S* at the beginning of my name and surrounded it with stars, like it was special. I wanted to open it, but I didn't want it to be over too fast. So I sat on the edge of the tub and held it against my heart.

Just to make sure Mamie stayed away I made some retching sounds and flushed the toilet.

Then I slipped my fingers under the torn flap and unfolded it. My stomach felt fluttery and my heart was beating fast and loud—maybe I *was* getting sick.

Pulling the envelope open, I looked inside. There was only one thing in there, a little record, one of them with the big hole in the center that only plays one song on each side. Patti Lynn's sister, Cathy—we called her Fatty Cathy when we was mad at her—had a lot of them. Fatty Cathy's records sat under her record-player stand in a wire rack that held them on their edges. They looked like a big, black Slinky. Patti Lynn and I wasn't supposed to touch them. But we did.

If a record was scratched, it bounced the same word over and over until you went over and picked up the needle. I didn't want to take a chance of scratching this one, so I reached in and hooked my finger through the hole and slid it out, slow and easy. The label was bright yellow and had a rooster on it. The word *SUN* was a rainbow over the rooster. Course I was only seven back then and couldn't read all of the words, but I knew. I knew what it was. Momma had made a record, just like she'd said she was going to! "Baby Mine" was the song. Under the song was *Lucinda L-a-n-g-s-d-o-n*. Under that it said *D-E-M-O*.

"Baby Mine." Momma had only one baby. Me!

I got so excited I nearly threw up for real. Momma had a record. She was getting famous. Pretty soon she'd be coming to get me and Daddy.

We didn't have a record player at our house. I was gonna have to wait until I could take it to Patti Lynn's to hear it.

That night, I wanted to put the record under my pillow, just to be close to it and make sure it was safe, but records scratched and broke too easy—Patti Lynn and I had found that out. We'd told Cathy one of the brothers had done it. Easy enough—those brothers of Patti Lynn's was always breaking stuff. Instead of under my pillow, I put Momma's record back in the envelope and hid it in the very bottom of the very back of my summer-shorts and T-shirt drawer. Mamie wouldn't have any reason to get in there 'cause it was February.

The next day, I went to school like normal, even though nothing was normal anymore. Momma was famous. She was coming to get me.

Mamie just seemed happy that I wasn't still throwing up.

All day long, I felt like I had bees in my belly. That afternoon Patti Lynn had her momma call Mamie and invite me specially to come over. Mamie thought Patti Lynn's momma was the most "cultured" woman in Cayuga Springs—whatever that was, it was good, I can tell you that. Patti Lynn's momma and Mamie played bridge together with a bunch of other ladies. When Mamie hosted, we had to just about clean the whole house with a toothbrush and buy only brand-name snacks from the Piggly Wiggly. I can't remember one single time that Mamie said no when Patti Lynn's momma invited me to do something.

At four o'clock, Patti Lynn and I sat in the purple bedroom she shared with Cathy and played the record. It was Momma all right. I closed my eyes and listened, pretending she was in the room, not just coming from a scratchy-sounding speaker. It was the most beautiful song I ever heard.

I'd had Patti Lynn hide the record at her house so no one would find it. From that day, every time I went to Patti Lynn's and we could get the bedroom to ourselves, I played that record. One day that song stopped being on the outside of me and moved deep inside. It was there all of the time, especially when I was feeling particular lonely.

That night, locked up in the little room in Eula's house, I fell asleep humming that song to myself.

Me and Wallace and Eula had breakfast, grits and eggs. I even got to go out with Eula and get the eggs right out from under the chickens. It was fun until one of the hens got mad and pecked me good on the hand. I told Eula I liked the grocery store better, where the farmers brought in the eggs and did all of the chicken fightin' for me. Eula found that particular funny for some reason.

Those chickens, flappin' and peckin' to keep their eggs before they even turned into baby chicks, told me that every momma wants her baby. Eula's story 'bout finding James like that just seemed wrong. Could it be true? Or was she just a little crazy, too? The more I thought about it, the more confused I got.

As we finished breakfast and Eula and I cleaned up the dishes, I studied her. She didn't act like she had a screw loose. In fact, we had a right nice breakfast, even with Wallace at the table. But that big, new bruise on Eula's upper arm and the way she was careful not to look at him told me I was right. He wasn't a nice man at all.

I really liked Eula and didn't want to get her in trouble for taking James. Once I got to Nashville, Momma would help me sort out what to do. Momma would know a way to find out who James's mother was, then figure out how we could get her baby back to her without sending Eula to jail for kidnapping.

But that was all for later. Now it was time to go.

I folded my dish towel and set it on the drain board. "Thank you for helpin' me out and feedin' me." I stood tall as I could and headed toward the front door.

"Stop right there!" Wallace's voice was extra grumbly this morning, making him sound even more like a bear.

I kept walking out the front door and climbed into the passenger seat of the truck. My mouth was dry and I all the sudden needed to pee—that always happened when I got real nervous.

The screen door squeaked open and Wallace thundered across the wooden porch. I paid no mind; I just slammed the truck's door and sat looking out the windshield.

To keep from peeing my pants, I counted my breaths. One. Two.

Wallace yanked open the passenger door so hard I was surprised it didn't come off in his hand. "Get out."

"My momma is waitin'. You only need to take me to the highway. I'll get a ride from there." My insides was wobbling like Jell-O, but I didn't look at him.

The front door squeaked again. "Wallace," Eula called, her voice meek as a mouse. Even I knew that wasn't gonna get the bear's attention.

"Get. Out. The. Truck." I could tell he was gritting his teeth, but I didn't look at him.

"Wallace." Eula's voice was sweet, like she was singing to baby James. "I told you it was gonna be all right, now. She goin' to Nashville. She ain't coming back round here. Right, Starla?"

I am white. I am the boss of what happens here. "That's right. I'm moving to Nashville permanent. I got no reason to come back." That didn't sound quite forever enough, so I added, "I won't never be back." I didn't tell them that I couldn't never come back.

Out of the corner of my eye, I could see the big hulk of Wallace step back from my door.

He's getting in. He's takin' me to the highway.

But instead of walking around the truck, he went toward Eula. I chanced a peek as he grabbed her by the shoulders and shook her.

"You done it. If'n you didn't take that baby, that girl could go on her way to her momma and everything be fine. But you done stole that baby. This is on you! You hear me? On you!" With his last words he shoved her hard, flinging her away from him. It was everything I could do not to jump out of the truck and onto his back, scratch his angry bear eyes out. But I knew if I did, I'd never get away from here. And he'd be even madder at Eula.

Eula stumbled, but kept her feet.

Wallace started to turn toward me. I snapped my eyes back to the windshield. I had to blink twice 'cause tears kept wanting to get out.

Breathe. One. Two. "It's time to go. I don't want my momma sendin' the police lookin' for me."

If he was worried about somebody finding out Eula took James, it stood reason that he wouldn't want the police nosing around searching for a little girl.

Wallace moved surprising quick. He grabbed my arm and yanked me from the truck so fast I didn't have a chance to get my feet under me. I ended up on my knees, my arm up by my ear, pinched in his big hand. It hurt, but I wasn't gonna let him know that.

Eula's soft steps came closer, hesitant, like a deer checking if it was safe to come from the woods.

He pointed at her. "Stay away! You know what needs be done."

"No, Wallace! Please!"

"Get back, woman!" He shook me a little, and I hung there like a rag doll at the end of his arm. "Sometimes I think you's dropped on your head as a baby! There ain't but one way out of this now."

"She just a little girl, nobody goin' pay her no attention." Eula's hands clasped beneath her chin.

"She a white girl. You know they don' ask a colored if a white girl tellin' the truth afore they strike. They be all over us. Even if they ask, you done stole that baby." He shook his finger toward the house with the hand that wasn't digging into my arm.

"She won't tell!" Eula cried, her hands out, palms up, pleading.

"I won't!" I shouted. "I won't tell! I don't care 'bout no baby!"

"I keep her! Keep her in secret!"

He breathed deep; his whole body shuddered when he let it out. He swung his free hand and landed Eula in the dirt. "This on you."

He started to drag me toward the woods.

"No!" Eula screamed from down on the ground. Her arms reached toward me.

"I won't tell! I won't!" I twisted, but Wallace held firm. My feet dragged in the dirt. "Let me go! I just wanna go to Nashville!"

Eula crawled after us. Crying. Begging.

My insides turned to water. I shoulda broken that window and run last night while I had the chance.

6

Everything after that slid by so fast, it wasn't much more than a blur in my head. Somewhere, out beyond Eula's crying and the *thud-thud, thud-thud* of my heartbeat, I began to hear something else.

Wallace heard it, too, 'cause he stopped dead still and his head snapped up. I could hear the roughness of his breath as it rushed through his nose. His hand gripped my arm tighter and his eyes narrowed to slits.

The sound rose and fell, swelled and shrank, until I recognized it. Dogs . . . huntin' hounds.

Quick as a rattler, he reached down with the hand that wasn't holding me and jerked Eula up off the ground. She came to her feet like she was one of those string puppets. I was pretty sure if Wallace let her go, she'd have gone flat back on the ground like just like a puppet, too. Her crying slid to whimpers.

Wallace's eyes was crazy, with so much white showing they looked like cue balls.

I opened my mouth to scream, but nothing came out.

Before I could blink, he drug the both of us toward the house. He started moving while I was half on the ground; I didn't have a chance to get on my feet, and Eula wasn't even trying. My shins slammed into the steps, tearing chunks of skin off and setting them on fire. I sucked in a breath to keep from yelling out with the pain; all bullies got worse when you let them know they were hurting you.

Eula's dragging feet caught the rug in the living room. It rolled up like a butter curl behind us. Wallace shoved us into the little bedroom where James was sleeping.

We landed in two heaps on the floor.

Just before Wallace locked the bedroom door, he warned us we'd both be sorry if we made a sound. I believed him. From the look on Eula's face, she did, too. I'd seen her scared of Wallace before, but there was something sharp and new to this scaredness.

I started to see stars. I sat there for a second, sucking air back into my fear-pinched lungs.

Eula scooted on her backside until she was shoved in the corner beside the door. She pulled her legs up to her chest and held tight with both arms. Her eyes didn't look like they was seeing anything around us. Somewhere deep in her throat, a thin, little whine rolled around, almost too quiet to hear.

I looked down at my scraped shins. That just made them hurt worse. It also made me wonder what Wallace would do next. I couldn't think about that. If I let fear get locked in my head, I wouldn't be able to think at all. And if I couldn't think, and Eula was all messed up, we were goners.

I'd been so surprised by Wallace's viciousness that I didn't fight my best—and Eula was too scared to fight at all. I had to do better, be faster, smarter. Meaner.

Mamie had smacked me before, and I'd been knocked down in a fight on the playground, but I'd never been jerked around and dragged like I wasn't even a person at all. I wondered if Wallace treated Eula like this all the time. Maybe she had tried to fight once—Wallace was so big, and poor Eula wasn't more than skin on bones, she couldn't beat him, or even get away most likely.

"Eula?" Her eyes were like glass. I'd never seen a grown-up woman so helpless and scared. She'd just switched off, like she wasn't even on the inside of herself anymore.

The sound of the hounds yippin' and howlin' was close now, maybe even in the yard. I jumped up and looked out the little window, but couldn't see nothin' but trees and a couple of squirrels scared up 'em by all the barking.

Kneeling back in front of Eula, I asked, "Who's comin' with the dogs?"

Her eyes stayed empty.

"Eula?" I touched her cheek and turned her to face me. There was a muddy place where her tears had mixed with the dirt from when she'd been knocked to the ground. "Who's comin' with the dogs?"

I heard Wallace's grumbly voice mixed in with the yappin' of the dogs. But I couldn't hear any other person.

"Eula!" I said, more of a sharp hiss than a yell. I couldn't yell until I knew who was outside.

She blinked. Then her eyes shifted and looked at me.

"Who is it? Who come with the dogs?"

She swallowed hard, like there was something blocking her throat. "Prob'ly Shorty. He come by most days."

"He huntin'?" Which would mean he had a gun he could use to fend off Wallace once he got to rescuin' us.

"He don't hunt, not no more. Not for years. Just got the one arm."

Dang, most likely no gun, then. I chewed my cheek for a second. "He white or colored?"

Her brow wrinkled and she looked at me like I'd gone crazy. "Why would he get dragged behind a car and had his arm tore off if he was white?"

My stomach went sour and I tried not to think about someone's arm being tore right from its socket like that. It seemed there wasn't no limit to the meanness of some people. I felt sorry for that man, but even sorrier for me and James and Eula. A man like that wasn't gonna be interested in making Wallace mad by rescuin' white children. 'Sides, with only one arm and no gun, he wouldn't have a chance against the bear.

I flopped backward and looked at the plank board ceiling. If only Eula hadn't taken James. Then Wallace would be happy to take me out to the highway and never see my white face again; he wouldn't be so scared of Shorty findin' out I was here and blabbing it all over. Or even if James had been a colored baby.

A while passed before the dogs seemed to settle down. Then I heard one of them snufflin' and rubbing the underside of the floor. There wasn't any latticework to keep animals from getting underneath the house. If only dogs could save a person—they don't care if you're white or colored.

I finally sat up and made myself ask, "What did Wallace mean when he said you know what's got to be done?"

Eula looked like she'd switched mostly back on. "He calm down now. Everythin' goin' be all right. You see. Just goin' take some time." She nodded and breathed an "Uh-huh." Then a few seconds later, she whispered, "We be fine."

She crawled over to James. Her gentle hands smoothed his blanket as her hunched shoulders curved over that baby. I felt like I'd turned invisible and started to wonder if she was going away in her head again.

"Eula?"

She started humming, soft and low and oh so sweet. Her head tilted sideways and her eyes stayed on James. It was like she thought she could make the rest of the world go away by just ignoring it.

And right that minute I understood; there was something broke deep inside Eula. Like maybe she hadn't been able to feel right in her world the same way I never felt right in mine—her without a baby and me without a momma. And I wondered if baby James could fix her.

No. Not in this world. Nothing good could come of a colored woman and a white baby. Wallace knew it, sure as day. He'd called her stupid, but she wasn't stupid. She was just empty. Empty and needing a baby to fill her up.

I crawled over behind her and rested my cheek against her back. Her bones was sharp under her skin. Her humming vibrated in my head.

I patted her on the shoulder. "We are gonna be fine, you and me and James. We just gotta get away from Wallace."

The humming stopped like somebody'd pulled the plug on the radio. Her body snapped up straight and I could swear she was holding her breath. "What'd you say?"

"I said we'll be fine once we get away from Wallace."

She turned around so fast that I fell backward onto my elbows. "Now you listen here. I ain't never leavin' Wallace."

I felt like I'd been punched in the chest. After the horribleness we just went through, I couldn't believe she'd stay. "Why not?"

"You don't understand nothin', so don't go talkin' like you do. You just a child, you don't know nothin' about bein' a wife . . . or a colored woman."

"But he's so mean to you! You can come with me to Momma's. She'll help you get a job in Nashville. You don't need Wallace."

"Wallace, he take care of me." Her face got softer. "He always take care of me."

"But—"

"Shush now! You don't know him. He jus' worried 'bout me. He a fine man. I wasn't nothin' till he with me. Nothin' but a throwaway." She sat there for a minute and her eyes got all faraway. "I was sixteen when we met . . . and so shy." She shook her head and sighed. "So shy I couldn't look a man in the eye—even an ugly one." She leaned close and chuckled, like we was sharing a joke. "And Wallace, ahh, you shoulda seen him; the girls all hovered round him like butterflies round a flower. And the men, why, they step right careful round him. Nobody mess with me once I with Wallace."

I wanted to say that nobody needed to 'cause Wallace was doing enough messing hisself. But the way she said it made me think she'd seen a world of hurt even before Wallace. So I just clamped my jaw tight.

"I didn't think he even know I was breathin'. But one Saturday night up in the balcony of the movie house, he come and sat right down next to me—even though there was plenty of empty seats. He smiled so handsome and handed me a bag of popcorn." She smiled in a remembering way. "I was so nervous I couldn't even eat it. Took it home and ate a few pieces every day for a whole week."

I decided I would never, ever eat popcorn again.

"Wallace, he grow up with a hoe in his hand, jus' like every other colored man in Mississippi. But Wallace, he made a life for hisself! One that didn't just sit there and wait for what was handed out." She smiled, like Mamie did when she talked about my granddad. "Had a job with a good wage at the charcoal plant. He work hard, was tall and handsome, and proud. So proud." Her eyes clouded over and her voice slid low. "That pride what bring him down. Down so low he never the same." She sat up straighter and squared her bony shoulders. "But he always take care of me."

She reached out to brush my hair away from my face, and I hated that her touch made me feel weak and better all at the same time.

"We be a family now, us four—a secret family." Eula cupped my cheek with her work-rough hand. "Good Lord, God Almighty, take care of His own," she whispered, as if church-grateful for her devotion being rewarded.

I thought for a minute. Maybe I ought to start praying direct to the Lord, since he seemed to be winning here over my baby Jesus.

"He done give me more than jus' baby James," Eula said. "He know you need a momma, too."

My back stiffened. "The good Lord already gave me a momma. She's waitin' for me in Nashville."

"Is she?" Eula's eyes looked straight into the dark pit of my soul where all of the half-truths hid. "I think your momma maybe been gone a long time." She tilted her head back, peered down her nose, and seemed to look deeper yet. "I think maybe she don't even know you comin'."

The bitter truth of that snatched the breath from my lungs, drained away my strength to load another lie. I just sat there and stared right back at her with my lips locked tight.

Eula tried to draw me close, but I pulled away. "There more to bein' a momma than growin' a child in your belly. Some women just ain't made for stickin' it out." She didn't say it hateful, like Mamie when she talked about Momma, but it still got my back up.

"It ain't like that with Momma!" I felt a tear roll down my nose. "She misses me."

"Course she misses you, you her child. But no matter how much missin' some mommas do, they still can't be a momma the way the good Lord intended. And I take real good care of you." Eula sat there while my hurt swirled with anger, making a knot of feelings so tangled and strong I could hardly breathe.

Then she said, "Yes, the good Lord take care of His own. Trust Him."

I was so mad my whole body shook. Eula thought she was better than my momma—when she was just a colored woman. And she tried to make me think this was all God's doing.

The skin on my neck prickled. "I trust God." My voice was raspy. Then it slid even lower, so low I wasn't sure Eula heard when I said, "But not Wallace."

I didn't want to talk anymore. I went over and laid down on my pallet, facing the wall so my back was to her.

I didn't turn over when I heard Wallace unlock the door a while later and let her out. Sometime after that, I smelled something sweet, like a pie baking, sneakin' under the door. I wondered if Eula had more to deliver to Cayuga Springs. I wondered if Wallace would even let her out of the house to do it if she did.

Then I worried she *would* leave . . . leave me and James here alone with Wallace.

That thought made my insides pucker. I waited and worried, but the truck never started up. Time passed. Eula come back in, but sat down next to James and didn't talk to me. My fear stewed and boiled and finally began to cool some. But it was still there, like bitter on the back of my tongue after eating a bad pecan. I had a feeling it would stay that way until I was safe away from Wallace.

Eula didn't so much as turn an eyelash my way. She sat beside baby James's basket, humming a church song and rocking. It was like I'd gone invisible. I told myself that was okay, since she was so good at seeing inside my head, I didn't want her to figure out what I was thinking 'bout doing.

I didn't much like being mad at her. But she was just too stubborn and determined to have a baby to see what was obvious as frog's eyes. Wallace didn't want to keep me as family. No, sir. Wallace wanted me gone to Jesus.

I told myself, I am white. Wallace can't really do me in.

But I knew better. Nobody knew I was here. I could get buried in the woods and nobody'd ever find me.

My head hurt and my throat felt like it had a big rock stuck in it. The afternoon passed with me and Eula staying invisible to each another and her coming and going with James. Wallace's voice on the other side of the door got running slow as an August river, and I knew he was back in the juice. I kept my mind on how I was gonna get away from here and to my momma—who did want me, no matter what Eula said. Getting away, that's all I let myself think about; not what I was gonna tell Momma about baby James, or about the empty place inside Eula that needed filling so bad that she'd steal a white baby.

7

Finally, it got dark and the house quiet. The wind came on, not fast and hard, but soft and easy, pushed ahead of a summer storm. The trees whispered with it. The old boards of the house sighed like they was too sad to stand another day. Through the flutterin' leaves I could see the on-and-off glow of heat lightning. I could still see the moon playing peekaboo through the leaves, so the clouds hadn't come on yet.

I couldn't hardly be still. My skin felt all jittery and my feet twitched with needing to move. I had to make sure Wallace was good and asleep, but couldn't wait until James was crying for his bottle again. I sure hoped a baby couldn't starve to death in the time it took me to walk to the highway. It was a fact, James had to come with me; I had to get him back to his real momma. I was mad at Eula for staying with Wallace, but I didn't want her to get into trouble. If I took James, she wouldn't, 'cause nobody would ever know she took him. She might have been wrong in going about it, but all Eula wanted was a family, and a person shouldn't get an arm tore off for that.

After I made it to the highway, I was gonna have to have a good story solid in my head. So while I waited, I played with some ideas.

Me and James was orphans. We'd been living with our old grandpa in a shack near the river, but he died of . . . of . . . being old. Now we was going to live with an aunt in Nashville, but there wasn't no money for bus fare.

Me and James's parents left us at a gas station because they didn't have any money to feed us. They told us to go to a church, and the church people could send us to live with our aunt in Nashville.

Me and James had a sick momma. She died. We were supposed to go to Nashville on the bus, but somebody stole the bus fare Momma had left us so we could go live with her sister. That's why we had to hitchhike.

Me and James was running away from a daddy who beat us to go live with our nice aunt in Nashville.

James had been kidnapped by some white people (which was a whole lot more believable than a colored person taking him . . . and it'd keep Eula out of it). I stole him from the kidnappers when they stopped for a picnic lunch. Then I hid in the woods with him until they gave up looking for him and went on. I was going to Nashville to live with my momma, but James needed to be taken back to Cayuga Springs to his people. That one seemed best.

Finally it was time. I could hear Wallace snorin' steady through the wall. I put on my socks and shoes, then got up real quiet and put my ear to the wall that met with Eula's bedroom. Wallace's snores vibrated against my ear like a bee. I wondered how a hateful man like that could fall asleep so peaceful under a picture of Jesus.

I tiptoed to the window and tried to wiggle the rusted latch, but it still wouldn't budge—I'd hoped my spit might have soaked in and loosened it.

I felt a hornet's wing flutter of panic just under my heart and I started breathing too fast. Sweat popped out on my top lip and I was near to comin' out of my skin. The feeling was worse than when I'd by accident got locked in the trunk of Mamie's car.

My feet wanted to run. My mouth wanted to scream.

I pinched my eyes shut and gritted my teeth—couldn't let Wallace hear me, couldn't show my hand, no matter what.

Eula thought it would all be okay if I just stayed. But I'd seen that crazy look on Wallace's face when he'd yanked me from the truck. That kind of crazy liked to hide behind a mask and you never knew when it was gonna come out.

I went back to working on the window, but the dang thing was gonna be stuck till the devil served popsicles.

Looking out at all that dark, I tried to get a fix on what I'd do once the window was open. Eula had been right about one thing: country dark was different than town dark. It swallowed up everything, hiding all sorts of awful things—catamounts with their bloodcurdlin' wildcat cries and sharp claws, swamps filled with snakes, bears, bats . . . I hated bats.

But I was beginning to hate Wallace more. Truth be told, I was more scared of him, too.

What if I broke the window? Could I do it without waking Wallace and Eula . . . even worse, waking baby James? More than anything, I needed him to keep quiet.

If I hit the glass with my elbow wrapped in that knit blanket, maybe it wouldn't make so much noise. I knew I was only gonna get one chance. Once Wallace knew I was trying to escape, he'd probably tie me up. A man like that might keep me tied up forever—like a dog. Tears got in my eyes. I couldn't cry. I couldn't. I would get out of here if I had to chew my way through the walls.

I grabbed the blanket from the cradle, my hands shaking like they did before I did a dare.

One chance. That's all I was gonna get.

I unfolded the blanket until it was just in half. I bent my elbow on my right arm and put the blanket over it. It fell off twice before I got it over and held tight underneath with a hand extra-clumsy from nervousness.

I pulled my elbow back, took a deep breath, and held it. With my eyes squeezed shut, I said a prayer to baby Jesus and hit the window with my blanket-padded elbow.

It didn't break. But I heard something that sounded like little pebbles falling onto the outside sill. I bumped it again, kinda easy, and heard more pebbles. Looking out, I could see little, dark chunks of glazing on the sill. Mamie had had to hire a man to put new glazing on our garage windows; she said if she hadn't, the glass woulda popped right out!

I dropped the blanket and pushed all around the edges of the glass. One corner moved.

Ho-ly cow.

I pushed it just a little harder and more glazing broke loose. I could feel the wind seepin' in right under the glass. It didn't take long before the entire bottom of the glass moved just a little when I pushed it. I couldn't tell how much glazing still held it, and I couldn't figure out how in the heck I was gonna get it out and not have it crash onto the ground outside. But I was gonna get out! If I heard Wallace coming, I'd just jump out and run—I couldn't do James any good by staying once Wallace was onto me.

I pressed against the glass, a little harder . . . a little harder . . . a little harder. Then it moved—too much!

Before I could even suck in a breath, it was falling to the ground and my hands were sticking out in the night, shaking hands with the wind. The glass landed with just a sharp clink and a soft thud.

For a minute I held still, not even breathing, listening for angry bear steps heading my way. But all I heard was Wallace snoring (thank you, baby Jesus). I closed my eyes and finally breathed. I stuck my head out the window frame. The pane was laying on the ground in two triangles.

The window was high enough from the ground that I would have to slide out backwards and lower myself from the sill. But how was I gonna get baby James out? The opening was too small for both of us, especially since he couldn't hang on by hisself.

For a second, I thought about leaving him there in the corner in his basket. Just drop down and make a run for it. Once I got to Momma, she could call the police and report a kidnapping. Trouble was, I couldn't tell anybody how to find this place. The second problem was that Eula would get punished. I kept thinking of that man, Shorty, who'd been dragged behind a car. And not long ago I'd heard about a colored church being set on fire with people inside. If people would burn down a church and drag a man until his arm came off, what might happen to Eula?

James had to come.

If I picked him up out of that basket, he'd probably wake up. If he woke up, he'd most likely start squallin'. Even Wallace juiced up couldn't sleep through that.

I studied for a minute. That basket was just big enough to hold him, soft and oval with a handle on either side that Eula used to carry him around. I got me an idea.

Sliding the knit blanket through the handles, I lifted the basket, testing to see if it'd hold. It did. I balanced the basket on the window frame, praying the whole time for James to keep on sleeping.

An owl hooted close by and I about jumped out of my skin—and almost dropped James out the window.

After swallowing my stomach back to where it was supposed to be, I lowered James and his basket to the ground. Then I slid through the window, letting myself down real slow and careful so I wouldn't step on him or the glass.

My toes touched the ground, but I could barely feel them because my whole body was tingly with nervousness. I pulled the blanket out of the handles, picked up the basket, and, although I wanted to run flat out, I tiptoed around the house, glad for the noise of the wind. Once I got past the old truck, I held the basket handles against my chest and took off, trying to run without jigglin' James's liver right out.

I ran as far as I could without my lungs burstin'—which wasn't all that far 'cause James and his basket took away all my speed. Then I slowed to a walk. I wanted to stop and get my breath. I couldn't risk it. I had to keep moving. I had to get to the highway before Wallace woke up.

In the darkness, the woods beside the lane might as well have been brick walls; everything was wove so tight together that a person couldn't squeeze through without takin' off a good layer of skin. So I walked on one of the ruts made by the truck tires. For a good while all of the night noises had been covered up with me trying to catch my breath, but before long I was hearing everything—tiny animals running through the brush, scared by me as much as they scared me right back; a tree giving off a squeaky groan when the wind blew harder. Daddy said trees making that sound could fall right down any minute. I couldn't tell where that particular squeaky tree was, so I just kept walking, hoping to be out of the way when it fell.

Lucky, I didn't hear any bears.

But a catamount don't make noise when it's movin'. I gripped the handles tighter and tried to go faster, ignoring the knife stabbin' me between my shoulder blades and the stitch in my side.

If I didn't make the highway by sunup, I wasn't sure what I would do. If I kept to the road, all Wallace had to do was get in his truck and he'd be on us. If I hid, waiting for dark, baby James would starve for sure. Out here, if he started crying, we'd be easier to find than the sun in the sky—you could hear a catamount cry for miles, I reckon you could hear baby James even farther.

A big gust of wind swished past, blowing my hair into the corners of my eyes. I shook my head, but I was sweating so bad it stuck like glue. I put the basket down to push the hair away. The big knot of pain between my shoulder blades didn't let up one bit. I decided to try carrying the basket on one side, like Eula did. I looked up, trying to see the tiny flecks of the moon through the trees. It was gone. I hoped it was just covered up with clouds and not gone because morning was about to happen.

Then I heard it, thunder rollin' across the sky. The wind kicked up and settled, and kicked up again.

I picked the basket up with my right hand and started walking. I had to lean to my left to keep balance. The basket bounced against my right leg something awful. Afraid I'd bounce that baby wide-awake, I moved the basket across my stomach and wrapped my arms around the whole thing, which seemed to hurt less than bending my elbows and holding it by the handles.

Suddenly the walls on both sides of me opened up and my feet hit the gravelly road. Somehow I'd made the curve and not noticed.

I turned right, back the way I'd come with Eula in the truck, toward the chip and tar road—even though that way passed through the swamp. I didn't know what was to the left and I couldn't just run all over the place lugging baby James. I was tuckered out already.

I'd taken about two steps when the first, fat raindrop hit me in the face.

8

Whistling past the graveyard. That's what Daddy called it when you did something to keep your mind off your most worstest fear. Ghosts and zombies had nothin' on Wallace the Bear, so I wished I could whistle. Maybe by the time I finished my song, I'd be through the storm, away from Wallace, safe on the highway, picked up by some nice preacher on his way to Nashville to give a Sunday sermon.

But I couldn't whistle, even though both Daddy and Patti Lynn had tried to teach me. So I always had to do my whistling in my head. And the storm that let loose was the worst ever in the history of the world.

The easy wind got wild. Dirt and twigs hit me like hot pepper, stinging my skin, especially my raw shins. When the lightning flashed, I could see the wind bend the trees nearly halfway to the ground, then toss them back. Long grapevines reached out from where they hung from branches, whipping me as I passed. In the places where kudzu covered the trees, they looked like giant monsters waving their arms and ducking their heads to eat whatever animal, or little girl, passed by. The wind shoved me this way and that, so I when I leaned against it, it just switched around and pushed me from another direction.

Then the rain really started. It came so hard that even with my head bent down I had to squint my eyes. James busted out crying, the sound snatched up by the wind and carried who knows where, probably right to Wallace's bedroom. James did sound a little like a catamount, so maybe Wallace wouldn't pay any attention (please, please, baby Jesus).

I kept moving forward, my shoes squishing with every sloppy step.

A loud crack sounded over the storm, the sound of a splintering tree trunk. The tree crashed against others, a dinosaur in the woods. I stopped dead and squeezed baby James tight, waiting for it to hit, hoping it wouldn't be on us.

It wasn't, but it was close enough the ground shook under my feet.

I wished I'd left James in the bedroom; at least then he'd be dry and warm and he wouldn't starve to death. I hadn't even got to the swamp yet. Carrying James, I was moving like a turtle, not the jackrabbit Daddy always said I was.

The good thing about storms this strong was they didn't last long. It might rain for the rest of the night, but I could walk in the rain; heck, I couldn't get any wetter. Right now I was just glad not to be squished under a fallen tree.

I started to shiver. I hoped James wasn't too cold. He kept crying and was wiggly, making me hold the basket so tight I worried I was hurting him. Maybe if I sang to him, he'd be less scared. I didn't know any baby songs, so I sang "Row, Row, Row Your Boat." My voice sounded funny in the wild wind, but I think James liked it 'cause he quieted some.

Before long, the lightning flashes were less blinding and less often and the thunder moved off. The wind stopped swatting at the trees, but the rain still come down hard. When I started to feel so tired and hopeless that I wanted to just stop right where I was, I thought about being locked in a room, with Wallace and his craziness just outside the door.

In my miserableness I almost wished I was back home getting myself hauled off to reform school. Truth be told, Mamie's house probably wasn't all that different from reform school, all chores and punishment and wadded-up disappointment—just without the locked doors. Sometimes I thought that Mamie thought if she smiled at me once, I'd let loose all the bad behavior I had stored up in me—which according to Mamie was considerable. I never got anything I wanted 'cause everything I asked for was "trashy" or "foolish" or "a waste of your daddy's hard-earned money."

Mamie's. Reform school. It didn't really matter. But Momma's in Nashville, that was gonna be different.

I started doing a different kind of whistling in my head; thinking how Christmas was gonna be in Nashville. Daddy would come there instead of going to Mamie's (and Mamie wouldn't be invited; she could sit in Cayuga Springs in her perfect quiet, looking at her perfect Christmas tree without my handmade ornaments from school messing up the back side anymore). Momma and I would make cookies in the shapes of reindeer and stars, and I wouldn't get hollered at for getting sugar all over the floor. I'd get Sea-Monkeys and Sparkle Paints and a Barbie House (I didn't really like Barbies, but the house with all of its fold-together cardboard modern furniture was neat) and a record player with records by Elvis and and the Beach Boys and Martha and the Vandellas. Mamie was particular determined that I didn't listen to none of that negra music, but I liked it a lot when me and Patti Lynn listened to Cathy's records.

Thinking 'bout Christmas in Nashville helped for a while. Then James let loose and no amount of jigglin' or singin' made any difference.

"Sorry, but there's no food," I kept telling him, but either he didn't hear or didn't understand. "I'm sorry . . . I'm sorry . . . sorry . . . sorry." I kept mumbling it over and over. My feet kept moving but my mind kinda went to sleep.

I'm not sure how much time went by, but suddenly I realized the rain had stopped and James wasn't crying. I worried he wasn't alive anymore, had maybe starved clean to death. But I was too scared to look, so I just kept walking.

With my mind awake again, I noticed the ground under my feet had turned to chip and tar. The trees and brush that had made a tunnel of the road had disappeared. Naked trees, black on the dark gray sky with ghosts of moss dancing under their broken branches. Water licked right up to the edge of the road.

The swamp.

All sorts of things ran around in my head and I couldn't stop them: swamp monsters, water moccasins, gators. My skin puckered up with a fresh crop of goose bumps and I tried to make myself small and quiet.

I loved Vincent Price movies, but after this I was never gonna spend a quarter to see another one. Being scared for real was way worse than being movie scared.

How long had it taken Eula to drive past the brown water and bare trees? It didn't matter. It'd take me a lot longer, especially since I was dog tired.

Then I heard it. Birds chirpin' for the morning. I hadn't noticed, but a soft gray light was creepin' in. Silver mist rose off the water—just like in all of the scary movies I'd ever seen. I wished with all my heart we was out of this swamp.

Light got brighter. The sky streaked pink and orange in front of me. I looked over my shoulder and saw the sky behind me had blued up some but still showed a couple of bright stars. James started crying again. I was almost glad . . . at least he was alive.

I was getting hungry myself and started thinking about a nice big bowl of Sugar Frosted Flakes. I told my growling stomach to shut up. It didn't listen—probably couldn't hear over James's caterwaulin'. My arms started to cramp and shake and I could feel a blister rubbed on my left heel by my wet socks. I had to rest for just a minute.

Water was everywhere, so I sat right down where I was, Indian-style on the puddly road. I figured in the middle was farther for the snakes to crawl and I'd see 'em coming. It took a couple of seconds to unbend my arms. Once they got loosened, baby James kicked and the basket jumped and rolled over onto the road.

The basket had been folded so tight for so long, he didn't tumble out.

I set the basket upright and spread it open. His face was red as an August sunburn. His mouth was open to his gummy gums and his eyes squeezed shut. I thought he'd stopped breathing when he finally sucked in a big gulp of air, then screamed bloody murder.

I was just reaching in the basket to get him out when I heard a rough rumble.

Not thunder.

A truck was coming—and there was nowhere to hide.

The robin-egg-blue patch on the hood sucked all hope from my lungs. I didn't even stand up, just sat there watching those headlights getting bigger by the heartbeat. The only direction I could run was straight down the road, and I sure couldn't outrun a truck, no matter how rickety it was.

But this old truck wasn't creepin' along. It was coming fast, way faster than Eula drove. A big lump of surrender swelled up in my throat. Black, slimy fear wound itself around it, choking me till my ears rang and my chest hurt. A sob rammed up against that fear and it exploded from me, startling me with its loudness.

Once that first cry was loose, it took over my whole self and there wasn't nothing left to be but blubberin' defeat. I'd tried. I'd tried to save me and James. But now Wallace knew my hand. Tears blurred the hulk of hunched-up rust and headlights barreling my way.

I was gonna spend the rest of my life locked up in that bedroom, probably tied up, too.

The truck got closer, not slowing down.

Closer.

It wasn't gonna stop!

I considered letting death gather me under that truck.

At the last second, I kicked James's basket, sending it rolling to one side of the road. At the same time I threw myself backward to the other, rolling up and over my shoulders in a backward somersault. As I landed on my belly, head still on the road, I heard my feet hit the water. Had James landed in the swamp on the other side?

The wheels locked up and slid on the wet chip and tar, screaming like a giant bird. The spray splattered my face as the front wheel stopped right in front of my nose.

That wheel didn't have a hubcap. Why I noticed was a mystery.

My stomach felt like it was still back underneath that truck's dull, pockmarked front bumper.

I heard James squallin'. He wasn't underwater and the truck hadn't squashed him. I couldn't see if he was hurt. I couldn't see nothin' but that fat rubber tire and rusty wheel. It come to me then that I couldn't move even a finger, laying there with my breath echoing in my body and my eyes on that tire.

The door clunked and squeaked open.

My eyes shifted in their sockets. The shoe that hit the pavement next to me was big and brown.

Tears wetted my cheeks and I hated every one of them.

All the sudden, Wallace had me by the back of my shirt, yanking me up off the ground.

For a second I just hung there, limp with fear.

Fight!

My arm finally listened to my brain and I took a swipe at him. I could only reach his arm. It felt like I was hittin' a ham.

I opened my mouth to yell, Let me go! But all that came out was a shameful sob.

He gave me a little shake like I was a kitten he had by the scruff.

That knocked something loose inside me. All my muscles woke up. I fought like a catamount to get free of that man, twistin' and thrashin' and scratchin'. With a scream through my gritted teeth, I flung my legs, trying to land a kick.

He slapped my face. The sting of it sucked the air out of my scream and stunned my limbs into stillness. My eyes got blurry as I hung there at the end of his arm, half-sitting on the ground.

That's when I realized I wasn't the only one screaming.

Eula was coming up and over the side of the truck bed, her hair sticking up like tufts of steel wool, blood running down her cheek. "Stop! Wallace! Stop!"

He jerked his head around, looking surprised to see her.

He moved quick as a snake, whipping me around so my head was toward the water and slammed me down. I grabbed at the marsh grass and tried to pull against him, but my hands kept slipping.

Eula threw herself at him, but he flicked her off like she was no bigger than a bug.

"Don' make this worse than it gotta be!" he yelled while he pressed me against the ground. The back of my head hit the water.

I wasn't gonna get tied up. I was gonna die.

"Please, don't," I said, my voice so small I could barely hear it. My bladder let go; warmth ran up my back. My heart beat so fast I was dizzy. "I'll stay with you and Eula. I'll never tell about James. Never . . ."

His eyes rolled up in his head, looking to the sky. His voice was a harsh whisper when he said, "God forgive me, it gotta be done."

Eula was up again. She pulled against Wallace's shoulders, like a bird trying to move an elephant. "Please, baby. You not this kind of man, I know you ain't. You got a good heart inside you. I promise I'll keep her locked inside. I promise. Nobody know. Please, baby."

For an instant, his grip on my shoulders eased.

Then Wallace roared as loud as any bear and flung her away. She landed on her side and rolled into the water.

"I won't tell! I won't tell anybody!" I screamed.

The water came up over my ears. I strained my neck to raise my head.

"Don't look at me!" he shouted. "Close your eyes and don't you look at me!" His knee pinned my shoulders and his big hand pressed my forehead. Then he pushed.

I kicked and bucked my legs. I clawed his arm.

The water blurred my vision, but I saw him turn his face away. My breath ran out fast.

My mouth opened. Water burned its way in.

This is the end of me.

The hand on my head began to shake.

A lily pad floated into sight. It looked different from the bottom.

All the sudden, I wasn't scared anymore. Warm calm wrapped me up tight.

I was sorry I wouldn't see my momma again. Sorry I didn't tell Patti Lynn good-bye. Sorry Daddy'd have to be without his girl when he came home for a visit next time.

My eyes closed.

Please don't hurt baby James.

All at once, the hand and the knee were gone.

My face sprung up out of the water. I had to kick with my legs to keep from sliding back in. I grabbed a handful of tall grass and pulled. I coughed and wheezed as I rolled over. I heard my lungs squeal as air rushed in, burning even more than the water as it had inched deep into my chest.

I heard Eula splashing and slipping a few feet away as she tried to get out of the mud and water. It hadn't been her who made him stop.

Wallace sat on the edge of the road, not a foot from me, his elbows on his knees, the heels of his hands pressed against his eyes. His mouth was drawn into an awful openmouthed frown; a string of spit ran from his lower lip. He rocked and muttered, "Sweet Jesus, save me . . . save me . . . I can't . . . I jus' can't . . ."

I wanted to yell his damnation. I opened my mouth and all that came out was a sorry sob; a baby's sob. I tried to swallow it, but another bubbled up right behind it.

Wallace trained his eyes on me and raised his fist. "You's alive now, but you run again, I am gonna kill you . . . right after I kill that squallin' baby."

Never let a bully see you scared.

I tried to sit up but my arms were too weak to push.

Reaching deep for courage, I found there was nothing left to grab on to.

I wished I'd let that truck run over me.

I rolled onto my back and looked up at the sky, my own barking sobs filling my ears. Suddenly the sunrise turned inside out and time ran backwards, sending the sky toward darkness.

Baby James sounded farther and farther away.

Then everything faded altogether. I reached out and took that blackness by the hand, glad to go away from here. Away from everything forever.

9

I was rocking. I was warm. A soft hum brushed my ears, which seemed to be plugged up with cotton, making the sound far away. I knew it was close though, 'cause it vibrated against my shoulder. Momma?

Keeping my eyes closed, I tried to dig back deeper into sleep. I was safe. That's all I wanted to let in. But my body worked against me, waking up anyway, poking with soreness and pain. For a while I could ignore it. Then things started to prickle my mind. The storm. The swamp.

A cold wind blew the cobwebs from my head, pulling them string by sticky string, showing more than I wanted to remember.

Wallace.

Oh, dear baby Jesus, no.

The smell of woodsmoke and kerosene snaked into my nose. I was back in the hateful little bedroom. Trapped. Hopeless.

I felt like something was trying to claw its way out of my chest. The pain forced my eyes open.

I was wrapped in the quilt from my pallet. Brown arms wrapped around me. Eula hummed as she pushed the rocker slowly back and forth. My bare toes tapped the floor each time she rocked forward.

Eula smiled. "There now. You awake." She said it soft and sweet, and the sound of it made me want to cry.

I pressed myself back against her bony shoulder and stuck my nose down into the quilt. My eyeballs felt like they was likely to explode from the tears built up inside. But inside was where they had to stay. Blubberin' wasn't gonna help anything. My cheeks burned with shame, thinking on how I'd cried and begged out there on the road. I'd showed I was nothing but a scared little girl.

And now Wallace knew.

"It's all right," Eula cooed just like she did to baby James. "It be all right now."

A tornado sprung up in my chest, a wild swirl of black fear, red anger, and hot frustration. Those feelings spun so tight I couldn't tell one from the other. They sucked the air from my aching lungs and sent bitter shivers through me. Eula had known she'd stole that white baby. She'd known Wallace was crazy. He'd tried to kill me and here she was acting all sweet, like it was a regular day.

I threw myself from her lap. The water in my ears crackled and fluttered. Tripping over the quilt, I stumbled to the floor. As I rolled over, I caught sight of her face and a tiny bit of my anger went away.

Blood had dried on her cheek over a deep red-purple bruise beneath her brown skin. Her black hair stood in pointy tufts like a crazy clown hat. Her lip was split and swollen.

She had tried to save me.

No! I pushed the thought away. She was wrong! She could have driven right on by, kept baby James, and I could have been safe with Momma right now.

Baby James!

I looked around the room. The bulrush basket was in the corner, dirty and broken. No baby inside. "Oh no!"

"He all right. He sleepin'." Eula nodded toward the cradle.

All my muscles let go at once. "He's okay?"

She nodded. "And you, too."

"I am not okay," I said, mustering up just as much hatefulness as I could. "I'm not." I sounded more pitiful than hateful. "You never shoulda picked me up. You kidnapped me just like you did James!"

Her brow wrinkled and her eyes filled with surprise and hurt. She looked away. "No. No, it wasn't like that. Nobody want James. And you . . . I was worried you come to no good out there all alone after dark."

"Wallace tried to kill me! How much more 'no good' can it get?"

She began to shake her head, burying her fingers in her hair. "It wasn't supposed to—" She rocked a little. "You was supposed to go on to Nashville. Baby James supposed to stay with me. But Wallace, he so scared . . ."

"He's scared! I was the one who almost got drowned."

She sent a quick look toward the glassless window. "Shhh. Shhh, now. No need to be afraid of Wallace."

Just then the bear's hateful face peered in through the window, and the urge to throw up grabbed me so fast all I could do was lean over and heave onto the floor. My stomach squeezed and squeezed until my eyes felt like they was gonna pop. Nothing but a thin string came up. Then I got a coughing fit, which caused more heaving.

I realized Eula had come onto the floor with me. She rubbed my back, talking quiet the whole time. I shook her hand off. She didn't put it back.

When I could finally breathe again, I peeked out from under my eyebrows to see Wallace still staring at me. I couldn't tell exactly what he was thinking, but he looked . . . sad. Guess he was since he didn't get me all the way killed.

Eula whispered in my ear, "He only tryin' to keep me safe. He don't mean it."

Well, the look in his eyes when he'd pushed me under told me he did mean it. But I was too scared of starting trouble again to say that out loud with Wallace so close.

He put a wide board across the window and started nailing it in place. Every hammer blow was a fresh stab of hopelessness.

Eula held me by the shoulders and pulled me so I was sitting on the floor between her legs with my back against her chest. I was too weak to fight it. She wrapped an arm around me and rocked side to side as she spoke soft against my ear, "He stop hisself."

I remembered the hand suddenly gone. I remembered Eula still trying to climb up out of the swamp

I wanted to ask, Why? Why did he stop? But the words jammed up in my throat.

Then I remembered Eula coming up out of the truck bed when Wallace grabbed me up off the road. "Why was you in the back of the truck?" I whispered.

"Wallace goin' without me. I jump in when he turnin' the truck around."

I wondered if she'd cut her cheek and lip then, or if Wallace had opened them up for her before he got in the truck.

"I always keep you safe," she said as she brushed my hair back.

Eula was crazy if she thought she stood a chance if Wallace got it in his head to kill me again.

Another board thumped up on the window. The room was getting darker fast. And the rest of the world farther away. I was gonna spend the rest of my life locked up in this breathless room. No one would ever know what happened to me. I'd grow up. I'd never get a record player. I'd never get to work as a curb girl at the drive-in.

When I opened my eyes, I kept them on a gouge in the linoleum, the only thing that didn't have power over me.

Someday Wallace had to get old and die. By then would I be too old and crazy to ever live anywhere else but this hid-away house? Would I be like old Chester Potts out near the dump, crazy as a loony bird, shoutin' and swearin' at everyone who went by his house? Mamie said he was crazy 'cause he'd been born to strange folk and had lived locked away from people his whole life.

"It over," Eula whispered. "He understand now. It ain't Wallace's nature to—" She snapped her mouth shut, but I knew what she was going to say: kill, not in his nature to kill, murder. "We be a family."

"We're not family." My voice sounded so weak and broken that it made me mad. I decided I wasn't gonna talk anymore.

The last board went up on the window, washing us in dimness. The light we did have came in dull, flat slivers and got ate up before it reached deep in the room. Not only would I be crazy by the time Wallace died, I'd be blind like a mole in sunlight, too.

"Sometimes Wallace, he get lost," she said against my hair. "But he always find his way back."

Again I felt the palm of his hand pressing on my head, then suddenly letting go. What if he hadn't found his way back just then?

Didn't matter. Sooner or later I probably was gonna die here.

I pulled myself away from her and grabbed my quilt. I crawled to my pallet and curled into the smallest ball I could. Pulling the quilt over my head, I sank into a dark place where no one could touch me.

I don't know how long I laid there wrapped up in that quilt, hanging somewhere between sleep and feelin' sorry for myself. Truth be told, I didn't have a lot of experience with feelin' sorry for myself—not like being hoppin' mad, or feeling like I'd come out of my skin if I didn't try something. Those were plenty familiar. Feelin' sorry was a place for babies and wienies. I wished I could just go to sleep for a long time, but sleep wouldn't settle in.

Back home when I was too worked up at Mamie to get to sleep, I reached deep into my memories and pulled out one that made me feel happy. It was so old that it was worn down to sounds and feelings and not a real picture in my head. We—Momma, Daddy, and me—lived in our own apartment in the upstairs of a nice old lady's house. She gave piano lessons. I remember hearing the beautiful mystery of her music coming up thorough the floor. . . . I also remember the *plinky-plonky* sounds of her students. Daddy helped her by cutting the grass and whatnot so we could afford to live there (I don't remember that part, but Mamie tells me about it when she's mad at Momma for being lazy and irresponsible). Momma and Daddy had tucked me into bed, both of them together. My room smelled like baby powder and Momma's hair. Mr. Wiggles was soft against my cheek, held tight in the crook of my arm. Momma and Daddy were talking real soft in the other room, Daddy's voice low and kind of rumbly, Momma's light and happy. Momma laughed . . . not in a big ha-ha way, but quiet like water tripping over itself in a creek. Those sounds wound themselves together and wrapped me up, just like a blanket. My insides got all quiet, which didn't happen often 'cause my insides was always busy. I floated on the cloud of their voices. It was the best falling asleep ever.

I ran that memory over and over in my head, but it didn't do any good.

Later, when Baby James woke up crying, Eula came and took him out. She didn't bring him back. I was too broke down to worry about him. A dark, wet blanket had covered my mind.

Eula brought me food. I couldn't even look at it. I pinched my nose and breathed through my mouth so I couldn't smell it. She asked me how I was feeling and I ignored her. She sighed, patted my shoulder, and went away again.

Sleep stayed away, but the mind darkness came back.

At some point Wallace raised his voice so I heard it clear. "Gimme 'nother jar of that catdaddy."

Eula's soft footfalls were followed by the sound of the jar hitting the table. I kept my ears perked, since Eula said the juice made Wallace to forget hisself. I smelled baking again. Eula hadn't left, so I wondered how much pie two people—even if one of them was a giant—could eat.

Sometime later I heard him grouching around and Eula helping him to bed. The springs squeaked. Two shoes hit the floor. Once I heard him start snorin' good, I finally relaxed.

Crickets chirped and a hoot owl called from the trees. Eula tiptoed into the room and put baby James in the cradle

After she tucked him in, her footsteps stopped right beside me. I pretended I was asleep, eyes tight and breathing slow.

Just go away.

She got down on her knees and stayed there a long while. When I heard her whispered "Amen," I knew she was praying over me. Then her hand settled soft as a butterfly on my head. She let it stay there gentle and kind as she pulled the quilt away from my shoulders—I was hot under there, but pretended to sleep on.

"Oh, baby girl," she sighed. "I will keep you safe. No matter what."

Her lips brushed my hair and then she stood up.

I'd never been tucked in so tender. A tear rolled across the bridge of my nose, but I was careful not to sniffle.

I waited to hear the door open, but it didn't. Instead I heard her rustling, then sigh. When I sneaked a peek through tiny eye slits, I saw she was over by baby James's cradle, laying on her back with her arm over her eyes. She was so skinny she was barely a shadowy bump on the floor, except for that sharp elbow stickin' up.

As I listened to her breathing even out and slow, sleep finally come over me.

I felt him there right before I smelled his sour, juiced-up breath; right before the big hand closed around my throat. I tried to kick, but he'd straddled me, his weight settled on my stomach and his feet hooked around my ankles holding them to the floor.

Pain stabbed my throat. Air wouldn't come.

Eula!

My voice stayed silent.

I tried to buck, bow my back, but I was pinned.

A thudding swish filled my ears.

Help me, Eula! You promised.

My eyeballs felt ready to pop.

Promised. Promised. Prom—

A scream shot through the air, wordless, shrill and terrified.

Eula!

Wallace suddenly rocked to the side, his grip loosening enough that I jerked in a breath before he tightened it again. There was a crash. Eula's scream cut off.

No, no, no, no . . .

James cried, but it was getting farther away.

Suddenly the hand left my throat and Wallace's weight shifted to the side and he went limp. Something heavy thudded to the floor.

Air tore down my throat, hurting as much as Wallace's cruel grip.

Eula screamed, "Oh, Lord, oh, Lord, oh, Lord!"

Her hands pulled at my shoulders. I pushed with my feet. Once my legs were out from under Wallace, Eula wrapped me tight in her arms. I tried to pull away, needing space, needing air.

"What have I done? Oh, Lord, what have I done!" Eula's voice slid to a pitiful whisper. "Wallace?" She let go of me and crawled toward him. "Wallace? Wake up. I didn't mean—" Her words disappeared into sobs as she got up and ran out of the room.

I was still gasping when she ran back with towels and a lamp. She pressed the towels to the bloody dent in the side of Wallace's head. The light showed a dark puddle on the floor. Eula's iron skillet was next to him.

"Come on, Wallace. You be all right," she mumbled as she held a towel to the wound. "You be all right."

It didn't look to me like Wallace was gonna be all right ever again.

And I was glad.

Eula sat at the table across from me. Four pies was sitting between us. None of 'em been touched. The lamplight made her cheekbones stand out over the shadows below. Her eyes looked strange and I would have thought she'd gone away from herself again, except for her hands. They was restless and twitchy on the tabletop, twisting, drumming, palms sliding over the surface, then twisting again.

Neither of us looked into the little bedroom.

Once she'd figured out Wallace was good and dead, she'd covered him with a sheet and had me move baby James's cradle into the kitchen. She'd pointed to the table for me to sit down and then looked at my neck, her eyes streaming and hands shaking the whole time. Then she'd gone to the pump, wet a cloth, and wrapped its coolness around my burning throat. After that she'd spent a real long time just sitting there crying—even while she fed baby James.

He was asleep now, not knowing anything about what had happened. He was lucky. Lucky, lucky baby.

Mamie always talked about things that once done can't be undone, how I had to think before I acted, how one second could change everything in your whole life. She'd been talking about things like breaking Jimmy Sellers's nose and me getting locked in the trunk of the car. But now I saw it was more than that. Being almost killed twice had changed something deep inside me. I couldn't tell what exactly, 'cause it was just settling in. But I wasn't never, ever gonna be the same again.

The rooster crowed, even though it didn't look to be getting light out yet.

Finally, Eula's hands settled. She blinked and put one hand over her heart as she stood up. She wobbled just a bit and put her fingertips back onto the table. "Reck—" Her voice was low and raspy before it stopped altogether. She cleared her throat and focused her eyes on the door. "Reckon I'd best go get the law."

I couldn't believe my ears. "What!" My voice was croaky, but she understood me fine.

She sighed, then sniffled. "Tell I done killed Wallace."

"The law? You crazy? What about baby James?"

Her shoulders curved and she breathed deep, letting it out long and slow. She reminded me of a dog Jimmy Sellers had once kicked. "Don't matter now. I goin' to jail anyway."

I'd been doing plenty of thinking on my own while we'd been sitting there. Wallace was a bad man—no matter how he used to be when he and Eula met. Nobody should care he was dead.

"You only killed Wallace to keep him from killin' me!" My throat hurt like my neck was being wrung again and I had to stop and take a slow breath. I went on, more careful to keep my voice quiet, "The law can't lock you up for that."

"Maybe not. But they'll know 'bout James." She looked more brokenhearted about losing that baby than knockin' the life out of Wallace. "That'll get me worse'n jail."

I thought of that man Shorty getting dragged behind a car for being colored and shivered. I couldn't let something like that happen to Eula. "So you can't tell!"

Her brown gaze turned to me. "I done killed him." She caught a breath like she'd been running. "I got to tell." She turned away from the table and started toward the door.

"Wait!" I jumped up. "Just wait a minute. He ain't gonna get any deader if we think about this for a bit."

She came back to me and put a hand on my cheek. "You a good girl. But no thinkin' is gonna make a difference. I done it. Now you stay with James while I go."

I thought about taking James and running while she was gone. Then nobody'd know she took him. But then I wouldn't be here to tell the law how she saved me. I had to figure out something.

"No!" I grabbed her arm as she started to turn away. "Just . . . just . . ."

She looked down on me with a sad smile. "It be all right. You'll get to your momma"—she paused—"or wherever you supposed to be."

Momma!

I still had hold of Eula's arm, so I tugged her back to the chair. "I got it!" I made her sit. "You and me and James will go to Nashville! Momma'll help us. She'll be so grateful you saved me. She'll help us figure out what's best to do 'bout Wallace and the law."

It didn't look like I was changing her mind, so I pushed some more. "You'll know I'm safe with Momma then. And it'll give us time to think on it ourselves. We don't want to 'run off half-cocked.'" Which Mamie said I did all the time.

Eula didn't say anything.

"Do it for me," I said. "We'll figure out what do 'bout Wallace. I promise. But take me to my momma. Please." Momma would save Eula.

For a long while Eula just sat there, staring at the window that was just graying with dawn. My heart beat fast and I realized I was as scared for Eula as I'd ever been for myself.

Finally she looked at me and breathed out a long sigh. "I take you to your momma afore I go to the po-lice. I owe you that."

My knees felt wobbly. (Thank you, baby Jesus.)

IO

By nine o'clock we'd been bouncin' along in that truck for almost an hour. The air was like a rubber raincoat, which didn't help my rolly stomach one bit. Baby James seemed fine with the heat, sleeping on the truck's floorboard between my feet and wearing just a diaper. But Eula looked sickly as she drove so slow we coulda been outrun easy by a turtle. Even creepin' along, the truck rattled like we was probably droppin' parts along behind us. I didn't complain about our slowness. As Mamie was forever reminding me, I needed to count my blessings. At least Eula hadn't gone straight to the law like she'd wanted to. And we were moving away from that big dead body.

Before we'd left Eula's house, we wrapped Wallace up in a sheet and drug him down to the springhouse so he wouldn't rot so fast. I didn't know why Eula cared, but she did. It was a miserable job and we only got it done because it was downhill and we rolled him most of the way.

Eula's Holy Bible sat on the truck seat between us, its gold letters rubbed to a thin shadow and its worn-out, cracked-edged cover flappin' in the wind that rushed through the windows. That Bible had been the first thing Eula had insisted on bringing with us. She'd snatched it up and held it tight to her chest the entire time she packed everything else, like she was afraid to set it down. We brought the picture of grown-up Jesus from her bedroom, too. Course with her hanging on to that Bible like she was, I'd had to stand on the bed and take it off the wall. It was in the back of the truck now with her grip—which is what she called the little tan-and-brown suitcase she'd pulled from under her bed. I'd seen better suitcases in the alley trash. But it held her few things just fine. I can't say why she brought her church hat, though, if she thought she was going to the law as soon as we got to Nashville. My seeing it go into the suitcase had made me hope she'd come round to my way of thinking.

Once her clothes had been packed, we'd gathered up all of the food we could eat on the road, which wasn't much. When we'd finally walked out of that saggy house, she'd stopped dead and looked around. I guess she figured she'd never be back. If I was her, that would be okay with me; who wanted to be reminded of Wallace's meanness every morning when you opened your eyes?

I know it ain't Christian, but I was happy that man was dead. Truth be told, Eula should be, too.

I watched the trees, cotton fields, and crooked, tin-roofed shanties go by, chewing on my thumbnail, sorting out the details of my plan. Everybody knows the details color your words truth or lie, so I had to get them straight and keep them straight. Eula's whole life depended on it. Once I got it all laid out in my head, I'd have to convince Eula it was the right thing, which was gonna take some doing—even with her Sunday hat in the suitcase.

Out of the corner of my eye, the waving cover of Eula's Bible was trying to get my attention and make me feel guilty over my lie buildin'. I turned my head so I couldn't see it anymore. I hoped baby Jesus would understand; he couldn't want a woman as good as Eula to get punished for protecting a baby and a little girl.

Next to the Bible was Eula's pocketbook, which held all the money we had, four dollars and seventy-five cents from her pie delivery on the Fourth of July—three cherry, one buttermilk, and a chocolate chess. I only knew that 'cause Eula spent the whole time she'd been packing talking nonstop. Some folks was like that, all chattery when they was scared, so I'd just let her talk. Once we got on the road, she'd clammed up tight, even though she still seemed plenty nervous.

For a minute I let myself wonder where I might be right now if those people hadn't ordered pies from Eula. It turned out Nashville was a whole lot farther away than I'd thought. Eula said it would likely take at least two days—maybe longer since she wanted to stay off the highways as much as possible. How would I have made it on my own with no money and no food?

When I'd asked Eula if our four dollars and seventy-five cents would be enough to get us there, she'd just looked real determined and said we'd make do. Which sounded like we was gonna come up short. I wish we'd found the rest of her and Wallace's money. But Wallace kept it hid away and we couldn't find it anywhere. I think maybe he'd been lyin' to her about having it at all 'cause we even looked in the woodbox and the attic.

As we traveled old, worn-out roads with no traffic, Eula spent as much time looking in the rearview mirror as at the road ahead. Her body was so tensed up she looked like a spring wound a turn or two too tight.

"We ain't seen but one car since we left," I said. "You can pro'bly relax some."

Her eyes jerked to the rearview again. She sucked in a breath.

I spun around and looked out the cracked back window. "It's only a man in a car, not the sheriff." The car was coming up fast—well, fast compared to how Eula was driving, so he was likely going regular speed. It didn't slow up at all until it was almost on our back bumper. The road was narrow, but if Eula got as far to the side as she could, it could pass. "Wave him round," I said.

Eula shot a look at me like I'd asked her to give him the finger. "He white." Her hands tightened on the steering wheel and she sunk down into her shoulders like a turtle. She ran a nervous tongue around her lips and fixed her eyes straight ahead.

"He just wants to go faster," I said, looking over my shoulder. "Pull close to the side."

Eula slowed down more and edged closer to the ditch.

The car behind us got even closer. We were driving into the sun so I could see the man behind the wheel real clear. He had slicked-back hair and a hateful frown on his face. He leaned his head out the window and shouted, "You and your pickaninny get off the damn road!"

Eula hunched deeper into herself.

My red rage snapped on. I shot up out of my seat and perched myself in the open window, hangin' on to the wing vent to keep steady. I raised a fist and shook it at the man. "We got as much right to this road as you!" I pointed in front of us. "Go on round!"

"Starla!" Eula hissed. "Get yo'self back in here!"

"No!" I waved the man around again. "He's got plenty of room to go round." Just then there was a thud and we jerked forward. I almost fell out of the truck completely. Before I could get myself slid back in, it happened again. That man was running right into us!

Eula grabbed the hem of my shorts and I was planted back in my seat. "Stop provokin' him."

"He's the one provokin'!" I started up again but Eula grabbed my shirt. I swatted at her. "He can go round."

"You get us killed," Eula said, soundin' so desperate that I stopped trying to get away. "We gotta be careful if I gonna get you to your momma."

I felt a little bad, letting my red rage get going and forgetting about how Eula had said we were supposed to travel like we was invisible.

The car rammed us again, just enough to jerk my neck. "Why won't he just go round?"

"Let's hope he do." Eula's eyes kept shifting to the mirror. "Let's hope he do," she repeated in a breathy voice that warned me things could get a whole lot worse.

I felt a little nudge as the man's bumper touched ours.

Then we started to go faster.

Everything swirled up after that. Eula crying. Me hollerin'. The truck's nose tilting into the ditch. The sight of the man's laughing face. His shout of "Little nigger lover" as he passed.

Even before I could yell back at that man, we thudded to a stop. I hit the dash. Muddy water splashed the windshield.

Thank goodness I had my feet braced on the floor and didn't land on baby James, who was full awake and screaming.

I looked down. He was flipped over onto his belly. I didn't want to turn him over. What if he was hurt?

Eula squeaked, "The baby! Get the baby!"

I looked over at her. Blood was running from a gash over her eye.

"Baby!" She sounded so sharp I reached down and grabbed him up. I wasn't careful like I should have been and his head flopped some, but he looked okay to me.

Eula reached over and took him from me. After she looked him over, she asked me, "You okay?"

I nodded. "But you're bleedin'." I pointed to her forehead.

"No matter. Long as you and James all right." She ran her hands over his arms and legs again like she was making double sure.

"What was wrong with that man?" I asked. "Why'd he do this to us? We weren't hurtin' him."

Eula just lifted a shoulder and wiped the blood off her eyebrow with the back of a wrist. "Don't need no reason." She sounded more sad than angry.

I sat there for a minute, gatherin' up my thoughts and discovering I'd bit my tongue when we crashed. Jimmy Sellers didn't seem to have any reason for his meanness either. But Jimmy was a kid.

"Why ain't you mad?" I asked.

"Might as well get mad at the wind for blowin'. Some things just be what they be."

I crossed my arms and felt the hot pricks flair up again. "Well, I'm mad as a hornet. And I think you should be, too."

Eula just shrugged and fixed on soothin' baby James. Once he settled a bit, she held him in the crook of her arm and pushed the driver's door open. It was hard to do 'cause it was uphill now. It clunked into place and she shoved herself and baby James out. When I opened my door, it only went about eight inches before the bottom corner dug into the ground. It was enough for me to squeeze out though. I was up to my ankles in muddy water before I realized it. When I lifted my foot, it sucked my sneaker right off.

I fished around and found my shoe and was more careful when I lifted my other foot. Muddy shoe in one hand, I climbed out of the ditch and onto the road next to Eula. Too late I remembered it was bad luck to walk around with one shoe on and one shoe off. Not that I really thought my luck could get much worse.

We stood there looking at the truck for a long minute with the sun beatin' down on us and the sound of the cicadas whirring in the air.

"Think you can back it out?" I finally asked, not taking my eye off the rear tire that looked to be at least two inches off the ground.

Eula said, "Don't look like it."

I looked up at her. "Maybe if I push?"

Her eyes turned to me and she busted out laughing like I'd told the best joke ever.

"I'm strong!" I crossed my arms and frowned at her.

She kept right on laughing. "Oh, I know. Must come from that red hair."

Now I was even madder. "How can you just stand there laughin' when that man did this to us and we're stuck?"

"Sometimes laughin' is all a body can do, child. It's laugh or lose your mind."

I narrowed my eyes. She had lost her mind once already since I met her. Considering the choice, maybe I shouldn't be so mad about her having a laugh.

I sat down on the road and put my muddy shoe back on.

11

We'll just wait a spell," Eula said. I held baby James while she climbed up into the back of the truck and got the brown grocery bag holding our food. We hadn't had breakfast. But with Wallace's bashed-in head still in my mind and us just being run off the road, I wasn't hungry. She stepped off the back bumper. "Someone'll be along."

I looked down the long stretch of empty road and doubted it. Truth be told, I wasn't sure I wanted anyone to come along after what that man did to us.

"Too bad we're hidin' from the law or we could get that man into some trouble for what he did."

Eula made a sound like she was choking. "Oh, child, the law wouldn't do nothin'. A white man can do pretty much whatever he wants to a colored woman and a little girl—even if the little girl is white. It the way things are round here."

"He wrecked us! That's gotta be against the law. It don't matter if you're colored and I'm a kid."

She sighed and shook her head. "You think what you want. We can't go to the law anyway, so no sense in gettin' all worked up over it."

I was so wound up I wanted to break something . . . like that man's nose. I gritted my teeth and felt like I was gonna come out of my skin. "Maybe we should just walk."

Her head snapped up and she looked like she was disappointed in me. I was used to that look, but for some reason it felt particular bad coming from Eula. "Child, I done told you it's two days' drive to Nashville," she said, not sounding prickly like I thought she might. "Walkin' won't get us there. We wait."

Baby James started to fuss for his bottle, so I gave him a little jiggle until Eula had it ready. I think he liked me 'cause he sounded like he was trying not to cry.

"What if—?" I cut myself off and fixed my eyes on the road.

"What?"

I was all shook up inside. And even though I still wanted to scratch that man's eyes out, there was something hopeless inside me, too. "What if the next person comes along is like that man in the car?"

She stood in front of me with a frown on her face. "It ain't right that you had to see such hatefulness. Ain't everybody like him." Then she set her shoulders square. "We just trust the good Lord to send someone kind and respectable our way."

It was plain Eula had more faith in the Lord than I did. Which was a wonder; from what I'd seen, she had plenty of reason not to.

We sat down in the shade. We fed baby James one of the bottles Eula had wrapped in towels soaked in springhouse water and waited for the good Lord to do his work.

I spent some time splitting long blades of grass plucked from the ground, my mind asking a whole string of questions that was probably best left alone. I was most curious about Eula's change since we drove away from her house. While we'd been there, she'd been skittery-jittery about killin' Wallace. She'd never stopped talking. Once we left in the truck, she went more inside herself. Now she was acting almost normal, like Wallace was just back home and not dead. I wondered why. Did she figure out Wallace needed killin' and wasn't feeling so bad about it now? Was she still set on going to the law once we got to Nashville?

I found a foxtail grass and pulled it from its skin. As I chewed on the soft, green stem, I watched Eula feed baby James. I couldn't ask about Wallace, but I couldn't keep all of my questions plugged inside my head any longer. "Who do you think baby James's momma is?"

Eula tilted her head to the side and looked at that baby with so much love it made my throat hurt. I wondered what it would feel like if someone looked at me like that.

"Someone young and scared, I imagine," she said.

"Why scared?" It seemed to me that anybody old enough to have a baby ought to be grown-up enough to leave scaredness behind—unless they lived with a man like Wallace, that is.

"Maybe all alone," Eula said. "Maybe too many mouths to feed already."

There was a girl in my class who said she didn't have a daddy, just a momma. I'd asked her if her daddy died, but she pinkie-swore she'd never had one, that her momma never even got married. When I'd asked Mamie about it, she'd said ladies didn't ask those kinds of questions. She was in a mood, so I knew not to argue that I didn't want to be a lady. Wish I had, maybe I'd know now and have one curiosity taken care of. I almost asked Eula about it now, about how a woman can have a baby and not a husband, but considering Eula done killed her own husband today, I decided it probably wasn't a good idea.

Then I thought on her other idea about James's mother. The LeCounts next door had five kids. They weren't rich like Patti Lynn's family and they all got plenty to eat. Truth be told, their dinners always smelled a whole lot better than what Mamie cooked up. Then I thought about the Pykes; ten kids, all black haired and gray eyed. They was all skinny and pale, kinda like I imagined that ghost would have looked at the haunted house. The Pykes I knew always had snotty noses, even in the summer. Mamie said the ladies auxiliary did a lot to help out the Pykes because they was dirt-poor.

I wondered if James could maybe be a Pyke. He was too little and wrinkly to tell if he looked like one. Then I wondered if the Pykes had throwed away other babies before him.

Eula had told me it was better if I didn't know where James come from, but things had changed considerable since then. I decided it was worth a try to narrow down if maybe he was a Pyke. "You find James in Cayuga Springs . . . where you was deliverin' pies?"

Maybe if she still didn't want to answer about James, the pie question would get it out of her by accident. Mamie had got plenty of things out of me by asking two questions at once like that.

Eula looked at me with her eyes all squinty. After I'd almost given up on an answer, she said, "I did."

I looked at baby James again, trying to see if his hair looked like it was gonna sprout in black like a Pyke. "But you don't know who his momma is?"

She shook her head. "Suppose we'll know soon enough after we get to Nashville." There was a little shimmy of her shoulders right then, like she'd shivered even though it was hot enough to boil a bullfrog in a pond.

I stopped asking about James. But my mind didn't want to stop thinking about him. It seemed impossible, someone throwin' away a baby, no matter how dirt-poor they was. Baby James was noisy and a pain in the be-hind, but I wouldn't just leave him on a church step and not know what was gonna happen to him or who was gonna take care of him.

Something Eula had said come back into my head. She'd said she'd been nothin' but a throwaway before she met Wallace. I knew she wasn't throwed away as a baby 'cause she knew her momma and daddy. But was being a throwed-away person why she was so fixed on keeping James even after she'd seen he was white?

"You got any brothers or sisters?" I asked.

She gave me a look like I'd asked something I shouldn't have. She swallowed and looked away before she turned it around on me. "Do you?"

I shook my head. "Wish I had a brother like one of Patti Lynn's—she's my best friend back home. Those boys can pull a real good gag and they got some of the goriest stories. Patti Lynn thinks they're awful, but I think they're funny. I wouldn't want her sister, though." I frowned. "Even with her record collection. She thinks she's hotsy-totsy." I made like I was patting my fancy hairdo. "Not to mention she gets hair-pullin' mad when Patti Lynn and I snoop in her stuff. The boys don't care."

Eula made a little grunt in her throat. "Sister might be better. Even a hair-pullin' one. Not all brothers are like Patti Lynn's." Eula's eyes got far away.

"You got one? A brother?"

Her eyes came back from whatever past they'd been busy seeing. She curled her nose and snorted. "Charles. He just like Pap. No-account. Ain't seen him in years. Might not even be alive no more." Something in her voice said she hoped he wasn't.

Right then, she stood straight up, looking down the road. "Here come!"

I jumped up and looked. A truck was coming from the direction we'd been headed. It was lots better'n the one in the ditch; it looked to have all of its red paint and it didn't shout out rumbles and rattles.

Before I could stop her, Eula walked out into the bright sun that was blisterin' the road, shading her eyes with the hand not hanging on to James. My stomach balled up tight as the truck slowed down and stopped.

Careful.

She stopped just like she could hear my mind, keeping the ditch between her and the truck. Her shoulders got acting all turtley again. She stood quiet and still.

The man's arm resting on the door was so brown I couldn't tell right off if he was light-skinned colored or suntan-skinned white. Maybe Eula couldn't either. When he stuck his head out the window, the shade of the straw hat hid most of his face. He was wearing overalls and a shirt with the sleeves rolled up. His brown chin and cheeks were covered with white stubble. Then he tipped his hat back on his head and showed he was white—which before this morning would have been a comfort.

I held my breath and got my feet ready to run and help Eula if he got ornery.

"That your truck?" he asked.

Eula nodded real slow, keeping her eyes down.

"Y'all okay?" he asked in a voice that didn't sound like it yelled hateful things. "Nobody hurt?"

She nodded again.

Well, that wasn't any help, her not talking like that. What was that man to think, we were okay? Or we were hurt? We didn't need extra questions.

I hurried out of the shade and stopped beside her. "We're fine, sir."

He looked surprised to see me; right before he got all squinty, that is. "I seen you before little girl?"

Eula got stiff beside me.

I shook my head, real definite. "No, sir. We ain't from around here."

Eula made a little sound in her throat and I bumped my shoulder into her as a warning to keep quiet. I went on, "We're on our way to live with our aunt in Nashville." Then I hung my head and looked real sad. "Me and James's momma died last week."

That sound came from Eula again, a little louder this time, like words was about to pop from her mouth. I bumped her again.

"Oh, a shame to hear that. My sympathy," the man said, touching the brim of his hat. "How'd y'all end up in the ditch?"

I didn't need to lie about that part. "Some man run us off the road 'cause he hates coloreds."

The man just nodded.

"Can you get us out?" I asked.

"Reckon I can give it a try."

He moved his truck around so its back was at the edge of the road, facing the back of Eula's truck. As he was doing this, I said real quiet to Eula, "Since you got no stomach for truth-stretchin', you'd better go back to the trees and wait until we're ready to go again."

"Can't leave you alone with a stranger."

I rolled my eyes. "I didn't ask you to go back to Cayuga Springs, just get too far away for bein' asked questions. I'll tell him James can't stay in the sun. Go. 'Fore he gets out."

Eula walked back toward the woods, but stopped as soon as she was standing in the shade. Her eyes stayed on me like a momma hen's.

"We thank you kindly for your help," I said to the man as he pulled a chain from his truck bed.

He just stood there staring at me for a spell. "How'd you get those marks on your throat?"

Uh-oh. I hadn't thought about Wallace leaving marks along with the soreness. "A bear," I said quickly. "I was runnin' from a bear. Got hit in the neck with a limb."

"A bear?"

Dumb! Dumb! I shoulda waited till I thought of something better. Course the man didn't look like he believed me. Who would believe a little girl could outrun a bear?

I laughed a little and put my hand over the marks so he couldn't study them too close. "Well, we was playin' bear. My friend was the bear."

"Oh, I see."

I held my breath for a minute. Then he knelt down behind Eula's truck and I was pretty sure he was done asking about my neck.

"This your momma's truck?"

My heart jumped. Why couldn't he just pull us out without all the questions? After a second, I decided there was no law against a colored owning a truck. "No, sir. Belongs to our maid. She been with us my whole life. Momma don't . . ." I looked down at my feet like I was trying not to cry. "I mean, Momma didn't drive." A good lie needs particulars.

The man sent a look over at Eula. I was afraid she'd do something to ruin my story, so I started making crying sounds and snifflin' real hard. For a second, the man looked like he didn't know what to do. Then he patted me on the shoulder (I could tell he wasn't used to kids 'cause he did it like he was slappin' a watermelon) and then crawled under the back bumper with the chain. When he come back out, it had been hooked on something under there.

Two minutes later, Eula's truck was back on the road and pointed toward Nashville.

"Tell your colored woman it doesn't look like any real damage," he said. "But I'd have it checked at a garage first chance you get, just to be sure."

"Yes, sir. We will."

He looked toward Eula again. "Y'all be careful." He looked down at me, right deep into my eyes. "Things are mighty touchy right now. Mind that you don't go lookin' for trouble by takin' your maid where she's got no business bein', you understand?"

Trouble seemed to find me well enough on its own, but I just nodded.

"And get to your aunt as quick as you can."

That one gave me goose bumps. I stood up taller. "Thank you, sir."

I watched him drive away, his words shootin' around in my head.

I remembered the news stories on the TV. Somewhere in Alabama a colored crowd had been blasted with a fire hose by the police because they wouldn't leave the streets. President Kennedy sent soldiers with guns to Ole Miss last fall when a Negro was trying to go to school there. There'd been lots of talk and whisperin' by the grown-ups beforehand. Then riots started and some people got killed. Grown-ups wasn't whisperin' anymore after that. They was yellin'.

Mamie had explained that some coloreds were stepping out of their place, stirrin' up trouble; that everybody—colored and white—was happy with keeping things separate, and it wasn't the president's business to tell Mississippi what to do. It had all made sense then. But after hearin' about Shorty and that man puttin' us in the ditch, I wondered. Eula hadn't been doing anything but driving down the road.

"Things are mighty touchy right now."

Once the man who helped us was gone, I waved Eula back toward the road. I decided not to tell her what he had said. His warning was for me. It was my job to keep Eula safe.

12

Eula kept letting the truck drift from one side of the road and to the other, like someone who didn't know how to drive. The further we went, the worse she got. Tick, tock, right, left. We was like the tail on the cat clock in the Sunday-school room.

She gripped the steering wheel so hard her skinny arms shook.

"There's no cars. You don't need to be so scared," I finally said. I was getting tired of rocking like a boat. Baby James seemed to like it though 'cause he was sleepin' like a log. "Maybe I should drive." I never had, but I couldn't be worse than Eula.

She shot me a look. "Now that just what we need, gettin' stopped by the sheriff 'cause you behind the wheel. Travelin' invisible, remember? And I ain't scared. Somethin' wrong with the steering."

We went on like that for a while; swing and rock, tick and tock, Eula driving slower and slower. She even stopped dead when a car passed us going the other way—which was probably good 'cause it kept us from ticktocking smack-dab into its side.

"Keep your eyes peeled for a service g'rage," she said.

"Ain't been nothin' but trees since we got out of the ditch. I think I'll see a g'rage easy enough."

She looked over at me and laughed. The minute she did, the truck headed toward the ditch. "Whoa!" She jerked her arms and snapped her eyes back on the road.

Finally I saw something other than trees. A marker for Copiah County. Right after that there was a sign with a cartoon man wearing a string tie and a white hat: COL. CLEAN SAYS—KEEP MISSISSIPPI BEAUTIFUL. It was getting to be against the law to be a litterbug—which was a person who throws trash and whatnot out their car windows.

And right after Col. Clean was a rusted metal sign with letters so far gone I couldn't read but a shadow of the biggest, Quigley's. I pointed. "There's a g'rage!"

Eula huffed. "I see it."

"Well, you told me to watch!"

"Reckon I did." Eula slowed down—which I woulda thought was impossible and still be moving—and pulled into the dirt lot. Even though we rolled in real slow, a cloud of dust popped up behind us.

Quigley's wasn't like the service stations in Cayuga Springs, with their shiny buildings, bright red Coca-Cola machines, and big, round lights with green dinosaurs or blue-and-white PURE on top of pumps. This one was bare wood gone silver. Just one rusty gas pump sat in front, and it didn't look like it would spit out a drop of gas. It was the really old kind that you had to hand-pump the gas into a big jar at the top before you filled your car. There used to be one like it at the closed-up filling station out on the edge of town, near the haunted house. Last year some kids broke the glass jar and beat dents into the metal. I think it was Patti Lynn's brothers. They used that filling station as a clubhouse where they smoked cigarettes and looked at magazines. Patti Lynn and I knew about it because one day we followed them like Nancy Drew. It was one of our favorite things to do.

Eula shut off the truck and waited.

The place looked empty, but the front door was open, so I guessed someone must be here. On one side of the building was a big pile of old tires; on the other there was a bunch of wrecked cars with missing parts and broken glass. Both sides had tall weeds that had caught every scrap of trash dropped by a litterbug and brought by the wind. I wondered what Col. Clean would say about his sign being right in front of this place.

A droopy, brown hound dog came from behind the building and stared at us. His face was gray and he looked like he had the mange.

"I don't think anybody's here," I said, hearing nothing but the dog panting and bugs buzzing.

Just then, somebody came out of the door. I expected a man just as old and run-down as this place and the dog. But a tall, skinny teenager with a giant Adam's apple and a good crop of pimples come out. He walked past the dog that had flopped down right there in the sun like he couldn't go another step.

He walked up to my window, not Eula's. He peered past me with squinty, soot-colored eyes, then looked back at me. "We don't sell gas no more."

Eula just kept looking out the windshield, so I spoke up. "You fix trucks?"

"Some."

"Can you fix this one?"

"What's wrong with it?"

"Well, that's what we need you to tell us." This boy was dumber than a stump.

"I mean," he said, real snotty, "what's it doin'?"

"Actin' broke."

He rolled his eyes like I was the dumb one. "Makin' noise? Fartin' smoke? Chuggin'?"

"Eula says it's the steering. Goes this way and that." I fished my hand back and forth in front of me.

He didn't say anything else, just dropped down on the ground. I leaned out my window and watched him use his heels to scoot under the truck. He didn't even have any tools with him.

Wasn't half a second later he scooted back out and stood up. He knocked the dust off his backside with one hand. "Nope. Can't fix it."

"You didn't even try!"

"Got a bent tie rod. Need a new one. I don't got one."

"You ain't bein' very helpful," I said, working to keep polite. Mamie always said you get more flies with honey than vinegar—which meant be nice and folks will be nice back.

He shrugged. "Don't got the part."

"Can you get one?"

"Maybe I could." He looked at Eula again. "Cash money only."

Eula finally spoke up, but she kept her eyes faced forward. "How much?"

He scratched his head and I expected cooties to fly out. "Prob'ly round ten dollars—plus puttin' it in."

Ten dollars! I sucked in a breath and looked to Eula.

"We just keep drivin' on this one," she said as she started the truck again. "Thank you, sir."

I wondered how she could carry on a conversation and never once look at the person she was talking to. Mamie always told me that was rude.

"Suit yo'se'f." He looked at me with his sooty eyes; truth be told, he looked kinda sooty all over. "It's gonna break though."

"How long we got?" I asked.

He shrugged.

Eula ground the truck into gear and nodded at the boy, then pulled away.

"Wait," I said, but Eula kept going.

The boy shouted after us, "Sounds like you got a bad clutch, too!"

"Mmmm-hum." Eula's answer wasn't no more than a sound deep in her throat.

"Maybe we can get him to fix it for four dollars and seventy-five cents," I said. "We can promise to send him the rest later."

She was back to fighting the steering wheel. "He say, 'Cash money.' Won't give credit to a colored," she said as if it had come down off the mountain in stone.

"But we're gonna get stuck broke down out here in the middle of nowhere."

Eula dipped her chin, real determined again. "We see how far we get. The good Lord will provide."

I didn't see how the good Lord, or baby Jesus, could fix a broke truck. "We won't make it to Nashville."

"We will," she said, like there wasn't a bit of doubt.

"Not if the truck is broke!"

"Might as well be broke if we can't buy gas to make it go down the road."

I got a little hiccup of panic. "Do we even have enough money to buy the gas to get to Nashville?"

She looked over at me. "I get you to your momma."

"But—"

"Might have to find me a little work on the way, but I get you there."

Eula finding work meant mixing in with people—not being invisible. I thought about all the sheriffs and police in every town between here and Nashville. There had to be hundreds.

"Like a job?" Then the questions just kept coming and I couldn't stop them. "How long will it take to get enough money? What will me and James do while you're working? Where we gonna stay? What if the police are on the lookout for me? What if Shorty comes by and finds Wallace dead before we get to Nashville?"

The second I said Wallace's name, the stiffness and determination run out of her like water out of a knocked-over glass. Her face crumpled up and she started shaking all over. Why did I have to say it?

By the time she pulled over on the side of the road, she was crying like a baby. She jumped out of the truck and ran a ways before her legs looked to give out and she sat right down in the weeds.

I got out of the truck and ran after her. I went to my knees and put my arms around her. "It's gonna be okay. Please don't cry."

But she did. For a long while her shoulders shook in my arms. I wished I could take his name back, let Eula go back to the place inside her head that made it so she didn't have to think about her killin' him.

"You only did it to save me," I said real soft as I rubbed her back. "I was gonna be dead."

A sob come from somewhere down around her toes. She fell to the side, sinking out of my arms, covering her face with her hands and making the most pitiful sound I'd ever heard.

I leaned my face close to hers, even though she couldn't see me with her hands in the way. "Please, Eula. Please. Stop crying. We're gonna be okay. We'll get enough money. We'll get to Momma and she'll fix everything."

Eula curled into a tighter ball and didn't even seem to notice I was there anymore. She was broke again and I wasn't sure I could get her back. And even if she did come back, she was so mad at me for making her have to kill Wallace that I bet she'd never ever talk to me again.

I sat down, looked down the empty road, and wondered if this was the end of Eula and me and getting to Nashville.

13

We sat there a long time. Eula stopped crying after a while, but then just laid there staring at the sky like a dead person. Nothing I did made her look at me—not talking or touching or jumpin' up and down or hollerin' that my hair was on fire. First I thought it was just 'cause she was so mad at me. But then not even baby James's crying got inside her head. I had to change his diaper myself and couldn't figure out how to fold it right, so it ended up kinda wadded up between his legs. Then I fed him another bottle. We only had four left, so I knew some of our four dollars and seventy-five cents was gonna have to go to buy milk for him. That was if we ever got to a place that sold milk. Eula had picked her road for travelin' invisible real good. There hadn't been one car go past since we left the garage.

I'd eaten some of our food and tried to feed some to Eula, but she'd kept her dead-person eyes, even when I held a bit of corn bread right to her lips. Baby James was sleeping again under the trees 'cause it was too hot in the truck. I'd taken Eula's suitcase and emptied it so he could have kind of a bed that would keep the ants and whatnot off him.

Finally, the sun went below the trees, but I knew there was still a lot of light left in the day (thank you, baby Jesus). It was less hot, but the air started to fill up with buzzin' skeeters. I went back to the truck and got Eula's spare slip and put it over the suitcase to keep them from bitin' on James. I was careful to make sure it stayed up off his face so it didn't smother him. Then I was left to smackin' and swattin'. I didn't know there was this many mosquitoes in the whole of Mississippi. I wondered if the skeeters eating Eula up would wake her. I decided not to cover her up so they could find her faster.

All of the sudden Eula sat up and blinked, kinda surprised, like she was just now seeing she was still in the world. I don't know if a skeeter was what done it, but I was real glad for whatever made it happen. I held still and waited, not wanting to scare her back inside herself.

She sucked in a big breath, then blew it out. After that she looked up at the sky and frowned.

I kept holding still.

She sat there for a long bit. Finally, I walked over to her, real slow and easy. Then I said real soft, "Eula?"

She looked at me and I could tell she was back to being herself.

"You okay?" I asked.

"I reckon we'd best be goin'." She said it like she'd only been sitting there for a minute and not disappeared into herself for half a day, not giving two shakes about what happened to me and James. I know I shouldn't have said Wallace's name, but we coulda got ate by a bear while we was sitting out here and she was . . . gone.

She stood up and brushed the grass off her dress.

I was half-mad. The other half of me was just happy she wasn't acting dead anymore. I didn't know which one would come out if I opened my mouth. So I didn't.

She looked at me, then her eyes went to the truck, where the door was hanging open and baby James wasn't inside.

"Where the baby?" Her eyes showed so much white I thought they was gonna pop out of her head.

I pointed over to the suitcase.

She hurried right over there like she was saving him from a fire and snatched the slip off. She let out something between a hiccup and a laugh. Then she looked back at me. "He good."

That's when I realized that she'd been thinking he was covered 'cause he was dead or something.

I was just starting to tell her that it was no thanks to her that he was okay, but before I got out the first word, she asked, "You cover him up like that?"

I nodded.

She came at me, real purposeful. She was already mad at me about Wallace. Maybe now she was madder thinking I coulda smothered baby James.

She grabbed my head between her hands before I could duck away. Then she pulled my face close to hers, like Mamie does when she's real worked up scolding me.

My heart got faster. "I was careful about—"

Her grip tightened. She put a big kiss right in the middle of my forehead, then kept my face between her hands and smiled at me. "You are a gif' from God, child. A true gif' from God." She glanced back over at the baby. "You done real good takin' care of him, Starla. Real good."

I was so surprised that I almost asked if she'd got over being mad at me for making her kill Wallace, too, before I remembered I'd made up my mind not to say his name again until after we got to Nashville.

Instead, I said, "I fed him, too. He burped real nice."

She patted my cheeks, then went and picked up James. "Jus' grab that grip and we be on our way."

For a minute I just stood there watching her skirt swish around her legs as she walked through the weeds toward the truck, wondering how she could just go on and off like a lightbulb. Here and gone. Crazy and calm. Comin' out of her skin and la-di-da, just a regular day.

"Come on now," she called over her shoulder.

I grabbed up the suitcase and followed. Grown-ups was real complicated. And Eula was the most tangled-up one I'd ever tried to figure out.

It got full dark. The clouds had been getting thicker for a while, but Eula said they wasn't rain clouds. I don't know how she could tell. I studied them trying to figure it out and noticed the sky ahead of us was different than the rest.

"How come the sky's lighter gray up ahead?" I asked.

"A town sits up there. Streetlights are shinin' on the cloud bellies."

"What town?"

She shrugged.

Since we'd left her house, she'd been acting like she knew where she was going. Now I was worried. "Do you even know where we are?"

"We in Mississippi."

"Ugh!" I rolled my eyes. "I know that. How do you know we're headed toward Nashville?" She'd taken lots of different roads, most of them dirt, all pretty much the same far as I could tell.

"Knowed the roads close to home. Once those run out we been goin' mostly north, sometimes east. We just keep doin' it and we gonna hit Tennessee."

"You sure? We been goin' north and east, I mean? How can you tell?"

"Sun rise in the east and set in the west. Easy from there."

"What about when it's dark?"

"Moon does like the sun."

"What about when the sun's straight up? Or you can't see the moon?"

"I just know, can't explain why."

"Mamie says I should know like that. But I don't."

"Who's Mamie?"

Dang. Eula done guessed already some about my momma—her not knowing I was coming. If she found out that my grandma was sitting back there in Cayuga Springs—way closer than Nashville even though we'd been creepin' along in that direction for a good part of a day—she might just turn around and take me back there. That'd be bad trouble for both of us.

I fished around and pulled out one of the stories I'd been gonna use when I run away with baby James. It only needed a little changing up.

"Mamie's my grandma I lived with." Building in some truth always made the best and easiest-to-remember story. "She died last week. That's why I'm going to Nashville." Uh-oh, I was sounding a shade too happy—truth be told, I was happy to be away from Mamie. But she wasn't really dead. If she was dead, I reckon I'd be sad. "I cried all my tears already; it was real sad when it happened."

Please, baby Jesus, don't let her ask how Mamie died.

"Why didn't your momma take you back with her after your Mamie's funeral?"

Oh, boy. I needed to be a whole lot better in thinking ahead when I asked baby Jesus for something.

My mind spun like a top, then it come to me—and it wasn't even a lie. "Well, you see, Mamie wasn't her momma. That'd be Granny Ida, and she died a long time ago, back when my momma was little. I only know her from pictures. Mamie was my daddy's momma; so Momma didn't come down for the funeral 'cause she had to work." Then I added a good particular. "She sent flowers though. They was pink, Mamie's favorite color."

"Mmm. How 'bout your daddy, then? He just let you walk to your momma in Nashville all by your lonesome?"

"Daddy works on an oil rig way out in the Gulf, so he couldn't come home for the funeral neither. That's why he can't take care of me hisself. They don't allow kids on the rig."

"Sound like a mighty small funeral." Eula's voice sounded suspicious—even after I'd added the part about crying and the flowers.

"It was." Then I perked up a little, like I was rememberin' the good parts. "But it was real nice. All the church ladies made supper and the whole choir sang." I'd never been to a funeral, so I was walkin' a narrow rope here. I did know that Mamie always made food and took it to the church for funerals, and the choir sang at every church thing I'd ever been to, so I had to be at least part right. If Eula called me out, I'd just tell her white funerals must be different from colored. What could she say to that?

Eula let the truck get even slower than turtle speed. "Starla." She looked over at me.

"It's okay, Mamie was old, so you don't need to feel bad."

Her eyes stayed on me instead of the road. I could feel them like they was shootin' tiny arrows at me. I looked out the windshield and squirmed a little.

"I'm pretty sure I know a made-up story when I hear one."

I kept my eyes on where the headlights lit up the road in front of us. They zigged and zagged, shining on the weeds on one side and then the other. Eula seemed to be used to the crazy steering now, 'cause she didn't head to the ditch when she fixed her eyes on me.

"Guess you don't." I lifted my chin. "You just get me to Momma, then you'll see." I had to get to Momma. And I sure couldn't let Eula go back to Cayuga Springs until I had it figured out how to keep her from getting locked up in the pokey.

Eula sighed real long and heavy. "Reckon I will."

We went along for a while. The light spot in the sky didn't seem to be getting closer. I was real tired and wished we'd get to there so we could go to bed. Then a thought sprung on me like a hop-toad. Where did people with no home and no money go to sleep at night?

Clunk!

The front of the truck dropped lower on my side, at the same time it veered toward the side of the road, making a *thud-rub-thunk* over and over. It only went a few feet before it stopped moving altogether.

I looked over at Eula. The little bit of light from the dash showed her eyes was big again.

"Guess that pimple-faced boy was right," I said. I picked up baby James, then unlatched my door. I slid out, extracareful to hang on to James until my feet hit the ground. Lucky we wasn't in a ditch this time.

Eula shut off the engine, but left the headlights on so we could see some. It didn't take two seconds for the bugs to start swarmin', ticking and snapping as they beat themselves silly against the headlights.

Eula and me met up in front with the bugs. We stood together looking at the truck like it was a dead animal. I kinda felt like we should say a prayer over it or something.

"How far you figure the town is from here?" I finally asked, keeping my eyes on the truck.

"Prob'ly a mile or so."

I noticed she kept staring at the dead truck, too, like maybe she could use her mind to make it come back to life. But the front wheel on the right side was sitting whopper-jawed enough I knowed that wasn't gonna happen.

I sighed. "Guess we'd best get goin'. Should we take your suitcase and the food, or leave 'em here?"

She stopped looking at the truck and turned to me. "We ain't walkin' into town in the middle of the night. What we gonna do when we get there? Knock on somebody's door?"

"Sure, why not?"

She made a little tisk noise that made me prickle.

"Once when my daddy was comin' home from the Gulf," I said, "his truck broke down and he stopped at a house where a real nice man and his wife let him stay over. Then they gave him breakfast and helped him fix his truck the next morning. Maybe someone would help us fix our truck, since we don't have enough money."

"Well, your daddy wasn't tryin' to travel invisible 'cause o' the law. And he weren't colored, neither. We don't know that town. Nobody gonna open their doors to us tonight."

"What we gonna do then?"

"We got enough milk for James. We got food." She looked up at the sky, where the chip of a moon was trying to get through the clouds. "With the Lord's blessing, we got good weather. We camp."

"We don't have a tent."

She made another tisk, like I was dense or something. "Too hot for a tent. We got the perfect place in the truck bed. High enough to keep the snakes away; we see the stars if they get out."

"What about bears? Truck bed ain't a pedmint to them."

"A what?"

"A pedmint. You know, somethin' too hard for them to get around."

I saw her head bob and her bright teeth showed. "Maybe you mean a *impediment*?"

Well, crap on a cracker. I thought I had it right. Patti Lynn and I had been hiding behind the couch listening to her sister talk on the phone when I heard it. Since Cathy had had to explain it to the boy she was talking to, I figured me using it would sound extra-smart. I'd been saving it up to use on Daddy when he came home, to show him even with my bad grade in arithmetic I wasn't stupid. Mamie always said I was dense as swamp mud when it came to arithmetic.

"Bears can climb," I said.

"If we put the food inside the truck and put the windows up, no bear's gonna bother us."

"You sure?"

"Uh-huh. Bears got way more important things to do than sniff around a skinny woman and a couple of chil'ren. We ain't got enough meat on us to fill him up."

"What about a catamount?"

"Oh, well, now, a catamount just can't help but holler once it gets dark, let ever'body know where he is. We'd hear him in plenty of time to lock ourselves in the truck."

"You just sayin' that so I'll shut up and sleep in the truck bed?"

She looked at me like she could see right inside my head . . . she was getting real good at that. "You ain't ever slept outside?"

I shook my head. I'd been outside after dark plenty . . . but sleeping and not knowing what was sneakin' up on you was crazy.

She grinned at me. "It's real nice. You gonna like it."

Turned out, I did. We was settled in the truck bed with baby James tucked into the suitcase, me and Eula laying shoulder to shoulder. The clouds broke up and there was plenty of stars, more'n I'd ever seen. The night was jumpin' with sounds, birds and bugs mostly. And tree frogs. Nothin' that sounded like a bear or a catamount.

Pretty soon, I heard a train whistle. It made me think of the one that blew nearly every night as I was going to sleep in my bedroom back home. Our house wasn't right near the tracks, but after the whistle if I listened close, I could hear the rumble as the train rolled through town. I wondered if it was the same train farther down the tracks. It made me feel far away from Cayuga Springs for some reason. My feelings was all mixed up about that. It was what I wanted. But there was things I was going to miss. Maybe that nighttime train whistle was one of them.

After a bit Eula started talking. "See how nice it is out here? Back when I was a little girl, sometimes Pap'd get in one of his moods—the hot weather seemed to bring 'em on—and me and Momma'd walk right out the door with nothin' but an old quilt and her clean uniform for the next day. We'd walk two miles to the judge's house—that was where she worked you remember."

It wasn't a question, but I nodded. I remembered right clear. I remembered about her momma working for a respectable family, and about the dresses used to make the quilt I'd slept with, and how sad Eula was that she couldn't recall the stories that went with the pieces of cloth.

She went on, "It was outside Jackson. Oh, they had a big spread. Lots of land." Her voice sounded like she was smiling, enjoying the memory. I thought that was nice, kinda like how I felt when I remembered my momma and Daddy's visits home. "We'd sleep right out under the stars and nobody ever even knew we was there. It was nice, sleepin' out with Momma, even if Pap was in a snit. He never got to swingin'—at least while Momma was alive—but the man never would let a body sleep if he wasn't done railin' and carryin' on. Once he tied me and Momma to straight chairs in the kitchen and throwed water in our faces if we fell asleep while he was preachin'. He got goin' on a lot about the Lord in them days."

"What about your brother?" I asked. "Did he go to the judge's, too?"

"He always stayed with Pap."

"Why?"

She was quiet for a long while, like she was having to think real hard. "Momma said it was to keep Pap from comin' after us. But I think . . ." She sighed. "I think that boy never did nothin' that wasn't selfish."

We got quiet then. The sound of the tree frogs seemed to get louder. I was just about asleep when I heard Eula. She was crying, real quiet, like she didn't want me to hear.

I knew what it was like, needin' a cry but not wanting anybody to know. But what if Eula didn't feel like that? What if she needed comfortin' like baby James?

I wasn't sure what to do. Our arms was pressed against each other still. I finally moved just enough to slip my hand around hers.

She squeezed tight and I squeezed back.

I fell asleep with my hand in hers and the stars floating over my head.

14

I was being chased by Jimmy Sellers on his bicycle and a bear. It was dark and cold. I was running so fast that my feet hit the ground hard. With every step, a pain shot through my head. I could hear the bear growling and the card clapping in Jimmy's spokes. They was getting closer, closer, closer . . . then all of the sudden, something snatched me right out of that dream and I opened my eyes.

Things hit me one at a time, but real fast:

I was still breathing hard.

My head still pounded with the echo of my running feet.

It was still dark.

The moon was out from behind the clouds. It had moved a good distance across the sky.

It wasn't Jimmy's bicycle clapping. It was my teeth chattering like the plastic windup kind from the dime store.

Lucky the bear stayed back in my dream.

I was curled up against Eula trying to get warm. My head felt like horses was running around inside it, and when I moved, it got worse.

I must have moaned a little, 'cause Eula was up right quick. "What is it, child?"

My teeth was chattering too much to talk.

She put her hand on my forehead, then on each of my cheeks. "You burnin' up."

I shook my head and lightning struck inside it. "C-c-c-cold." I felt so bad I wished I was back asleep being chased by a bear.

"Lord A'mighty." She sat there for a minute like she was thinking. "Got no aspirin. Can you get up and walk?"

I wasn't sure, but I said I could. With the truck broke, it was the only way I was gonna get to something to make me feel better. I started to stand up, then got all tippy. Eula grabbed hold of me right before I fell over the side of the truck bed.

"Whoa!" She kept her hands on my shoulders. "Maybe you should lay back down while I walk in the direction of that town. Be better not to have to explain why I got a white child with me anyway. First house I see, I get you some aspirin. Can't be far."

"No! Don't leave me!"

She looked at me for a minute, like she was deciding.

"I c-can w-w-walk." I didn't care how puny I felt, I wasn't staying out here alone not knowing when Eula'd be back.

"Child, you can't even talk." She tried to make me sit back down, but I stiffened my legs.

"Th-that's-s-s jus' 'cause I'm sh-sh-shiverin'. I can w-walk. Y-you said it can't be f-f-far."

"All right. Don't much want to leave you here alone, anyhow. Sit back down so I can put your shoes on you." She did. The one that had been covered in mud was stiff and kinda crackled, but she got it on my foot and tied. Then she got me stood back up and kept one hand on my arm as she reached outside the truck gate and undid the hook—there was only the one on the passenger side, the driver's side done rusted away. We'd been listening to that gate rattle all day.

It dropped down and she helped me out. She made me sit on the ground while she got back up in the truck bed and collected baby James.

She tied him onto her with a sling made out of the same slip I'd used to keep the skeeters off him. Nobody could tell if he colored or white in there.

Eula put her hands under my arms and helped me stand up. She didn't let go until she was sure I wasn't gonna topple over. Then she wrapped one arm around my shoulder and hooked her hand under my arm, holding me close to her side. We started down the road, stepping together like we was in a sack race—but real pokey. Every time my feet hit the ground my eyeballs feel like they was gonna shoot out. But I didn't bellyache about it 'cause I was scared she'd leave me where I was and go on without me.

It felt like we went a long, long way, across a little creek and past a field, but Eula said we hadn't done much more than a quarter mile when we seen a mailbox post with two beat-up mailboxes sitting on a cross T. Two tiny houses sat back a ways on either side of a rutted drive. They was still dark, but we heard a rooster crow somewhere near.

"Farm folk rise early," Eula said. "We wait just a bit, let 'em get roused afore we go knockin' on their doors."

My head hurt so bad I wanted to cry. My throat felt like I'd swallowed hot charcoal from Patti Lynn's daddy's grill, and I wasn't sure I was hearing anything in my left ear—Eula was on my right, so I couldn't be sure. I didn't think an aspirin was gonna make these giant miseries go away, but sure wished I had one to try.

I was just ready to drop down and lay on the ground when Eula said, "There now." We started up the lane, toward the house on the left that had a light shining in the window—not bright, more like Eula's oil-flame lamps.

When we got closer, I saw these wasn't much in the way of houses, just one-room shanties really. The front step of this one was mostly rotted away, so we stayed on the hard-pack ground and Eula reached high to knock on the door.

I was thinking on the nice man and his wife that gave my daddy a place to sleep. I hoped this house had at least one empty bed. All I wanted to do was crawl into it, cover up, and get warm.

As we waited, I got real dizzy, so I sat down on the ground behind Eula.

The raggedy curtain on the window next to the door moved. Two little heads with tiny braids sticking out all over peeked out and looked down at us—little colored girls. I was glad; we weren't gonna have nastiness toward Eula from some cranky white person. A bigger head showed up over them in the top pane. Then they all disappeared. We waited for the door to open.

It didn't.

Eula knocked again. "Sorry to bother y'all so early," she called through the door. "We be needin' a little help."

There was a space between the door and the floor where the yellow light from inside showed. I could see the shadow of somebody's feet on the other side. "Please!" I said, the word tearing up my throat. Then quieter I said, "Please help us."

The door swung open. A man stood looking down at us. "Sorry. We got nothin' to spare." He started to close the door.

Eula surprised me when she reached out and pushed against it and kept it open; especially since this man was every bit as big as Wallace. "We don't need money . . . or food. Truck broke down and the child is sick. If we could just have a couple of aspirin to bring her fever down, we'd be mighty grateful."

A woman came up behind the man and peered around his shoulder. She put an arm out to keep her children back. "What's wrong with him?"

Eula said, "Nothin' catchin'. And she's a girl."

"How you know it ain't catchin'?"

"We don't need to come in. If you could just spare the aspirin, we'll be on our—"

"That child white?" The man was leaning out the door, squinting at me.

"Yes," Eula said. "She in my care."

The door closed . . . hard.

I saw Eula's shoulders rise and fall with a deep breath. Then she turned around and walked toward the other house. I stayed sitting where I was.

There still wasn't any lights on over there. When she knocked on the door, it squeaked right open.

"Hello?" she called. "Hello? Anybody 't home?"

A small voice called out from the door of the house with the lights on, "Nobody live there."

Just as soon as I turned my head, the girl disappeared from the door with a little squeal, like she'd been pulled away. The door closed up with a bang.

I was so cold; I brought my knees up and wrapped my arms around them. It didn't help. I was shaking so hard my muscles started to hurt. If the sun would just get up, I knew I'd be warmer.

Eula pushed that squeaky door all the way open. Before I figured out what she was doing, she and baby James disappeared inside.

"Wait!" What if that little girl wasn't telling the truth? What if somebody got surprised and shot her? Everybody on a farm had a shotgun.

I jumped up. Pain shot though my head. I was so dizzy that I stumbled forward and landed on my knees.

"Eu-Eula!"

She didn't come back. She didn't call out. I didn't hear no gunshot.

I tried to get up again, but slower. My head pounded, but I didn't fall over from dizziness. I started for the open door and realized something wet was on my cheeks. I musta been crying from being so miserable. I sniffed and wiped my face dry on my T-shirt sleeve.

This house had a porch. Thinking of the rotted step on the other house, I stepped up on it real careful.

"Eula?" I started in the dark doorway.

Eula was headed back out at the same time and we ran smack into each other. I don't know who screamed the loudest, me, Eula, or baby James (since he was tied on her front, I slammed right into him). My own scream felt like it came out of my throat with bear claws.

"Oh! Oh, my! Oh!" Eula sounded like she couldn't catch her breath. "Goodness!" She put her arms around baby James and started to jiggle him. "Shhhhhh. Shhhh, now. It's all right."

It wasn't all right. I bit my lip to keep from crying again.

"Place is empty, but I checked in case there was somethin' left we could use. Been picked too bare even for mice to bother. We keep on down the road a piece. Next house can't be far."

"Why can't you go back there?" I pointed to the house with the lights on and the little girls inside. "And make them give us some aspirin."

"Because that ain't the way Christian folks behave. C'mon, now, let's go."

I stomped my foot. "Is it Christian to let a kid be sick and not help? Why do we care if we treat them Christian-like if they won't help us?"

She leaned down so she was looking right in my eyes. "You hear me, child. You can't use other folks' bad behavior to excuse your own. When we got a choice, we keep Jesus in our hearts and don't do nothin' that would make him ashamed."

"Why won't they help us?" I sounded like a crybaby, but I couldn't help it. "Why did he slam the door when he saw I was white?"

"Same reason some white folks slam the door when they see I'm colored. Some folks don't see nothin' but your skin. It ain't right, but it's the way people are." She bundled me close to her and started us back toward the road. "C'mon now. Sooner we start walkin', the sooner we get you some aspirin."

When I looked back toward the house with the lights, those two little colored girls were back at the window. One of them raised a hand and waved.

The sun was coloring the sky orange and blue when we come to the edge of town. I heard a train somewhere on up ahead. The street was lined with houses that looked a lot like Eula's, some a little better, some closer to the shacks we'd just been to. There wasn't any sidewalks. Some of the yards had grass, some didn't. Two or three houses had folks on the front porches. All of them colored. All of them stared at us.

Disappointment near choked me. What if all colored people hated me? I mean, before Eula and Wallace, I hadn't really knowed any that wasn't obliged to be nice on account of they was working for whites . . . and Wallace sure hated me. I was tuckered out and felt so rotten, I didn't think I could walk any farther to get to the white part of town.

Eula was seeing inside my head again. "Not all colored are like that man; just like all white folk aren't like the man who run us off the road." She led me right up to a house covered in dark green shingles, the kind that usually go on a roof. An old man was sitting on the porch in a rocking chair smoking a cigarette.

"Excuse me, sir," Eula said. "Could you spare us some aspirin? We travelin' and our truck broke down. We'd 'preciate knowing a g'rage for a tow, too."

The man blew smoke out through his nose and fixed his eyes on me. The whites was yellow and he looked like a dragon with that smoke shooting out of his nostrils. "Got no aspirin. The Lawd does my healin'." He picked a bit of tobacco off his tongue, then he pointed down the road with his cigarette between two knotty fingers. "Three g'rages in town. I recommend Polsgrove's. Least likely to steal you blind."

I didn't know why Eula was bothering asking about a garage. We didn't have money to fix the dang truck anyhow.

"Thank ya kindly," Eula said, and turned us back to the street.

The man called after us, "If y'all're lookin' to doctor, there's a drugstore four block on. But I'd recommend prayer."

Eula looked over her shoulder. "I think we could use both."

There had been a woman with a baby on the porch of the house catty-corner across the street when we'd stopped to talk to the old man. She'd gone inside. Her front door was closed.

The lady at the next house said she was sorry she couldn't help us—right after she gave me that same squinty look the man in the shanty had—and closed the door.

My knees was starting to get wobbly again. A couple of times things got a little gray around the edges. I didn't tell Eula 'cause while she looked for help, I didn't want to be left alone where folks all looked at me like I was one step above a worm. What if there was a colored like that white man who run us off the road? One that did more than just look at me hateful?

"Maybe we should just go on to the drugstore," I said—or at least I thought I said it.

Eula stopped and looked at me funny.

"What?"

"Maybe we shouuuuuld . . . ?" she said; so I guess I only said half.

"Go on to the drugstore."

"Someone'll help. We need a place for you to rest. It's too far back to the truck. And we need milk for James."

Just like he was listening, baby James started to make little fussing noises—the ones that come before he got to be a red-faced screamer.

No one came to the door of the next two houses. My feet got tangled up and all three of us nearly fell down the steps of the last. Baby James was crying serious now.

When we got back to the street, I sat down and held my head in my hands. "I can't go no more." I didn't care anymore if colored folk went by and said all sorts of hateful things to me. I didn't even care if they did worse.

"You there!" a lady's voice called from across the street.

"Oh, no," I said, not even looking up. It was bad enough when they ignored us, but now somebody was yelling for us to get on.

"Y'all need some help?" When I looked up, a white-haired colored woman was coming down off her porch and heading our way. She was little but moved like she meant business. Everybody we'd seen so far was either half-dressed or wearing a housecoat, but she was dressed and her hair was pulled up nice and neat. She wore wire-rimmed glasses that flashed in the morning sun.

When she got closer, she looked at me. "That child is ill."

"She is," Eula said. "Fever. We'd be obliged if you could spare some aspirin and maybe some water?"

The woman made a tut-tut noise as one of her hands came my way. I ducked. Pain shot through my head and I squeezed my eyes closed.

"It's all right," she said real kindly. "I just want to help you up. We'll get you inside and see what we can do to make you feel better."

I gave her my hand and she hauled me to my feet. She looked at Eula. "Baby sick, too?"

"No. He hungry though."

"I imagine you are, too," the woman said. "I can't imagine what brought y'all here in such a state, but it doesn't matter. We'll get all that sorted out later."

Now we were walking toward the lady's house. I wondered what Eula would tell her when they sorted it all out, 'cause it couldn't be the truth. But right then all I wanted to do was to lay down and die.

Once I was on the lady's couch with a cold cloth on my head, I began to think maybe I wanted to live after all. That was the last thing I remember thinking as the darkness pulled me under.

15

Thunder woke me; the long, rolling kind that comes from far away, then goes over and rattles the windows. Angels bowling. When I opened my eyes, the window I saw wasn't home. Things started to get untangled in my head, one kinky string at a time. I'd run away from home. The law was after me. Wallace the bear was dead. Me and Eula and baby James were going to Momma in Nashville.

I wondered if Mamie'd already got used to me not being "underfoot." I wondered how long it'd be before Daddy come home and found out I was gone—they only radioed out to the oil rig was if there was an emergency, and I didn't think Mamie considered my running off an emergency. She probably wouldn't want Daddy to get started looking for me, neither. The longer I was gone, the harder I'd be to find. I didn't want Daddy to be upset. By the time he got to come home again, I'd be with Lulu, and she could tell Daddy to come on up and live with us in Nashville. That way he wouldn't have to worry at all.

I looked at that unfamiliar window again. It was tall and wide and had lace curtains that moved with the breeze.

Un-uh. Not breeze. A fan was sitting on the table near my head; it moved from side to side, the hot, sticky air dragging across my skin. Outside was the calm that sat in front of a July storm, the kind of cloudy stillness that said you'd better get you and your bicycle on home before a gully washer let loose.

Lucky I was safe inside, but inside where?

I tried to sit up, but was weaker than a baby bird. My mouth felt cottony and my lips were all cracked and sore.

I got myself up on my elbows, which was hard to do with spaghetti arms. The couch I was on had been covered with a sheet. I wasn't wearing my clothes, but had on a white cotton nightgown that was too big for me. Oh, no! I looked at my wrist and found my Timex was still there. (Thank you, baby Jesus.)

I was in a strange living room with a turquoise-painted piano against one wall. When I tried to call Eula, my throat was too dry to make a noise.

My head got fuzzy, so I laid back down.

"Starla?" The voice came through the doorway before the lady did. She was almost as short as me. Her skin was smooth and dark, like the buckeye Momma had sent me from Nashville for good luck. The lady's hair was pulled back tight from her face in a bun. She wore a bright yellow skirt and blouse and a yellow bracelet; she reminded me of a white-haired bumblebee. She even had a kind of buzzing energy bouncing off her, like she was used to being busy all the time and didn't like being still.

She looked kinda familiar. But I didn't know many colored folk up close—except Eula, Patti Lynn's Bess, and Ernestine next door with the LeCounts.

"You're awake!" she said, smiling like I'd done something special. "Thank the Lord." She put her hands together like she was praying and looked up toward heaven. Then she walked a little closer and looked at me real close. "Your eyes have lost that glassiness, too."

I opened my mouth to talk but only got out a choked whisper that didn't sound like a word at all.

"Let me get you some water. You have to be parched." She went back the way she'd come.

I listened for some sound from baby James or Eula, but the only thing I heard was the refrigerator door open and close, a glass clinking on the counter. And more thunder.

The woman came back, helped me sit up, and handed me a glass of cold water. It was the best water I'd ever swallowed, even better than from Eula's mason jar out on that hot road. I gulped it until the lady reached out a dark hand and tipped it away from my mouth. I noticed her palm was as pink as mine.

"Best not to take too much at once." She took the glass from me and set it on the table with the fan.

I swallowed down what was in my mouth and wanted more. When I tried to talk this time, something came out. "Where's Eula and baby James?"

The lady sat down on the coffee table right next to Eula's wore-out Bible. She put her hands on her knees and smoothed her skirt. "James is napping in the bedroom bureau drawer. We had to make do since this house has never had a baby."

"You don't have grandkids?"

She shook her head. "No children, so no grandchildren. My students are my children."

I looked at the piano. It was so old the keys were yellow; one of them didn't even have the white cover on it anymore. "You give piano lessons?"

"I teach elementary school; grades three, four, and five. Our school is so small, they're combined." She tilted her head. "You look to be about that age."

"I'll be ten in September." Then I realized I couldn't just blurt out things without thinking. My age wasn't a secret, but plenty else about me was. I didn't want to get to spilling my guts or spinnin' tales until I knew what story Eula had told. "Where's Eula?"

"Well now, she's found some employment. She'll be home in time for supper. She didn't like leaving you, but I assured her you were in good hands with me. I understand your truck needs fixing before you can resume your trip."

"How'd she find a job so fast?"

"Oh, child, it's Saturday. You've been buried under a fever for nearly a week."

A week? "I don't remember anything, 'cept camping in the truck, then walking and walking . . . Oh! You're the lady who come out of the house to help us!"

She nodded. "Cyrena Jones. You may call me Miss Cyrena instead of Miss Jones since you're living right here under my roof. And your name is Starla. Lovely, just lovely." She reached over and fluffed my pillow. "So tell me, how did you and your brother come to be traveling with Eula?"

I smelled a rat. This was just how Mamie got me to tell her things that she already knew the answer to, checking to see if I was telling the whole truth, nothing but the truth. I think she learned it from *Dragnet.* And if this lady thought James was my brother, then Eula must have told her some story. "I'm so tired." Which was the truth. I yawned just to make sure she believed me and put my head back on the pillow. "Eula pro'bly told you ever'thing anyhow."

She looked right square at me, using her teacher eyes. I think all teachers learned that look in teacher school and used it to draw kids out of a lie. "You're very fortunate to have had Eula helping your family—and lucky she's so devoted that she embarked on this trip alone with you children. Things are . . . unstable. And in this town . . . well, it's very bad at the moment. I can think of all sorts of things that could go wrong—considering."

She didn't know the half of what had already gone wrong.

"Yes, Miss Cyrena." I wanted to be agreeable and polite, her taking us in and all, but I'd never heard of white folk calling a colored woman *miss.* Bess was Bess, and Ernestine was Ernestine. "We're real lucky havin' Eula—me and James."

"James and I," she said in her teacher voice. Guess the colored-teacher school taught the same things as the white-teacher school.

"James and I are real lucky." That just sounded wrong, like I was trying to be hoity-toity like Patti Lynn's sister, Cathy.

Miss Cyrena sighed a little. "I'm so very sorry about your grandmother."

"Thank you." I put on a sad face. Whatever Eula had told her, I was surely supposed to be sorry, too. Had Eula told her Mamie was dead, like I'd said when we were in the truck? Or had she invented a story of her own to explain why she was travelin' with two white children and no money.

I decided to pretend to sleep until Eula got here so we could get our stories straight. I closed my eyes and folded my hands on my chest. A nice sleepin' pose—like Snow White after she ate the apple.

For all of her rules and politeness, Miss Cyrena didn't have much respect for a sleeping sick girl, 'cause she kept right on talking. "Eula is quite a remarkable woman. She slept on the floor right here beside you every night. Did all of the doctoring herself—even though I offered to pay for a doctor visit when I learned your funds are limited. I'm afraid I was little help other than offering aspirin. You see, as many children as I've nurtured and seen grow up, I've never nursed a sick child. When children are sick, they don't come to school. But Eula knows so much. She figured you'd gotten ill from your fall into the river while you were playing. And she knew just what you needed to bring you back to health."

Now I knew part of the made-up story. But it wasn't much help; I sure didn't think Eula woulda told Miss Cyrena that Wallace tried to drown me in the swamp.

"She used vinegar and hot compresses on your ear, then she put in some garlic oil and plugged it with a cotton ball. I'd never even heard of such a thing, but it worked. Before long you'd stopped moaning with pain. She spooned slippery elm tea into you like you were a baby bird. Kept you propped up when your breath got rattly. Made a tent over you and kept putting pots of hot water under it so you could breathe the steam. She's smart, that one."

I nodded. I wondered what Miss Cyrena would think if she knew the main reason Eula probably didn't want a doctor was 'cause we was lawbreakers travelin' invisible.

I kept my eyes closed.

"But there's something about her. . . . I think she has a lot of fear bottled up inside. Big fear." Miss Cyrena sighed. "Has something happened to her, do you know?"

I finally opened one eye. "She seems fine to me . . . just like always. I'm real tired." I closed my eye. I sure wasn't gonna tell her 'bout Wallace's meanness 'cause I'd have to explain where Wallace was now. And I didn't feel right telling stories about Eula's momma and pap to a stranger.

"Oh, of course, dear. I just want to help Eula. I feel in my heart she needs it. But I can't get to the crux of the matter. She's very . . . quiet."

"She's always like that. It's her way," I said without opening my eyes.

"Hmmm," Miss Cyrena said, like she was thinking—and not about being quiet. "When you arrived, she said she'd already called your mother and told her of the delay. If you were my child and ill, I'd figure out a way to get to you. Would you like to call your mother now—tell her you're getting better?"

My eyes sprung open. "That'd . . . that'd be long distance." Even if I had the money and wanted to, I couldn't call Momma. I didn't know her number. I didn't know her address. I'd planned on hunting her down once I got there because of her being famous. I figured if I had trouble, I could find Sun Studio, where she'd made her record, and they could tell me where to find her. "'Sides, she's . . . sick herself. That's why she can't come get us."

"I see." Miss Cyrena said it in that way teachers have, saying they see when they think they see more than you're telling them. She started out of the room, then stopped and turned to me again. "Just one more thing. When I sent the neighbor boy to the garage to bring your things from the truck, Eula's suitcase was the only one in it." She stopped talking for a second, like she was waiting for me to explain why I was travelin' to live with my momma with only the clothes on my back. But I was too smart to fall into her quiet trap and kept still. "Eula figures someone took your and James's things before the tow truck got there." Another of those sneaky quiet spots. "Once you're better, I'll take you to the church and we'll see if we can get some clothes for you and the baby from the charity box. That'll get you by until you can travel on to your mother."

I mumbled something and closed my eyes like I couldn't help falling asleep. Then I tried to breathe slow and deep. I'd only meant to pretend so she didn't ask me more questions. But the real thing got ahold of me and the next thing I knew I woke up and the room was getting dark. Miss Cyrena was standing at the front door looking out, her yellow dress light against the shadows around her. I could smell that it had rained.

I rubbed my eyes, then looked around. "Where's Eula?"

"Not home yet."

"I thought she was supposed to be home by supper."

Miss Cyrena stayed real still. "She was."

"Why are we in the dark?" The fan was electric, so I knew she had lights.

"Better to watch outside this way."

The way her voice sounded gave me a little rush of goose bumps. "Why you need to watch outside? When Eula gets home, she'll walk right in, won't she?"

She moved then and came to stand beside the couch. "I've asked Mrs. Washington from next door to come and sit with you and James for a bit."

Right then I heard the back door open and close. "Cyrena?" the voice wasn't much over a whisper, and it sounded nervous.

"I'll be back shortly."

"Where you going?"

"To look for Eula."

"I'm comin' with you." I started to get up, but got so dizzy I had to stop as soon as my feet hit the floor beside the couch.

"No." Miss Cyrena put a hand on my shoulder.

"But—"

"Shh!" She pushed me back onto the pillow. "You're still too sick. Now just lie back down and Mrs. Washington will bring you some tea and toast." Miss Cyrena started out of the room. Then she stopped. "Leave the lights off."

"Why?"

"Do as I say." She sounded almost mad. Then she added, "Please. It's important."

Then she was gone.

I tried to get up again. As soon as I stood up, my knees turned to jelly and I had to sit right back down. I couldn't do nothing but sit in the dark and worry about Eula—and wonder why leaving the lights off made any sense at all.

16

The worry must have wore me down 'cause I woke up to voices in the kitchen. Mrs. Washington was talking, even though she had sat with me in the dark while I ate my toast and not said a word. She didn't like me.

"What's wrong with her?" Mrs. Washington asked.

Was she asking about me? Well, she coulda found out herself if she'd just opened her mouth while she was sitting here, instead of acting like we didn't both speak American.

Miss Cyrena's calm voice said, "Just sit here, Eula. I'll get you something to drink."

I sat straight up. Eula was back! I started to get up and hurry to the kitchen, but just then Miss Cyrena asked, "Is Starla asleep? She doesn't need to hear any of this."

I froze like a rabbit.

"Yes. The baby's back down, too," Mrs. Washington said.

I heard Miss Cyrena's sharp footsteps coming toward the living room. If there was something she didn't want me to know, the best way to find out was to play possum until I heard what I needed to hear. Real quick, I laid back down and closed my eyes.

When I heard her footsteps leave the doorway again, I got off the couch, nice and quiet. I was a little dizzy, but better than before I ate the toast. I made it to the kitchen door by holding on to the furniture to keep my balance. I plastered my back against the wall by the door, then slow and easy peeked around the jamb. I was real good at this, having had a lot of practice spying on Patti Lynn's brothers.

The only light burning in the whole house was the tiny one on the back of the stove top. It was just bright enough that I could see the funny way Mrs. Washington was staring at Eula. I could only see Eula's back. She was sitting at the table with her head bent and her face in her hands.

I wanted to hurry in there to see what was wrong, but kept myself still. They'd clam up for sure if they saw me. Or they'd make up some story that even a three-year-old wouldn't believe.

Mrs. Washington leaned close to Miss Cyrena and whispered, "I told you strangers would bring trouble. You gonna keep on goin' until the Klan burns your house and runs you out of town like they did Purnell Morgan? You got a good job . . . a life. Why you want to risk it?"

"Shush! Trouble was here long before I, or Purnell, allowed strangers in our houses. We'd all just been putting up with it."

"It ain't worth it," Mrs. Washington said, shaking her head.

Miss Cyrena looked like she was getting her back up. "This"—she pointed toward Eula—"tells me it is worth it. If we don't take some action, this kind of thing will never stop. This woman just went out to earn a day's wage and now look at her!"

I bit my lip. What had happened to Eula?

Now Mrs. Washington looked to be getting her back up. I edged out a little farther, maybe get a better look at Eula; those two women were staring at each other so hard, they weren't gonna notice me.

Eula was so still I thought maybe she'd gone inside herself again.

Mrs. Washington said, "All you and your N-double-A-CP friends are doing is making things worse!" Her whisper was sharp. "More outsiders always bring more trouble. Nothin' is ever gonna change in Mississippi."

I was getting all antsy-pantsy. Why couldn't they stop talking about strangers and N-double-A-CP, whatever that was, and talk about Eula?

"This has nothing to do with the N-double A CP," Miss Cyrena said.

"You don't think so? I suppose you don't think it had anything to do with Tober Bryant getting beaten within an inch of his life, either?"

"It wasn't the N-double-A-CP who beat him and left him bloody in the road! It was the Klan . . . and the Klan has been doing wrong long before the N-double-A-CP showed up. Besides, Tober knew the risk and he decided it was worth it."

I was itching to jump into the kitchen, get a look at Eula, and ask what trouble they was talking about. But I held tight, listening.

Mrs. Washington raised her chin and humphed. "I reckon we're never gonna see eye to eye on this."

"Probably not." Then Miss Cyrena put a hand on Mrs. Washington's arm. "Thank you for staying with the children." Her voice had lost all of its mad, just like that.

"I did it for you, not for them."

"I know. You're a good friend."

Mrs. Washington put her hand over Miss Cyrena's. "Have a care, Cyrena." Then she went out the back door.

Miss Cyrena turned around and I had to duck out of the doorway.

"Now, how about that something to drink?" Miss Cyrena asked Eula.

I held my breath, waiting. Hoping she hadn't gone inside herself. Miss Cyrena wouldn't understand. She might even send Eula to a hospital—or the loony bin. I couldn't let that happen.

I was just about to go through the door when I heard Eula say in a faraway voice, "Maybe some tea?" She didn't sound normal, but at least she was talking and still in the world.

A cupboard door opened and closed. "I think some of Kentucky's finest might do you better tonight."

"Don't care for hard liquor," Eula said in her tiptoe-around-Wallace voice. "Tea be fine."

I heard a bottle clunk on the counter. "Sometimes it's best to let hard liquor care for you. I'll add just a splash to your tea. It'll calm you." I heard the kettle fill. "As for myself, times like these call to forego the tea." I heard the cap come off a bottle and something glug into a glass. "Bourbon straight up. The school board would be mortified."

A chair slid across the floor. Then it creaked; I figured Miss Cyrena sat down.

The kitchen stayed quiet. I wondered what they were doing in there, not talking, but was afraid to peek around the corner. I was getting real shaky, so I slid down and sat on the floor.

Finally, the teakettle whistled.

"Ah," Miss Cyrena said, "there we are." The whistle stopped. The refrigerator opened and closed. She clattered some dishes and silverware. "I added honey and milk. You won't even taste the bourbon, but it'll calm your nerves."

The cup and saucer rattled onto the table.

Miss Cyrena's chair creaked again. It was quiet for a second, then she sighed. "Don't get the wrong idea. I really don't drink much. Lately occasion has called for it."

The teacup and saucer made some noise.

I started to think they wasn't gonna say anything interesting at all and I might as well just walk on in there, admit I was awake, and get a look to make sure Eula hadn't got a new black eye or something.

Then Miss Cyrena said, "The men who followed you . . . they were white?"

Eula must have nodded 'cause Miss Cyrena said, "I thought as much. Why did you feel you had to hide?"

It was quiet again.

"Eula, did they hurt you?"

"No." Eula's voice was so soft, I barely heard it.

"Did they threaten you?"

The teacup rattled and I heard Eula take a slurpy sip.

"Eula?"

"I didn't want 'em followin' me back here . . . to you and the young'uns."

"So they did threaten you."

Eula didn't say anything.

I listened close. Her breathing changed, getting noisy and deep. In my head I could see her face, the way it had looked when she figured out that Wallace wasn't getting back up. It was that kind of breathing, the kind you did to keep from screaming.

"Ain't them followin' like that a threat?" Eula finally said. "Went on for blocks. I even turned round and went back the way I come and they stayed just over my shoulder like the devil's shadow."

It hit me hard. Eula's keepin' a secret. A secret about what all them men done to her—or what she done back to them. Eula was used to being bullied and scared. Why, most of the time she just went on about her business when Wallace was doing regular bullying. If she went and hid, it was 'cause of more than followin' like the devil's shadow. It was 'cause she'd seen the devil.

"It certainly seems like a threat to me. Although I'm afraid the sheriff won't think so."

"No sheriff!" Eula then lowered her voice. "I was prob'ly just worked up from what they done earlier. No need for the sheriff."

"Earlier? You didn't say they'd bothered you earlier."

"T'weren't nothin'." The teacup clattered a little.

"Eula, you hid behind those stacks of sour-smelling milk bottles on the loading dock of the dairy for two hours. I think it must have been something."

I heard Eula sip her tea again.

"I won't call the sheriff, Eula," Miss Cyrena said. "But I'd like to know what happened."

Eula sighed. She sounded real tired.

"Please," Miss Cyrena said.

"When I was workin' in Miz Clark's front flower beds, they come by in a truck."

I leaned so I could see into the kitchen. I was so low, I saw mostly legs. Miss Cyrena's knee was jumpin' like a jackhammer. I knew how she felt, all jittered up inside and no place to put the aggravation. Happened to me a lot.

Eula went on, slow, but steady enough I was pretty sure she was gonna stay in the world. "Passed two or three times before they stopped right in front of Miz Clark's, hung out their windas, and hollered round some—like they do; nasty man-talk. I could tell they was in the juice real good. I kept my head down and ignored 'em, like always." Eula stopped for a second. "Then I heard one of the truck doors open and a foot hit the ground. One of 'em yelled for me to look at him when he talkin'."

"Oh, dear."

"I held myself still, tryin' to decide if I should get up and run or stay put, when I heard the screen door squeak. Miz Clark, she come out on her front porch. I was afraid she was gonna fire me, 'cause of the trouble I was causin'. But that weren't what she had in mind. She had a shotgun—ain't never seen a white woman hold a shotgun. She yelled at them men, 'Y'all get your white-trashy selves back in that truck and get on down the road. Leave my woman alone, else I'll have to use this.' Then she cocked the gun and put it up to her shoulder."

Miss Cyrena slapped her palm on the table so hard and sudden, I jumped. "That's why I respect that woman! No man is going to get away with any mischief while she has her eyes open. So, did they leave?"

"Uh-huh. Didn't see 'em no more while I was at Miz Clark's."

"But when you left? They followed you?"

"I think they been waitin'. I hadn't got two blocks when that truck got to creepin' up 'hind me—" Eula stopped talking suddenlike, just the way she did when she didn't want to tell everything.

Her head shook and she put her face in her hands.

"Eula?" Miss Cyrena's voice got softer. "Eula, I need to know . . . in order to protect you—and the children. You must think of the children."

Something changed in Eula's shoulders right then, she looked like she got smaller. She said, real quiet, so quiet I leaned forward and almost lost my balance and fell through the door. "You know what them kinda men're like."

"Oh." Miss Cyrena's leg got going faster. "Did they . . . ?"

"Tried . . . but I got away."

Did they what? Tried what? If I went in and asked, I knew they wouldn't tell me. Why did grown-ups have to talk with so many blank spots?

"How?" Miss Cyrena asked.

"Eye pokin'. They was pretty drunk and clumsy."

"Good . . . yes, good." Miss Cyrena sounded like she wasn't sure it was good at all. "Tell me about this truck. New or old? What color was it?"

"Not new, but not old. Red-and-white. Had a Confederate flag painted on the hood."

Miss Cyrena hissed. "Jenkins brothers. Mrs. Clark was right, those men are white trash. Worthless, do-little scraps of humanity. Make themselves feel important by picking on women and children—and of course, Negros." She paused. "I only hope . . . well, it's good you hid and they don't know where you are."

I felt my red rage coming on, not strong as usual 'cause I was sick. Why did everybody have to be so daggone mean to Eula? After I got better, I was gonna find that truck and break out its headlights.

"How did you lose them and manage to hide?" Miss Cyrena asked.

"Now that's somethin' I learned as a young'un; gettin' away and hidin'. Learned it real good."

Miss Cyrena's voice dropped so quiet I had to listen hard to hear when she said, "You've had a difficult life . . . more than most of us, I imagine."

My ears perked up then. I'd been more and more curious 'bout Eula and her pap and her no-account brother. I already knew more than I wanted to about Wallace.

But Eula didn't say anything to ease my curiousness. She just said, "Think I'll only take backyard or indoor work from now on."

"Yes, I would. Once those ruffians set their sights on you, it's usually best to stay out of their way. And they'll have a grudge to carry now, too. Never known them not to get their revenge." Miss Cyrena was quiet for a second. "I think I have a better idea. Why don't you use my kitchen to make baked goods? That green-tomato pie you made was the most delicious I've ever tasted, and the hot-milk cake . . . my, oh, my. Mrs. Washington went on and on about that peach cobbler I took over to thank her for the collards from her garden. You could probably sell things to the coffee shop and restaurants and not have to work outside of this house at all. I could do the sales and delivery—even the shopping. You won't be exposed at all."

"Can't until I earn enough to buy bakin' supplies."

"I'll front you the money."

"No, ma'am. I couldn't take any more from you than I already have."

I couldn't be still any longer. "Do it, Eula," I said, walking into the kitchen. It would keep Eula safe while we got our money built up so we could fix the truck and get on to Nashville. "It's a good idea. And I can go out and collect bottles along the roads, turn 'em in for the refunds. You shouldn't be out where those men can get at you."

"Starla! I thought you were sleeping," Miss Cyrena said. She put her arm in front of her glass, like she didn't want me to see it.

Eula reached out an arm and motioned me close. I stepped right up next to her and looked at her face. She didn't have any more cuts than the ones Wallace had given her, which was healing up nice. A little of the antsy-pantsy left me.

She wrapped an arm around me and touched my forehead with her other hand. "No more burnin'." She smiled. "You better, child. You better." The gladness in her voice made me feel special—like she'd felt poorly 'cause I felt poorly. I got a sudden attack of being ashamed; she was in so much trouble 'cause of me.

I laid my head on her shoulder. Her arms wrapped me tight and I was all the sudden taken by a cryin' fit.

"Please, Eula," I said against her shoulder. "Please do like Miss Cyrena says."

Eula petted my hair and rocked me. "Shhhh. Shhhh, child."

I jerked away. "I mean it! It ain't safe for you out there with those men and the N-double-A-CP."

Her eyes got wide. "You been listenin' awhile."

I nodded and wiped my eyes. "What is the N-double-A-CP?"

Miss Cyrena said, "An organization to help Negros get their full rights as citizens of this country."

"Like what?"

"Voting without harassment. Equality under the law—not separate rules for Negros and whites; no separate schools or toilets or bus seats."

"Oh." I couldn't imagine a school with white kids and colored kids all mixed up. "Mamie said everybody likes it the way it is—not just whites, coloreds, too."

"That's what most white people say," Miss Cyrena said. "They don't want it to change."

"Colored do?"

"Not all, but that's because they've been taught to be afraid."

Eula pulled me back against her. "All right, that's enough worry for one night. Time you get back to sleep."

"Please say you'll bake and not go out to work," I said. "Please."

Miss Cyrena said, "You'll make money faster baking than doing domestic work."

"And I can help," I said.

"It's a good plan, Eula."

For a long while Eula was quiet. Then I heard her sniffle. "It's a good plan." She patted my back. "Now get you back to bed, child. We bakin' tomorrow."

As she tucked me in my couch-bed, I said, "I'm sorry."

She tilted her head; the moonlight glittered in her eyes. "What you mean?"

"I'm sorry I'm causin' you so much trouble."

"Now you listen to me. I spent my whole life wantin' to take care of children. You a blessing, not a burden." She looked at me hard. "Don't you go forgettin' that."

She patted my shoulder and left me alone. As I fell asleep, it come to me that that was the first time anybody had ever told me I was a blessing.

17

I got up the next morning and it looked like Eula had been up all night baking. I bet she'd used up everything in Miss Cyrena's kitchen that could be made into a pie or cake. And she didn't even have a single order yet.

I stood there looking at them all lined up on the table. "How come you baked all these?"

Eula was at the counter, her hands deep in a mixing bowl, sweezing and patting, squeezing and patting. "Sometimes I just gotta bake."

"What's this one?" I pointed to a pie that kinda looked like apple, but not.

"Green tomato, for Miss Cyrena. She near ate the last one all herself." Eula leaned close. "So I reckon it might be her favorite."

"That one pumpkin?"

"Sweet potato."

"And that?" I pointed to a round cake with a hole in the middle.

"Surely you know apple-dapple cake?"

I shook my head. "Never seen a cake with a hole."

She raised her eyebrows. "Angel food?"

I shook my head.

"Well, we got our work cut out for us. You gotta know what they taste like if'n you gonna make 'em."

I eyed the table. There was lots of things that didn't look familiar.

"We gotta eat 'em all?" I was all for sweets, but even I couldn't eat all these, even if I had a week.

"Miss Cyrena said she'd take some in town, maybe give out a sample to some of the restaurants and a couple of her friends. Try to scare up some business."

Then it hit me. Eula said I had to know if I was gonna make 'em. "Am I helpin'?"

"You want to?"

I nodded. This'd be almost as good as when I got to Nashville and got to make Christmas cookies with Lulu.

"Good. A lot of soothin' come from bakin'. Get your hands washed and down in this here dough." She wiped her hands on her apron and stepped back. "We makin' a chess pie."

"Shouldn't I use a spoon?" I asked before I plunged my hands in the bowl. "Mamie always said to keep your fingers out of what you're makin'."

"Oh, no, child. Gotta get your hands deep in a pie crust. That how you know when it right. Just gotta barely hold together. Too wet and it won't be nice and flaky."

We spent the rest of the morning making that chess pie. Eula explained to me how you had to use ice water when mixin' the crust. She showed me how to put it in the pie tin and brush it with egg white and prick it with a fork and bake it for a few minutes before adding the filling—which was mostly eggs and sugar, but had cornmeal in it!—to be baked. That made for a nice crisp crust, she said. But it was only for a chess pie. Every pie, it had its own special trick. I wanted to learn them all

Eula was right, baking was soothin'. Too bad baby James was too little to do baking, maybe he wouldn't cry as much.

The baking business in Miss Cyrena's town turned out to be real good. So good that I didn't even have time to go out and collect bottles for deposit money. I was a little sorry 'cause I missed being outside.

Me and Eula . . . I mean, Eula and I (Miss Cyrena was real picky about the way we talked in her house) started rolling pie crust and mixing cake and muffin batters first thing in the morning, even before we ate breakfast. When I bellyached about being hungry, Eula told me I was lucky that Miss Cyrena had a nice new electric mixer or breakfast would be even later.

Even though I had to wait for breakfast, I was glad Eula had decided to do baking instead of going to work at people's houses and whatnot. I could keep my eye on her and know she was safe. Besides, if she hadn't, I might never have found out something about myself. Turned out, taking care of babies wasn't my only gift. Eula said I got me a special gift for rolling pie crust, too. She only had to show me how to do it once. And then she helped me with my first one by putting her hands over mine and letting me get the feel for how hard to press the rolling pin and how to go this way and that to make the dough a circle. In the four days we'd been baking, I'd only rolled one too thin and had to start over. Eula said that messing with the pie dough—she called it "working" the dough, but I was the one working, so it didn't make any sense to me—too much made it tough and not nice and flaky, so I was real careful from then on.

I wondered, what other gifts I got bottled up inside me? That question had started to gnaw on me some.

That Thursday morning, my wondering was bigger than ever. And so was the orders. Folks in Miss Cyrena's town must eat an extra lot of cake and pie on Friday and Saturday, so Eula said we had to work extra-fast—which made our conversationing time shorter. We wouldn't get to sit at the table and have a banana and a glass of milk while we waited for a batch to come out of the oven. That was my favorite time of day, me and Eula at the table talking with the timer ticking behind our words. I'd already found out she'd been a maid to three different houses with kids before she switched to baking. When I asked why she changed families (Bess and Ernestine sure had stayed put with their families), she'd got real quiet before she said it was 'cause she loved them babies too much. She said that was the reason she changed to baking, too; too much baby love. That didn't make a lick of sense to me, but she got some tears stuck in her eyes, so I didn't ask any more about it.

Even though our conversationing time wasn't gonna be, I was determined to get my questions asked about my gifts. Just as soon as we had the pie dough getting cold in the Frigidaire and the first cakes in the oven, me and—Eula and I finally got to sit down and eat our grits and eggs and fried bacon. Miss Cyrena said Frosted Flakes was nothing but sugar, and a growing child needed protein. I'd been growing just fine on Frosted Flakes so far, but didn't argue 'cause we was guests in her house.

Even though I was starvin', as soon as Eula finished saying grace, I got right to it. "Eula, you got any more special gif's . . . other'n pies and babies?"

She stopped with her coffee cup halfway to her mouth. She shook her head. "Reckon not . . . none that I know 'bout anyhow." She blew on the coffee, then took a sip.

"When did you know 'bout the ones you got?"

"Well now, the babies come early, when I helpin' my cousin take care of the littler cousins while their momma worked."

"How old were you?" I was wondering if I was late in finding my own gifts, or right on time.

"Changed the first diaper when I was four." She wrinkled her nose and waved her hand under it. "Stinky one, too." She laughed a little. "You find out someday. Them new baby ones like baby James has ain't so bad yet. I was takin' care of 'em all on my own by the time I was nine." She picked up her knife and nodded for me to start eating, too. "Time short, eat up."

I felt a little disappointed. I thought having the gift before I was ten was real special.

I swung my bare feet, liking the feel of the linoleum swish, swish, swish with the tick-tick of the timer as I thought. I put a big bite of eggs into my mouth.

As Eula buttered her toast, she said, "Soothed the colic in the baby when I was eight. The rest just come a little at a time."

"How'd you know 'bout the pies?" I asked. My mouth was full, but Miss Cyrena wasn't in the room to scold me.

"Here's the thing 'bout gif's." Eula stopped buttering her toast and looked straight at me. "A body don't know how many the good Lord tucked inside them until the time is right. I reckon a person could go a whole life and not know. That why you gotta try lots of things, many as you can . . . experiment."

I took a bite of bacon, forgetting that I always saved it for last because it was my favorite.

Mamie always made me do the things she wanted me to do, which was never the interesting stuff. Whenever I asked to do something, she said I'd make too much mess, or too much noise, or it was dangerous, or I'd break something, or people would think I was unladylike, or think I was trashy. Why, if I hadn't met Eula, I might never have found out about the babies or the pie crust.

"How do you know what to try?" I asked. There didn't seem to be enough time to try everything. What if I was trying race-car driving (dangerous, unladylike, *and* trashy) when my gift was really doctoring animals?

She looked at me like I wasn't getting the point. "Why, when your mind gets curious 'bout somethin', you know you should experiment. You a white child, you can do anything you want!"

I snorted. "You don't know my mamie." I realized too late that I wasn't stickin' to my story. I held my breath for Eula to say something, but she didn't even look my way, so I reckon she was so caught up in talkin' gifts that she missed it.

"I ain't sayin' doin' it right the second it pops into your mind. Rules keep a child safe. But as you growin', the chances gonna be there for you. Why you can be anythin' when you grow up."

The way she said it got me thinking. Mamie said girls grow up to be secretaries or nurses or teachers and then turn into mommas, and that's their job for the rest of their life. But my momma was famous for being a singer. She must have tried things that weren't secretarying or nursing to find out she had a gift.

Right then I got a little sick feeling in my belly. She had been a momma . . . but had to leave to get famous. Do you have to choose one or the other?

Eula said, "You got all sorts of gif's hidin' inside you. I can tell."

"You can?"

"Clear as the sun in the sky!"

"What are they?"

"Ohhh," she said real serious. "They don't got names yet. That's the part you have to find out with your experimentin'."

The timer went *ding!* Eula got up to check the cakes with a toothpick; that's how you could tell if they was done. As she did, she patted my shoulder. "Jus' remember, they's all there inside you, waitin' to be found."

I sat there finishing my breakfast, feeling around inside to see if my mind got curious about something.

Curiosities started snapping like popcorn.

That afternoon, when Miss Cyrena was loading up her car to make deliveries, I decided I'd had all the being indoors I could tolerate. She'd pulled her car right up to the back door so she didn't have to carry the cakes and all to the driveway on the side of the house. I followed Miss Cyrena out, even though the going-out rule was: only with permission, which was most always given after dark and only for the backyard. Truth be told, I was turning even whiter on account of I never got to be in the sun. If only I had my bicycle! I'd be able to ride away from this neighborhood where I stood out like a polar bear mixed in with regular bears. I would ride and ride and ride, until my legs fell off.

"Can I come?" I asked. I'd brought a cake with me so I'd be helpful. I handed it to Miss Cyrena.

She took the cake. Her eyes flickered toward the house and back to me. "Oh, I don't know if that's a good idea."

"Please? I'll stay in the car. I won't be a bother at all."

She took the cake and put it real careful in one of the boxes Mrs. Washington's son, Cletus, had made to carry the cakes and whatnot. "It's not that you'd be a bother! You're always such good help. It's just that . . ."

I knew what she was thinking. 'Sides me sticking out like a polar bear, there was the Jenkins boys in town. We hadn't had no more problems from them, probably 'cause Eula was staying hid inside Miss Cyrena's and they couldn't find her. Course Miss Cyrena had said they like to pick on kids, too, so I couldn't argue that I was white and they'd leave me alone.

"If I see that truck with the Confederate flag on the hood, I'll hide down on the floorboard."

Her eyes got squinty behind her glasses. "You heard it all, didn't you?"

I nodded. "So I know to stay away from them. See? It's good."

"It's not like hide-and-seek, Starla. Those men are cruel and dangerous."

"Miss Cyrena, I'm gonna go crazy if I don't get outta here."

After a second, she smiled just a little. "Well, we can't have you going crazy, can we?"

I held my breath.

She nodded. "Go tell Eula you're coming with me."

I jumped and turned around at the same time and ran into the house before she could change her mind.

She called after me, "And change your clothes. Put on that nice dress we got you from the church."

I run upstairs to change—since I slept on the couch and didn't have a room myself, I kept my clothes up in Eula's room. I stopped when I heard Eula laughing. Since we'd been at Miss Cyrena's, Eula had changed some. Her smiles come more easy and she acted less like she was afraid of her own shadow. But laughing had still been a rare thing.

I walked slow and quiet and peeked in the door. Baby James was laying in the middle of the bed and Eula was telling him a story. Course James wasn't big enough to pay any attention, but Eula was having fun anyway. She made her hands act like butterflies and bumblebees and Brer Rabbit. Those critters did the silliest things . . . which is why Eula'd been laughing. All the sudden she looked up and saw me. Her smile come quick and bright and changed everything about her.

"C'mon in and you can hear the story, too," she said, patting the bed beside her.

I went in. "I gotta put on my dress. Miss Cyrena said I could ride with her to make deliveries."

For a second Eula's brow wrinkled. "She think that a good idea?"

"I'm stayin' in the car." I grabbed my dress and yanked off my shirt. I had to get back out there before Eula decided to try to change Miss Cyrena's mind.

She surprised me by not arguing. "Well, now, you be careful . . . and mind Miss Cyrena."

My dress went over my head.

"Let me button you up."

I turned around so Eula could. While she did, I watched her in the mirror. Her hands used to move nervous and twisty all of the time, but now they were slow and steady, sometimes even still. Her mouth had got softer. And her shoulders sat square instead of curved in.

"You're different." I said it before I thought.

Her hands stopped buttoning and she tilted her head. "Different?"

I nodded. "You're . . ." The right word stayed hid, then all of the sudden popped into my head. "Happy."

Her smile and eyes was soft, like when she looked at baby James sleeping. "I reckon I am." She touched baby James's face, then put her hands on my shoulders and pressed her cheek next to mine. We looked at each other in the mirror. "Havin' somebody to love does that for a person."

All Eula had ever wanted was a baby. I wondered if she would have been happy all along if her babies had lived. "But . . ." I didn't want to take away her happiness, but, as Miss Cyrena always said, we have to be practical. "You can't keep him." I said it real soft, like that would make it less hurtful.

She squeezed my shoulders. "I ain't just talkin' about James."

My breath swirled around in my chest and my stomach tingled. It was like Eula's happiness come through her hands and seeped inside me, too.

"'Sides," she said, still smiling, "love don't need to be in the same house. There always be love inside me for you and James, no matter where we are." She buttoned the last button and turned me around. She smoothed my hair down. "There now. You look real nice. Best not keep Miss Cyrena waitin'."

As I hurried back down the stairs, I felt like a different person than when I'd come up.

When we pulled out of her driveway, Miss Cyrena said, "I'll take a little detour so you can see the school where I teach. This part of town is called the Bottoms. It's low and prone to flood, which is why most of the colored live here."

"Why would you want to live here if it floods a lot?"

"The colored don't choose to live here. It's where they're allowed to live."

I got to thinking. Most of the colored in Cayuga Springs lived in one neighborhood, too. Mamie had said it was because they liked to stick with their own kind. Miss Cyrena made it sound like they didn't have a choice.

"What if you wanted to live somewhere else?" I asked.

"It would depend on where that somewhere else was."

"Like if it was in a white neighborhood or a colored?"

"Yes." She stopped for a minute, like she was making up her mind about something. "That's something that many of us are trying to change. We want Negros—all people—to have all of the same choices available as whites."

I thought about how mad Mrs. Washington had sounded when she and Miss Cyrena were talking about the N-double-A-CP. "Doesn't Mrs. Washington want that?"

Miss Cyrena looked at me like she was surprised by my question—and not good surprised. I held my breath, afraid I'd made her mad and she was gonna take me back home.

"Everybody wants equal rights, Starla. Everybody. They don't all agree on how to make it happen . . . or about how much misery they're willing to take on to get them. It's a complicated world and takes dedication and a willingness to take some risk to evoke change."

Miss Cyrena was starting to talk confusing. But she still got me thinking. Eula had said that because I was white, I could do anything I wanted. I started to feel a little guilty about my skin, even though I couldn't help the way I was born.

I sat up straighter and looked around. "It's real pretty here, lots of trees. I'd live in the Bottoms if I lived in your town."

Miss Cyrena looked at me with sad eyes. "You have a very good soul, Starla." Then she said, "There it is. My school."

I looked on both sides of the street but didn't see a school. "Where?"

"Right there." She pointed to a building on my side of the street. It looked like an old church with all of the colored windows taken out and plain glass ones put in.

As we passed, I looked to see behind it. "Where's the playground?"

"The children play in the back and side yards. We don't allow them to play on the side where the alley is."

I turned in my seat so I could see behind the school as we passed. Most of the grass was worn away. "Where's the swings? And the tetherball poles? And the monkey bars?"

"Our money is all used up buying books and supplies. There's none left for playground equipment."

"Oh." I felt real sorry for those kids.

"We get by. The children are used to making their own fun. It encourages creativity. And Mr. Baker is very good at organizing games. We do have some balls for kickball, dodgeball, and such."

I thought about the swings at my school. Everyone always raced out the door to get one at recess. Course the boys like Jimmy Sellers didn't. They took their sweet time, then pushed out whoever was in the swing they wanted and took it. They were real good at not getting caught by the playground-duty teacher, too.

"Do you have bullies in the colored school?"

Miss Cyrena looked over at me. "The colored school is filled with children who are just like the children in the white school. Some good as gold. Some shy. Some real smart. Some struggle with letters and numbers. And, yes, there are bullies. And just like in the white school, we try to change their ways."

I thought on it for a minute. It sure didn't seem to me that anyone at my school was trying to change Jimmy Sellers's ways. He knew just what to say to the teachers, just how to smile and "Yes, ma'am" until they believed his bull-hockey stories. I was real glad he was going to Jr. High next year.

I wondered if the teachers at the colored school were that dumb, too. Since Miss Cyrena was a teacher, I guess asking her would be disrespectful.

"What school do you attend?" Miss Cyrena asked. "I mean, *did* you attend when you were living with your grandmother."

Eula had told me that she told Miss Cyrena the same story I told her: my grandma had died and I was going to live with my momma in Nashville. But Eula was even smarter about it than me. She didn't say she was our maid, 'cause we couldn't afford a maid if we couldn't afford money to send me to my momma. Eula told Miss Cyrena she'd been helping my sick grandma as a Christian charity, on account of Eula's cousin being a maid for a friend of my grandma's. It made sense to me. But I didn't know where she said my grandma and I lived.

"Oh," I said, real easy, "I went to the elementary school."

"Which one?"

Uh-oh. "There's only one in town," I said, like that was the only answer. Then I asked a question to change her thinking. "Where are we taking the first cake?"

"Slattery's Diner. Luckily for Eula, their baker is down with the shingles. They've ordered nine pies and two cakes."

"Nine?" That only left one pie for somebody else—plenty of cakes though.

"That's their specialty. Everyone in town goes there for pie."

Miss Cyrena slowed the car down all of the sudden, way down to creepin'. I looked up and saw we were crossing the railroad tracks.

"Don't want to upset the cakes. That system Cletus designed works well, but we can't be too careful."

I'd watched when Cletus Washington put the stacking wooden boxes into Miss Cyrena's trunk. He'd also made some for the backseat. The trunk one fit like a puzzle, and I figured he was real smart to make it. I was surprised when I found out he didn't go to high school, even though he was fifteen. Instead, he worked at the lumber mill and knew all about wood. He wanted to build furniture someday. I bet he'd make real good furniture.

After we crossed the railroad tracks, we passed Applewhite's Dairy. I wondered if that was where Eula had hid on the loading dock when she'd been running from the Jenkins brothers. We passed a few other businesses: a propane-gas bottler, the Ford car dealer, a little orange-painted root-beer drive-in with a covered place for the cars to pull under to stay out of the sun and rain, the Chevy car dealer, a produce market with big baskets of watermelon and cantaloupe out front. And then the houses started getting bigger, with good paint and nice grass. There were lots of them, not just a few like in Cayuga Springs.

Once we got to the center of town there was a yellow-brick courthouse with giant, round columns in front. As we drove around the block, I could see that even though most of the building was square, parts of it was round, too, like when they was building it they couldn't make up their minds.

There was a Sears and Roebuck store, two jewelry stores, a JCPenney, two grocery stores (Miss Cyrena said there were two more on the edge of town; one of them was the colored grocery where she bought our baking stuff). We passed a brick library with light posts on each side of the front steps and a green-tile roof, three drugstores (Miss Cyrena said two of them had lunch counters), a Goodyear store that took up a whole corner, a Ben Franklin five-and-dime, and lots of churches. They even had a hotel! And that's just what I could see. Miss Cyrena said there was a new "shopping plaza" out by the fairgrounds that had stores, too.

We turned onto a street that had a big patch of grass and trees down the center. Cars went one way on one side and the other way across the grass. It was real pretty.

"Here we are," Miss Cyrena pulled into an angled parking place. "You wait here while I take in the baked goods."

I was itching to go into the drugstore two doors down; curious if they had different penny candy than the one in Cayuga Springs.

"Starla," she said in her teacher voice. I could feel her looking at me.

I took my eyes off the drugstore and looked at the front window of Slattery's Diner. The special today was chicken fried steak. "Huh?"

"Look over here at me," she said.

I did.

"Stay in the car."

I nodded. Plenty of people was on the streets, women with hats and pocketbooks and kids mostly. Maybe I'd just ask one of the kids about it.

"Don't talk to anybody through the windows, either."

What good was it to be in town if I couldn't find out anything?

"I mean it. This town might be bigger than where you're from, but it's still small enough that people talk. We don't need a dozen questions about why you're here with me."

I crossed my arms and slumped down in the seat. "Might as well have stayed home."

"I can take you back home right now and come back to make my deliveries." She had her teacher brows all raised up like they do when they pretend they're letting you make a decision on your own.

"Okay, okay."

Miss Cyrena went into Slattery's. I looked up and down the street. A kid came out of the drugstore wearing wax lips and holding a sucker that was about six inches long and looked like it was made of coiled ribbon candy. It was striped and shaped like a long, skinny cone. I'd never seen one like it.

That got my curiosity going.

I looked at Slattery's. No Miss Cyrena yet.

I had to hurry if I was gonna shoot down there and take a look at that candy section. Once me and Eula was making some money, maybe I'd be able to take a dime, come back, and buy one of them twisted suckers. I hoped they was only a dime. No way to know without looking.

I jumped out of the car and closed the door nice and easy, just in case Miss Cyrena had her teacher ears pointed this way. Once when we was in first grade, Patti Lynn and me was talking to each other across the aisle just by movin' our lips, not even makin' a whisper. Mrs. Kessler heard our lips movin'. She made us both stand at the front of the class until recess. Teacher hearing was as good as Superman's.

I hustled myself right on down to the drugstore. Lucky the candy was near the front. Most of the stuff was the same as Adler's had. But there was them long, skinny suckers wrapped in clear cellophane, sticking up out of a box made special with holes for the sticks. They was all different kinds of stripes. I was wonderin' if every color was a different flavor when I heard a dog scream—a scream, not just a yelp. That dog was hurt bad.

I run out of the store. There in the middle of the street was a black-and-white dog limpin' over to the curb, holding one of its back legs up off the ground. A truck was driving on, not even stopping after hitting it.

My red rage exploded. I took off running after the truck.

It slowed down.

Maybe it was coming back! Maybe the driver just saw what he done and was coming back down the other side of the grass.

But he turned left.

I run at a diagonal across the grass, puttin' on my jackrabbit speed.

"Hey!" I yelled. "Stop!"

The truck slowed down just a little and a guy with long hair hung his head out the window.

I heard Miss Cyrena calling me now.

"You hit that dog!" I yelled at the man.

He gave me the finger and sped up.

I slowed down. I couldn't catch him now.

Miss Cyrena was yelling my name, her breath making it bounce. I turned and saw she was running my way.

"He run over that dog!" I said, pointing toward the drugstore.

A man was putting the dog in his car. The sound of the dog's whimpers made me flash hot all over again. If I'd been sitting in the car like I was supposed to, I could have jumped out in front of that truck and stopped it.

"You should have stayed in the car." Miss Cyrena was mad enough that she was grittin' her teeth.

"But—" Drugstore or not, I'd have been out on the street when that poor dog screamed.

She took me by the arm and hurried me back toward her car. "No buts. There are plenty of people out here to worry about that dog. And you just drew a dangerous amount of attention to us."

"So what?" I said, getting my back up. I wasn't sure if I was more mad at that man for hitting the dog, for me not catchin' him, or Miss Cyrena for making such a fuss. "Nobody knows me."

"They all know me." She opened the passenger door and set me down. She looked down at me with her lips all pinched up. "And that truck you were just chasing belongs to Jobie Jenkins . . . one of the men who bothered Eula."

My mouth come open. "But I didn't see no flag."

"Of course you didn't. You were chasing it from behind."

My stomach flipped over. "But . . . but . . . they don't know I'm with Eula. So everything's okay."

Miss Cyrena took a big breath. She was shaking. "Probably so. As long as he didn't see me chasing after you. Then they'll know how to find you if they want."

She closed my door and walked around the car. When she got in, I said, "I'm sorry. I didn't mean to make trouble. I'm so dumb!" I hit my head with the palm of my hand, like I could knock the troublemakin' part out.

She looked at me and sighed. "Oh, Starla." Then she touched my cheek. "It's your generous and caring heart that made you go after that man. That's nothing to be ashamed of. I'm sure everything is fine. I doubt he noticed me."

But as she turned the key to start the car, I caught the worried look in her eye.

Miss Cyrena stopped at a gas station and gave me a dime to buy a bottle of Co'Cola from the red cooler out front. When I lifted the lid and stuck my hand down in that icy water to pull out a bottle, I wanted to jump in with my whole self. Between my red rage and my shame over making trouble, I was plenty hot.

I fished out a sliver of ice and run it on my neck. Then I pried off the cap with the bottle opener on the side of the cooler. I took such a big swig, it burned my throat going down.

Miss Cyrena drove us to a park near her house and stopped the car under a tree. There wasn't any kids playing, but I could see why. This park didn't have swings or anything, just a worn path between invisible bases where some kids had played baseball. Miss Cyrena said the city didn't come mow in this part of town very often, so the men in her neighborhood took turns doing it. She said some of them only had a nonpower mower; some no mower at all.

"How do they cut the weeds"—I couldn't call it grass—"then?"

"They use an old-fashioned scythe."

When I didn't know what that was, Miss Cyrena explained it. It sounded real tiring.

"They must like their kids a lot," I said.

"They do it for the community. We have to look out for each other, especially when things are difficult."

"Are they difficult now?"

She sighed and nodded. "And only going to get worse I'm afraid. Change doesn't come without struggle."

"Change? Like what you was talkin' about the other night?"

"Um-hmm. The fight for civil rights is just now sparking. They'll be a firestorm before it's over."

I thought of the TV news film I'd seen back in Cayuga Springs of colored people getting drug off stools at a lunch counter, and another where they was attacked by police dogs. I asked if that was what she meant.

She spent some time telling me about the things that the N-double-A-CP was doing and how much trouble they was getting in.

"Just in the South?" I asked.

"Most, not all. Have to start where the problem is the most glaring, then it can spread."

"I don't want you or Eula to do it. I don't want you to get chewed by police dogs or yanked out of a store and arrested."

Miss Cyrena looked at me and put her hand around my shoulder. "You're a good girl, Starla. Don't ever let your pure heart change."

I wasn't sure how a heart could change, but didn't want to talk about such frustratin' stuff anymore—especially while I was staring at the pitiful colored-kids park. I drank my Co'Cola and thought about how maybe when I got older I could help get some swings for this playground.

After a bit, Miss Cyrena started talking again, this time about Eula's pies and all the people that might be customers. It was a nice time and got my jitters settled down some.

Then we drove back and delivered the rest of the stuff, to two restaurants and three people's houses. We kept our eye out for that Jenkins truck, but never saw it. Miss Cyrena said that we could probably shed our worry. I think she was just saying that to make me feel better.

I sure hoped that dog was okay. I kept thinking it belonged to some kid who'd go to bed crying tonight.

The last house on our delivery was Mrs. Clark's, where them Jenkins boys had bothered Eula while she was working in the flower bed out front. That flower bed was particular pretty, and I knew it was 'cause of Eula's hands working in it. I was real curious to see what kind of woman scared off three fellas with a shotgun, but Miss Cyrena made me stay in the car again. I stretched my neck to see Mrs. Clark when she answered the back door, but a colored maid took the cake from Miss Cyrena.

After that, Miss Cyrena drove me out to see the new "shopping plaza" and the fairgrounds. The shopping plaza turned out to be a one story string of stores with glass fronts all stuck together with a big parking lot out front. And then I saw the fairgrounds and nearly peed my pants.

"A carnival! Oh, Miss Cyrena, can I go?"

"It doesn't look like it opens until later." She sounded like she was glad. I had a feeling she'd have said no if it had been open. I didn't deserve it after all the trouble I caused today.

But it wasn't open, anyhow. All of the rides were quiet and still and the only person I saw was a man in an undershirt coming out of his little camper-trailer, scratching his big belly. I couldn't even smell any caramel corn or hot dogs.

"I was supposed to go to a carnival last summer—with my friend P—Polly." Whew, I almost said Patti Lynn's name. "I saved up my allowance money and collected bottles for refunds for three months so I could buy ride tickets and a candy apple."

"You didn't go?" Miss Cyrena asked.

I shook my head.

"Why not?"

I shrugged.

"Starla?"

I looked out the window. "'Cause I got put on restriction for forgettin' to take out the trash." Now Miss Cyrena knew I was always trouble.

"That was all? The trash?"

I nodded. It still got my insides all knotted up when I thought about it. I'd been so careful not to sass and to keep my room picked up and everything all week. I'd even been extra-helpful to Mamie, doing extra chores without even being asked. But that darned trash and the ants that found it was what done me in.

"This one don't matter," I said the truth. "I don't have any money anyhow."

"I suppose not."

Miss Cyrena was quiet the rest of the way back to her house. I was so tired by the time we got there, I ate my supper and went straight to bed. As I was falling asleep, I tried to imagine what that carnival looked like all lit up and full of people, the air filled with calliope music and the smell of sweet cotton candy.

18

We spent Friday baking again. Eula said if business kept up like this, we might have enough money to pay Miss Cyrena back, fix the truck, and go on to Nashville in another week and a half. I'd decided not to ask for a dime for that stupid sucker. A dime could buy us a half gallon of gas.

I was glad me and Eula'd have more time baking. Eula promised I could run the mixer next time. Besides, Momma didn't even know I was on my way, so she wouldn't be worried.

By five o'clock, we was done with our orders for the day and the car was loaded up. Eula was rubbing her back and tilting her head from side to side to stretch her neck. My feet hurt—Miss Cyrena said they wouldn't be if I'd just wore my shoes. I told her that if I had, I'd just have a different misery; hot, swollen, stinky feet. She and Eula laughed and laughed. I think every one of us was in a good mood now that the work was almost done.

I wanted to go with Miss Cyrena to make deliveries, but poor Eula looked dog-tired and I'd have been ashamed to leave her there with sticky syrup on the counter, flour on the floor, and every pan in the house sitting dirty in the sink. Miss Cyrena promised I could go on Monday; that perked me up some. Maybe I'd see that black-and-white dog again and know it was healin' up okay. She said that if the Jenkins boys was gonna do anything, they'd have done it by now. It was most likely the one that hit the dog hadn't give me, or that dog, another thought—that's the kind of fellas they was, hard and selfish.

A while later when Miss Cyrena got back from deliveries, she brought the dirty pie tins she'd collected from Slattery's. She dropped them into the sink where I was washing the last pan.

I gave her a cross-eyed look. "Can't I do these tomorrow?"

"Never put off until tomorrow what can be done today," she said.

I didn't like that one bit. We didn't have no baking tomorrow since we got all of the weekend orders done. There'd be plenty of time to wash nine pie tins. I opened my mouth to say so, but she used those teacher eyes on me. I rolled my eyes and started washing again.

She nodded at me like she was proud of me not sassing. Then she said, "Eula, would you help me with something outside for a minute?"

Eula put down the floor mop and followed her out the back door. The window over the sink looked out on the driveway. I leaned up on tiptoe, but couldn't see them. I listened real careful, but couldn't hear them talking.

I dropped my dishrag in the soapy water and tried to keep my drippy hands over the sink as I took a step backward, leaning as far as I could to see out the back door. They was clear back near the hedges that was the end of Miss Cyrena's yard. They had their backs to me and Miss Cyrena was talking steady and serious.

I got worried. Was she getting tired of working for nothing but a thank-you? Was she telling Eula it was time for us to find someplace else to stay till we got the money to fix our truck? Had Miss Cyrena somehow found out about Eula doin' in Wallace?

Just then, I heard baby James start to cry in his sleeping drawer. Neither Miss Cyrena or Eula looked like they heard him, even though the bedroom window was open and sure I didn't know how they couldn't.

I shook the suds off my hands and wiped them on my shorts as I headed to get him up and change his diaper, feeling kinda mad that they was out there just talking while I had to do all the work.

Being mad was better than worrying over what Miss Cyrena was saying.

When me and baby James come back to the kitchen, Miss Cyrena and Eula was standing side by side, looking like they had a secret.

"You tell her," Miss Cyrena said to Eula.

"You the one makin' it happen. You tell her." She sounded kinda peculiar.

My heart climbed right up into my mouth.

"What? What's happenin'? Is it bad?" I gave baby James a jiggle as he started to fuss more for his bottle.

After one last look at Eula, Miss Cyrena said, "You've been working so hard, helping with the baking and the baby. And it's summer, when children should be having fun. So"—she paused—"we've decided to take you to the carnival."

Eula nodded and looked like the cat that got the cream.

I closed my eyes for a minute, letting the words sink in. We wasn't being throwed out. The law wasn't coming to get Eula.

"Starla?" Miss Cyrena said. "Are you all right?"

I let out a long breath. "Yes, Miss Cyrena." The idea was sinking in. I was finally going to a carnival! "Yes, I am!" Eula came and took baby James and got a bottle out of the Frigidaire. "When?" My feet were itching to get my shoes and go.

"Tonight," Eula said. "Right after we have a bite of supper."

I looked from Miss Cyrena to Eula. "We're all going?"

"Well, no. Although it's Friday night and sure to be busy enough not to stand out, we decided it best for Eula to stay home with baby James."

"In case the Jenkins boys are there?"

Eula gave me a look that was sharp enough to put my eyes out. "I don't want to hear no more 'bout that. It's not for a child to worry on. 'Sides, I don't like carnivals."

"Everybody likes carnivals!" I said.

"I don't." She did a little shiver, like she'd just walked into a spider's web.

"How come?"

"Don't hold no happy memories for me." Then she smiled real big. "But you gonna have fun, fun, fun."

Then it hit me like a bucket of cold water. "I don't have any money for rides or games." What fun would it be to go and just watch other folks have fun?

"It's my treat," Miss Cyrena said. "Every child should go to a carnival at least once."

I looked at Eula.

She nodded. "She right. You need to make your own good memories."

"Let's get supper over with," I said.

We all laughed. I was going to a carnival and I was gonna bring back enough good memories to share with Eula that she would get over not liking them.

Miss Cyrena parked the car so far from the fairgrounds that there weren't many other cars parked along the street. A couple of groups of people walked past, but they was so excited about getting to the carnival they didn't give us a look.

"I think it's best if we walk in separately," Miss Cyrena said. "I'll stay close, keep an eye on you. Don't even think about me being here. We shouldn't look like we're together. With so many children here, you'll blend right in."

"Okay." I felt in my pocket to make sure the two dollars she'd given me was still safe.

"We'll meet back here at the car at, say, eight thirty?"

I looked at my Timex. Even after all of the rain and whatnot, it was still working just fine—Takes a Licking and Keeps on Ticking. "Can we stay till nine? Pleeeease?"

"You'll have to pace yourself to make your money last."

"I will. I want to see everything before I decide what rides to go on anyway. And I want to watch people play all of the games, too. If it looks easy, I might try to win a stuffed animal like P—my friend's brother did one year."

"Oh, I'd avoid those games. They're made to look easy, so they can take your money."

"I wanna watch anyhow." I opened my car door.

"Nine o'clock, then. Have fun."

As I started walking toward the carnival, my stomach got tight and wiggled around a little. I wanted to run, but was afraid Miss Cyrena wouldn't like running to keep me in sight. I checked over my shoulder to make sure I wasn't going too fast. Miss Cyrena was a ways back. She shook her head to remind me I wasn't supposed to look for her.

Pretty soon I saw the Ferris wheel sticking up above everything. It was even taller than a house! Its spokes had colored lights that flashed when it stopped and stayed lit when it went around. It wasn't dark yet, but them lights was bright enough that they showed up real nice against the sky. My stomach got wigglier.

I walked through the grassy parking area. I passed a little boy tugging on his daddy's pants pocket to get him to go faster, and a man with a little girl sitting on his shoulders. I used to ride on my daddy's shoulders like that when I was little.

I got a funny tingle on my neck. I sure hoped Eula and me got to Nashville before Daddy came home again. I didn't want him to get worried.

The breeze blew a sugary smell past me and my mouth watered. Would I get a candy apple, or cotton candy? Or maybe I wouldn't buy a treat at all and just ride as many rides as I could.

The crowd got thicker as I got closer. Finally, I was there with it all right in front of me. There was so much to look at. It was all movement and sound and smell. A bell rang. Men shouted to get people to play their games. Music came from somewhere. A whirring siren came from right next to me. It was a ride that spun a line of seats backwards up and down over little hills. It went faster and faster. Lightbulbs over the top of it spelled H-I-M-A-L-A-Y-A. Must have something to do with mountains, 'cause the riders and cars disappeared behind a wall painted like giant, snowy mountains for a few seconds before they came flying back out.

While I was walking and watching that, a man called out, "Hey, Red! Come win a goldfish!" He stood in a booth with lots of tiny fishbowls that held orange and a few black fish. He held a bunch of little hoops. "Just toss a ring over one and he's yours! It's easy."

"No thank you, sir." I kept walking. I wasn't gonna waste my money on getting a goldfish. Our truck was already full with Eula and James and me. And you had to feed a goldfish. We was having enough of a time feeding us. Now, a teddy bear was different. A teddy bear didn't eat nothin'.

While I was looking up in a trailer window where a man was swirling blue cotton candy onto a paper tube, I tripped over something. It was a long, snaky-looking cable running across the ground. When I really got to looking, I saw they were everywhere. It made it hard to study things while I was moving, so I stopped and looked around some from where I stood. Once I'd seen everything I could from there, I moved and stopped at another place. By the time I'd gone all around the carnival to check it out, it was seven thirty.

There were two different booths where you could win a teddy bear. One where you had to pop balloons by hitting them with darts—you only got three for a dime, but the balloons were pretty close together. The other one took knocking over stacked milk bottles with a baseball—three balls for a dime. I could chuck a rock pretty good and had pretty fair aim, so maybe I'd try that one. I was gonna wait until the end though, so I didn't have to carry Teddy on all of the rides.

I took my money to the little wooden ticket booth. I had to wait in a long line, but finally got up there and bought ride tickets with all of my two dollars, except the ten cents I was gonna use to win Teddy. I decided to skip the treat. I'd get a chance at cotton candy or a candy apple before I'd get a chance to ride a ride again.

Since I'd never been on a carnival ride and I wasn't too crazy about being high up in a tree, I decided to try a low-to-the-ground one first. It couldn't be a baby one, though. I picked the Tilt-a-Whirl.

I had to wait in line. When I climbed up the steps and onto the wavy platform, the man running the ride pointed me to a car that already had a boy with blond hair sitting in it.

"Somebody's in that one," I said, and started to walk on to the next one.

"Too busy tonight for single riders. You go with him."

I didn't want my first carnival ride to be ruined by someone who might be a wienie and scream like a baby the whole time. I studied him for a second. He looked like he was maybe in fifth or sixth grade.

I asked him, "You been on this ride before?"

He grinned, not snotty, but kinda nice. "I been on all the rides before."

I turned to the man running the ride. "Okay, I'll go with him."

"Darn right you will," he said. "Now get in, you're holding up the line."

I got in and sat as far from the boy as I could. The man loading us pushed the lap bar across us and I put my hands on it. It was sticky.

"I'm Troy," the boy said. "My friend got sick and went home, that's why I'm by myself."

"Why'd he leave?" Nobody'd leave a carnival.

"Threw up after the Himalaya."

"Oh."

"You don't get sick on rides do you?" he asked.

"No! Never." It wasn't a lie.

Right then, the ride started to move. Slow, but in just a second, our car spun around in a circle, making my stomach jump out of my body. Then it started to go faster. I grabbed the bar tighter.

Troy didn't scream, except to yell, "Faster! Faster!" every time we passed the man who ran the ride. After the first spin, I was yelling it, too. Sometimes our car would spin up so we was facing the center of the ride, then stop and hang there for a second before it whipped in a circle so fast everything around us got blurred. That ride was the most fun I'd ever had.

I couldn't believe it when it started to slow down and our car swung one last time, then rocked to a stop.

"That's it?" I said. "It was so short!"

"Yeah." Troy pushed the lap bar up. "They're all that way."

I just sat there. Maybe if I didn't get out, I could go again.

The man walked around the platform. He stopped by me. "Out."

"I wanna go again."

"It'll take another ticket. Since there's a line, you gotta go wait anyhow."

"Come on!" Troy was outside the ride waving his arm at me. "Let's do the Scrambler!"

I jumped out of the car and ran around the platform to the stairs.

"Hurry up." Troy pulled a long string of red tickets out of his pocket. He musta had more than five dollars' worth! "This way."

The Scrambler didn't look exciting enough to waste a ticket on. Troy got in line, but I stayed back.

"Come on—" Then he looked at me funny. "What's your name, anyway?"

I couldn't tell him my real name like I could if it had been Kathy or Debbie. Instead of risking a made-up name that I might forget, I said, "Red."

"Well, come on, Red."

"I don't think I want to ride this one."

"Yeah, you do. It's fun!"

I looked at the Scrambler again. It looked boring.

Just then, a kid coming out of the exit bent over and threw up all over his shoes.

I jumped in line with Troy.

Turned out, the Scrambler was as fun as the Tilt-a-Whirl. The first time it looked like our seat was going to slam into one of the seats on another arm, I screamed. But it was just an optical delusion—which is something that tricks your eyes into believing something that's not true. And no matter how hard I tried, I couldn't keep from sliding over and mashing Troy against the edge of the seat.

When we got off that ride, I asked, "What's next?" Troy seemed pretty good at picking out rides.

"Ferris wheel."

"I'm gonna take a break. I'm using my tickets pretty fast."

"Go ask your mom and dad to buy you more."

"They aren't here."

"Oh. Well, you're gonna want to ride this one. You can see everything from up there." He grabbed my hand and pulled me along.

As we waited in line, I looked up at those seats, rocking way up at the top. My skin started to itch and my mouth got dry. "I'm gonna go to the bathroom while you ride this one. I'll meet you after."

He looked at me and his eyes got squinty. "You're scared."

"No, I'm not. I need to go to the bathroom."

"Scaredy."

"Am not."

"Then ride with me." He lifted his chin like it was a dare. "You can go to the bathroom after."

"Next up!" the man loading yelled.

Troy used his dare stare on me.

I sucked in a big breath, pushed past him, and sat in the seat waiting to be loaded.

Troy sat next to me, and the man locked the bar in front of us. I held on to the bar and kept my eyes on the teddy bears waiting to be won across from the Ferris wheel.

We went up backwards and real slow, stopping as the seats were loaded. I felt like I was gonna pee my pants. When we got up high, I held real still and told Troy if he rocked it, I was gonna break his nose. He musta known I'd do it, 'cause he sat still.

After I'd made it around once, I started to feel a little better about it. You really could see everything from up there, church steeples, the water tower, the whole carnival . . . and the people looked so little. I didn't think I could see as far as the Bottoms though.

As we got off, Troy said, "You liked it, right?"

"Sure." I liked it okay. And I'd got over being scared of being up high, too. Good thing, 'cause the next thing we rode was the Paratrooper.

We rode more rides and walked for a bit, watching the games and whatnot. It was weird, hanging around with him. We wasn't friends. We didn't talk much. But we stuck together anyhow.

When we stopped, we were standing right in front of the Bullet. "This one next," he said.

I looked up at the thing. The car on the end of a long arm swung back and forth, back and forth, getting higher each time until it went upside down and on around. I didn't like it.

"I've only got one ticket left. I want to save it for . . ." I looked around; we'd ridden everything scary. "For the bumper cars."

He laughed so loud the people around us stopped and looked at us. "You're kidding, right?"

I looked at the Bullet again. Up high was one thing. Upside down up high was a horse of a different color.

Troy was staring at me.

Well, I'd found out I wasn't scared of a whole lot of things lately. Maybe this would be like the rest.

We got in line. And Troy looked at me like I'd gone and done the biggest dare ever . . . like he was proud of me or something.

I made it to the second swing before the screams I was holding in busted out. "Let me off!" I stomped my feet because my hands couldn't let go. "Let me off! Letmeoffletmeoffletmeoff!"

All my screaming didn't do nothing but get a bunch of people to stop in front of the Bullet and watch.

When it finally stopped after what felt like an hour, a horrible hour, I got off. I couldn't tell how far the ground was from my feet when I took a step. Lots of people stood there laughing. Troy was one of them.

"You're not as nice as I thought you were." I shoved him and walked away as fast as I could considering I was walking like Eula's broke truck, this way, then that, not able to keep a straight line.

Troy called after me, "Hey, Red, don't be sore! You did good."

I ignored him. I'd wasted my last ticket and people were laughing at me.

I was too mad even to win my teddy bear. I walked away from the rides and back toward the parked cars.

"Red!"

I walked faster, right past a man in a deputy's uniform. I got madder yet; I needed to be more careful. Lucky, he was looking the other way.

After being in all those lights, it seemed extra-dark out in the parking area. After a few seconds, I got so I could to see better. I was deep in the parked cars when I saw it. The red-and-white truck with the big Confederate flag on the hood.

I thought about the meanness of those Jenkins boys, how they'd scared Eula. I thought about that poor black-and-white dog. I thought about all those people laughing at me. I thought about being scared.

I picked up a rock and broke one of the headlights. The sound of it shattering and little pieces of glass hitting the bumper made me feel better. I took aim at the second headlight. Just as I was about to swing the rock, someone grabbed my arm.

19

My breath stuck and my heart jumped. I gripped the rock tighter in case I could use it and got ready to kick and scratch my way free of the Jenkins boys.

I spun around.

"Starla!"

My foot stopped just before it hit Miss Cyrena's shin. My breath finally came loose.

"What's gotten into you?" Miss Cyrena's voice was low and hissy, not much more than a whisper.

"It's the Jenkins boys' truck. They deserve to get some of their own meanness back."

"Two wrongs do not make a right."

Hadn't I heard that a million times? I jerked my arm free. "Well, it's three," I said real sassy. I wanted to smash the other headlight, one for Eula and one for that dog. But I didn't.

"Let's go," I said. All my good memories about the carnival were ruined now. Ruined by Troy. Ruined by those laughing people. Ruined more by the stupid Jenkins brothers.

I threw down the rock and stomped away. "I ain't sorry I did it."

"Now, young lady—"

"Red!"

I stopped and looked over my shoulder. That doggone Troy started to run toward us.

"You okay?" he called. "That nigra botherin' you?"

"I'm fine. Go away!"

Troy was getting closer.

I took off, not worried 'bout Miss Cyrena keeping up. She made a sound like Mamie makes when she's exaserbated with me, but I kept going. I zigged and zagged between cars, trying to lose Troy. I heard Miss Cyrena huffing along behind.

All of the sudden, there was a shout. "Hey! You little pissant! You busted my headlight!"

"No, I didn't!" It was Troy's voice.

I started to run and heard Miss Cyrena's steps get going faster.

I hoped them Jenkins boys believed Troy . . . or maybe I hoped they didn't. It was his fault I went on that ride. And he'd laughed at me.

Then my conscience got on me and I stopped. I couldn't let them beat Troy up for something I did.

When I turned around, Miss Cyrena was right there, breathing hard.

"I gotta go back," I said.

"You can't go alone. And I can't go with you." It was the first time I'd heard Miss Cyrena sound like she didn't know what to do.

"I have to tell 'em Troy didn't break their stupid headlight. I'll say I saw somebody else do it." Kinda true. "You wait here."

"I don't think—"

"Just stay hid. We don't want them boys to know we're together and maybe find Eula."

"They might recognize you from town."

"So what? Far as they know, I'm just some kid worried 'bout a dog. You said yourself, they didn't pay no attention to you bein' there. I'll be right back." I walked off, listening for her following.

She didn't. (Thank you, baby Jesus.)

When I got back to the truck, one of the Jenkins boys—who wasn't a boy at all, but a man with a beard and everything—had Troy by the neck of his shirt. The man had dark hair and was near as big as Wallace. Next to him was the brother who'd hit the dog. They didn't look like brothers at all 'cause the dog-hitter was skinny had light hair that was almost girl-long.

"Stop!" I yelled. "He didn't do it."

The big brother looked my way. "You know this kid?" Now I saw the third brother step out from the other side of him. This one wasn't much bigger than an eighth grader and looked too young for a beard at all.

I shook my head. If they thought I was Troy's friend—which I wasn't—they'd figure I was just trying to get him out of trouble. "Ain't from around here. I saw someone else break it. Went that way." I pointed back toward the carnival.

All three of them Jenkinses looked off that way. I did, too. That's when I saw that danged deputy heading toward us.

"What's the trouble here?" he asked, shining a flashlight on the brother holding Troy. "Let loose of that boy, Jobie."

The man let Troy go, but in a rough way that made him stumble backward. I could tell them boys were every bit as bad as Miss Cyrena had said. "Someone busted our headlight."

The deputy put his light on the truck. "So I see." He moved the light to Troy's face. "You do this, son?"

"No, sir. I was just goin' by." He looked at me and for a second I was afraid he was gonna tell them I did it, but I don't think he'd been close enough to see.

The light moved on to me. I couldn't see nothing but its brightness.

"And you?" the deputy asked.

The light-haired brother who'd give me the finger pointed at me. "I bet she done it. I seen her in town yesterday. She—" He stopped talking, realizin' probably he'd have to admit he run over the dog if he kept on.

"No, sir, I didn't," I said. "I seen someone run off that way, though." Then to make a good lie I added, "A kid . . . with dark hair and a white T-shirt."

"How old?" the deputy asked.

I shrugged. "Didn't see him from the front, or close at all. He was kinda tall and skinny." Seen plenty of them at the carnival.

He put the light back on Troy. "You see him?"

Troy shook his head, his eyes still big 'cause the scared hadn't left him yet. "No, sir."

The deputy finally pointed the flashlight down so it didn't shine in anybody's eyes. "I'll keep an eye out," he said to the Jenkins boys. "You fellas can get on your way."

"But who's gonna pay for this busted light?" It wasn't the Jenkins who'd had ahold of Troy, it was the young one. Even little as he was, he looked the meanest of 'em all.

The deputy's light shot back up and shined in the young brother's face. "Now, Jesse, you and I both know a headlight is cheap, and you and your brothers have gotten by with a whole lot worse, so count yourself ahead and go on home. I don't want to see you back at that carnival lookin' for someone to hold accountable. That's my job."

For a minute everybody just stood there, looking at each other.

The deputy put a hand on Troy and turned him around. "You go on back to your evenin', son."

Troy took off so fast, he was gone before I could blink. I knew I should take off, too, but my eyes were stuck on them Jenkins boys. Were they bad enough to sass a deputy? Or worse?

"Get on now," the deputy said.

The brother who'd had ahold of Troy spit on the ground, then opened the driver's door and got in. The dog-hitter went around and opened the passenger side. "C'mon, Jesse."

Jesse took a step toward the deputy and I held my breath. He got his chest all puffed out and said, "Only 'cause we was leavin' anyhow." He turned around and spit on the ground, too—I'm pretty sure just 'cause the older brother did—then got in the truck and slid to the middle.

The truck started up before the last brother got in.

The deputy put a hand on my shoulder and made me step back. It was a good thing, too, 'cause those boys tore out of there so fast I bet they'd have run over my toes.

The deputy stared after the truck, mumbling something I couldn't understand.

I decided it was time for me to make like a banana and split. I started to move, but his hand tightened on my shoulder. "Hold up, there."

"Yes, sir?" I said, sweet as pie, but my heart started thudding and I could feel sweat start.

"You said you're not from here?"

"No, sir. I mean, yes, sir, that's what I said."

He put that flashlight on my face again. He seemed to be looking particular hard at my hair. "What's your name?"

My mind went blank as the chalkboard on Monday morning. I couldn't come up with a single name.

"You got a name, don't you?"

"Yes, sir. Nancy."

"Nancy what?"

"Nancy Drew, sir." Ohm'gosh, he'll never believe that. "But people call me Red," I added just in case he'd heard Troy hollerin' after me.

"Hmm." He got that look like the jig was up but he wasn't letting on. "Where you from, Nancy Drew?"

"Out in the country; next county over." My brain was finally working again. Best keep things as general as I could.

"Where's your folks?"

"Visitin'. They're supposed to pick me up out on the street at nine o'clock, so I better go."

He looked at his watch. "I'll walk you."

"No need, sir." I tried to back away, but he didn't let go.

"Oh, I think there just might be. I want to meet your folks. You see, we got a report of a runaway girl . . . redhead 'bout your age. I wouldn't be doin' my duty if I didn't check you out."

"They might be late. They ain't very reliable to be on time."

"I'll wait."

"Suit yourself." I started walking toward the street with his hand on my shoulder. I glanced around, hoping Miss Cyrena stayed out of sight until I figured a way out of this. But here she come, from a couple of rows of cars over.

I had to do something.

We was coming up on a sawhorse barricade. Some people walked on the other side of it.

"Oh, no!" I yelled, and pointed. "He's stealing that lady's purse!"

Just as soon as the deputy looked that way, I shoved him as hard as I could with my shoulder. His feet got tangled in the legs of the barricade. I took off in the other direction, not even looking to see if he went all the way down.

There was lots of shouting. I cut through parked cars, ducking low so nobody could see me. Finally I got to the bushes that were at the edge of the fairgrounds and hid in there. I hoped Miss Cyrena got the point and went to wait for me at the car.

I was crouched down, fanning away skeeters, when I heard something. "Psssst. Red? Red, you there somewhere?" Troy was whispering. I could tell he was moving closer.

I held still and tried to see him through the leaves.

He called again. He was on the street side. I peeked out and saw him just past me. He was on a Sting-Ray bicycle.

"Red," he whispered. "Where are you?"

I didn't say anything and he got a little farther away, but he was moving real slow.

"C'mon out. I owe you one. I'll ride you outta here."

I sure could get back to Miss Cyrena's car faster on his bicycle. I could hide near there and wait for her to show up.

I stuck my head out. "Here," I whispered.

He swung his bike back around and stopped right in front of me. "Get on."

I took a look up and down the street. Nobody seemed to be looking our way. I heard plenty of commotion, but it was still back across the parking area. I had to hurry.

I got out of the bushes and onto the banana seat behind him and held on to the bar on the back.

"Which way?"

I told him and picked up my feet. "And fast!"

He stood up and pedaled. We was flyin' away from the fairgrounds.

Once we got to a dark place, he slowed down a little. "I never seen a girl do nasty to the Jenkins brothers before. Or knock over a policeman. Why'd you do it?" He was a little out of breath, but he kept pedaling.

"None of your beeswax."

"Oh, yeah? I'll just take you back then."

He started to make a U-turn. "No!"

"Then tell me." He swerved back around.

I figured we were only a block or so from Miss Cyrena's car. If he gave me trouble, I could just push him and his bike over and take off. But that seemed wrong, considering him saving me and all.

"He thinks I'm a runaway girl."

"Are you?"

"No."

"Then why'd you shove him? You coulda just had your parents tell him."

"I live with my grandma."

"So?"

"I wasn't supposed to be at the carnival."

He put on the brakes and skidded to a stop. "You are a runaway girl!"

I didn't say anything. He'd been nice to me . . . mostly. I didn't like telling him lies.

"Man! I knew you were brave! I never met a runaway before. Why'd you run? Your grandma beat you? Where you goin'? How you gonna live? Ain't you scared? How come—"

"I can't answer all them questions."

"Why not?"

"That's part of bein' a runaway . . . secrets." He thought it was neat to be a runaway, so he oughta respect the rules.

"Oh, right. Where am I takin' you then?"

We was away from traffic and the lights of the fair, on a street with just a few big houses with big yards. Miss Cyrena's car was parked less than a block away; I recognized the house with the curlicues all over the front porch and the pointy-roofed room at the corner like a castle.

"I reckon here's just fine." I got off and walked over to the sidewalk. "Thanks."

I heard shoes clicking this way. I spun around and saw Miss Cyrena coming so fast that I didn't think she even noticed Troy.

"Starla! Dear Lord, what have you done?" She used that mad-hissy whisper. "Get to the ca—" All at once, she stopped talking and moving. Guess she saw Troy.

"It's okay. He helped me get away."

"Oh, child. Nothing is okay. Not now."

The awful sound in her voice made my stomach flip worse than it did when I was on the Bullet.

20

We was sitting at Miss Cyrena's kitchen table, the room lit only by the little light on the stove while the rest of the house stayed creepy dark. That made me the most worried, Miss Cyrena keeping the house dark like we were hiding.

Eula and me had just spent the last half hour telling Miss Cyrena the truth, at least the truth about Eula. Even the parts about her finding baby James on the church step and doin' Wallace in. Eula told me we owed Miss Cyrena being honest. Well, Miss Cyrena thought I was good and helpful. I didn't want her to be disappointed in me by finding out I was running to keep from going to reform school. So I kept to my story: my poor grandma died and we were broke, so I was hitchhiking to Nashville to my momma when Eula found me. Eula didn't know better so she couldn't say different.

From then on, I did most of the telling, especially the parts in the swamp and what come after. Eula spent most of that time holding her belly and rocking herself back and forth. She kept sendin' looks at the stove, like she was wanting to get up and start baking.

"Oh, dear Lord." Miss Cyrena had been saying that a whole lot. "Well. My. I thought something like this might be at the heart of matters. I know an abused woman when I see one. But had no idea it was this extreme."

Eula looked down at her lap, ashamed. But the shame was on Wallace, not her. Didn't she see that?

I got up and stood behind her. I put my hands on her skinny shoulders and said, "He needed killin' for sure, otherwise I'd be dead. Prob'ly baby James, too."

Miss Cyrena seemed worked up some, but not about Wallace getting killed by a skillet. "I've seen plenty of men like Wallace. They're just biding their time here on this earth until the devil comes to collect them. It was his time and he'd earned it."

Eula got stiff. "He weren't always that way. I was no more than dirt till I was with him. He protect me."

"I'll bet he made sure you never forgot it either," Miss Cyrena said, kinda snippy. When Eula flinched, Miss Cyrena reached over and touched her arm. "I know you didn't see the violence and need for control in him in the beginning, but I'm sure it was there. Nothing you did turned him into such an abusive man. And you . . . well, you just didn't see your own value before that. It's an easy thing for a woman to overlook. We're taught from the cradle that men rule."

"No." Eula was shaking her head. "No. I was nothin'. And I'd been bad. But I paid. Paid and paid before Wallace save me."

Miss Cyrena looked at me with an eyebrow raised.

I shrugged and shook my head.

"Who made you pay?" Miss Cyrena asked real quiet. "Who did Wallace save you from?"

I could see it in Miss Cyrena's eyes; she wanted someone to get paid back for hurting Eula, for making her feel like a throwaway. I did, too. It was like when Jimmy Sellers picked on Prissy Pants, but lots stronger. And there in that kitchen, there wasn't anyone to go after, no matter how bad my red rage got. So I waited with Miss Cyrena, neither of us hardly breathing. The truth was about to bubble out and we didn't want to scare it back inside.

For a second, I thought Eula was gonna tell us. Then she shook her head real slow and lowered it. I felt the shame creepin' back on her, thick as tar.

Miss Cyrena got up, walked around the table, and got on her knees in front of Eula.

"Tell us, Eula," Miss Cyrena said, holding Eula's hands. "We know you're a good person . . . a caring person. The way you've put yourself at risk for these children is testament to that. We're all victims of our lives. Things happen that can ruin us if we hold them in. Tell us. You need to let it out so you can be strong again."

Eula sucked in a big breath. Her shoulders kinda shook as she let it out. "I weren't never strong."

"Look at me, Eula," Miss Cyrena said.

It took a minute, but Eula looked up.

"No one could have done the things you've done to protect Starla and James if she wasn't strong. You're strong, so strong."

Something changed on Eula's face. "You think so?"

I hugged Eula tight from behind. "Yes! You're strong." I'd seen her weak, so weak that most people wouldn't come back from it. But Eula always came back. That was strong. My daddy always said being brave wasn't not being scared. Being brave was keeping going when you were. Somehow, Eula always found a way to get on.

Miss Cyrena said, "Now gather that strength and throw away that secret you've been carrying. You're not alone. Not anymore. Nothing you say is going to change all Starla and I know you to be."

Eula sighed, sounding tired and brokenhearted. After a bit she said, "Pap and my brother knowed the wrong I done. Not a day went by without them punishin' me—even after I'd already suffered the worst punishment. But Wallace, he saved me from them. For a while I thought I was free." She looked down at her hands, rubbing one another in her lap. "'Cept God wasn't done with me."

"Go on," Miss Cyrena said.

Eula sniffed and turned her head to look at the wall. "It don't matter now."

I thought about all of the things Eula had told me, and all of the sudden I had an idea. "Was it about a baby?"

She stood up so fast the chair leg scooted over my toes.

Miss Cyrena rocked back and sat on her heels, startled.

"How you know?" Eula's eyes held me like she'd caught me stealing.

"All your troubles been 'cause of babies." I threw my hands up. "Babies. Babies. Babies. Takin' baby James from that church step. Gettin' fired"—she hadn't used the word, but it was pretty clear to me—"'cause you loved the white babies too much. God taking all your babies before they was born."

"Not all," she said, as she sat down hard in the chair. "God didn't take 'em all. That's why He punishin' me, I didn't protect him."

"Protect who from wh—?"

Miss Cyrena shushed me.

I almost sassed her; I took care of Eula, and Eula took care of me. That's the way it worked. Miss Cyrena was just Miss Cyrena. But if I got in a fight with her now, I'd never know about Eula's baby.

"Charles done took my baby boy . . ." She started crying real hard.

"Charles?" Miss Cyrena asked.

"My brother." It came out *bruuuuuuther* 'cause she was crying so hard.

"Your no-account brother took you and Wallace's baby?" My palms itched my hands up into fists. Wallace didn't deserve a baby for sure, but Eula did.

Eula busted out crying harder.

Miss Cyrena said, "Go get a tissue."

"You go," I said. "I'll stay here."

Miss Cyrena shot me a teacher look so sharp that I ran fast as I could to the bathroom and back just to get it done and get on with Eula's throwing away her secret.

I handed Eula a Kleenex. She cried solid for a few minutes. It was real pitiful, but I didn't know what to do. Miss Cyrena just patted Eula's knee every now and then. I put my hands back on her shoulders and patted her, too.

After a bit, all that patting got her calmed down.

"Sorry." She blew her nose. "It been a long time since I let myself think 'bout him."

"Who?" I'd lost track. "Wallace, Charles, or the baby?"

Miss Cyrena moved her lips but didn't say out loud, The baby. Then she asked Eula, "Do you want to talk about him now?"

"I ain't never told no one. Not even Wallace."

"How could Wallace not—"

"Shhh, let her talk," Miss Cyrena said. "Just let her talk."

I leaned forward and wrapped my arms around Eula. My hands locked together over her heart, and I rested my cheek on her head. Her hair was coming loose from where she kept it pulled back. It was springy and a little rough under my cheek. I liked the different feel of it.

"That baby come from bein' a fool and lovin' a boy from the family my momma work for," Eula said.

Miss Cyrena frowned and her eyes got strict.

Eula held up a hand. "I know what you thinkin', Miss Cyrena, I know. But I was jus' fourteen, and so in love. He so kind and handsome, jus' sixteen hisself. Treat me like a person." Eula looked at Miss Cyrena. "You know what I mean . . . a person . . . not just a colored girl."

Miss Cyrena's eyes got rid of their strict and just looked sad as she nodded.

"Didn't everybody get mad at you and him?" I'd never seen a white and a colored get married. Eula didn't say that right out, but he was her baby's daddy. I can add two and two.

"Nobody know. Everything stay a secret. Even the boy didn't know 'bout the baby. My momma died unexpected and I couldn't go to his house anymore." She sighed like she was real tired. "One day I finally work up the courage to go see him, but his momma say he gone to a fancy military school somewhere, might never be back. The way she looked at me, I could tell she knew somethin', but she just closed the door and I never see her again. So there I be." Eula's hands dropped to her lap, limp as dead fish.

"You poor child," Miss Cyrena said. She grabbed both of Eula's hands and held tight. I just hung on, pressing my cheek against the side of her head and resting my chin on her shoulder.

"You managed to keep the pregnancy hidden?" Miss Cyrena asked.

Eula nodded. "Pap and Charles didn't pay much attention to me once Momma gone, long as I kept dinner on the table and their clothes washed. Didn't get real big; loose clothes kept my secret fine. When he born, Pap was off somewhere. But I heard Charles come home. I wadded up a towel and stuffed it in my mouth to stay quiet, but I couldn't keep the baby from cryin'. Charles come in, see him, and go crazy. Not jus' because I had a baby, but because that baby so white. He cuss and stomp, and I tell him that ain't gonna change the baby's color, so he jus' gonna have to get used to it. He said Pap was gonna beat me. I told him I'd take my beatin' from Pap since I knowed I done wrong, but he'd better go away, leave me alone. He left, slammin' and cussin' the whole time. Baby and I fell asleep.

"Next thing I know, I was yanked out of bed by my hair. Once Pap done with me, I crawled back into bed, bloody and bruised, fed the baby, and cried myself back to sleep. Then, when I wake up . . ."

She shook her head and got up, leaving me and Miss Cyrena with empty hands and tears on our cheeks.

Eula walked to the back door and looked out to the dark night, wrapping her arms around herself like she was cold, even though it was still daytime hot in the kitchen. For a minute, I stood there like my feet were nailed to the floor. Then I walked over to her, slid my arms around her waist, and hugged her tight. "It's the same as with Wallace, the shame is on Charles, not you."

She didn't turn, but her hands closed over my arms at her waist.

I heard Miss Cyrena move behind me. I wanted to tell her to stay away, but all I could do was feel the quietness of Eula's crying and the pain of missing her baby. The chair creaked and it stayed just Eula and me, like it was supposed to be.

Charles took her baby. Maybe he left it on a church step. Maybe that's the real reason Eula picked up baby James.

After a bit, Eula got straighter and breathed deep. She kept still, but started talking again. "Charles said he give the baby to a family movin' up North, where a mixed baby had a chance. But Charles was too mean to ever do anythin' that kind. I'd seen the hate in his eyes when he looked at my child." She stopped.

I was just about to ask what she thought Charles really did with him, sure she would tell me he'd left him at a church. But she spoke before I could ask. Her voice was slow and stuttery. "Ch-Charles was m-mean to the bone. Once he d-drown a wh-whole bag of p-p-puppies . . ." All of the sudden her body jerked and kept twitching with sob after sob.

I heard Miss Cyrena blubber a little, too.

"No!" I said. "He couldn't have hurt a baby, no matter how no-account he was. He couldn't!" I held Eula tighter. "Your baby is a boy up North, growin' up fine. He's happy with a family. He has to be."

She shook with a breath and squeezed my arms. "Every day I pray that's so. Every day."

We was all quiet for a minute.

"Charles and Pap got a whole lot meaner after that. Till Wallace stop them."

I wanted to ask what Wallace did to stop them. I wanted to ask, since the baby was white, why didn't Charles give him to the baby's daddy—or his daddy's momma, like I lived with Mamie. I wanted to ask what else her pap and Charles had done to her. But when I opened my mouth, Miss Cyrena stood up right fast and pulled me away. Her cheeks were shiny wet.

"Do not ask her anything more." Miss Cyrena's fingers dug into my arms. "Not a single question, do you understand me?"

I leaned my head closer to her and whispered real quiet, "But you said she needed to get it out so she could be better."

"And she has. If she needs to tell more, she will. This has been very, very hard for her. She'll need time now. Lots of time and lots of love."

I looked at Eula. Her head was bent as she blew her nose, but something about her was different already. She looked a little less folded in on herself.

Miss Cyrena took my chin and made me look at her. "Time and love. Nothing more."

I nodded.

Miss Cyrena made us all cups of tea. For a while we just sat at the table in the almost dark, not saying a word, drinking hot tea that just made us sweat. But it gave us something to keep busy with while we let Eula soak up our love.

I wanted to say something to make her feel better, but I didn't know what words could have that much magic. I just sat there brushing my feet back and forth on the floor, waiting for something . . . waiting . . . I don't know for what.

Miss Cyrena was finally the first one to talk. "More tea?"

Me and Eula both shook our heads.

Then there was more waiting. I put my elbow on the table to prop up my head on my hand. Miss Cyrena didn't even scold me about manners.

My eyes was sleepy, but I was too jittery inside to go to sleep. It felt like the whole night went by, but when I looked at the clock, it was only ten after eleven.

"All right, then." Miss Cyrena sat up straighter and got on her teacher voice. "We're going to have to deal with the issue at hand. With the police knowing Starla's in town and that boy seeing her leave with me, it won't take them long to start looking in the Bottoms. They know me and my involvements, they'll start here first."

"But Troy pinkie-swore not to tell," I said.

"We don't know that boy, so we don't know he'll keep his word," Miss Cyrena said. "Besides, if the Jenkins boys find out he knows, they aren't above beating it out of him. Plus, we don't know for certain that none of them saw you and me in town together yesterday. They might just put it all together. . . ." She was back to her knowin'-what-to-do self. And truth be told, it made me feel a whole lot better. I thought of her after I'd chased that truck and it finally come to me how scared she was. Scared for me. Scared for Eula. And maybe even scared for herself.

Eula nodded. "True." She stood up. "Me and the children'll get our things and go now. You been too kind for us to stay and bring trouble."

Miss Cyrena looked startled. "Trouble and I are well acquainted, so don't worry on that account."

"He'll stay quiet," I said. "I know he will. He helped me get away. 'Sides, we ain't got enough to fix the truck and buy gas yet." Turned out

Polsgrove's Garage might not steal you blind, but they charged plenty to tow and fix Eula's truck.

As much as I wanted to get to Momma, I liked our baking business and sleeping on Miss Cyrena's couch. Anyway, it made sense to take longer to get to Nashville, just in case the police were looking for me up there, too. If it took us long enough to get to Momma's, they'd get tired out and forget about me. And the longer we were away from Wallace, the more likely people would believe someone else done killed him after we left. It was smart to stay hid out. "We can stay here and do baking for a few more days—until we can get the truck fixed."

Miss Cyrena looked at me so serious that my skin got all prickly. I knew things weren't going back to the way they were.

"We must deal with the reality of the situation, not hang on to what we hope will or will not happen. The stakes are too high. But you're not leaving here until we have everything figured out . . . a plan to keep you all safe. It has to be tonight. The law will not look favorably on me housing a white runaway—"

"I ain't a runaw—" I jumped out of my chair and stood with my whole body stiff. She heard the police call me that, but I couldn't let her believe it. She'd send me back to Cayuga Springs for sure.

"I'm speaking. You may have your say when I'm finished." She looked me in the eye and waited until I nodded. "I know most runaways have a reason for their actions, and I wanted to give you time to tell Eula and me the full truth. But time has run out. Ideally I'd check things out before you left me, make certain you really do have a mother in Nashville, but as things stand, I can't. As long as Eula is escorting you, Nashville is still your destination. We just have to figure out how to get you there in short order." Miss Cyrena looked at Eula. "Perhaps it would be best to leave James here with me. I can arrange for him to be taken to the police and returned to his family."

"He was give up!" I said. "Eula told that true, nobody wants him."

"That doesn't matter, child. Eula had no right to take him in any case."

"You can hide him while we stay and build up our money," I said. "It won't be long."

Miss Cyrena shook her head. "There's no hiding in the Bottoms."

"I'll leave by myself," I said. "The police ain't lookin' for Eula, just me. I started out for Nashville by myself anyhow." As soon as I said it, my chest felt like it'd been hit by a baseball bat. How could I leave Eula and not make sure she was all right? And baby James . . . But I was the one they were looking for. "Nobody knows about Wallace. If I go, they won't bother Eula, right?"

Eula and Miss Cyrena both said, "No!" at the same time. Then Eula finished, "You ain't goin' anywhere alone."

"That's a fact," Miss Cyrena said.

"If you don't go to Nashville with me, maybe they'll never find you," I said. "Maybe they'll decide somebody else killed Wallace and you can go on livin' here with Miss Cyrena bakin' pies."

"What about James?" Miss Cyrena asked. "How are we to explain a white baby?"

"You said you'd take him to the police, have him give back to his momma." As soon as I said that, I got a cold spot in my belly. Baby James needed me as much as Eula did. How could I let him get handed off to just anybody? What if they couldn't find his momma? What if she was a bad person? But if it kept Eula out of trouble . . . My thoughts was getting all tangled again.

"If Eula stays, that will be impossible. There will be too many questions. I have connections, but there's a limit to how much they can do." Miss Cyrena got up and started to walk back and forth across the kitchen. "No. We have to get you two out of here. I've got some money put by, but it's in the bank and I can't get it until Monday. Then it'll take the time to fix the truck . . ." She shook her head. "No. That just won't work."

"We ain't leavin' James," I said. "He'll go with us. Momma will figure it out. Eula said he was abandoned. Nobody's looking for him. Momma can say she found him on a church step."

Miss Cyrena stopped for a second. "It might be better if a white woman handles getting him to the authorities."

I nodded. "Momma will take care of it. She's famous, and famous people can do things."

Miss Cyrena started to say something, but closed her mouth back up.

Then she started pacing again. "As for Wallace's death, perhaps no one will investigate. Awful things happen to poor black men all of the time and the police look the other way. If they do come after you, you acted in self-defense, Starla can testify to that. But James must be turned over to the authorities long before it comes to that."

"You right," Eula said, but it was so quiet that I could barely hear her. "But I ain't sure I can live with that. I done wrong and need to account."

"Eula, the only one who needs to account is Wallace. And he's before his maker doing that right now. If you hadn't acted . . ." Miss Cyrena stopped. "Well, things would have been worse, so very much worse."

She went over and hugged Eula tight. She was so much shorter than Eula her arms went around Eula's waist and her head was against Eula's chest. They stayed that way for a bit. I stood and watched, feeling again like a polar bear with regular bears.

Miss Cyrena let Eula go. "You're welcome to come back to me, once you have Starla to her mother and James safely in the hands of the authorities. I can help you get set up with a new life somewhere. Here in town if you like."

"Eula's staying with me and Momma!"

Eula stayed quiet, but she looked a little unsure.

"One step at a time, Starla. Eula needs to know she has options. She's spent her whole life being told what to do. It's time for her to have the right to choose."

I felt a little bad then. "Yes, ma'am." Eula loved the baking business. She wanted a baby like James, but she'd kinda got stuck with me by accident. It made me a little squirmy wondering what she would choose.

"All right," Miss Cyrena said. "We just have to figure out how to get you there quickly and safely."

She fetched a step stool, then opened the cupboard and reached high on the top shelf. When she climbed back down, she had a coffee can in her hands. "I've probably enough in here for bus fare and still leave you a little extra. Of course, you can't leave from here. I'll drive you to the station in Jackson. We'll leave before light. Hopefully we can get you on an early bus and you'll be in Nashville by tomorrow evening." She started moving around the kitchen and talking faster and faster. "I'll pack lunches. You two will have to pretend not to know one another. We'll wrap James up so nobody can see he's white." Then she looked at me. "But first we'll have to deal with that hair."

"Huh?"

"Your hair. It's too easily spotted; makes you stand out." She hurried out of the kitchen. Eula and I looked at one another as we heard her ratting around in the bathroom. When she came back, she had a towel with black smudges all over it in one hand and a box in the other. "Lucky for you, I color Mrs. Washington's hair for her; she's so sensitive to the fumes she has to sit with her eyes closed and her nose pinched, but that woman is so vain." Miss Cyrena shook her head. "If it gets rid of gray, it should tone down that red."

I covered my hair with my hands. Mamie had threatened to dye my hair lots of times, saying it might take some of the wild out of me. Each time I'd got more attached to its redness.

I looked at Eula. "Don't let her."

She said, "Couldn't we just put a hat on her?"

"It's over ninety degrees out. That would flag her up more than her red hair."

Eula shook her head real sad as she took the box from Miss Cyrena.

An hour later I was looking in the bathroom mirror at a girl who didn't look like me. I put a towel over my hair and I came back. I took it off and looked at the black-haired me again.

Mamie was wrong. I felt wilder inside than I ever had.

Me and Eula was upstairs packing up our stuff with the curtains closed, lit up only by a flashlight. Miss Cyrena was downstairs in the kitchen feeding baby James so he'd be ready to travel.

All the sudden, there come a holler from outside, awful name-callin', then a crash and a flash of light. I was close to the window, so I jerked the curtain open. Right before Eula yanked me away, I saw the Jenkins truck speed away. The one headlight made me sure. They was still hollerin'.

I heard Miss Cyrena running toward the front of the house.

"Fire! Fire!" Her feet thudded back toward the kitchen. "Fire!"

Eula and me near knocked one another over trying to get down the stairs first. I stopped dead at the bottom in front of the open door. Flames was lickin' across the porch floor.

Eula pushed past me and run to the kitchen, just as Miss Cyrena come running back with a soup pot full of water.

"Starla! Water!"

That snapped me back to myself. I run to the kitchen. James was laying on the floor, squallin' 'cause he wasn't done eating.

By the time I grabbed a pan and was back to the front door, Eula and Miss Cyrena was headed back to the kitchen. I flung water onto the fire and saw people on the other side, flingin' water themselves. After I'd made three trips, the fire was small enough some man come up on the porch and stomped the last flickers out. I heard glass crunching under his shoes.

"Now you gonna listen to us?" he asked, kinda nastylike considering Miss Cyrena was the one whose house got fire throwed at it.

I wished I'd broke out both headlights, then them Jenkins boys wouldn't'a been able to see to drive down to the Bottoms tonight. I started to shake a little. What if we'd been asleep like we was supposed to be? Would that fire have ate the whole house? Would we have got out?

Cletus was standing just off the steps. He was looking at me funny.

I couldn't tell if he was sorry for me or mad at me. Some of the others were looking at me, too, their eyes white in the moonlight.

I turned around and went back inside the house. But I kept my ears outside.

"You not gonna be satisfied till they burn you to the ground." I recognized Mrs. Washington's voice.

I wanted to stomp out there and tell them it was my fault, not Miss Cyrena's. But all of the sudden the whiteness of my skin made me too ashamed.

21

Miss Cyrena parked her car around the corner and two blocks away from the Jackson bus station. We'd been careful when we left Miss Cyrena's at four o'clock in the morning. Careful nobody was following, especially somebody with just one headlight. Miss Cyrena figured four o'clock was 'bout the safest time to bolt. She said the drunk ones was too far gone and it was too early for anyone else to be up and out.

She'd been right. We didn't even see a car moving—except for the milkman's truck—as we drove out of that town.

Now the sun peeked up over the tall buildings. There were so many of them! Jackson was the biggest city I'd ever seen. I wanted to jump out and take a look around, but Miss Cyrena said we had to follow the plan—and me looking around Jackson wasn't in it. I know I'd already caused Miss Cyrena enough trouble by doing what I wasn't supposed to. I'd self-promised not to disobey her again. I did hope I'd get back here someday. I wanted to get up high in one of those buildings and see how far I could see. I wondered if people looked like bugs from up there. I bet you could drop water balloons from a window, duck back, and never have anybody know where it come from.

Then I got a thought. Nashville was a city. Would it have tall buildings, too? Maybe Momma lived in one and I could try my water-balloon idea before we moved to our big house with horses and whatnot.

"You all wait here while I go and purchase tickets," Miss Cyrena said. "That way you won't be seen together near the station." She turned around and looked over the seat at me. "Do you remember everything I said?"

I nodded. Then I safety-pinned the note on my shirt that Miss Cyrena had printed before we left her house. I felt like a stupid baby wearing it. It had my pretend name and my momma's famous name:

Sarah Langsdon
Destination: Nashville / Lulu Langsdon
Emergency call: 601/KL5-2942

It was Miss Cyrena's phone number. If somebody called, she was going to pretend to be my grandma I'd just visited.

"I know you can fabricate a whale of a story, Starla," she said, looking serious, "but please stick to the one we discussed. If I get a call, it's important that our stories match."

"I know. I know." Miss Cyrena's story was boring; a dumbbell could remember it. I had been visitin' my grandma in Jackson and was headed home alone on the bus to Momma. Big deal. I could think up something a whole lot more exciting; this story didn't even have anybody dyin' in it.

She turned back around. "All right then. Here I go." She opened the door and we watched her walk down the street toward the bus station.

I was kinda excited, this was my first time on a bus, 'cept for a school bus anyhow. Lula didn't seem excited. She seemed nervous, looking around like she expected somebody to come and arrest her.

"Stop lookin' so guilty, you'll give us away. We're just gonna be riding a bus," I said. "Easy as pie."

She looked at me. "Remember when we bakin', and what I say about overworked crust? You and me, we done pushed our luck 'bout as far as a body dare. We overworked crust. Things ain't gonna turn out good."

"Once we're on the bus, what can happen? We'll get to Nashville by tonight and find Momma."

"I hear 'bout plenty that happen on a bus. Plenty. Specially to colored."

"What you mean? What could happen on a bus even if you was colored?"

"You right. Nothin' gonna happen on the bus."

"But you said—"

"You got that ad-dress from your memory yet?" She shifted and put her arm on the back of the seat to see me better. I shook my head and my cheeks burned. I only had to come up with one thing, one thing, to help us get to Momma, and it was hiding from my brain. Miss Cyrena had been worried about where we was gonna go once we got to Nashville. I'd told her that my momma was famous and would be easy to find. She said that wasn't good enough. She wanted an address. That's when my brain got stuck. I couldn't think of one thing about Nashville—even the name of the recording studio on Momma's record disappeared. I told her Mamie never let me write to Momma, so how could I know an address? Then Miss Cyrena had asked if I got mail from Momma. I don't know why I didn't think of the return addresses on my birthday cards before. Trouble was, every card had had a different address and I didn't pay much attention—Momma was supposed to come and get me. I wasn't supposed to have to find her.

I'd been closing my eyes and trying to picture the last birthday-card envelope in my head, just like Miss Cyrena said to. I remembered a street that started with a *B* on one envelope. And another one with a street that was a number. I didn't remember which one came first, or the whole name of either one. Miss Cyrena said to watch the street signs when we got to Nashville, in case one made my memory come back.

Eula reached back and patted my knee. "It'll come." But her face didn't look like she believed it.

I was just getting ready to make Eula tell me what happens to coloreds on the bus when I saw Miss Cyrena. She was almost running back down the street. Her pocketbook bounced against her hip and her hat slid sideways. She held two tickets in her glove. (Even though we'd had to hurry when we left her house, she'd made sure she was presentable so nobody'd give her "a second look.")

We got out and met her on the sidewalk with our suitcases, Eula with her grip and me with one from the charity box. Miss Cyrena called it an "overnight case." It looked more like a box than a suitcase. It was black patent leather with a picture of Barbie on the top. I had a little canvas bag with baby James's stuff from the charity box, too. And, course, our sack lunches.

"No time to waste." Miss Cyrena handed one ticket to me and the other to Eula, who was getting baby James wrapped up in a thin blanket from the charity box, so no one could see his face. "The bus is boarding. It's not an express, so it'll take longer. But it'll get you out of town immediately."

She took the baby's bag from me and handed it to Eula. I wished I could go with her so she didn't have to juggle all of that stuff. But Miss Cyrena had been real clear on her plan.

"Eula, you go first." She grabbed Eula in a hard, quick hug. "Bless you. And remember what I said about coming back."

Eula nodded. "I can't thank—"

Miss Cyrena shooed her on. "No thanks needed. Just keep your head down and stay safe."

Eula picked up her grip and hurried away. She held baby James so tight to her chest, I was afraid he might not be able to breathe.

Miss Cyrena said to me, "Keep that phone number." She tapped the note on my shirt. "Call me if you have any troubles. Collect."

She looked up. Eula had turned the corner

"Now you. Remember the story. Your grandma dropped you at the station and had to get on to work." She nodded as she talked, like she was agreein' with herself. "I called the bus station from a pay phone and told them you'd be traveling alone and to inform your driver."

"Yes, Miss Cyrena."

"And don't even look at Eula. That shouldn't be a problem at the segregated stations. But on the bus, you need to treat her as you would a stranger. Once you get to Nashville, walk out the front entrance to the bus station, turn right, and walk two blocks. Eula will meet you there."

"I know. I know."

"And if you don't find your mother—"

"I will!" She'd been getting my back up with all this talk about my momma not really being in Nashville, not being famous enough to find.

She closed her eyes for a second. "But if you don't, go to a Baptist church—a colored Baptist church. Someone there will help you."

"I got it!" I wasn't nervous, but she was making me get that way. I just wanted to get on that bus and go.

I was surprised when she grabbed me in a hug. It was over almost before I could blink. "Take care of yourself. Take care of Eula."

"You don't need to tell me. I'll always take care of her."

She nodded. "Go then. Before the bus pulls out without you."

That thought put fire under my feet. I ran as fast as my Red Ball Jets would carry me.

The silver-and-blue Greyhound bus was running, but the door was still open. I climbed up the steps. There was two seats on either side of the aisle, not hard benches like the school buses we rode on field trips, but nice, soft chairs. Most of them had people already in them. The inside of the bus smelled as stinky as what come out behind it. The driver stood there looking out from under his uniform cap with his hand out like he wanted money. Eula was carrying our money. I only had the dollar Miss Cyrena give me in case of an emergency, and he wasn't getting it.

"Your ticket, miss?"

"Oh!" I'd forgot it was in my hand. I gave it to him.

He looked at the stupid note on my shirt. "You the one traveling alone?"

"Yes, sir. Going home from Grandma's." I pointed to my note and shut my mouth fast, to keep the details that my mind was making up from coming out.

"Don't wander far from the bus when we stop. Restroom and right back. Is that understood? I run a tight schedule and don't have time to hunt you down when it's time to pull out."

He didn't have to be so grouchy about it. I bit down hard to keep from saying that out loud. Miss Cyrena would be mad if I got in a fight before we even left the station. I nodded.

"All right, then." He lifted his chin for me to go on.

I leaned this way and that, looking for Eula and James. I didn't see them. They shouda been on by now! It had to be the right bus, it was the only one at the curb. I turned, ready to get back off and find them, then I heard James cry. I knew James's sound. It couldn't be no other baby.

They was clear at the very back, stuck in the corner. Eula's head was bent like she was trying to get small as she could, but I saw her Sunday hat over the seat backs. A couple of empty seats were around them. So I went down the aisle, looking to sit as close as I could.

"Hold on, missy," the bus driver called. "Up here. Where I can keep an eye on you."

I turned around. There weren't any people coming on behind me. "It's a free country. I can sit wherever I want. I ain't a baby."

His eyebrows shot up. "Is that a fact? Well, this is my bus and I don't want an unsupervised white child sitting in the back." The way he said "the back" made it sound like it was full of snakes or something. "Get up here." He pointed to a seat in the second row.

I heard some coughing in the back of the bus. It was Eula.

I turned around and went to the second row, but I didn't sit in the seat he pointed to. I went across the aisle and excused myself to the lady on the aisle so I could get to the window seat. I sat down with my lunch sack and my suitcase on my lap.

The lady sat back down next to me. She was smiling.

The driver wasn't.

He reached across the lady. I flinched, but he wasn't going after me; he grabbed my suitcase and slid it on a rack up over the seats. "Behave yourself."

I waited until he turned around before I stuck my tongue out at him.

The lady looked like she was trying not to laugh. She reminded me of Mrs. Knopp from Sunday school. Except she smiled more. She tried to get me to conversationing, asking about where I was going, my grandma, and whatnot. I answered a few questions, then told her, nice and polite, that I was sorry but I was real tired from getting up so early for the bus.

She smiled and told me to just close my eyes, she'd wake me when we got to a rest stop.

The window was slid open in front of our seats. I laid my head on the glass next to me and pretended to go to sleep, holding my lunch on my lap so it wouldn't slide off.

After a while I opened an eye and looked out the window, but it was my reflection in the glass that I saw, not the fields on the other side of it. The new, black-haired me looked like a stranger staring back. Miss Cyrena said the color would go away someday and my hair would get red again. As black as it was, I didn't believe it. For some reason that made me want to cry. Mamie would be glad; but lately I hadn't been thinking too much about Mamie. If I saw Troy again, he wouldn't know me. I closed my eyes so I could pretend I was Red again—just a girl at a carnival riding the Tilt-a-Whirl.

Thinking about that made me think on how my carnival got ruined. Eula had said carnivals didn't hold any good memories for her. I wondered what happened that ruined hers. Had it been no-account Charles? Her pap? Or her white husband? Or something else?

I bet it was no-account Charles. He ruined everything.

Miss Cyrena had been right. It was gonna take forever to get to Nashville; we had to stop at almost every town we went through to let some people off and more people on. The first time we did, in Canton—which reminded me a little of Caygua Springs—the bus driver looked at me and said this wasn't a rest stop and to stay right where I was. He'd tell me when it was okay to get off.

I told him I didn't even want to get off the stupid bus.

He looked perturbed, but I didn't care. He didn't have to be so dang bossy just 'cause I was a kid.

The bus was on a real highway, number 51, not the back roads me and Eula traveled on, so it was a little more interesting. Not only was there the towns, there was signs along the road. Billboards trying to get you to stop at a restaurant, or a motel. Colonel Clean had some reminding you not to be a litterbug. But the ones I liked the best wasn't just one sign, they was a string of little ones all spaced out, telling a rhyme. You had to keep your eye out to get the whole rhyme—but they all ended with the same last sign BURMA-SHAVE. They was for some sort of shaving cream. They was all so good, I remembered them:

A shave / That's real / No cuts to heal / A soothing / Velvet after-feel / Burma-Shave

Past schoolhouses / Take it slow / Let the little / Shavers grow / Burma-Shave

If you dislike / Traffic fines / Slow down / Till you / Can read these signs / Burma-Shave

They sure stuck in my head. Why couldn't I remember Momma's return address then?

After a while, when we was between towns, the brakes hissed and the bus rocked as it turned off the highway into a gravel parking lot. It pulled to a stop in front of a white-painted cinder-block building with rounded corners and big front windows. A sign sticking up from the top of the roof had writing in a neon light: RIEDELL'S DINER.

I looked at my Timex. It sure seemed later than nine o'clock in the morning. Yesterday had run into last night, and last night had run into today with just a nap in Miss Cyrena's car.

The bus driver grabbed the silver lever and opened the doors. "All right, folks. Thirty-minute rest. Restrooms inside for whites. Behind the building for colored. Y'all might want to get some breakfast while you're here. Riedell's has the best biscuits in the whole of Mississippi."

Ha! That driver never ate Eula's biscuits.

"They don't serve colored. Thirty minutes."

There wasn't anyplace else around, just a couple of houses and a cow pasture. I wondered where the colored people were supposed to eat if they were hungry.

I left my lunch bag—full of enough food for a whole day—on my seat, thinking I might just have me a snack from it when I got back on. If one of the colored folk was hungry, maybe I'd share. I wondered if that's what Eula'd meant about stuff happening to coloreds on the bus, that they never got to eat.

That made my other questions start poppin'. I'd already been itchin' to find out if Charles ruined Eula's carnival. The questions about her before Wallace met her in the movie house had been piling up. I was tired of waiting—what if I forgot one? So when I got outside the bus, I pretended to be interested in some of the rocks from the parking lot for my pretend rock collection. Since I'd talked to the lady on the bus and nobody even gave us a look, I figured it'd be okay to talk to Eula like she was a stranger; that's what Miss Cyrena said, Eula was a stranger. It'd look most normal if I asked her about her baby while we walked to the building at the same time.

Eula and James was the last to get off the bus, even after all the other colored people. Her eyes got big when she saw me, but she didn't turn her head. She just walked on past like I was invisible.

I had to hurry to catch up. "Lady. Lady, your baby a boy or a girl?"

She took one quick look over her shoulder. "He a boy, miss." Then she squinted her eyes at me. "He sick. Might be catchin', so you best stay away."

I thought about the empty seats around her. That must be how she kept people from asking to see him.

"Oh, I never get sick," I said real loud, in case anybody was listening. "And I just love babies."

She kept going, headed to the corner of the building where a sign with an arrow pointed toward the colored restrooms. I stuck with her.

Once we got around the corner, I asked, "Was it Charles that ruined your carnival?"

She looked around. But all the colored folks were already behind the building, and the whites stayed up front.

"You and me ain't supposed to be together. Get on up to the white restrooms and take care of your business."

"Tell me and I'll go." There wasn't nothin' to do on the bus but listen to what was buzzin' in your head. I couldn't stand sitting there the rest of the day not knowing.

"Why you got to know this now?"

"'Cause I do. So was it?"

"No. Now get on." She jerked her head toward the front of the building.

"What was it, then? What ruined it?"

She rolled her eyes and huffed. "Child, remember what Miss Cyrena told us."

"Nobody's payin' us any attention." Nobody'd seen James was white. We was far from the Jenkins boys and there wasn't any police around. What did it matter? Since she was so overworried, I gave her a reason to spit it out. "Tell me 'fore anybody comes back this way."

"You like a dog with a bone." She looked like she'd like to give me a swat. "I just had an unpleasant time, that's all."

"The rides make you sick?"

"Didn't go on no rides."

"Well, why didn't you like it?"

"I jus' didn't."

"That ain't true and I ain't going back up front till you tell me. Was it while you lived in Jackson with your momma?"

She started talking real fast. "Me and Momma down south visitin' my aunt. Weren't supposed to go to the carnival, me and Cousin Henry. But I talk him into sneakin' out."

"Did Charles tell?" I knew he had to have a part in it.

She shook her head. "Jus' me and Momma visitin'. Up in Jackson, they a night just for colored at carnivals. But not in Henry's town. We shoudn't'a gone. It was—bad." Her eyes were watery; she was holding a secret. "Now I told you. Get on." She started walking again.

"What happened? What'd they do to you and Henry?" I hadn't asked Eula about babies when I should have; I wasn't gonna let this secret ruin her, too.

She turned around right quick. "They beat Henry so bad he never walk right. Strip his bloody clothes off him and hang 'em on the fence by the road; a warnin' to others might have ideas about comin' to the white folks' carnival."

I felt like a hundred red rages was wound up inside me. "And you?" I was shaking. I could hear my own breath puffing through my nose. "What'd they do to you?"

"They too busy draggin' Henry off to bother me." The way she said it gave me goose bumps. "I run for help, but couldn't get no one to come. When I got back, Henry naked on the ground. I help him home. Had to watch his face swell and his momma cry over him." Tears wet her face, but she didn't look stronger like she had after she'd told about her baby. She looked . . . broken. "That was worse than bein' beat my own self."

She turned and walked on down the path that led to the colored restrooms.

I wished Miss Cyrena was here. Eula getting this secret out didn't make her feel better at all. I musta done it wrong.

I followed along behind her, my questions all bottled up behind a big lump of shame. I wanted to tell her I was sorry. Sorry for making her tell. Sorry about Henry. Sorry about the Jenkins boys. Sorry Charles stole her baby. Sorry. Sorry. Sorry.

Then I saw where the colored passengers were lined up and got even sorrier.

Down the dirt path was a crooked outhouse that looked ready to fall down. Not a lick of paint on it, except for the words COLORED DINING ROOM over the door.

All of the sudden it hit me why Eula was nervous as a cat in a roomful of rockers and Miss Cyrena told me to stay away from her on this trip. The law finding us wasn't the only danger. Sometimes colored got picked on just 'cause they was colored in a white place—like eating places, carnivals, and bus seats.

I went back and got on the bus and sat there with a blackness rolling around inside me.

When Eula got back on, I couldn't look at her. I pretended to be picking something out of my lunch sack—even though I felt too sick at my stomach to eat.

22

I reckoned lots of colored restrooms were nasty like that, since that was one of the things Miss Cyrena said needed fixing by the N-double-A-CP. Truth be told, I'd never thought serious about it before our stop at Riedell's. Now every time I watched Eula and baby James go toward one, I hoped they wasn't as awful as that outhouse with its nasty joke on the outside. I was almost curious enough to go look a couple of times, but we was travelin' invisible again.

No, that wasn't the truth at all. I didn't look 'cause I was afraid of what I might see.

I couldn't explain the tangled-up way things was making me feel. Mamie said I'd understand when I got older. But the older I was getting, the more confused I got.

Last month, me and Mamie had been watching the news when a story come on about a colored man getting shot in his own driveway. "Agitators! They brung death on that man," Mamie had said. "We didn't have trouble like this before the agitators. Things are the way they are for a reason. And everybody here is happy with it. Those outside agitators need to stay home where they belong."

I just kept thinking about that man shot in the back, bleeding in his driveway in the dark. He sure wasn't happy. And his kids had been right inside the house. I couldn't even think about my daddy getting shot dead just outside our house.

"Agitators," Mamie had said again. "Things were fine till they started comin' down from the North, stirrin' up trouble, tryin' to make their ways ours."

That had got me thinking. I'd never been to any other place. Weren't things the same everywhere? When I'd asked Mamie, she'd snorted cigarette smoke out of her nose and said, "Point is, it's none of their damn business." Mamie didn't cuss a lot, so I knew she was real worked up. She leaned close and pointed the two fingers holding her cigarette at me. "That's the point. Not if it's the same or not."

That night I wasn't gonna ask any more questions. Mamie was mean enough without getting her worked up. I stayed confused about if it was the same everywhere until I met Miss Cyrena.

Now I got to thinking again. Miss Cyrena didn't seem like an agitator, stirrin' up trouble. She was a nice lady that helped people who needed it, people like me and Eula. She helped the N-double-A—CP, too, so they probably needed it for a good reason . . . like that nasty colored restroom at Riedell's and Eula's cousin Henry getting beat bloody 'cause he wanted to go to a carnival. Miss Cyrena said things were better for the colored up North, but still had room for improvement.

Once the bus had got going again, I got to thinking hard. Colored water fountains never had a cooler like most of the white ones did. Didn't colored people like cold water when it was hot as the hinges of Hades? And Miss Cyrena's school. No swings. All kids liked to swing, so I bet the colored kids didn't think things was fine the way they was.

Just as I was thinking that, we passed a sign that said WELCOME TO TENNESSEE. I sat up straight and looked out the window. Thank goodness we were almost to Momma!

The lady next to me must have been paying attention to me. She pointed to the stupid note on my shirt. It was getting dirty and crumpled some. "We're only halfway to Nashville."

"But we're in Tennessee!" I said.

"And we've spent all day so far in Mississippi. States are big. It takes time to get across them."

Now that was a disappointment. I got in my lunch sack and pulled out an apple.

Pretty soon we come on Memphis. It was even bigger than Jackson.

I asked the lady next to me, "You been to Nashville? Is it bigger'n Memphis?"

"Why, I live in Nashville. Have all my life. And, no, it's not big as Memphis, about half the size."

That made me feel some better. I wasn't sure how easy it'd be to find anybody, even if they was famous, in a city big as Memphis. Just then, I realized I'd ruined my story of coming home to Nashville from visiting Grandma in Mississippi. I closed my mouth and decided not to open it again until after I was off this bus.

We stopped at the bus station to trade some passengers and "use the facilities." We were north of Mississippi, but still there was a colored and a white waiting room. I wondered how far north a person had to go for it to change.

We left the station and chugged through stoplights for a while. Then an interesting thing happened. We made a turn and climbed a hill up to a giant road. Even though I wasn't talking to her anymore, the lady next to me told me it was an inner state highway and it was brand-new, the very first one in Tennessee. They were building them all over the United States. She said on inner states we didn't have to stop at stoplights and whatnot, so we'd travel much faster.

I was all for that, but just nodded and made sure I kept my face toward the window. Inner state roads really was amazing. We went over roads just like they was rivers. Other times we was the river running under another road. The lady was right, we never stopped at all.

Turned out inner state highways might be fast, but they got real boring. I fell asleep PDQ.

The lady next to me shook my shoulder. "We're here."

I straightened up and looked out the window. Well, crap on a cracker, the bus was pulling into the station. I'd slept past all of the street signs that might have started up my memory.

I yawned and rubbed my eyes. My neck hurt and was stiff.

The driver said, "End of the line for this bus. Check the board in the terminal for transfer departures."

"Is Lulu Langsdon picking you up?" the lady asked, pointing to my note.

I forgave Miss Cyrena right then for making me wear it. Momma was famous.

"Yeah, she is." Course I'd ruined my story, so I couldn't tell the lady Lulu was my momma, and that made me a little sad. But the good thing was I didn't need them street signs to shake my memory loose after all. "You know where she lives?"

"Oh, no. I don't know her."

"But you've heard of her, right?"

She tilted her head. "No. Should I have?"

"She's a famous singer."

She smiled. "This town is full of them."

That wasn't good news at all. And there was something funny about the way she said it, too.

She stood up and got my suitcase off the shelf over our seats and handed it to me. She bent over and looked outside the bus. "Do you see her? Is she here yet?"

I looked at the folks on the sidewalk like I was having a time with all the faces. When I thought I'd been looking long enough, I said, "Yep, she's here."

She leaned over closer to me. "Which one? Is she a relative?"

"She's my aunt." I scooted off my seat like I was in a hurry to get off and see her.

The lady looked like she was gonna ask another question, but the man standing in the aisle behind her cleared his throat real loud.

She said she was sorry and got herself off the bus. I waited until I saw her hug a man in a brown hat and walk away before I stepped into the aisle. I was slow enough in getting off that nobody but the colored were left and they were all standing waiting for me.

I hurried off the bus and into the station. I know I was supposed to find the front door, turn right, and walk two blocks before I met up with Eula, but I'd slept past all of the street signs that were supposed to make my memory work.

I looked around. Over on one side of the room I saw an old-fashioned, wooden phone booth. I went over and got inside. When I closed the door, a little light came on. The phone book was chained to the booth so you couldn't steal it. And it was so thick!

I went to the *L*'s. There were several Langsdons. I ran my finger down the line, skipping to first names that started with *L*. My hands started to get sweaty and I felt a weird tingle at the bottom of my spine. LaRoux . . . Larry . . . Leonard . . . Luther . . . Martin.

I started to feel sick.

I flipped to the *C*'s. There was only one Claudelle: John.

Maybe the lady on the bus just didn't like music. Momma was so famous she had an unlisted phone number—probably a private line, too, where you didn't have to worry about somebody in another house listening to your conversation.

I got out of the phone booth. Not far from me was a guy with a guitar case talking to a man with cowboy boots and a funny tie that looked like it was made from a shoelace. A guy with a guitar had to know something about the music business.

I walked close and pretended to be reading the rules under the yellow-and-black fallout-shelter sign.

They were talking music all right.

Mr. Boots was saying, ". . . the Idle Hour? Oh, it's on Sixteenth, right near Music Row."

Music Row! Now that sounded like a place where I could find Momma.

Mr. Guitar said, "Got me a gig there tonight."

Mr. Boots said, "Well, break a leg, kid."

I didn't think that was very nice.

Mr. Guitar headed to the front doors.

I waited for him to get gone, then went to the ticket lady and asked how to get to the Idle Hour by Music Row.

She looked down at me over some little half-glasses. "Ain't you a little young to be hangin' out in a bar?"

A bar? "Um, I ain't lookin' for the bar. I'm lookin' for Music Row. My momma wants to know. She's waitin' in the car. Figured the bus-station people would know where everything that's in Nashville." There, that should take care of Mrs. Nibby Nose and her curiosity.

"Uh-huh." She sighed. "Your momma gonna be a star?" She leaned over. "She gonna replace Patsy Cline?" The way she said the name it was like she was saying Momma was gonna replace Jackie Kennedy . . . ridiculous like.

I didn't want to get into a big talk about my pretend momma, just in case Mrs. Nibby Nose would get it into her head to run outside and talk to her in person. "Music Row?"

"Your momma won't find anybody there. It's Saturday night. Recording businesses won't be open till Monday morning."

My stomach felt like a rock.

"If your momma's interested in country music, she should already know ever'body'll be at the Opry tonight. Since she don't, you might encourage her to look into a different profession." The last bit was real snippy.

I crossed my arms. "You know where it is, or not?"

She huffed and made her mouth pruney. "Sixteenth and Seventeenth Avenues, south of Division."

"How far's that from here?"

"'Bout fifteen, twenty blocks. Out Vanderbilt University way." She lifted her chin toward a map on the wall. I noticed she had two black hairs sproutin' out from a mole down under there and thought it fit her witchy self just right.

"Thank you, ma'am." I stepped over and looked at the map. It had a pin with a red ball in it that said it was the bus station. Nashville spread out all around it, covering the big map. I followed the avenue numbers until I found Sixteenth. It was gonna be a long walk with baby James and two suitcases. A real long walk.

Another red pin was stuck not near as far away from the bus station. The label said GRAND OLE OPRY. Reckon everybody getting into Nashville wanted to know where it was.

I headed out the front door of the station and turned right. I could see Eula on the corner two blocks down, her grip sitting on the sidewalk and baby James bundled close. She was staring my way. When I got closer, I saw she was standing under a sign for a city bus stop with a few other colored folk.

A bus chugged up and opened its doors. All the other coloreds got on. I heard Eula saying", "Thank you much, I'm waitin' on someone. I be gettin' the next one."

I hung back until the doors closed and the bus pulled away.

"I was beginnin' to worry you got yourself lost in there," she said.

I shrugged. "Who you talkin' to?"

"Some of the locals headin' home from work. I needed to know where to find the colored part of town, in case we need that Baptist church."

"Oh, we won't be needin' the church. We'll find Momma at the Grand Ole Opry." I explained to her all I'd found out in the bus station.

"But we don't know where that place is," she said, looking around her like directions might spring out from around a corner.

"I do," I said, wishin' I could show off to Mamie that I'd figured it out. "Fifth Avenue. Near Broadway. I saw it on a map."

Eula looked up overhead at a street sign, picked up her grip, and said, "This way."

"How do you know for sure?"

"Avenue numbers get bigger this direction."

"How we gonna know which way to turn on Fifth?"

"We get it figured out." She was already moving. "Hurry on up. Gettin' late."

My Barbie case bounced against my leg as I hurried to catch up. I couldn't believe I was this close to finding Momma.

Lucky it was summer, otherwise it woulda been dark by the time we got to the Opry—which turned out not to be a building called the Opry, but in the Ryman Auditorium. It looked a lot like a big, fancy brick church with pointy-arched windows and everything. Out in front, and stretched way down the block, was a long, thick line of people waiting to get in. Eula was getting skittish as a cat in a dog pound, but I wasn't giving up and going to the colored church yet. Just look at all these people lovin' country music. If Momma wasn't here, somebody had to know who she was and how to find her.

I asked the first kind-looking lady I come to if Lulu Langsdon was performing tonight. She frowned and said she didn't think so, but there was a poster near the door with the names of who was. She didn't act like she'd ever heard of Lulu.

Momma wasn't listed on the poster, so I went back to the line. Eula had parked herself near the alley and was watching me like a nervous momma bear—Daddy said they was the most dangerous when they was looking after their cubs. There wasn't any way that Eula could ever look dangerous, but she did look tight and jittery and didn't take her eyes off me.

I worked my way down the line, went almost a whole block, but nobody knew Lulu. The line started moving and people got too interested about getting inside to talk to me. It was getting on toward dark and I'd promised Eula we'd get us a bus for Jefferson Street before the streetlights came on. Besides, James was fussing and we was down to our last bottle of milk.

I drug myself back to her and we walked out onto Broadway to catch a bus—her new colored friends from the bus stop had told her how to get to their neighborhood and where to find the Mt. Zion Baptist Church.

"Get your jaw up off the ground," she said. "We find your momma. Tomorrow another day."

"But the only thing goin' on tomorrow'll be church . . . and I don't know where Momma goes for Sunday service."

"Well then, that'll give you somethin' to pray for tomorrow morning . . . that we find your momma on Monday."

That's when it hit me. We'd had some pretty hard times since we got to Miss Cyrena's, but Eula hadn't gone inside herself once since that first day after Wallace got killed. And them Jenkins boys was way worse than me just saying Wallace's name.

Now she was the one trying to keep my spirits up. I wondered what had changed, but didn't get the chance to ask. The bus pulled up and we climbed on. Eula had to sit in the back, and the closest white seat I could find was three rows ahead of her and James.

23

The bus dropped us off on Jefferson Street. I knew to get off because Eula coughed three times behind me, but by then the only other white person on the bus was the driver, so it didn't really matter.

Everybody I saw walking on the street had a brown face. I was a polar bear again. But this time nobody looked at me with hateful eyes. They didn't look at me at all. People was dressed nice, laughing and talking, going into restaurants and movies, just like white people do on Saturday nights in Cayuga Springs.

Eula had given James his last bottle while we were on the bus, so he was quiet again. She looked up and down the street when she stepped off the bus beside me.

"There, now. There's a store on the next corner."

She was looking real tired from being up all night and lugging James and her grip around all day, so I reached over and took her grip from her. "I'll carry this for a while."

She smiled down at me, and some of the tired seemed to fade. "Why, thank you, child." She said it like nobody'd ever offered to carry her load before.

We bought some canned milk and walked to the Mt. Zion Baptist Church. Eula's new friends had said it was the best colored congregation in Nashville, involved in the community and always looking out for those in need. Well, I reckon that was us all right. They even had a special group called the Rescue Band. I liked the sound of that; it was a way better name than the Ladies Auxiliary. One of the women from the bus stop said she would tell Reverend Freeman to expect us.

It hit me then that the colored at the bus stop were a whole lot nicer than the colored in Miss Cyrena's town . . . but maybe they were nicer 'cause none of them had seen me. I was keeping Eula from finding a place to fit in, a place that might make her forget all about turning herself into the law for killin' Wallace.

I pondered while we walked. Maybe once we found Momma and Eula didn't feel so responsible for me, I could convince her to go back to Miss Cyrena's or come back here to Jefferson Street, where folks treated her nice. We hadn't talked about Wallace for a long time. I hoped she was forgettin' him.

It was getting serious dark by the time we saw the church. It sat on a corner. It was brick with long steps up to the doors. It looked pretty much like any of the white churches I'd ever seen. Cayuga Springs colored churches were all made of wood.

Eula walked right up to the front door of the church, like she wasn't afraid of nothing.

The door was locked.

She knocked.

We waited, but nobody come. We went back down the front steps and followed the sidewalk to the corner, past the stone box with the glass door that held the announcement board. It had Reverend Maynard P. Freeman's name and the time of Wednesday and Sunday services. There was also a line that said *All of His flock welcome here.* I hoped they meant it.

I looked up as we walked down the side of the church. It looked dark inside.

Eula went to the door that went to the reverend's office and knocked, but nobody answered that one either.

She came down the steps slow and thoughtful. "We wait a spell."

"What about baby James's bottles?"

"I find a hose bib and get him all fixed up. Can you watch him while I do?"

I nodded and we got ourselves set up on a little strip of grass behind the announcement board. We figured it was better than sitting out in the open on the steps where somebody might come by and ask about my whiteness. Eula walked around the building looking for a water faucet while I changed James's diaper. His cord—Eula had explained to me all about how a baby's cord feeds it before it's born—had finally falled off. I was glad; that dark, shrivelly thing was nasty nasty. Now he had a nice little belly button, just like a real person.

I'd thought it was dark when we'd settled in, but it got darker, specially behind the announcement board. Our eyes was plenty adjusted, still, I'd'a felt better with some light.

Eula said the reverend'd be here soon. But we waited and waited and he never come. We got James all settled down to sleep in Eula's open grip. I was getting real hungry. We'd already ate all the food Miss Cyrena had packed. But if Eula wasn't gonna complain, neither was I.

She musta been doing some mind reading 'cause just about then she pulled out an apple and handed it to me.

"Here you go. Tide you over till the reverend come."

I'd finished my second apple on the bus. I thanked her and took it, but before I took a bite, I saw that she didn't get another one out. "What about you?"

"I'm not hungry."

I knowed that couldn't be true. I handed it back. "Me neither."

She pushed it back toward me. "Eat it. You growin'."

I took a bite. Then I handed it to her. "We'll share. You're too skinny."

She shook her head. "Your family won't like it."

She had that right. Mamie'd have a conniption. I shrugged. "Whose gonna tell 'em?"

She looked kinda sly, then took the apple and bit it. We grinned at each other like we was sharin' a secret, or pullin' a practical joke. I liked the feeling.

We was still passin' it back and forth when a teenager come past. We'd agreed not to draw attention of anybody but the preacher when he come—just in case not everybody round here ignored polar bears. So we sat still.

He must have seen or heard us though 'cause he said, "Who that?" I could see him stand up taller. When he turned his face our way, his glasses flashed some moonlight.

I looked down at my lap, afraid my white face'd show up too much.

He took a step, but it wasn't in our direction. He stepped into the street. "I don't want no trouble. You hear? Leave me alone." He took two more steps backward and then turned and run as fast as I'd run after shoving Mrs. Sellers.

I sat there with my breath coming fast.

I heard Eula let loose a long breath, but her body didn't relax none; I could feel her tight muscles where our shoulders touched.

"You think he was scared of a bully?" I whispered.

"Mebbe. Or white folks. Sometimes men get nice and juiced on Saturday nights. Like to come to the colored streets and make trouble."

I'd heard enough to know that if they did, there wouldn't be any law stoppin' 'em. I decided if whites did come, it was gonna be up to me to protect Eula.

"You settle down and sleep now, child. I wake you when the reverend get here."

No way was I going to sleep now I knowed there was trouble out. But I didn't want to make Eula more scared. So I leaned my head on her shoulder and pretended, but my eyes stayed wide-open.

Every time there was footsteps out on the street in front of the church, I felt Eula get stiff, like she was readyin' herself to fight. But everybody just crossed the street and went on by. As time went on, there got to be less and less people. My eyes kept getting heavy, but I forced them back open.

I was kinda drifting off when I heard them, a whole lot of feet running our way. I started to jump up, but Eula grabbed my arm and held me still. "Shhh."

A man shouted, "We gonna get you sooner or later. Might as well take it now." He was out of breath and his voice shook as his feet hit the ground.

A figure turned the corner and started down the middle of street in front of us. Before he took three more strides, four men was on him, knockin' him to the pavement. I thought I saw a glint of glasses as he hit the ground.

There was the sound of fists hitting skin. But the worst sound was the huffs as the blows landed and the low growls and whimpers of pain.

I wanted to do something to help that boy. If only I had me a big stick—

Just then baby James started to squawl. Eula snatched him up right quick, but one of the men beatin' on the boy stopped and looked our way.

James kept squallin'. The man started toward us. "Come out here."

Eula shot to her feet. "Stay put!" she whispered before she walked out to the street with James in her arms.

I was getting up when I saw clear that the man was colored, not white. I stopped.

"Well, now, look what we got here." He had that thick-tongued sound of being in the juice.

The other men stopped beatin' on the boy, but he didn't get up to run off again. He rolled around on the ground making some awful noises.

"What is it, Pudge?" one of them said.

The first man come closer to Eula. "We got us a woman like to breed, is what we got."

"Do say?"

Now all the men were facing Eula. Her voice was shaky, but loud, "We just waitin' for Reverend Freeman. He be here any minute."

"Well then, we best get our business done." The first man, Pudge, reached for her.

Eula jerked away, but the man snatched her by the shoulders.

I shot out, hollerin' at the top of my lungs. I grabbed at the arm of the man holding Eula. It was so big and strong, I ended up swingin' on it like a monkey bar.

"Ho there." Somebody grabbed me by the waist and wrapped his arms around me, my back pressed against him. I kicked and wiggled, but he just laughed. "Why this one's white!"

"Damn, too bad. We coulda got ourselves two for one."

"Let her be!" Eula shouted. "Let her be and I'll do whatever you want. No fightin'. I take care of all of you."

"Well, we like some fight in our women, don't we?" the third man said.

"Let her be," Eula said, her voice still strong. "Whatever you want. Just let her be."

"Ain't like we could diddle her, now, is it?" the man holding me said. His breath was real bad.

"No, sir, not if we want to go on breathin'." The one holding Eula was laughin' now. "Lucky we got us this one."

I jerked myself enough to get loose and flung myself at him.

One of the other men snatched me back.

"Starla, stop!" Eula held baby James out to me. "You need to take James around and sit on the front steps. Don't come back around here. I come and get you in a bit. It's all right, they ain't gonna hurt me."

The man put me down, slow and careful, in case I got wild again.

I wanted to hurt them as much as they'd hurt that boy. But there was four of them—and they was mean.

"Yeah, you go on, girl. You give us any more trouble and we won't be so nice to your woman here."

Eula looked at me. "Don't provoke, Starla. It be all right now. Take James."

My mouth was dry and my heart was beating so hard it hurt. I looked up and down the street, but nobody was in sight.

I took James. Eula had covered his face with the blanket. I don't know why, but he'd stopped squallin'.

"Sticks, you go round there and make sure she stay where she supposed to."

"I got as much—"

"You get your turn. Get on." It was clear, Pudge was the boss.

Sticks wrapped his hand around the back of my neck and squeezed. Then he shoved me, not toward Jefferson Street, but toward the alley behind the church. I dug in, but he gave me a little shake and squeezed harder. "Don't make me carry you."

I moved as slow as I could.

My red rage wasn't enough to save us. The boy on the road started moanin' again. I couldn't help him neither.

The man tried to hurry me along, so I stopped dead at the start of the alley. I wasn't going on my own. He would have to carry both me and James if he wanted me to leave Eula.

The men was laughin'.

I wanted to cover my ears, but couldn't with James in my arms. I couldn't do nothin' but hold him close and start to cry.

The blare of a car horn made me jump.

"You there!" It was a man's voice, deep and strong and sober. A car door opened. Sticks took off down the alley. I heard other feet running, too.

The police?

"The good Lord'll have his day!" the deep voice shouted. "You run all you want."

I spun around.

The car was sitting at the corner, driver's door open, the dome light shining in the empty car. A man shorter than Eula stood by her side. I could see the white of his preacher's collar under his chin.

He looked up and saw me. "Come, child. Come now. We get you inside. Those miscreants won't bother you anymore."

The reverend helped the boy up from the street. I could see his bloody face in the glare of the headlights. It hurt to look at it.

The reverend picked up the boy's glasses from the pavement and handed them to him. "You want to come on in, son? Or you want me to take you home?"

The boy mumbled something that must have been *home* 'cause the pastor took the boy and set him in the passenger seat of his car. He rolled up the windows and locked the doors before he come back to take us inside.

As he took us to the church basement, Reverend Freeman apologized for being so late. One of his flock was on her way to the gates of heaven and he had to see her home. He also apologized for those men, even though it sure wasn't his fault. He said they was young and angry and took their anger out on the weak. He hoped to someday bring them to the Lord and help heal their souls.

I didn't think there was any fixin' men that mean.

The reverend got us cots set up and told Eula that the little kitchen was stocked and we was welcome to anything we wanted. He invited us to Sunday service, but didn't act like he was making us go to pay for our beds.

After he left, I asked Eula what them men was about to do.

"Nothin' but talk nasty; words not fit for a child's ears. Reverend Freeman come afore they had a chance to even to that." She petted my hair. "I don't want you to think of them ever again. Reverend's right, the good Lord will have his day." She wiped her palms on her skirt. "You hungry?"

I shook my head. All that nastiness outside had scared my hunger away. I wasn't sure it'd ever come back.

She made me lay down and took my shoes off. "You sleep now. Tomorrow we celebrate the Lord and all his goodness."

I wondered again how Eula could be so sure about the Lord. He seemed to let her fall into the path of plenty of bad folk. I was plenty mad at the Lord for letting it happen, too.

Maybe it was 'cause He hadn't let any of those bad folk do their worst. Maybe that's the way Eula looked at the Lord . . . like he'd saved her from worse. I tried to think on it some more, but my brain was so tired it slid right down into sleep.

I woke up to the smell of baking. Opening my eyes, I saw it was still dark. The light was on in the tiny kitchen over in the corner of the basement. I got up and walked to the door. Eula was pulling a cookie sheet out of the little oven.

"Why aren't you asleep?"

She looked up, startled. "Makin' a thank-you for the reverend. I'll replace the ingredients on Monday afore we leave to find your momma."

I looked at the countertop. "You must think he really likes cookies."

"Well, the whole church is bein' hospitable, so I reckoned we could put some out at the service."

She started to put flour into the mixing bowl again. I'd seen how big this church was; she already had more'n enough cookies.

"Ain't you slept at all?"

She shook her head and added a pinch of salt.

"You gonna sleep?"

"Can't. But you get yourself some rest now."

I started back to my cot, then stopped. I looked over my shoulder. Eula was humming.

I went back in the kitchen. "My daddy says that when you do somethin' to distract you from your worstest fears, it's like whistlin' past the graveyard. You know, making a racket to keep the scaredness and the ghosts away. He says that's how we get by sometimes. But it's not weak, like hidin' . . . it's strong. It means you're able to go on."

She looked up. "Your daddy sounds like a smart man."

"I think that's what your bakin' is, it's your way of whistlin'. Ever' time something really bad happens, you start bakin' . . . like it takes your mind away from the scaredness."

She wiped her hands on a towel, then come over to me. She held my face in her hands and looked right into my eyes. "I ain't strong, not like you, Starla. I live my whole life scared."

"That ain't the point, the scaredness. The point is you find a way around it. You're plenty strong. Look at all that happened to you, and here you are, still takin' care of me and James. You could have stayed with Miss Cyrena forever. But you didn't." I touched her cheek. "You're strong, too."

I turned around and left her then, a little embarrassed by blabberin' on.

I fell asleep listening to the sound of Eula working in the kitchen. It was almost as good as my best fallin'-asleep memory of Momma and Daddy at the piano teacher's house.

24

We had a real nice Sunday. Everybody at Reverend Freeman's church acted like it didn't matter that my skin was white. The reverend said a sermon that talked all about how Jesus forgives us no matter what wrong we done. Lots of folks said, "Yes, brother," and "Amen." I took Eula's hand and squeezed it, hoping she got the message and didn't worry no more about killin' Wallace—that man was too mean for God to care. We sang hymns, which was mostly the same as my white-church hymns, but they sounded a whole lot prettier in this church for some reason. Maybe that's why Eula felt about the good Lord like she did; music in a colored church was real upliftin'.

Then we was asked to a potluck dinner in the basement to celebrate Mrs. Thomas's ninetieth birthday. She even let me and all the children help her blow out the candles on her cake—there was so many it looked like the whole cake was on fire. Everybody loved baby James. There was so many hands wanting to hold him, I didn't hardly get to touch him all day. But when it was time for him to get fed, I was the one to do it 'cause he knew me best. Eula worked with the ladies serving and cleaning up after. I liked seein' her so happy, talkin' and smilin'—she seemed a lot less shy than she had when we was getting used to living with Miss Cyrena. Maybe it was being away from Wallace for so long.

That made me wonder how his body was holdin' up down there in the springhouse. We'd been gone from Eula's house over two weeks. I knowed she still felt bad about leaving him like that 'cause I heard her crying in the night over it, beggin' God to take his soul.

I decided to stop thinking about Wallace 'cause it started up the bees in my belly.

After the dinner, everybody sat around talking and whatnot. Then a man got out a banjo and started to play. He was real good. Some of us kids got to clapping and dancing.

After he'd played all his songs—I knowed that to be the case 'cause everybody asked for more, but he said he didn't know no more—I got to thinking about music and my momma.

As he was putting his banjo back in its case, I went up and asked him, "You know a lot about music?"

He smiled. "Run though my veins like blood."

"Well, my momma is a famous singer. Maybe you heard of her, Lulu Langsdon, or maybe Lucinda Claudelle." I had to make sure I gave all her names, just in case.

"A singer, you say?"

I nodded.

He rubbed his chin. "Don't recall that name."

"Well, me and Eula are lookin' for her. I was hopin' somebody could tell me where she lives." I tried not to sound too disappointed, but I wasn't sure what to try next. Our money was running out and Eula hadn't bought the ingredients to replace the church's yet.

"Some of the music folk mix it up—only when they's playin' though. Most the white musicians hang out down on Broadway . . . near that Opry of theirs." He puckered his lips like he was thinking hard. "Might try a place called Tootsies. Might be somebody know of her there. They don't open till afternoons though. Music people are mostly night owls."

Tootsies? Now that name poked my memory. I dug deep trying to remember when I'd heard it.

Nobody talked about Momma when I was around, so it had to be when I was sneak-listening to Daddy and Mamie. Think. Think. Think.

Yeah, Tootsies! It was when Daddy and Mamie was talking in secret; after Daddy come home and said he'd heard from Momma and she was working again.

I run and told Eula what I'd remembered.

She grinned bigger'n I'd ever seen. "Well, now we know where we're headed tomorrow. I told you the good Lord'd show us the way."

I just let her think that it had been the Lord and not the banjo man; it seemed to make her feel good.

Turned out Tootsies on Broadway was easy to find. It was purple. The whole name was Tootsies Orchid Lounge, which must mean a bar, 'cause it had beer signs in the window and said nobody under twenty-one. Neither me or Eula could go inside, which made a particular problem in talking to people and finding out about Momma.

It was late afternoon when we got there. We'd had to wait for baby James's washed diapers to dry before we could pack up and leave the church.

I told Eula, "Go on down and wait at the corner." After all the misery I'd caused her, I'd made up my mind I was gonna be extracareful she didn't get caught with baby James. It'd been risk enough her and me walking here together draggin' suitcases after we got off the bus from Jefferson Street. But it turned out in this town, lots of folks toted cases of some sort.

"Ain't leavin' you standin' here with all them men drinkin' right inside," she said, a real stubborn look on her face.

"It's daylight. And I ain't goin' in. You'll be able to see me from down there just fine."

She hugged James close and took a quick look around. "What you gonna do?"

"I'm workin' on some ideas. But you standin' with me just makes for more explainin'."

"I ain't leavin'."

"We got to find Momma today. We don't want folks askin' about James. And we're outta money." After buying ingredients to stock the church and more milk for James, the bus back to Broadway picked us clean. Neither of us wanted to take more from the church unless we had to. I pointed toward the corner. "So get on down there and let me find Momma."

Just then a bus rumbled by with its brakes hissing. I'd never seen one like it. It didn't say Greyhound or Trailways on the side. It was silver and green and white and had a lady's name on it instead. Loretta Lynn. I'd heard of Loretta Lynn. She was a famous singer at the Grand Ole Opry—which was right around the corner. Patti Lynn's momma listened to the Opry on the radio—Mamie didn't allow any music 'cept Bible music on our radio. I figured it was 'cause she didn't want Momma singin' in her house.

The bus turned out of sight and I wondered if Momma had her singin' bus yet. I decided to go to the Opry again if we didn't find out about Momma at Tootsies.

"You're wastin' time," I said to Eula.

Eula puckered her mouth, picked up her grip, and walked down the sidewalk a ways, but stopped before she got to the corner. She turned around and looked at me, like to say, I ain't goin' no further.

The door to Tootsies was standing open. I heard someone playing a harmonica somewhere inside. But it was so dim in there, I couldn't see much from where I was. I kept getting closer until I was right at the doorway. I stood there for a minute, with my shoulder against the doorframe, waiting to get used to the light.

The place was foggy blue from cigarettes and it smelled like sweat and smoke. The walls was all cluttery with pictures and whatnot. I wondered if there was a picture of Momma in there.

The long bar was on the left side close to the door. A lady wearing glasses and a green print dress stood behind it. She looked more like a Sunday-school teacher than a bar lady.

"Pssttt!" I leaned so far my head was inside the door. I figured you had to have your whole body inside for them to call the police if you wasn't twenty-one. "Pssst."

The lady looked up and squinted. She waved her dishrag to shoo me away.

"You Miss Tootsie?"

Some of the people sitting at the bar looked up. The lady walked out from behind it and come to the door. She brought the rag with her. She put her hands on her hips and looked down at me. "You're too young to be hangin' round a bar, young lady." She pointed to my Barbie suitcase. "What are you up to?"

"I'm looking for my momma. She's a famous singer, and I heard all famous music people come here."

The lady smiled. "That they do." Then she cocked her head and got kinda frowny. "What's your momma's name?"

"Lucinda Claudelle. But her famous name is Lulu Langsdon."

"Huh." Her chin went up and she flipped the rag. "I reckon *famous* means different things to different people."

"You know her?" I asked, my mouth getting dry. It was hard to breathe. Did she still have a ponytail? Would she recognize me with my black hair?

"I know Lulu Claudelle. She doesn't have kids."

I stood up straight and looked her in the eye. "Well, here I am, so I reckon she does."

She raised her eyebrows, like she was surprised I'd sassed. "Where'd you come from?"

"I been livin' with my mamie."

"And where is that?"

"Cayuga Springs." I could tell the truth 'cause I was in disguise with my black hair. "If you'll just tell me where Momma lives, I'll be on my way, ma'am."

She looked at me for a long while, like she was making up her mind. "Wait right there for a minute." She went back inside. There were lots of people; once she got deep enough in the bar, I couldn't see her anymore.

I glanced down the sidewalk. Eula was standing there, looking nervous as a toad in front of a lawn mower. I smiled and gave her the A-OK sign.

She didn't look any easier. I could see her frowning brows right clear.

Then I got to wondering if Tootsie was getting Momma's address or calling the police. My heart got to gallopin' and I backed up from the door and made myself ready to run, just in case.

In just a bit I saw Miss Tootsie go back behind the bar. I was ready to call to her when I saw someone shovin' through the crowd, coming fast toward the door. She had on a checkered blouse and black slacks like Laura Petrie wears at home on *Dick Van Dyke*—but this lady was out in public. Good thing Mamie wasn't here, she'd have a conniption fit.

The lady's hair was so . . . big. And it was so blond it hardly had any color at all. She looked like her head had been wrapped in white cotton candy.

Disappointment started to get on me, and right then I realized I'd been hoping Momma was actually here. But then I thought, maybe this lady knows where Momma lives, that's why Miss Tootsie went to get her.

My stomach flipped like it did on the Bullet.

The lady stepped out the door and onto the sidewalk. She leaned right down in my face, bringing the smell of cigarettes and perfume. "Where in the hell have you been for the past two weeks?"

I was so surprised I couldn't get any words out.

"And what did you do to your hair?"

How could somebody this mean be friends with my momma? My hair might be black, but I still had red rage inside. I leaned right back at her. "I just wanna know where my momma is."

"For God's sake, Starla, I am your momma."

25

I blinked, trying to look past the crazy hair and raccoon makeup and see my momma. I hadn't seen her since I was three, sure, but this lady didn't look nothin' like what I remembered, or the old picture of her. Nuh-uh. This was just a trick to make me stay here long enough for the police to come.

"Liar. My momma has red hair. And she'd never talk that mean to me!"

The lady put her hands on her hips, took a big breath, and looked like she was getting ahold of her temper. "How'd I know your name if I'm not your momma?" She tried to put her hands on my shoulders, but I jerked away and started to run.

"Starla! Wait!"

I kept going. Eula was grabbing her grip off the sidewalk watching me come.

The lady yelled, "I gave you Mr. Wiggles."

I froze.

"I sent you a buckeye for good luck."

I looked over my shoulder. That lady could not be my momma.

Coldness fell over me like rain. I turned around real slow.

"Come back here." Her voice cut deep, way deep.

Right then, I felt Eula standing right behind me. "You all right?" she whispered.

I swallowed. "That's . . ." I couldn't make myself say it.

"Your momma." Eula didn't sound near as surprised as she should have.

I couldn't make my feet walk back to that lady, so she come to us.

"Now who's this?" she put one hand on her hip and pointed at Eula with the other.

"Eula," I said, trying to find some of my starch. "She brought me here. Made sure I was safe."

"Well, it would've been nice to know! Everybody's been crazy with worry. Your daddy had to come in off the rig—missed two weeks' work." Momma looked hard at Eula. "It took two weeks? And you didn't think of callin' and tellin' anyone she was safe?"

Soft as a mouse, Eula said, "I'm sorry—" The Eula I'd seen with the church ladies was gone.

"It ain't Eula's fault!" My hackles come up. "How was we supposed to call you when you ain't in the telephone book?"

Momma's mouth got tight. Something about that look hit me as real familiar. My stomach got a cold spot in it. I took a step backward and bumped into Eula.

People were looking at us real curious as they passed.

Momma grabbed for my arm, but Eula wrapped her arm across my shoulders from behind me and pressed me close. Eula said real quiet and polite, "If you don't mind me sayin', ma'am—"

"I do mind." That tightness come back to Momma's mouth. "I got no idea why you brought her here when you shoulda taken her back home. But you can get on your way now." She flicked her hand like she was shooing a stray cat. Then, like the words were hard coming, she said, "Thank you for bringin' her."

"Don't you treat her like that!" I said, leaning toward Momma.

"No you listen to me, missy, you watch your mouth." Momma put a finger in my face. "You won't be talkin' to me like that over some negra woman."

"But Eula—"

"Enough! I gotta call your daddy and get back to work."

"But—"

The smack come before I even saw her hand moving. It wasn't hard, but took me by surprise. I sucked in a breath and it stuck in my chest. I bit my lip to keep from crying. Everything was moving so fast, and not in the direction I'd been expectin'. Eula's arm stayed locked around me and I felt some steadier. But she was just a colored woman. If Momma wanted to drag me down the street by my hair, Eula couldn't do nothin' about it. And right then, the look in Momma's eyes said she might do just that. Something fluttered in my memory for a second, but skittered back into the dark, a roach under the refrigerator.

Baby James started to cry. We'd fed him already and he'd been sleeping fine. He knew something was wrong.

I was afraid Eula'd let go of me to comfort him, but she held tight.

"I don't have time to stand out here foolin' around, Starla." Momma said. "Thank the woman and come on."

She reached for my arm, but I jerked away, bumping Eula a little and making James holler louder.

If I just left Eula standing out here with James a'squallin', she was sure to get into trouble. We had to get James to his family. Momma had to help. And Wallace . . . I still hadn't got Eula convinced not to turn herself in to the law. All the sudden that big, dead body was just about all I could think of.

"I can't leave her. There's—things you need to know about. Things you gotta know." Once I got it all explained, Momma would help her. "She saved me."

Momma had said everybody had been worried, which meant even if she was surprised to see me, she'd be grateful Eula'd saved my life. But I sure couldn't just blabber right out here on the street that Eula'd killed her husband.

Now people weren't just staring, they were stopping.

"I ain't goin' anywhere without Eula." I made my legs so stiff my knees were knots.

Momma's raccoon eyes got so narrow I couldn't see any of the green anymore. Then she huffed. "Fine. Y'all come on." She turned around and pushed past a lady with hair as big as Momma's, but it was coal black; they coulda been salt and pepper shakers.

"What're you lookin' at?" Momma said, and gave the lady the stink eye and marched down the street without looking to see if we followed behind.

When I unlocked my legs, my knees got so wobbly I almost fell down—from standing stiff, not 'cause I was scared of my own momma.

Eula nodded for me to start moving. "We here now. Got no choice but to get on and tell the truth."

"You just let me do the tellin'." I had a "truth" all worked out in my head. I sure hoped it went better than my ideas about findin' Momma.

Eula picked up her grip. We followed Momma. James screamed louder.

We didn't go far, just to an upstairs apartment in a building a few doors down from Tootsies. It was one big room with a little kitchen folded in one corner and not much more than a lumpy couch and the foot of a bed peeking from behind a yellow, flowered curtain. Through an open door, I could see a bathroom sink with a rusty streak under the faucet and a dull mirror that was spotted black.

I wished we was back at Mt. Zion Baptist with the banjo music and the smell of cookies in the basement.

"You live here?" I asked.

"No, this is my vacation home." Momma spun around. "Jesus Christ, Starla, of course I live here." The way her hands moved, jerky and fast, made me flinch, even though she wasn't swingin' at me.

I felt a little dizzy.

James still didn't like the way things were going. The high ceilings and wood floors made him sound like he was crying in a barrel. The noise seemed to make Momma more jittery. Again, I got a feeling that I'd seen Momma like this before, and it didn't turn out good.

Eula gave James his sassy and he quieted some.

Momma stayed jittery. "Sit down." Momma pointed to the table with two chairs. She still didn't look like Momma at all—except for the nervous hands. She grabbed a pack of Winston cigarettes off the table. She pulled a matchbook from where it was tucked in the cellophane wrapper and lit up. She sucked until the tip glowed bright orange, then blew out the flame with her smoky breath and tossed the match into the kitchen sink. It sizzled as it landed in a pile of dirty dishes. "I got to call your daddy."

"Not yet! You can't call Daddy till I tell you what happened. We need to make a plan."

I reckoned since he'd come off the rig, he could move up here right away and get a new job. With all of us up here, it'd be easier to keep Eula from the police. I hoped he didn't get all worked up about me taking my just desserts. I'd hate to have come all this way and end up in reform school anyway. At least he and Momma would be here waiting when I got out. And I'd still be able to save Eula. But I had to get the story out to Momma first, so she could make sure Daddy understood before he come . . . or spilled the beans to the law in Cayuga Springs.

"I need to get back to work," Momma said. "It's busy and Tootsie can't take care of the crowd by herself. And I can't afford to lose the tips."

"You singin' there?" I asked, knowing I was getting distracted, but I was real curious about Momma's life. The singin' was the only part of her I recognized.

"I'm workin'. How you think I get the money to send Mamie to take care of you."

Now that rubbed me the wrong way. "Daddy sends Mamie the money to keep me."

She rolled her eyes and gave a laugh that sounded like a dog's bark. "Well, I'm not surprised the old bitch kept it to herself, much as she hates me." Momma stopped herself. "For your information, I send money for you almost every month."

If she did that, she must love me. Right?

She reached for the phone sitting on a table made of bricks and boards at the end of the couch.

I shot up off the chair and put my hand around her wrist to keep her from picking it up. "No!"

"The sooner I get your daddy called, the sooner he'll get here to take you home and he can get back to work. We ain't made of money, in case you hadn't noticed."

"I ain't goin' home. I'm livin' with you now."

She looked like I'd said a swear word and let go of the phone.

I let go of her wrist. "I just need to explain—"

"You can't live here, Starla."

I blinked, feeling like she'd slapped me again. "Why not? You're my momma."

"For one thing, there's nobody to take care of you."

That was the silliest thing I'd ever heard. "I'm almost ten, I don't need takin' care of during the day. Even when Eula gets a job, she'll be here at night when you're singin' someplace."

Momma sighed real hard and touched my hair. "You belong in Cayuga Springs. Besides, there's no room for you and a colored woman and her baby in this apartment. There's barely room for me and Earl."

"The baby ain't stayin'—Wait a minute." I looked around. "Who's Earl?"

"My husband."

"Daddy's your husband. His name's Porter, not Earl."

Momma's face got so soft I almost recognized her. "Dear Lord, they never told you."

"Told me what?" I almost covered my ears.

"Your daddy and I are divorced—have been for almost six years. Earl's my husband now."

"No!" The whole room was spinning. Everything in Nashville was wrong, wrong, wrong.

She tried to put her arms around me, but I jerked away. "It ain't true."

"It is. I'm sorry nobody told you. Your daddy should have."

A hiccup surprised me. I blinked to keep from crying. "Well, I still can't go back to Cayuga Springs."

"Of course you can. Mamie'll be mad for a while for you runnin' away, but she'll get over it—"

"No!" Things was getting blurry. "No!" I stomped my foot. "If I go back, they'll send me to reform school. And Eula and baby James . . ." I made myself tall, like I did when I was trying to stand my ground with Wallace. "We ain't goin' back!"

Momma grabbed my arm. Her fingers dug in worse than Mamie's. "You listen here." The words kinda hissed out. "You've caused everybody enough worry. I don't know what trouble you got yourself into, but you can't just run off and make life what you want it to be."

"Why not? You run off and made life what you wanted it to be!"

The slap came fast and hard. My head jerked to the side and my cheek caught fire.

Eula had me then, wrapped up in her arms and spun away from Momma. James was caterwaulin' across the room.

"I'm calling your—God! Somebody shut that kid up!" Momma gave a frustrated look toward James and stopped with her hand halfway to the phone. "That baby's white."

It finally got in my head that if Eula had me wrapped up in her arms, baby James was left alone over by the table. He'd kicked the blanket off and was more cherry red than white, but nobody would mistake him for colored.

I pulled away from Eula. "That's what I need to tell you." I swiped my nose with the back of my hand. "Eula's husband kidnapped me and baby James both." I heard Eula gasp, but kept talking. "She had to kill—"

Momma held up a hand and turned away. "Stop right there! I don't want to hear any more. Not another word." She leaned close. "Not another blessed word!" She picked up the phone. "You both go over there and sit back down. And do somethin' about that baby!"

Eula hurried to comfort James.

"But, Momma—"

She swooped back in my face. "Enough!" She gritted her teeth and flung her hand toward the table and chairs. "Get. Over. There."

I drug myself back to the table on feet too heavy to lift off the floor. This was worse than the nightmares I had when I was sick at Miss Cyrena's. Oh, I wish we'd just stayed there and kept baking. I'd rather spend the whole rest of my life hid in the dark from the Jenkins boys and the law than go back to Cayuga Springs. Then my worst, most awful wish come, and my throat hurt like I was being strangled. I wish I'd never found Momma in Nashville.

Eula plugged a bottle into James's mouth and he got quiet.

All I could hear was my pounding heart and the *snick-shhhhh, snick-shhhh* of Momma dialing the phone.

"Porter, she's here." She listened for a minute. "Yes, she's fine." She listened again. "Oh, for God's sake, I don't know and I don't want to know. You're supposed to be taking care of her, so you get your ass up here and take this mess off my hands before Earl gets back tomorrow night." Her face started to get red. "No, he still doesn't know, and that's none of your damn business. You get up here by noon or I'm puttin' her on a bus." She slammed down the phone.

The sharp bang shattered my heart like a bottle hitting the sidewalk.

26

I didn't look at Momma again. I shut off my memories, too. They was as unreal now as Lulu, the lady she'd turned into. I sat there in that chair with the sharp pieces of my heart falling down and cutting my gut, my ears ringing, and my body turning to stone. Beyond the ringing I heard Lulu bossing Eula. There's food in the fridge . . . use the bologna not the bacon . . . I don't want to see any mess when I get back . . . keep that baby quiet . . . *do not* answer the phone . . . make Starla take a bath . . . she can sleep with me . . . you know not to use the tub, but I don't mind if you take a sponge bath . . . be sure and leave your towel separate . . . she'd better be asleep when I get home . . . make sure y'all are packed to leave first thing. Every order made me slide farther away, made the ringing get louder.

Then she left for Tootsies.

I hated her.

After I heard the door close behind her, I got up off the chair and headed toward the bathroom. As I passed Eula, she tried to talk to me but I shook my head and kept going.

She respected me not wanting to talk, but her face looked sad and I heard her sigh.

Just before I closed the bathroom door, I turned around and said, "You can use the bathtub."

I locked the door and turned on the water to fill the tub.

I made it so hot that I had to get in real slow. I wanted it to hurt; wanted my outside to feel as bad as my inside. I sat there for a long time watching my skin turn redder and redder. I thought about all of the nights I'd dreamed of the day I'd see Momma again. I thought about how stupid I'd been to think I could be happy and living with my family glued back together in a big house with laughin' and horses and a dog and a good Christmas like the one on the *Andy Williams Show*.

Finally my insides was as fiery as my skin. I liked the burn and hoped it took everything I'd been wishing for and turned it to ashes.

Then it come to me. Maybe Momma was just surprised. Maybe she'd been so worried about me that she was wound up tight inside and was just letting off steam. It had to be a shock, me showing up safe and sound after over two weeks. Yeah. That had to be it. She'd come home from work after a while and we'd sit down and have a nice talk. She'd say she was sorry. She'd listen to my story about James and Eula and she'd fix everything so Eula was safe.

I remembered the way her nails dug into me . . . and I remembered how it sparked a memory I pushed away. Had I made her this mad before? Back when I was really little?

Something I'd heard Mamie say come back to me. ". . . shook her till Porter come and snatched that baby from her. What if he hadn't been there? That girl isn't fit to take care of a baby. . . ."

No. Mamie said all sorts of lies about Momma.

A flash came back to me. Momma's face was right down in mine . . . and ugly-mean. She was yelling. There was a red splash of nail polish across the bathroom floor. I was a bad girl. She jerked me hard. Bad. Bad. Bad . . .

I slid all the way down and let the water come up over my head, but her voice went on. On and on and on.

I held my breath and it got farther away. I laid there on the bottom of the tub looking at the wavery bathroom on the other side of the water.

All the sudden I saw Wallace's face. I jerked myself up; floppin' so much that water sloshed all over the floor. I sucked in a breath.

Footsteps ran across the apartment. "Starla!" Eula wiggled the doorknob. "You all right, child?"

"Fine," I said in a croaky whisper. Then louder: "I'm fine."

She didn't say any more, but I didn't hear her leave the door.

I closed my eyes and rubbed my face. All the sudden, a cryin' fit got hold of me. I wadded the washcloth over my mouth to keep Eula from hearing. I cried on and on, more than I could ever remember. I got worried that maybe I couldn't never stop.

But the sobs finally turned into hiccups, my tears into burning eyes. By the time I was back to my real self, the water had gone cold and my toes was all shriveled.

I felt some better.

When I come out of the bathroom, Eula was at the kitchen table. I don't know when she'd left the bathroom door. She didn't ask what had taken me so long. She just took me over to the couch and sat us down. Then she took my comb and worked the tangles out of my wet hair. She hummed nice and soft while she worked. Even though my hair was black, my scalp was tender like it was still red, but Eula didn't make those tangles hurt as much as when Mamie worked on them.

I closed my eyes and concentrated on her humming, her long fingers moving through my hair, the brush of her breath on the back of my neck. Some of the anger got less tight inside me.

"Let's leave," I said, keeping my eyes closed. "Right now. Let's go back to Miss Cyrena's."

For a minute, Eula stayed quiet. I hoped she was making plans on how to get back there.

Then she sighed. "You know that ain't the right thing to do."

"Why not?" I turned and looked at her. "Nobody cares. Nobody wants us except Miss Cyrena." I hated that it was true, that Momma had meant what she'd said. If we left now, I wouldn't have to know for sure. Once Momma was back, it'd be too late to run.

"What about your Daddy?"

I shrugged. I didn't want to think about him right now. Truth be told, Daddy wasn't never home and Mamie hated me. Patti Lynn . . . well, my insides was too raw to think about never seeing her again.

Eula looked at me for a long while; her eyes was sad as I'd ever seen them. "I know you disappointed in your momma—"

"She's horrible! And she ain't my momma no more."

"She always be who borne you. Nothin' change that. 'Member I told you, there more to bein' a momma than birthin' a baby. And some women just ain't made for it. Your momma surely is one of those." Eula shook her head, real sad. She held my face in her hands and got so close we were nose to nose. "That your momma's shortcomin'; it got nothin' to do with you and the good person you are."

I felt my chin start to shake. I bit my lip, and when I blinked, I felt a tear roll down my cheek. "I'm not good. I never do nothin' but make trouble."

Eula sat back with her eyes wide. "I never heard anythin' so foolish."

"It's true! I'm always gettin' put on restriction and sent to the principal's office. Mamie says I'm sassy and disobedient—and I reckon she's right. I leap before I look and I got me a real bad temper."

"Well, now, we can all do better. That's why we get up every day, to try and do better with the good Lord's help."

"Mamie says I'm just like Momma! What if it's true?" I could hardly breathe after those words got out.

Eula looked real serious. She was shaking her head slow, like she was considering. "We all a little like our mommas, but you ain't your momma. I'm sorry for sayin' this, but she a disappointed and selfish woman, ugly and hateful inside. Maybe she always that way, maybe life hammered her into it. I can't say. But what I do know is you and me, we been through some things together. Hard things. And I ain't never seen you act selfish. You fight for what's right. There's nothin' to be ashamed in that. You take care of James and me when we need it, even when it'd be easier to just leave us. I see that you a beautiful person inside—most beautiful I ever met."

I wanted to believe her. But I couldn't. For one big reason. And that reason made me sure she was just trying to make me feel better. I pulled up all of my braveness. "I run away, just like Momma. And . . ." I swallowed but my mouth was dry. "And if it wasn't for me, you wouldn't have killed Wallace."

His name surprised her, I could tell. She sat there for a minute quiet and still. It didn't look like she was going inside herself, but I couldn't be sure.

Her whole body was shaking a little and her voice was low and strict when she said, "I never want you to say that or even let it into your head again. What happen with Wallace was 'cause of Wallace and 'cause of me. Our trouble been brewin' a long while. After I took James, disaster comin' like a freight train whether I picked you up on that road or not. What happen with Wallace is on me, not you. Not you!"

She grabbed me in a hug so ferocious, the love reached clean to my bones. She kissed the top of my head. "Truth is, you save me, child. You save me as sure as the sun rises. Sooner or later, he gonna kill me, or James, or both of us. I know that now. And I know that because you give me the strength to see it."

We stayed quiet for a bit, hanging on to each other. Then she said, "I know I gotta pay for what I done. But I do it with an easy heart. Never you feel any sorrow over me." She pulled me away from her and put her hand under my chin. "You hear me?"

"They can't lock you up for savin' me. They can't."

She smiled then, soft and kinda sad. "Maybe not. We just wait and see what justice bring. I'd kill that man again and again if he tried to hurt you. So maybe I am a sinner in the Lord's eyes. I find out when I meet him, and that the only judgment that means anythin'."

"Daddy will help you." Right then it came to me that maybe I didn't know Daddy; I sure didn't know Lulu. And Mamie'd probably have the law waiting to take me off to reform school when I got back. She sure wouldn't help Eula. Mamie would wish that Wallace had done got me out of the way for good.

"You should leave," I said. "Without me. That way nobody'll be lookin' for you."

Eula shook her head. "Ain't you been listenin'? You and me come this far, we finish this together."

I tried to swallow but my throat closed up.

"Together." She nodded and kept her eyes on mine until I nodded, too.

Eula made me go to sleep in Lulu's bed. It made my skin all crawly to think of her laying her fake blond hair on one of these pillows. I laid there until I heard Eula feed James and tell him a sweet good-night, same as she done with me. I hoped James wasn't as wound up inside as I was. I worried I'd still be awake when Lulu come home. I didn't want to see her face ever again.

But the night moved on and Lulu didn't show up. The apartment stayed hot. The street outside stayed noisy. Music come out of the doors of the bars and met on the street before coming up and in the window. The voices of men and the laughter of the women made me wish we was sleeping in the bed of Eula's truck. I heard a fight. Eula fed James again. After I heard her get back on the couch and start snoring real quiet, I finally picked up my pillow and went around the curtain.

The light from the street made the room look like it was just a rainy day and not nighttime. James was laying on a folded blanket on the floor at the foot of the couch where nobody would step on him. He was just wearing a diaper. Eula was on the couch. She wasn't wearing her nightgown, but had put on one of her baking dresses like she was ready to get up and run if need be. Her Sunday hat and nice dress she'd worn on the bus sat on top of her grip. At least she wasn't wearing shoes.

I got down on my knees and studied her for a bit. Her hair stuck out from her head like a dark halo. I kinda wished I'd just stayed quiet in that room at her house and let her be my momma; let her and Wallace and James and me be a family, the way she'd wanted.

It was a silly thought. Wallace wasn't never gonna let that happen.

I laid down on the floor and put my head on my pillow.

I'd just closed my eyes when Eula whispered, "I feel bad for your momma."

My eyes sprung back open. "Why? She's so awful."

"'Cause she'll never know what she missin' in not knowin' you."

Eula's hand come over the edge of the couch and I took it.

We stayed that way, just bein' for a while, before I finally fell asleep.

27

A three-rap knock woke me. I jumped up, my heart skitterin' along like a startled rabbit. It took me a second to figure out where I was. The couch was empty. Eula was at the table feeding James his bottle.

Thump, thump, thump. It wasn't a knuckle knock, it was a fist.

I looked toward the curtain that hid most of Lulu's bed. Feet were sticking out, red toenail polish looking like stoplights. Nasty and bossy as Lulu was, I was surprised she hadn't woke me up and made me go get in her bed when she come in. I almost wish she'd tried.

The knock was louder the third time.

I got up and peeked around the curtain. Lulu's hair was wild, her raccoon eyes smeared and her mouth hangin' open. "Someone's at the door," I said. She didn't open her eyes. I poked at her foot. "Lulu. The door."

She rolled over and covered her head with the pillow.

I turned to Eula. She looked nervous, but put James down—he didn't like his breakfast interrupted and started to bawl. She motioned for me to stay back, then went and opened the door just a crack.

"Sorry, ma'am. Must have the wrong apartment." It was Daddy.

My bruised heart wasn't ready to see him, but I come up behind Eula and pulled the door open all the way.

Daddy almost didn't look like Daddy. His hair was all messy and his face had some beard on it. But his eyes were the most wrong. Daddy's eyes was always laughin'—Good Time Charlie, some folks called him, even though his name wasn't Charlie at all. But now his eyes was red and bloodshot and had dark circles under them. I held my breath, waiting for him to start yelling.

His eyes lit on me and changed. "Starla! Thank God!" He picked me up off the floor and squeezed me tight before I even saw him moving. He kept saying over and over, "Thank God. Thank God. Thank God."

I wrapped my arms around his neck and my legs around his waist. I buried my nose in his neck and breathed him in. He was still Daddy. (Thank you, baby Jesus.)

He felt skinnier, but his shoulders were still strong and his arms hard as rocks like always.

I heard him sniff and that broke my tears loose. We cried some. Then he set me down. He wiped his face with his hands, and his beard made a scratchy noise. Eula handed me a Kleenex. When I took it, I saw she was crying, too. The only one who wasn't was James, 'cause she'd picked him up again.

Daddy looked at James, his white face against Eula's brown arm. I could tell he was trying to figure out where James come from. Maybe since Lulu was married now, he thought maybe James was her baby.

That made my stomach feel sick. I hoped no baby ever had to have Lulu for a momma.

Daddy didn't ask about James, though. Instead he looked past us into the little apartment. "Where's your momma?"

I pointed to the curtain. "Lulu is sleepin'." I was never gonna call her Momma again.

His face changed. He looked like a storm. "Get dressed. We're leavin'."

"But, Daddy, I need to tell you somethin'."

"You can tell me on the way. Get dressed."

"I can't go without Eula and James."

He looked at me. "James?"

"The baby."

He looked at them. "Why not?"

"'Cause they need our help." I thought of Miss Cyrena and of those folks at Mt. Zion Baptist, how they helped just 'cause we needed it, without asking a lot of questions. I wanted Daddy to be like that. "Eula done saved me from gettin' killed."

"Killed!" His eyes got big. "Last night? Here? What in the hell happened?" He looked like he wanted to break something.

"Not here. Back in Mississippi. She kept me safe in gettin' here. That's what I need to tell you—"

"Quiet out there!" Lulu sounded like her tongue was thick and sticky.

"What happened!" Daddy was getting riled. It was an unusual thing.

"I had to run away so I didn't get sent to reform school, but got kidnapped almost right away—"

"Shut the hell up!" Lulu again.

Daddy looked mad enough to stomp snakes. He stalked over to the end of Lulu's bed. "Don't bother yourself to get up." I'd never heard Daddy sound so . . . nasty. "In case you're at all interested, we're leavin'."

"Porter?" Lulu mumbled his name, like she wasn't sure it was him.

"Jesus, you reek of booze! As far as I'm concerned, you just burned your last bridge. One night! One fu—One night and you couldn't stay here and take care of her?"

Daddy being so mad at her made my heart float.

"Hey, I had to work!" Now she sounded awake. "It ain't my fault she showed up here! If your mother had been doing what we pay her for—"

"Pay her for? Is that how you see it?" He made a real disgusted sound. "You make me sick." He kicked the foot of her mattress, then turned around and run his hands through his hair. After a second, he said, without looking at Lulu, "You might want to drag your ass out of bed, since you probably won't make any effort to see your daughter again."

"Fuck off." The sheets flounced like Lulu was covering up her head.

Daddy come stompin' back to me. "Get your stuff, you can change in the car. You can tell me what happened on the way."

"But Eula—"

He looked at her. "You want to come with us?"

Eula nodded and held James tight.

He pointed to her grip, all packed and ready to go—just like Lulu had ordered. "This yours?"

Eula nodded again and he picked it up.

I grabbed my shoes and Barbie suitcase and we was out the door lickety-split. Daddy slammed it behind us. His jaw kept working and his breath was real rough. We went down the stairs and got in his car. He started it up and drove off, so anxious to get gone he didn't even ask where baby James come from. I reckon by now he'd figured he wasn't Lulu's.

As we drove away, I was busy inside—hoping Daddy's being mad was all on Lulu and not me, getting my story organized, worrying 'bout Daddy getting Eula fixed up with the law, worrying 'bout baby James and what was gonna happen to him. I kept worrying about those things so I didn't have to think about that horrible person who used to be my momma. It didn't come to me until we'd gone six blocks that I didn't even say good-bye to Lulu.

After seven blocks, I decided I didn't care.

Daddy didn't say a word for fifteen minutes. He just drove, then pulled into a parking lot, told me to get dressed, and got out. I real quick put on my dress, 'cause it was fastest and I could put it right over my pj's. Then me and Eula and James followed him into the diner.

The waitress brought coffee for Daddy and orange juice for me. Eula and baby James was at a little table way in the back. Daddy told the waitress to let Eula order whatever she wanted and bring him her check. Then he said to me, "You said you were almost killed. Did you mean that or were you exaggerating?"

I was so glad he didn't want to talk about Lulu, I almost sounded too happy when I started my story. "It's true! It was a kidnapper, Eula's husband, Wallace. He kidnapped me and James both. Eula had to save me with a skillet—"

"Whoa, whoa, whoa!"

Dang! I'd been planning this for days; how I was gonna explain all nice and careful, but when that first word come out, the rest was right behind it. All because of Lulu. I hated her even more.

My insides felt like Jell-O. What if I'd already messed it up? I took a deep breath and got ready to start again. I had to get this done right. And I had to do it while we was separated from Eula, in case she decided to be contrary about what I was gonna say.

I got my mind organized to start over. I thought about asking baby Jesus for help, but it seemed wrong, since I'd be bendin' the truth some.

"Afore I get tellin' what happened, you gotta promise not to stop me to ask questions or scold me. I know I done wrong and gotta get consequences." This was the first thing I was supposed to say. "But you listen to everything so we can help Eula."

"After what you just told me, I reckon it's best to start at the beginning."

That's when it come to me that he probably already knew about some of it from Mamie. But Mamie would make me look as bad as possible. Daddy had to know my side so he really understood.

"Okay, but I mean it, Daddy. You gotta hear it all. No interruptions."

He made an *X* over his heart like we did when we was swearin' to keep a secret from Mamie.

"Mamie pro'bly already told you 'bout my gettin' put on restriction for breakin' Jimmy Sellers's nose."

Daddy kept his eyes fixed on mine and tilted his head. He turned his palm up and flipped his fingers, telling me to come on and tell it. I was some disappointed, but not surprised. Daddy always made me tell him what I done wrong my own self, even if Mamie had already told him and punished me.

"It's gonna take a long time," I said.

He folded his hands around his coffee cup, raised his eyebrows, and waited.

I told him about Prissy Pants—but I called her by her real name so I didn't sound snotty—and Jimmy Sellers. When I got to the part where I punched him, it looked like Daddy was fighting a smile, but I couldn't be sure. Daddy never smiled when I lost my temper and leaped without lookin'. I told him I apologized to Mrs. Sellers and tried to act like I meant it. Then I explained how much I love the Fourth of July and the fireworks and how Mamie always punished me with the worst possible thing. I was glad I'd made him promise not to interrupt, 'cause he'd say that's what punishment was supposed to be; if Mamie did something I liked, it'd be a reward. He always said that when I complained about Mamie's unfairness.

Then I had to tell him about breaking restriction and Mrs. Sellers finding me, and me pushing her down, and I was really glad he couldn't say anything. His eyes was doing enough scolding.

"I didn't want to go to reform school, like Mrs. Sellers was sayin', so I run off. I figured Mamie'd be happy to be rid of me anyway."

Daddy opened his mouth and I gave him the stink eye. He closed it. Daddy always kept his cross-heart promises.

The waitress brought our breakfasts, but I wasn't hungry anymore.

"I was gonna come to Nashville to live with Momma. But I didn't know then that she'd turned into Lulu." I shivered. "If I had, I might'a gone back home and waited on the front steps for the law to come get me."

"Starla, she's always been—"

I held up my hand. "Daddy!" Truth be told, I didn't stop him because of his cross- heart promise, but because I didn't want to hear that she'd always been Lulu. If I got to thinking about that, I'd be a goner and not be able to finish my story. And I didn't want to cry in front of Daddy, not over Lulu . . . ever.

He blinked and nodded. "Sorry."

I spun a story about Wallace grabbing me off the road and him taking me home. I said he'd already had James with him. From there on I tried to stick close to the truth. As long as Wallace was the one who took James from the church steps, Eula should be okay. I still wasn't sure how we'd get around the law when it come to Wallace's deadness, but Daddy'd think of something.

I took a glance at Eula. Her fork was moving her food around, but

I didn't see any leave the plate and go to her mouth. From the way her eyes kept peekin' from the side, I figured she was working hard not to watch what was going on at our table.

I kept talking, wanting to get it all out as fast as possible. I explained how Wallace had seen some colored girl leave James in a basket on the step of a church. And that Eula couldn't have babies and wanted them more than anything. Wallace seeing that colored girl leaving that bundle was God telling him this baby was for Eula. It shoulda been okay 'cause James was supposed to be colored and not wanted by anybody.

"On his way home, he musta decided I'd make a good kid for them, too."

Daddy was frowning. I wasn't sure he was believing me, so I added that it turned out Wallace was plum crazy, and once he got home and Eula made him see how much trouble they was in for taking white children, he went crazier yet with being scared.

"First we was locked up," I said. "Eula tried to take us back to Cayuga Springs, but Wallace was sure the white folks would come and murder them both and stopped her. He was big as a bear, and mean as a snake. Eula was afraid of him before I ever got there, but she tried to help me anyway—and got hurt while goin' about it, too."

In my mind, I made like I was telling a story that happened to somebody else; otherwise, when I come to the next part, I'd'a been too shook up to talk at all. It was better if Daddy didn't know how scared I'd been.

I told Daddy about me escaping in the night with baby James, and his eyes got so wide I thought they'd pop right out. I could tell he wanted to talk, but he kept his promise—until I told the part about Wallace coming after us and trying to drown me in the swamp.

His fist hit the table and he said, "JesusfuckingChrist!" so loud that everybody in the diner looked at us.

I started to shake a little and forgot that I was telling about somebody else. Then I looked over at Eula, sitting there, stiff and tall, with her eyes white and her hands working in her lap. I pushed feelings of not being able to breathe and the picture of Wallace through the water out of my mind. I couldn't let Daddy stop me here. "You promised," I said.

He got up and walked outside. I saw him through the window, pacing back and forth, running his hands through his hair and then wrapping them behind his neck and looking up at the sky. My stomach hurt like it was being poked with knives. I couldn't go make Daddy feel better 'cause I had to get my own self back to where it wasn't me in the story.

Finally, Daddy come back in and sat back down. He took a deep breath closed his eyes and breathed out long. Then he nodded for me to go on.

"Well, I reckon it's obvious he didn't get me killed." It helped to talk sassy. "He stopped and cried around that he couldn't do it, and then took me back and locked me in that room again. But Eula was worried still, so she stayed in there with me. Later, when Wallace got all juiced up—the moonshine—he come in and tried to finish me off. But Eula killed him with a skillet." I was quick to add, "She didn't mean to kill him. She just wanted to stop him from hurtin' me and he ended up dead after one whack."

"Oh my God." Daddy looked kinda sick and covered his face. I was afraid he was gonna throw up right there. I should feel sick, too. But truth be told, I got to feeling better the more I got out. Every word said Wallace couldn't hurt us anymore.

I switched sides in the booth and put my arm around Daddy. "It's okay. Eula saved my life, that's why we gotta help her."

"Why didn't you come back—"

"I ain't done."

He nodded, but still looked peaked.

"Eula, she wanted to go to the law right then and tell them she'd done Wallace in. But I made her take me to Nashville first, 'cause that's where I was headed and it was Wallace's fault I didn't get there. Eula's very interested in doing the right thing. We put Wallace in the spring-house to keep him cool. I just wanted to get away and change her mind about goin' to the law about it."

"Wha—"

"Daddy!"

He held up a hand and nodded again.

"Eula and me and James started out in her rickety truck. We was gonna make sure James got back to his family. . . . I was thinking Mom—Lulu'd help with that. And Eula was gonna turn herself in to the police when we got there, but I was still hopin' to convince her not to. Lulu was supposed to help with that, too."

I told him about how the truck broke down and I got sick and how Miss Cyrena took us in and all the rest of what got us to Lulu's apartment.

When I got done, he just sat there.

I went back to my side of the booth. "You can talk now."

Daddy was shaking his head, looking at his cold bacon and eggs. "Honest to God, I don't know where to start."

28

Daddy paid for three breakfasts that didn't get eaten. Mamie would have had a hissy fit seeing all that food go to waste. But I reckon my story sucked away Daddy's appetite just like it did mine. And he really must not have known where to start, 'cause he hadn't said a word after saying that. He'd just sat there for a minute, then picked up the bill from the table, slid out of the booth, and headed to the cash register. I had to pee so bad by then I had to run straight to the bathroom, which for some reason was at the front of this diner, not the back near Eula where it should have been and I could have let her know what I'd told Daddy.

I went as fast as I could, not even stopping to wash my hands. I needed to talk to Eula outside of Daddy's hearing. But when I come out, they was both already gone. I pulled the front door open. A lick of panic went over me when I saw Eula was already in the backseat and Daddy was behind the wheel. They were talking!

I run and jerked the car door open.

Daddy was saying, ". . . me about your husband and—what you had to do."

I looked at Eula and thought she'd stopped breathing for a minute.

"Sorry to keep you waitin'," I said, real cheerful. "Don't you need to use the restroom, Daddy?" I tried to tell Eula with my eyes that things was okay. But she kept looking at her lap.

He gave me a wrinkled-forehead look—which he didn't do often, so I had to respect it or else. "Not a question for you to be askin'. And you're interrupting."

Daddy said to Eula, "There's no way to repay you, but I'll do everything possible to see you're treated fairly by the police. I've got a friend who's a county deputy . . ." He stopped, like something just come to him. "Where's your house?"

She told him and he looked some relieved.

"Good. Maybe I can get Don to help us out then."

"I'm ready to take what's comin' to me, sir." She kept her eyes low and not looking direct at Daddy. "And I thank you for your kindness."

I wanted to tell her that she didn't need to be scared of him like she was most white men, but the scarder she was, the less likely she was to go spillin' the beans.

When Daddy turned back around and started the car, I pisst-whispered at her. When she looked up. I made like I was lockin' my lips together with a key. The look in her eyes made my stomach flip over. I wanted to jump over the seat and put my hands over her mouth.

"How much longer till we're home?" I asked, trying to get Daddy distracted.

"A few hours. Now shush. I'm tryin' to talk to Eula." He gave me a look and I closed my trap. I needed Daddy happy, not all mad at me. He pulled us back on the road, then looked at Eula in the rearview mirror. "You only did it to save her—like self-defense. The law should be on your side."

"Baby James might be harder to explain." Eula's voice was quiet, but not so quiet that Daddy didn't hear.

"I done told Daddy all about Wallace takin' him 'cause he thought you needed a baby." I made my eyes big and raised my eyebrows so she'd get the message. "And that Wallace was crazy."

Daddy looked over at me. "Starla, I'm pretty sure that part of your story was . . . modified."

My heart started to beat fast. I should have remembered Daddy always knew—even when I got Mamie to believe my truth stretchers. He didn't always say, but he always knew.

"It's what happened!" I said, knowing it was a waste of breath. "And Wallace was crazy!"

"A man like that wouldn't care if Eula had a baby or not, but if it helps Eula, that's our story."

My body got like Jell-O. (Thank you, baby Jesus.)

"I took him," Eula said, and my heart fell to my toes. "I did."

Before Daddy could say anything, I said, "But he was left on the church steps by a colored girl like I said—the white Methodist church. Eula thought it'd be bad for a colored baby to be left there, so she took him. And it was Thursday; Wednesday prayer meeting was over and it was a long way till Sunday. What if nobody found him? And she didn't know he was white until after she got out of town . . . he was all wrapped up. Please, Daddy! I know some awful things get done to colored folks. I can't let that happen to Eula. If you won't say Wallace done it, tell them I took him from the church! That'll be okay. I'm a kid—and white. I'm goin' to reform school anyhow." Somehow I'd started crying.

"Starla, Starla. Relax. We'll figure out somethin'." He patted my leg. "Nobody's reported a missing baby. Whoever sent him to that church doesn't want to get found out. And you're not going to reform school."

"I'm not?" I sniffled.

"Of course not."

"But Mrs. Sellers—"

"Has been worried sick since you ran off. Both her and Jimmy spent time with the search parties."

"Search parties?"

"The whole town's been lookin' for you, afraid you'd gone off somewhere and got hurt or lost."

"The whole town?"

He nodded.

I frowned. "Mamie is gonna be so mad."

"Might as well get ready for it." After a second he said, "How did you think you were gonna travel near six hundred miles on foot in the first place?"

Now that just made me sound stupid. "I didn't know it was that far."

I decided Daddy had some questions to answer himself. "How come you never told me you and Lulu was divorced?"

He sighed real long. "You were too young at first. Then"—he shrugged—"it just didn't seem to matter. Lucinda was gone and was gonna stay gone."

"Well, it mattered to me!" My ears caught fire. "All this time I been thinkin' good things about her, wishin' we was all together again. Thinkin' she loved me—" A breath jerked inside me, like I was gonna get a sob going. I gritted my teeth to keep it in. "She's horrible."

Daddy ran a hand through his hair. "She sent you birthday cards to show she loved you."

"Big deal. And she didn't when I turned six." Now that I'd seen Lulu, I knew that one didn't get lost in the mail.

"Baby, I didn't know—that you thought that way about her, I mean. You were so little when she left, I didn't think you remembered her hardly at all." His lips bunched and he shook his head. "I thought it was better you didn't know about her . . . how she is. I didn't want her to hurt you . . . but she has anyway."

Eula coughed a fake cough.

Daddy's eyes went to the rearview mirror. I don't know what kind of face Eula made; I was too mad and sorry to look. But right away Daddy said, "Your momma does love you, Starla. As much as she can love anybody. She's not like the rest of us inside. She can't show you like she should."

I didn't say anything. Couldn't say anything without blubberin'. Someday I might cry about Lulu again, but not for a long time. I had to hold on to the mad so the sad didn't drown me.

"How did you even find her?" Daddy said it, but it was more like to himself than to me. The light glittered in his eyes, like he had some tears wanting out. "I'm sorry, baby. I'm not very good at this. I was wrong not to tell you."

Hold on to the mad.

I crossed my arms. "Well, it sure woulda saved a whole lot of trouble." Without a place to go, I might never have run away for real at all. Eula'd never have picked me up. She and James could have stayed together out there in the woods—I stopped right there. Dreamin' about Eula and James being happy living out there with Wallace the Bear was as crazy as me thinking Lulu was famous and really wanted me and Daddy to live with her.

Truth be told, me and Eula needed each other—we had a gift together. If I hadn't run off, we'd never have found it.

I wouldn't give up on her—ever.

After a little while, I spent some time telling Daddy how hard Eula worked to get the money so she could take me to Nashville. I told him she was the best momma ever to me and James, even though she wasn't our momma at all and could have just left us when things got bad. Then I spent some time reminding him about how she'd saved me at least three times—first from dyin' of thirst on the Fourth of July, second from Wallace drownin' me in the swamp, and third time with the skillet. "Oh, and then when she got me well at Miss Cyrena's. I was pretty sick, so I reckon I could have died then, too."

Daddy had his elbow on the car door and was rubbing his forehead. He was starting to look sick again. "I get it, Starla. I already said I'd help her."

"But what if the police don't listen to you? What then?"

"We're just gonna have to take things one at a time. It'll work out."

I leaned closer and whispered, so Eula wouldn't hear over the wind coming through the wing vents and partway-open windows, "How do you know?"

"I don't. We just have to hope for the best."

That worried me. I'd been *sure,* not just hoping, that Momma would help Eula. But Daddy was sounding a little perturbed so I shut up. I leaned against the window, liking the way it vibrated against my head; then I started to change my plan.

I musta fallen asleep, 'cause I woke up when the car started to slow down. I was mad at myself; I didn't want Daddy and Eula talking without me. Then I saw where we were and about had a kitten.

"What are you doin'?" Daddy looked startled and I realized I'd yelled it.

"I figured we'd take a restroom break and get lunch—"

"No! Keep goin'." I never wanted to see Riedell's Diner again.

"But—"

"I ain't hungry. Go." I looked on down the road, feeling like Riedell's was a wild animal I was afraid to look square in the eye.

"Starla, what's going on?"

"That place is horrible. And"—I slid over to whisper—"they don't serve colored people."

He got back on the gas and we went on by. I slumped back in the seat. "Thank you."

Daddy kept his eyes on the road and nodded. "We'll find someplace else."

"Good. I'm hungry."

Daddy laughed and looked at me. "You are somethin' else, you know that?"

I just smiled back.

Daddy found us another place not far down the road. I looked for signs in the window that said WHITE TRADE ONLY or NO COLORED SERVICE, but didn't see any. It made me wonder why the bus stopped at Riedell's when maybe all the passengers could eat here.

"I'll run in and make sure this place is good," Daddy said. "Be right back."

Eula was changing James's diaper. "There now, little man, you all fresh."

I knew she wasn't gonna like my new plan.

"Eula, you gotta go. Now."

She frowned. "What?"

"I'll take care of James. You get out of the car and hide somewhere until we're gone. I'll tell Daddy you got in a car with some colored folks and run off."

"I do no such thing!"

"You have to. Then get to Miss Cyrena's. You'll be safe there."

"Safe from what?" Her mouth was all puckered.

"From the law." I got on my knees and leaned over the seat and flipped the back-door latch. "If they don't listen to me and Daddy, things could be bad."

"You not thinkin' straight. If them Jenkins boys find me, it for sure be bad." She pulled her door closed again. "I done made up my mind from the start. I take what comes, but I ain't spendin' my days hidin' like a river rat. I gotta tell what I done. If the law says I need punishment, that the way it'll be."

I unlatched the door again. "But you don't deserve to be punished! Get outta here."

She pulled the door closed and pushed the lock down. "Stop this foolishness. You make me get out here, I go straight to the law right now."

"You don't understand—"

"I do. I understand real clear. A body can't run from what they done. They carry it with them inside. It fester and spread like poison if it's buried. It gotta be out in the air where it can heal." She opened her palms to the sky. "Someday you understand that, too." She locked her eyes on mine. "I hope someday real soon." The look she gave me threw water on the hot coals burnin' inside me.

She's ashamed of me. That thought coming clear sucked the air from my lungs. I wanted to lay down in the front seat and hide my face.

Daddy come back and opened my car door. "Okay. Let's go in."

I spun around.

"Why are you cryin'?" he asked.

I got out and walked past him. "I ain't." I didn't stop until I was inside the restroom with the door locked behind me.

The roads started to get some familiar and I got to itchin' all over. Then I saw the water tower and my stomach tied itself in a knot. The sun was low, making the tank look orange instead of silver, and the paint that said CAYUGA SPRINGS look black and not blue, but we was home. I wanted to tell Daddy to stop the car and wait until dark before we drove into town. To let me out so I could run off. My ears got hot when I realized *I* was the one I wanted to keep safe from punishment. I was shameful and selfish, just like Eula thought.

"Does everybody know?" I asked.

"Know what?" Daddy looked at me. "That we found you?"

That wasn't what I meant. I wanted to know if everybody knew I run off to my momma and she didn't want me, but I couldn't make myself say it out loud. I nodded.

"Of course. Otherwise they'd have kept worrying and looking. We told Sheriff Reese and he spread the word."

"Oh."

"Why do you sound so disappointed?"

Right then we turned a corner and passed Patti Lynn's house. I sat up straight, hoping to see her outside, but the sidewalk and porch and driveway was all empty. A big yellow bow was on one of the porch posts. "What's that?"

Daddy smiled. "It's a sign that someone is waiting for you to come home."

"For me?"

"Yep. Mamie said it's something folks did back in the War; girls wore yellow ribbons for their soldiers. There was a song or a movie or something about it."

"Did Mamie wear one for Granddad?" He didn't come home from the War, so I wondered if she did, how she decided when to stop.

"I reckon she did, since she was the one who told me about it."

I turned in my seat to stare at the ribbon that said Patti Lynn missed me. It made me feel really good and more ashamed at the same time.

We drove the rest of the way home, going the same way Patti Lynn and I rode our bikes to each other's house. I wished Daddy could have just let me off at Patti Lynn's, where I was missed.

Our house didn't have a big, fancy front porch like Patti Lynn's. It had a cracked-up set of concrete steps without anything to keep the rain off you when you rang the doorbell. Out in the front yard was a sweet-gum tree. Tied around it was a yellow bow. This one wasn't big and puffy like Patti Lynn's, more like a stringy afterthought. But it surprised me that it was there at all. Then I remembered Daddy had been home from the Gulf for two weeks.

Knowing he missed me and didn't just come get me 'cause Lulu was throwin' me out and he didn't have a choice made me feel some better. I pointed at it. "You missed me, too."

"I did. But I wasn't the one who tied that ribbon there."

"Patti Lynn?"

He shook his head like I was being silly. "Your mamie put it there."

You coulda knocked me over with a feather. "She did?"

"Why do you sound so surprised?"

"Mamie hates me."

Daddy looked like he wanted to jump out of the car; he never liked arguing with me about Mamie. But he stuck. "No, she doesn't. She loves you."

"She wishes I wasn't never born, so I'd say she hates me all right."

His face got dark red under his tan. "Did she say that?"

Daddy sounded so mad, I almost lied. But Eula had said a person had to own up to what they done. "She did. Once . . . or twice, I don't 'member. She was mad."

Daddy was breathing real loud. It went on so long, I got worried. "Daddy?"

"She didn't mean it. She says a lot of things she doesn't mean when she's mad." Then he looked at me. "You get your stubborn streak from her, you know. Sometimes watchin' you two is like watchin' two mules standin' eye to eye in a road plenty wide for you to pass."

"I ain't like her. Not one little bit."

"Okay. Think what you want."

I crossed my arms. "I will." Then I caught myself with my lips all pinched up like Mamie's when she was exaserbated with me, so I smoothed 'em back out, careful not to look over at Daddy.

I wished I could go live with Daddy on the oil rig and Mamie could sit here and eat all of her special bridge-club snacks without me. I wouldn't have to go to school then either. I could maybe earn my keep by making beds or doing dishes. I was spinnin' such a good picture in my head, I was a little startled when Daddy said, "Mamie does love you. If she didn't, she wouldn't care how you behaved as long as you were out of her hair. She was a wreck while you were gone—she couldn't eat or sleep. She's just so afraid . . ." Then he stopped and scrubbed his hand over his face.

"Afraid of what?" I knew exactly what she was afraid of, she'd told me a hundred times. But I didn't know if Daddy knew.

Then I could see. He knew. He just didn't want to say it. Probably 'cause he was afraid of the same thing. After meetin' Lulu, I was some scared myself.

"Mamie just wants you to grow up to be a good person," he finally said. "To learn to live right, get along with people, and be happy."

"Ha!" I slapped my knee. "That's a good one. She's only worried about what people will think."

"There's more to it than that, Starla. Even if it seems like she's just trying to make your life miserable, she does want you to be happy. Part of being happy in life is accepting the rules. I've asked a lot of her . . . I didn't realize . . ."

"You asked a lot of me, too!" My ears was getting hot again. "I never wanted to live with Mamie. Nobody ever asks me what I want!"

All the sudden my door opened up. Mamie pulled me out onto the grass between the sidewalk and street. She hugged me tight. I could hear her breathing was ragged. Just when I started to think things was gonna be all right, she grabbed my shoulders, her fingers diggin' in, in that too familiar way. She got right so we was nose to nose and I knew what was coming. But it come so fast, I didn't get braced. She shook me so hard my teeth clacked together.

My head spun and my tongue bled copper in my mouth.

Such commotion broke out that I had a hard time keeping up with what was happening. Daddy yanked me away from Mamie at the same time Eula jumped out of the backseat. Baby James didn't like being left so he started caterwaulin'. Mamie first was crying to Daddy that she was sorry, then started shoutin' and swattin' at Eula to get away from her. Ernestine come running from the LeCounts like she expected a fire.

"Mother! That's enough," Daddy yelled. "Enough!"

"She's attackin' me!" She took another swat at Eula.

Eula wasn't doing nothin' but standing in between Mamie and me. She wasn't even looking at Mamie. If Mamie'd hold still for half a second, she might figure that out.

"She is not," Daddy said. "Calm yourself down."

Ernestine was standing off to the side, wringing her apron.

I spit the blood out on the ground. I was some mad at myself. I hadn't been caught that unprepared for a long time.

Daddy put his hand under my chin. "Let's see."

I stuck my tongue out. It was still numb and hadn't started hurting yet.

"Go inside and get some ice on that." He looked at Eula. "You and the baby go with her."

"That colored—"

"Stop! Just stop, Mother." As I climbed the steps, I heard him tell Ernestine thank-you and to go on home. Then he said to Mamie, "We need to talk."

29

The house was creepy quiet, the way it always was when Mamie was brewin' a storm. Usually I just went up to my room and stayed out of her way, but I didn't have to. Mamie had gone to her room—off the living room where it wasn't so danged hot—and slammed the door. I don't know what Daddy had said to her after I'd come inside, but when she'd come in, her face was red and her lips pinched tight. She didn't even look at me or Eula when she'd walked into the kitchen to snatch up her cigarettes and matches.

By the time Daddy come in, it was getting dark enough outside that Eula that had turned on the kitchen light. He went straight to the cabinet and pulled out three bowls and a box of Frosted Flakes—they was Daddy's favorite, too. "This'll get us by." He got the milk bottle out of the refrigerator. "I want you to eat and go to bed," he said to me.

"I ain't goin' to bed. Eula needs me when the sheriff comes."

"I think we've all had enough today. Tomorrow'll be soon enough for the sheriff." He looked to Eula. "You need anything special for the baby?"

"Need to mix up more formula is all."

"What do you need?" he asked.

I said, "Canned milk, water, and Karo syrup." My tongue was numb from the ice and *syrup* was *thyrup*. "We used reg'lar milk at Eula's house, but she says canned is better."

Daddy looked at me kinda surprised.

"I learned a lot while I was gone."

"I reckon you did." He opened the cabinet and shuffled some things around. He pulled out a can of Pet evaporated milk and held it up. "This?"

I beat Eula to telling him it was. Before I met baby James, I just thought canned milk was used in Mamie's coffee and fancy desserts—the ones only bridge club got.

"There's only one can." He looked a little worried. "Will that be enough for tonight?"

"He's just born and only takes a little dab at a time, Daddy." I laughed at his silliness. Eula had stopped even trying to beat me at an answer.

He looked at me like he did sometimes when he'd been gone for a long time and I'd grown a lot. Then he pulled out the Karo bottle from the cabinet and set it on the counter next to the milk.

I started to get up and mix it, but Daddy told me to sit down and eat, then I was supposed to take a bath and go to bed.

"I had a bath last night."

He frowned at me.

"Okay. Okay." Then I asked, "Where's Eula sleepin'?"

"She and the baby can have my room. I'll sleep on the couch."

"Mamie won't like it," I said, my stomach getting tight.

When he looked at me, he had a funny expression on his face, like he didn't really care what Mamie thought. I considered that for a minute. Daddy never did stuff to make Mamie mad. Truth be told, Mamie always thought whatever Daddy did was just fine and dandy, so maybe it was Mamie who was actin' strange. Everything was upside down.

I knew there was no way to not take a bath and get away with it—I'd tried plenty of times. So I hurried as fast as I could, not even waiting for hot water, or doing more soapin' than rubbing my chest with the bar of Lux so I could pass the sniff test. After I put on my pj's, I went to the vent that let the heat from the kitchen into the upstairs hall. It was closed in the summer, but the lever to open it was on my side. I moved it real slow and careful. I could see Daddy sitting at the table.

He was holding James while Eula was at the counter mixing formula. James looked really little in Daddy's arms, hardly big enough to be a baby at all. Daddy was looking at him. "Wish I could start over with Starla. I did everything wrong. All of it."

Eula stopped stirring and turned around. She didn't say anything, just waited.

He looked at Eula. "How bad was it for her . . . with Lucinda?"

I saw Eula's shoulders move, like she'd breathed a big breath. "Bad." She waited for a second, then said, "She broke that child's heart."

I laid my cheek against the wood floor. I didn't want to hear about Lulu or Nashville ever again. Some tears got loose. I let them roll off my cheeks and nose, making a wet place on the floor.

I was just thinking about getting up and going to my room before I had to sniffle when Daddy said, "How can I fix this?" I'd never heard him sound so small.

Eula stood there, quiet as a tree stump.

Daddy looked at her.

"It ain't my place to speak out," Eula said, and she turned to the counter again.

"Well, I sure as hell can't ask my mother! I had no idea she was so . . . rough. She was never that way with me." Daddy swiped his free hand across his face. "Starla respects you, your kindness. You must be doing something right. Help me. Please."

For a long while Eula just stood there stirring. Then she sighed loud enough I could hear clear up where I was.

I held my breath, wondering what she'd say . . . if she say anything.

Finally she said, "A child only want one thing; her momma and daddy's love. It don't take more'n that."

"I do love her!"

"Mebbe that so. But I ain't sure she knows it, not down in her bones where it count. Her momma, and what I see of her granny—" Eula cut off sharp, like she was afraid she'd said too much. After spending so much time with her, learning about her life, I understood why. But Daddy wasn't like most. He wouldn't get mad at her for answering his question.

His head bowed and he shook it slow. "I know . . . I know. I shoulda known before now."

Eula stood like she was getting some starch. "You know now. The question is, what you gonna do about it?"

I'd never seen my daddy cry, but I think maybe that's what he was doing right then.

I woke up in the middle of the night. I was hot and thirsty and my insides was busier than usual. I went to the bathroom and got a drink of water. On the way back to my room, I flipped open the register in the floor to check and see if Eula was down there feeding James. The kitchen was dark. I stopped at the door to Daddy's room. It was quiet. James was letting Eula sleep. I put my hand on the doorknob.

It wasn't right to wake her up. I shouldn't, I couldn't.

I'd just peek in, make sure she was all right. I opened the door slow and quiet, just enough for me to get my head around the edge. The moon come silver and bright through the window. I saw one of the drawers from Daddy's dresser was on the floor next to the bed. I reckoned James was inside. Eula was under the sheet, still and quiet. I was some disappointed. Temptation tickled me and I almost made a little noise to see if she roused up. I don't know why I was feeling the need to hear her voice. It was shameful selfish of me. Tomorrow was gonna be an awful day with the sheriff coming, and she needed sleep.

I pulled the door closed.

"Starla?" she whispered. "That you, child?"

I pushed the door back open. "Yeah."

"Can't sleep?"

"Uh-uh."

She patted the mattress. "Come on over here. Watch now, James on the floor."

"I see him." I tiptoed to the bed and laid down next to her. My insides felt less jittery right away.

Eula petted my hair. Each stroke of her hand smoothed out more jitters.

"What's botherin' you?" she asked.

"Everything."

"Can't be everything. You with your daddy. That good. You gonna see you friend Patti Lynn real soon. That good, too."

"Yeah."

"So it's somethin' else."

I reckoned it was. I hadn't been able to say exactly what had my insides so worked up, but all of the sudden it was clear as day. And Eula was the only person I wanted to talk to about it. "I been wonderin' . . . what if . . . what if Mamie's right?"

Eula made a sound like she didn't think Mamie could be right about anything. But she said, real nice, "'Bout what?" I reckon she'd had a lot of practice saying nice things when they wasn't what she was thinking at all.

"'Bout me turnin' into Lulu." There, it was out. My heart felt a little lighter, but still bounced around like a moth in my chest.

"You ain't like her." Eula sounded like she meant it—not shy or oversweet like she was just being nice.

"But her hair was colored. It's really red, like mine. And she run off . . . so did I. And Mamie said Lulu always leaped before she looked, just like me."

"You just a child and got some growin' up to do is all. I see you learnin' every day 'bout how to think things through. You ain't like your momma on the inside, not one little bit. Never will be. People is born one way or t'other. Life change a body some, but their nature stay the same. They might can hide for a time, but they don't change in their soul where it count. You kind and generous and protect the people you love. I bet your momma was never any of those."

I thought for a minute. "But you said Wallace wasn't always how I saw him. You said he changed."

She breathed deep and I felt her shift a little. "I said it. I did. But I was wrong. It's like Miss Cyrena say, I just didn't see him clear. I thought the fights he got into before we was married was 'cause he was protectin' me. I thought he wanted to know where I was ev'ry minute and who I was talkin' to was 'cause of love. I'd never had nobody fight to keep me safe, so I believed it. Law, I was wrong about a lot of things. I see only what I wanted to in that man. Maybe I just wanted to get away from Pap and Charles so bad. Maybe that what clouded my eyes. But since you come, since my time with Miss Cyrena, I'm thinkin' more clear every day. I remember it all, even what I don't want to."

After being with Wallace just two days, I didn't know how anybody couldn't see him clear.

Eula went on, her voice soft and slow, smoothing the uneasy prickles on my insides more and more. "The memories you got of your momma prob'ly a lot the same. You was just a baby. You see other mommas and think that's how yours was, too."

I thought about Lulu, the real Lulu, not the one I thought I was gonna find. I thought about when we was standing in front of Tootsies, when that tightness in her mouth hit me as familiar, and not good familiar. Could Eula be right? Had I made up all of the good things in my head? Had Momma always been made of sharp spikes and bristles?

How had Daddy ever loved her?

We got quiet and I kept pokin' around in my soul to make sure I knew what was in there.

Baby James started making those little noises he always made before he woke up. I knew me and Eula only had a minute.

"Who do you think his momma is?" I wondered if she was a spiky, bristly woman like Lulu. If she was, baby James was sure better off with us.

Eula sighed. "Reckon we might never know. Or we could know tomorrow."

"What will happen to him if they can't find out who she is?" I didn't want him to be an orphan like the boy in the book Mrs. Jacobi read us last year, Huck Finn. After the past few weeks, I knew for sure a kid can't just float down a river and have adventures that all turn out good.

"Then they find some new parents for him. Folks who really want a baby. A place where he'll be treated special."

"You sure?"

"It's what we gotta believe, child. What we gotta believe."

Before I fell asleep next to Eula, I spent some time praying to baby Jesus to please give James a nice family that would take real good care of him, especially if he had to go back to the woman who throwed him away.

30

Daddy made me and Eula stay upstairs while he talked to the sheriff. I'd been trying to listen at the hall register—even after Eula scolded me for eavesdropping. But the men was in the living room and I couldn't make anything out. When I didn't hear Mamie's voice at all, I went and looked out the window. Her station wagon was gone. I hoped she'd never come back.

Me and Eula was too nervous to talk, so we'd just been sitting quiet, worry chewin' our insides. When Daddy finally called us down, we looked at each other. She nodded at me and then picked up James. I took her hand and we left Daddy's bedroom. We walked slow, acting like we was marchin' to our death—which is what Mamie said when I was being poky about something I didn't want to do. When we got to the bottom of the stairs, Daddy was there. He smiled at Eula. I couldn't figure out if the smile said things was okay, or that he was sorry they wasn't. The four of us went into the living room.

Sheriff Reese picked his hat off his knee, stood up, and hitched his gun belt.

I stopped cold.

Daddy put his hand on my shoulder and nudged me forward. "It's okay."

The sheriff nodded to Eula, then waved his hand to tell us to sit on the couch.

He started off by looking down at me with squinty eyes. "You do know how much trouble you caused by running off, don't you? I had every deputy doing overtime. The state police got involved. Not to mention the hours and hours the townsfolk dedicated to lookin' for you. Then there's your grandma and daddy's worry. Your actions affected a lot of people."

Butterflies filled my stomach. My mouth and throat was so dry I couldn't hardly make a sound. "I didn't think—"

"I can't hear you. Speak up, now."

I cleared my throat. "I . . . I didn't think anybody would care I was gone."

Daddy sucked in air like he'd been hit in the stomach. "Starla . . ."

"Not you, Daddy. I was gonna get to Momma and then she'd call you and you could come to Nashville. We'd . . ." I stopped talking. I sounded like a stupid little kid.

Sheriff Reese crossed his arms. "Now you know. This is a small town. What happens here spreads wide ripples."

"Yes, sir."

"You were very, very lucky," he said. "Things could have turned out much differently. Do you understand what I mean?"

When I closed my eyes, my breath disappeared and I felt Wallace holding me underwater. My eyes snapped open and I gasped a breath. "I do, sir. I most surely do." Then I put in, "I was lucky to have Eula protectin' me."

He stared down at me for a long while, making me real uncomfortable. Then he said, "And do you think she's lucky to have you?"

I started to say yes, me and Eula had a gift together. But all the sudden it didn't seem like a fair trade for having to kill her husband with a skillet—no matter how bad a man he was—and travel to Nashville in a broke-down truck, and all the troubles along the way. I shook my head and stayed quiet.

"Mrs. Littleton," he said, looking at Eula.

I sat there, not hearing anything for a second. I couldn't believe that after all we'd been through, I didn't know Eula's last name. Littleton. Eula Littleton.

When my hearing turned back on, Sheriff Reese was explaining that he'd already sent a deputy, Daddy's friend Don, and the coroner—from listening close I figured that was somebody who picks up the dead people—out to Eula's place, and the sheriff should be hearing from him shortly. I didn't know what the sheriff needed to hear from Deputy Don about; we all knowed Wallace was dead. Then I wondered how fresh the springhouse had kept him, but didn't think I'd be asking.

Eula's throat worked hard to swallow. Her eyes stayed on the floor in front of her feet.

"Mrs. Littleton, I know this is hard, but I need to you tell me exactly what happened."

Eula's nervousness buzzed against my skin. I said, "He was tryin' to kill me! She had to hit him with a skillet to get him to stop."

It was hard to tell what the sheriff was thinking; his eyes seemed a little sorry for me, but his mouth was perturbed. "I have to hear it from Mrs. Littleton. Maybe you'd like to go upstairs and wait." It wasn't a question.

I scooted toward Eula till our hips and legs was touching. "I'm fine here, sir."

The sheriff looked at Daddy.

"It happened to *me*," I said. "It ain't like I don't know about it already." It felt good to be able to fight for something after feeling so low about being a bother.

Daddy said, "She can stay." He sat down next to me. We was three birds on a wire now. I didn't want the sheriff to shoot Eula off of it.

She tucked baby James next to her, snug between her leg and the arm of the couch. Then she wiped her hands on her skirt. I reached over and took one. I saw the sheriff look at our hands with a sour face. It made me want to take her other hand, too.

Eula let out a breath and told the whole story, right from the pie delivering that put her where she saw James dropped at that church.

I jumped up and stood in front of the sheriff, my hands in fists. "But Wallace took him!" I looked at the sheriff. "He did!"

Eula reached out and took one of my fists and pried it open until she could hold it. "We got to tell the truth—all of it. How a body to tell what comes out your mouth true or not if you don't always speak true?"

"But—" My throat closed up.

She pulled me next to her on the couch and told the rest of the story, just like it happened. When she got done, my face was wet and so was hers.

The sheriff looked at me then. "You agree? This how it happened?"

"Yes, sir. If she hadn't saved me—"

The sheriff said, "I understand."

"She was only tryin' to help both me and James."

"All right. That'll do." He didn't say it mean, but he meant business.

I pinched my lips together.

He asked Eula about the exact time she saw the baby—he never called him James—being left at the church and to describe the young Negro who'd left him. When she told that the girl had a little limp on the left side, my eyes near popped outta my head.

"That's Gracie!" I said, leapin' before I looked again.

"Gracie?" the sheriff asked.

I rolled my lips in. If Gracie left James at the church, she'd know who his momma was. I didn't want to get her in trouble. And I wasn't sure I wanted James to go back to his momma either.

"Starla," Daddy said, "you need to tell us."

I closed my eyes. My ears was ringin' and I felt kinda dizzy.

"Starla."

I opened my eyes. I could see Eula was scared, too—not for Gracie but for James. She said, "Secrets ain't gonna help James."

"She's Bess's girl. Bess works for Patti Lynn's family. Sometimes Gracie comes to work with Bess. And sometimes she works sweepin' porches for other folks."

"What other folks?" the sheriff asked, getting a little notebook out of his shirt pocket.

I shrugged. "Dunno."

The sheriff put away the notebook without writing in it and stood up.

I jumped up and put myself between him and Eula. "You can't arrest her!"

"You're a little spitfire, aren't you?" Then he looked at Daddy. "You got yourself a handful here."

"Starla," Daddy said, "the sheriff's just doing his job."

I kept staring Sheriff Reese right in the eye. My breath was coming fast, like I'd been running.

Daddy asked, "Can Eula stay here? I'll take responsibility."

Sheriff Reese put his hands on his hips and pursed his lips. "Well, she came back here on her own, told the truth—even though your girl didn't want her to. I suppose I can trust her not to run off before we get things sorted out."

I sat back down on the couch next to Eula, feeling like the muscles had gone out of my legs. Daddy walked with the sheriff to the front door. When he followed him outside, I got curious. Eula tried to stop me, but I sneaked up to the side of the front door and listened through the screen.

The sheriff was talking. ". . . talk to that girl. I'll send someone around from Child Welfare to collect the baby."

They can't just take him!

"What good will it do to send him off to some institution for a few hours?" Daddy asked. "You're likely to find his mother yet today."

"Got rules. It's outta my hands. Besides, if we do find the mother, I doubt the court will let the baby go back to her right away. Might not be fit." He paused like he was thinking. "I won't be to my office to call Welfare until after I've talked to this Gracie. That'll give you some time to get the womenfolk prepared. It's the best I can do."

Daddy must have nodded. Then he asked about the possibility of murder charges being made against Eula. The words turned me inside out. I think my heart stopped beating while I waited for the sheriff's answer.

"Can't say. Lots of factors to consider. Coroner's report. Investigation of the scene. Defense of a white girl. If it was a colored man done the killin', folks'd be scared of being murdered in their beds and I'd have trouble even getting an investigation done before people'd be pushing for maximum punishment of the law . . . or worse."

This made my mood swing two ways at once. It made it sound like my being white was what made me worth saving. And what did he mean, or worse? What would people do that could be worse than getting Eula arrested? Before I knew it, the sheriff's feet was going down the steps. I hurried back and sat next to Eula.

Daddy came back and stood in front of us. He told us about Child Welfare and how James was gonna have to go stay with them until things with his mother got straightened out. He put a hand on Eula's shoulder. "They'll probably be here by late morning or early afternoon."

Eula looked particular sad, but she nodded and picked James up. "Best make sure he's clean and fed then."

When she climbed up the stairs, she moved slow, like she was tired, like the fight of keeping me and James safe was all she'd had and now it was gone.

I felt more helpless than when Wallace was tryin' to drown me.

31

They took James at one fifteen that afternoon. I felt even sadder than I thought I would, seeing the sheriff's deputy and the Welfare lady drive off with him. It had to be worse for Eula, her wanting a baby so bad and all. I wondered if watching him go made her think of her too-white baby and how Charles gave him to somebody else—I kept the dark ideas about what might have happened to him out of my head. He was a boy. A happy boy with a momma and daddy who loved him. Just like I hoped James would be. I'd asked the Welfare lady if me and Eula could come and visit him later, but she'd said she wasn't sure where he'd be and it was a bad idea anyway. I'd been surprised that she wasn't keeping him with her. I thought that was her job.

Me and Daddy and Eula stood on the front sidewalk and watched until the deputy turned the corner and we couldn't see the car anymore. I saw Ernestine peeking out from the LeCounts' living-room window, watching it all happen. Eula was the first one of us to go back inside. When Daddy and I followed her, she asked Daddy if she could use the kitchen, she felt like doing some baking. She'd noticed some bananas need usin'.

I was proud when Daddy told her she was a guest in our house and didn't have to ask permission, she could do as she pleased. The kitchen was hers anytime she wanted. That made me feel better for about two seconds. Until I watched Eula creep through the living room and disappear into the kitchen, her shoulders folded in and her head down.

And she didn't invite me to come help like ususal. I reckon that said as much about how bad she was feeling as anything.

I hoped the law didn't punish her; James going away was punishment enough.

I'd asked Daddy about a million times how long it was gonna be until Sheriff Reese called to tell us about finding James's mother and what he was gonna do about Eula. Daddy finally got so prickly about saying he didn't know that I'd finally stopped asking.

The house filled with wonderful smells. I wanted to go to the kitchen, but I think Eula just needed to be alone with her baking.

Daddy had to leave for a while, but wouldn't tell me where he was going. When I kept asking worried questions, he told me it had nothing to do with Eula, so I could relax. I didn't tell him that part of me wasn't worried about Eula, part of me was worried he'd leave and never come back. Course that was silly. I knew Daddy wouldn't just disappear like Momma had. Still, I couldn't help my nervousness.

I heard his car start and pull away. I laid down on the living-room floor in front of the TV. The only thing on was stupid lady stories like *The Guiding Light* and *Search for Tomorrow*, so I turned it back off. Then I just laid there and looked at the ceiling, feeling too low to get up and do anything.

The only good thing was Mamie stayed gone.

In a bit, Eula come through the living room and said real quiet that the banana pie was cooling for dinner and she was gonna go up and rest a bit. She was careful not to look at me. Her shoulders didn't seem any stronger . . . I worried that losing James might not be able to be fixed by making pies. There might be things so bad that all the whistling in the world couldn't make them go away.

I wanted to take her hand, to help her like she'd always helped me. But I remembered how she'd left me alone in the bathroom in Nashville when I'd wanted to be by myself. So I just laid there.

After a while, there was a knock at the front door. When I saw it was Patti Lynn, I got up lickety-split to let her inside and pull her close for a hug. When we stopped huggin', we just stood there, not sure what to do next. We wasn't really neither of us huggers.

"What'd you do to your hair?"

"I had to make it black to hide from the law. It's really a long story."

"And you're gonna tell me every bit of it!" Then she looked more serious. "I'm glad you're back." For a minute she looked like she didn't know what else to say. Then she poked me in the arm. "Can't believe you'd run off without me!"

"If I hadn't been runnin' from Mrs. Sellers, I'd have taken you and my bike, too. Maybe even a bologna sandwich."

She laughed. "Oh, you shoulda seen her!" Patti Lynn made some crazy faces and jumped around like she had ants in her pants, shaking her finger and pulling her hair.

Things felt more right after that.

We sat on the couch, Indian-style, facing each other while I told her everything that had happened. Everything except about how horrible Lulu turned out to be. I'd spent so much time spinnin' stories about her and how her and me and Daddy was gonna be happy again, I just couldn't admit it . . . not even to Patti Lynn. I let her think that I come home because I wanted to, that I didn't like Nashville after all.

"Oh, my gosh! You're just like Huckleberry Finn!"

I got serious then. When I'd told her about Wallace, I'd played like I wasn't scared, but that wasn't right. I couldn't let her think running off alone was something a girl should do—even though Patti Lynn had a perfect family and didn't have any reason to. "Truth be told, it wasn't nothin' like that story. I wish I'd never left. I almost got killed and brung a lot of trouble to Eula, too." It made my chest hurt to admit it, but the sheriff was right.

"You love her like we do Bess?"

I smiled. "More." Then I got sober. "But I don't know if we'll be able to keep her with us. The sheriff is still considerin'."

"She saved you." Patti Lynn waved her hand like she was sure. "He'll let her be."

"I hope so." After what I'd seen lately, I knew better than to pretend in happy endings like they had in stories.

Patti Lynn spent some time telling me about the search parties. Then she went out and got a stack of newspapers from her bike; her new, purple Sting-Ray had a white basket with flowers on the handlebars. That made me think of Troy and his Sting-Ray . . . which wasn't purple but blue and didn't have a basket at all 'cause he was a boy. I wondered if he'd forgot about me yet.

When Patti Lynn showed me the newspapers, I couldn't believe almost all of them had my third-grade picture on the front. Every day there was an "Update on missing child, Starla Claudelle." As I went through them, I couldn't believe the things people thought might have happened to me: fell in a well, got ate by a gator, drowned in the river, climbed a tree and broke my neck, kidnapped by a crazy person who wanted to use me as a sacrifice in devil worship. After reading all that, I felt pretty lucky. Nobody even had a thought that I'd run off to my momma. In fact, the stories in the paper acted like I didn't even have one.

The other thing that knocked my socks off was how many people had nice stories to tell about me and said they were praying like crazy for the good Lord to keep me safe and bring me back home. Even Mrs. Sellers. There was a picture of her, too; she looked like she meant it.

One paper had a huge picture of Daddy and Mamie standing on the porch. Daddy looked scared. Mamie looked like she was bawling like a baby. I folded it quick, so I didn't have to look at it long, so I wouldn't have to think about Daddy saying Mamie couldn't even eat the whole time I'd been gone. She'd sure made herself scarce around here since I got back. So maybe it was just for show. I'd never been nothin' but trouble for Mamie.

All the sudden, I wanted to go out to my fort. But that was a place I didn't let nobody come, not even Patti Lynn.

"Wanna go for a bike ride?" Patti Lynn asked.

"Better not. Daddy and Mamie are gone. I'd get in trouble."

Patti Lynn laughed so hard she got tears in her eyes.

"What's so funny?"

"Since when are you worried 'bout gettin' in trouble?"

I started laughing, too. It did seem most ridiculous. Still, we settled for watching Popeye cartoons and playing checkers instead. I wished I had a Mouse Trap game like Patti Lynn instead of just this dippy checker game. But she didn't seem to care.

At the same time I heard Daddy come in the back door, the telephone rang. I hurried to answer it. Mamie never let me 'cause I wasn't polite enough. The way she wanted me to do it seemed silly. In the time I said, "Hello, Claudelle residence, Starla speaking," I coulda had a whole conversation done. I tried to remember to do it right, but every time I beat Mamie to the phone, I was so excited, I just got out "Hello."

It was Mrs. Todd. I figured she was calling for Patti Lynn to come home, but she asked to talk to Daddy. She sounded funny.

Daddy took the phone and nodded, saying "Yes," "Of course," and "I understand" a bunch of times. When he hung up, he clapped his hands together like he had good news. "Patti Lynn gets to sleep over tonight for you girls to catch up."

We was so happy we jumped up and down a little. We always had sleepovers at Patti Lynn's. Mamie needed her sleep. Mrs. Todd said that after five kids she could sleep through a bomb exploding.

Then I thought about Mrs. Todd's sounding so strange. "Is everything okay? None of the boys is in the emergency room?" Seemed like that happened about once a month.

"Everybody's fine."

Then I thought about the sheriff going to talk to Gracie. "Are Bess and Gracie in trouble?"

"Why would they be in trouble?" Patti Lynn asked. I hadn't told her the part about Gracie being the one to drop James at the church. And I didn't really know why I didn't.

"Everything's fine," Daddy said. "Now go wash up and we'll get some dinner going."

I took off running for the stairs, just in case Patti Lynn wanted to ask more about Bess and Gracie. Lucky, she was so excited about staying over, she forgot on the way up to the bathroom.

By the time me and Patti Lynn got back downstairs, Eula was in the kitchen with Daddy. She looked real sad while she emptied the baby bottle that was left in the refrigerator. She rinsed it over and over again. Then she set it in the sink and turned around.

"I'll just brown them pork chops, Mr. Claudelle, if'n that all right?"

"I'd appreciate it. I'm not much of a cook." Then Daddy set us girls to peeling potatoes. When Eula come over to inspect our work, she laughed, saying there wasn't much potato left when we got done with 'em, so we'd best peel a few more. The sound of her laughing made me have hope that she just needed to cook some more to get back to herself.

The three of us making dinner was almost as good as baking in Miss Cyrena's kitchen.

Then Mamie come home to ruin everything.

She stood in the doorway between the living room and the kitchen with her arms crossed and a lipstick-red frown on her face. Her pocketbook, white like her shoes, hung from one arm. "Who gave y'all permission to mess up my kitchen?"

Patti Lynn jumped—even though Mamie was always sweet as pie to Patti Lynn and her momma, Patti Lynn knew about the real Mamie. Eula spun around from the stove, meat fork in her hand.

"I did." Daddy was sitting at the table tucked in the corner by the door, looking at the newspaper.

Mamie's eyes stopped being all squinty and her frown went away. "Oh, Porter. I didn't see you there."

"I'd reckon not."

She set her purse on the table with a big sigh. "I'm just too exhausted to even think about makin' dinner." Like she couldn't see us standing right there doing it already. "I've been out calling all day, thankin' people for their kindness during our distressin' time."

"We're cookin' dinner, Mamie," I said, real cheerful. "You can go put your feet up." Which I figured to be her dearest wish in the world judgin' by her frequent mentioning she don't have time to do it "even for a second."

"I think I'll do that." Then she looked at Daddy. "Porter, we need to talk about findin' a place for that colored woman. Can't have the whole town knowin' she's sleepin' in our sheets."

Daddy turned the page in the newspaper. "She'll be gone tomorrow."

"Daddy!" I dropped my knife in the sink and stood in front of him with my wet hands clasped like I was praying. "No, Daddy. Pleeeease."

He smiled at me. "We'll all be gone tomorrow, Starla. I got us a place of our own today."

I was jumpin' up and down and squealin', but I could still hear Mamie start sputterin', "You're not serious! What about your job?"

"I got a new one. Right here in Cayuga Springs."

I heard Patti Lynn clap behind me. I was so excited I nearly peed my pants right there in Mamie's kitchen.

"Porter, don't be foolish!" Mamie put her hand on her hip, like she did when she was getting extra bossy. "You're just upset by Starla's running off." She shot me the stink eye. "Don't be hasty throwing away a good job like that. You can't begin to make as much money here."

"No. But we'll make do."

"Where are we gonna live, Daddy?" I hoped it was closer to Patti Lynn.

"I rented our old place, upstairs at Mrs. White's. I'll be working off some of the rent. The house needs a lot of repair—which is why the apartment is sitting empty; leaky roof."

"I don't mind a leaky roof," I said, afraid Mamie would convince him it was too bad to move into. "We can put a bucket under it."

But Mamie wasn't worried about Mrs. White's roof, she was worried about her own. "But I can't keep this house on what I make doing the books for Adler's Drug Store. I sacrificed a good job to stay home with—"

"That's my other good news." Daddy looked like the cat that got the cream, as Mamie said; which meant mighty pleased with hisself. "I ran into Mr. Brinker at the gas station today. He's in a tight spot at the real estate office. His receptionist quit last week with no notice. He was happy to know you'll be available right away. You can even keep the side job with Adler's with no problem. See, everything's working out great." Daddy was smiling, but it wasn't his Good Time Charlie smile; it was kind of an I-dare-you smile. I'd never seen him use it on Mamie.

"So she just runs off and end's up getting what she wants? Letting her work you like this is wrong, Porter. It just encourages more bad behavior."

I kinda gagged, ready to jump in and defend myself, but Daddy gave me the look and said, "I'm the one who'll have to deal with it though, not you. I thought you'd be relieved."

"I'm only thinking of what's best for Starla. With you working all day, she'll run wild."

It took some teeth grittin' after that one, but I stayed quiet. I didn't want to sass and make Mamie right.

"Mrs. White said she'll be happy to keep tabs on her after school until I get home."

"Well, haven't you been busy." Mamie put on her squinty eyes. "A person would think you'd at least have discussed this with me first. If you want to get a job back here, fine, but there's plenty of room in this house for all three of us."

I shook my head, but it was more like a shiver, so Mamie didn't notice, and made my eyes beg, Please no.

Daddy folded the paper and stood up. He put his hands on Mamie's shoulders and kissed her on the forehead. "I've already asked too much of you, Mother. I'm giving you your life back."

Daddy left the kitchen by the back door. Mamie looked like she didn't want her life back all that much. She grabbed her purse, spun around, and went through the living-room door When her bedroom door slammed, my smile popped out and I danced around just a little.

Eula was smiling, too. "There now, it as it should be."

That's when my happy flew out the kitchen window. If me and Daddy was gonna live at Mrs. White's, where there was only two bedrooms, where was Eula gonna go? All alone out there in that house in the country where all she'd remember was killin' Wallace with a skillet? She didn't even have her truck to get to town no more.

I ran out the back door to catch up with Daddy.

But he didn't have an answer for me. He reminded me we had to take things one step at a time. I was beginning to hate those words. He put his arm around me and give me a squeeze. "Things have worked out so far, right?"

I nodded.

"Well, then we have to believe it'll continue just the same. Eula can come stay with us until the sheriff says she's free to go."

"Go? Where? What if she doesn't want to go?"

He raised his eyebrows. "What if she does? We can't keep her here just because we don't want her to leave. Shouldn't she be the one to make her own plans?"

I didn't like hearing that, or the way he said it. Like I was being selfish. I thought about how happy Miss Cyrena was living with all her own people. How Eula got involved with the ladies at Mt. Zion. But I was Eula's people—all her people now that James was gone. I went back inside, hoping it took the sheriff a long time to make up his mind to let Eula go. Maybe she'd get so used to living with us she wouldn't want to leave.

32

The next afternoon I found out why Patti Lynn had to say overnight at my house—and it wasn't from Patti Lynn. Her parents must have made some big threats to keep her from calling, 'cause she always told me everything, even when the sheriff brought her brother Gary home after getting caught drag racing—and Gary didn't even have his license yet.

Mamie come home from her hair appointment real excited. She started talking even before her foot was in the back door. She said nobody was supposed to know, but it was all over town. Right then Daddy tried to stop her, but she was so worked up, she kept talking right over him. She said Mrs. LeCount was at the hairdresser, and that Bess had told Ernestine, and Ernestine had told Mrs. LeCount, that Gracie had told the sheriff that Patti Lynn's sister was baby James's momma! Mamie didn't call him baby James though, just "that baby," like she'd never met him.

"That girl is so chunky, who could have been able to tell?" Mamie said.

"But Cathy ain't married!" I said. "How'd she get a baby?"

"Thanks a lot, Mother."

Mamie waved her arms with her palms up, like she was laying something out in front of Daddy. "You want to do it all by yourself. Go right ahead."

Daddy took me outside on the back steps and he told me how Cathy could get a baby without a husband. He just kept talkin' and talkin'; all I wanted to do was get up and run to my fort. It was horrible. Awful. Impossible.

Finally, I reached over and put my hand over his mouth. "Okay. Okay. Okay."

He got quiet for a second and I thought it was over. I kept staring at the grass, hoping he'd get up and go back inside. Then he asked, "Do you have any questions?"

The whole thing was so terrible, I didn't even want to think about it. All I knew was that I was never getting any babies. I was just ready to make a run for my fort when another thought come to me. James belonged to Patti Lynn's family. Me and Eula was gonna get to see him all of the time—and Eula would stay for sure now.

I said it to Daddy, but I still couldn't look at him; might never be able to again.

"Starla, this is the Todds' private family business," he said. "We're not gonna talk about it with anyone. You understand?"

"But everybody knows already."

"Maybe, but that doesn't mean we're going to add to the gossip."

"But with James there," I said, "what am I supposed to do, pretend he's invisible?"

"Honey, James isn't going be there. The Todds are putting him up for adoption."

I did jump up then . . . and looked at Daddy. "No! They can't just throw him away again."

"Starla—"

"To who?"

"We won't know. That's always kept secret."

"But James is their family! He's a good baby. He tries real hard not to cry—"

Daddy grabbed my hands. "It'll be better for him. Cathy is too young to be a mother. She has to finish school. He'll be happy in his new family. And since he never knew his real momma, he won't miss her at all."

"Maybe his daddy wants him."

Daddy looked sad and shook his head.

"You knew last night! You knew and didn't tell me."

"Mrs. Todd was upset. She said more than she meant to, then asked me to keep it to myself. I had to respect that."

I stomped my foot. "It ain't right! James is special. We need to tell them. They'll change their minds. They just need to get to know him better . . . they . . . they . . ." All the sudden I was blubberin'. It happened so fast, I couldn't stop it.

Daddy scooped me up and pulled me onto his lap. I hid my face on his shoulder and, for the first time I could remember, cried without even trying to stop.

The Todds weren't just taking James away, they were taking Eula's reason to stay, too.

I spent the rest of the day in my fort. My secret Howdy Doody lunch box was right there. I hadn't opened it since July 3, almost three weeks, the longest time ever. But for the first time I didn't even want to. The things inside had been ruined in Nashville. So I just laid there, only moving when I needed to swat bugs. Lots of thoughts were marching around in my head, their plodding feet pounding against my skull.

I wish I knew where James was. I wanted to say a better good-bye to him and remind him that he's a good baby and that Eula and I woulda kept him if the law would let us. It was important for him to know that.

Then I got to thinking about what Daddy had said—not about you-know-what, but about Cathy being too young to have a baby, her needing to finish school and whatnot. I'd looked at Daddy's senior yearbook a lot while he was gone working. I liked seeing him in the football-team picture, the basketball-team picture, the baseball-team picture, and the track-team picture. Momma wasn't in the yearbook. Which should have struck me as peculiar before now, I guess. That yearbook was from 1954. I was born in September 1953. Course I knew Momma and Daddy got married when they was still in high school. But it had never all come together in my head until right then—after Daddy had gone on and on about people lovin' each other and sometimes they get a baby before they was married, and then they get married real fast before the baby is born. But sometimes they're not ready to be parents and they don't . . . like Cathy.

How could I have been so dumb?

Ugh. I was just like baby James.

Was Daddy sorry he didn't send me to get adopted? I sure bet Lulu was.

I spent some time trying to imagine living with a different momma and daddy, maybe even having brothers and sisters, in a different house, maybe a different town . . . with different friends. It come to me then, as bad as Mamie was, I didn't want any other daddy or best friend. I didn't want to go to a school where Mrs. Jacobi couldn't be my teacher.

If James could pick, would he want to stay a Todd no matter what?

Mrs. Todd was always so fun and nice, but what if she would be as hateful to him for ruining Cathy's life as Mamie was to me?

The whole thing made my head hurt worse.

Finally I heard Daddy calling my name. I stuck my head out between the leaves. He was on the front sidewalk.

"There you are," he said. "What are you doing in there?"

"Nothin'."

"Well, come on. It's time to go to the apartment. I've got Don's truck. Your bed and everything from your room is in it and ready to go. You can fix things however you want when you get there."

"What about Eula?"

"She's already there. Said she'd have sandwiches ready when we got back."

I couldn't really believe we was moving out of Mamie's house. I'd been wishin' for it for so long—not for exactly how it was happening for sure, but it was still a dream come true. It was gonna be me and Daddy and Eula from now on. I might miss my fort some. But I reckon I could ride my bike here and sneak in it without Mamie knowing.

"What about my bike?"

"In the truck."

"Mamie still mad?" I asked.

"She'll get over it."

Well, that just told me Daddy didn't know Mamie very good at all.

"Come on!" He sounded excited. He was smiling his real smile, too.

I started to leave my fort, but stopped and looked back at the Howdy Doody lunch box. Living with Daddy, I could take it and he'd never snoop inside. I stared at it for a minute, then I crawled on out and left it right where it was.

After we'd pulled away from Mamie's house, I asked Daddy, "You sorry you didn't get me adopted?"

He looked real surprised. "Why would you even ask that?"

I told him about my figuring out things while I'd been in my fort.

He pulled over to the curb. "Look at me, Starla."

I didn't much want to do it; what if he started talking 'bout that again? What if he started talking about Lulu? But I wasn't a baby. I had to have grown-up conversationing whether I liked it or not. I gritted my teeth and looked him right in the eye.

"Some of the best things in life come when you're not planning on them. It's important to see them for the gift they are."

That made me think of Eula and warmed up the cold spot in my stomach some.

Daddy went on, "I nearly died when I thought we might not find you. You're the best thing that's ever happened to me." He swallowed kinda rough. "I'm sorry if I ever made you feel otherwise. I just . . . I thought you'd be better living with Mamie because you're a girl and I wasn't sure I knew how to raise you right." He stopped and looked out the windshield for a second. "And maybe I wasn't as grown-up as I should have been. But I am now. It's you and me, kid, from here on." He reached out and touched my black hair. "You're my girl. I'd be lost without you."

I turned in my seat and looked out the windshield. My ears were hot, but not from being mad. "That's what I thought."

(Thank you, baby Jesus.)

That night me and Eula and Daddy sat on the living-room floor and ate bologna—and-cheese sandwiches on Wonder bread. They was the most delicious I'd ever had. I liked mine with mustard; Daddy had remembered and not just bought mayonnaise like Mamie always did.

Since our apartment was upstairs, it was real hot. But Mrs. White gave Daddy a big fan and it was blowing real good, so I wasn't sweatin' at all. I wouldn't have minded if I'd been sweatin' like a hog, as long as me and Daddy and Eula was in one place. As we sat there and I looked at Daddy talking to Eula, something peculiar come over me. I got the same feeling as when I'd been eating dinner with Patti Lynn's family, where everybody was having a nice time; a feeling of things being shiny and bright and just like they was supposed to be.

I bet it wasn't that way at Patti Lynn's tonight. I wished I could call her, but we didn't have a phone. Mrs. White had said we could use hers anytime, but truth be told, I didn't want to leave this apartment. Even if it was just to go downstairs. Even if it was to call Patti Lynn.

Daddy started his new job the next day . . . doing what he called being a grease monkey. I thought that was the funniest job I'd ever heard of until he explained it just meant he worked on cars down at the Esso station. Me and Eula spent the morning getting my room set up. We'd just finished when there was a thump-thump-thump on the floor.

We looked at each other.

Three thumps came again.

"We'd best go check on Mrs. White," Eula said, hurrying for the door that opened to a stairway built on the outside of the house.

I followed along. Mrs. White was real old, older'n Mamie. Her hair was gray with just a few black hairs left in it. She wore old-lady, tie-up shoes and a bib apron over her dress all the time. Daddy said one of the reasons she made the upstairs into an apartment was because she had bad knees and the stairs were troublesome to her.

Mrs. White was waiting for us at her back door. She had a broom in her hand and invited us into the kitchen. "Sorry to use this"—she lifted the broom—"but I just can't do those stairs, and it was more dignified than standing out in the yard yelling up at your window."

"We just happy you all right, ma'am," Eula said, smiling.

I felt real proud of her. A few weeks ago, she wouldn't'a said boo to a white woman unless she was forced.

Mrs. White set the broom down. "Well, I know Porter doesn't have much for setting up housekeeping. And I certainly have more than I need down here." She pointed to two boxes on the kitchen table. "I thought y'all might be able to use these."

I got closer and looked inside the boxes. One had some pans, some silverware, and some towels. The other had the neatest dishes I'd ever seen; the plates and bowls was all different colors, orangey red, yellow, green, what Mamie would call "cream," and dark blue. Mrs. White called them Fiesta dishes. Funny name. There was some glasses in there, too—but they was regular clear glasses like everybody had.

All the sudden I wished Daddy had brought my cowboy bowl from Mamie's.

"I'm sure Mr. Porter be happy to have 'em," Eula said, as she picked up the box with the dishes. "Thank you, ma'am."

"Please tell your daddy if there's anything else he needs, just ask," Mrs. White said.

I picked up the other box. "Thank you, Mrs. White."

She went and held the back-door screen open for us. "And, Starla, you're welcome down here anytime you want to watch television or use the telephone."

I'd been so excited about me and Daddy getting our place that I'd forgot we didn't have a TV. "Thank you, ma'am." I was some relieved not to have to miss my shows.

"It's just so nice to have other people in the house again. Since I stopped teaching piano, it's been too quiet."

I remembered the sound of her students and their music that skittered from fast to slow and back again, the up and down notes that sometimes sounded wrong. I reckoned I wouldn't miss hearing them, but the magic that come up when Mrs. White played was different. "Do you still play, Mrs. White?"

She laughed a little. "Not as well as I used to, but I'll keep at it as long as I can drag myself to the piano bench."

"Good," I said, following Eula around the corner of the house to our stairway.

After me and Eula got things put away, we went out to sit on the stairway. It was in the shade and the breeze was nice. I'd been thinking about Patti Lynn all morning. I got to worryin' maybe she needed to talk to me, with baby James and Cathy and whatnot going on. I wasn't sure she knew which house was Mrs. White's.

"I think I'll ride over to Patti Lynn's," I said, getting on my feet. "I won't leave you here by yourself long, I promise."

"You think that a good idea? Things bound to be difficult over there right now."

"But what if she needs me? She doesn't know where to find me . . . and I bet Mamie wouldn't tell her if she called to find out."

"I see." Eula sat there for a minute. "Maybe I oughta come too. I wait outside, course."

"It'll take too long to walk. And don't worry, I ain't breakin' any rules, I ride to Patti Lynn's all the time." I went down and got my bike from where Daddy had parked it underneath the stairs.

It felt good to ride again, my legs pumping and the wind in my hair. I took the long way to Patti Lynn's.

Turned out, I was gone even less time than I'd planned. Eula was still sitting outside when I got back. I put my bike back under the stairs, went up, and sat beside her. Then I parked my elbows on my knees and sat my chin on my fists.

"That bad, was it?" she asked, real soft.

"How come nobody is like they're supposed to be anymore?"

"Your friend havin' trouble?"

"She's okay, I guess. But her momma was grouchy and had the house all closed up and the curtains closed. She wouldn't even let me inside. Patti Lynn had to talk to me in the backyard. Then Mrs. Todd called her back inside after just a minute—and she sounded almost as mean as Mamie." I sighed. "They sent Cathy away. Not to the same place as baby James, though. She ain't gettin' adopted. She's livin' with some relation in Ohio." I looked at Eula and told her the worst part. "They said she can't never come home again. Patti Lynn cried when she told me—and she don't even like Cathy. It was terrible sad."

We sat there for a minute, Eula rubbing my back.

"Why'd they send her away?" I asked. "Everybody already knows what happened."

"They hurtin'. I'm sure they's doin' what they think best for Cathy."

I looked up at her. "Like when Charles give your baby away? You think he was doin' what he thought best for you?"

Eula looked at me for a long time. "Charles always mean to the core, so it hard to tell. But your friend's family ain't like that. So I'd say they got good intentions."

While I was sitting there thinking about the storm that was tossin' me and Patti Lynn's lives in different directions, I got a big knot in my throat. Somehow Eula musta known, 'cause she pulled me closer and leaned down to look in my face.

"What's goin' on in there?" She tapped my heart, not my head. And I reckoned that was the true source of my misery, not what I was thinking but what I was feeling.

"If I hadn't run off that day, nobody'd even know about baby James. Patti Lynn's family wouldn't be ruined. Cathy could have stayed home. You wouldn't'a had to kill Wallace—I know you said that ain't true, but it is."

"Child, the good Lord got plans for all of us that we don't know—and he always got his reasons. He want us to learn and rejoice in the good that come from his design."

"You said a person's gotta be accountable for what she's done. If it's God's plan, why should anybody ever get punished for what they do?"

"God's plan ain't a free pass. Uh-uh. He give us moments to make choices, and we make them. We accountable for those choices. God's job ain't to make our lives easier, it's to make us better souls by the lessons he give us. I tell you now, I wouldn't change one choice I made since I met you. No matter what."

"You're just sayin' that to make me feel better. No good come from what I done."

"That ain't true at all." She wiped a tear off the end of my nose. "They's plenty of good."

I shook my head.

"Well, you think on it for a spell. It'll come clear." She got up and left me on the step.

Piano music started to come out of Mrs. White's windows. It didn't just touch my ears, it seeped inside and wrapped itself around my heart. But things just wouldn't come clear.

I was still sitting there when Daddy come home from work.

33

Four more days went by without hearing from the sheriff. I started to believe maybe he'd forgot about Eula; started to believe she would just keep on sleeping in our living room on the cot Mrs. White had sent Daddy to fetch from her garage after his first day at work.

Sunday morning we dropped Eula and her Sunday hat off at the colored church in town. She didn't want him to drive her all the way out to the country church she used to attend. I hoped people at this church was as nice as the folks at Mt. Zion Baptist. If she liked the town church, maybe that'd be another good reason for her to stay.

Instead of my usual Sunday dress, I wore the dress Miss Cyrena got me from the charity box. Wearin' it made me feel less far away from Eula. As me and Daddy climbed the wide steps up to the big, heavy double doors at our chruch, I held his hand, even though it was babyish. The choir was already singing when we went in. I was glad we was late. I figured Daddy would sit in the last pew so we wasn't "such a spectacle," as Mamie called it when we was late, by walking halfway down the aisle to our regular pew.

But he kept right on going toward Mamie and her pink hat. She looked some surprised when Daddy tapped her on the shoulder to slide over. Since I was in church and supposed to be figuring out the lessons God was teachin' me, I reckoned it'd be bad to make a stink, so I just made sure I was sitting on the other side of Daddy.

I heard Mamie whisper, "What on earth is Starla wearing?"

"She looks fine—"

The preacher got up and started talking, so that was the end of that. I decided I was gonna wear this dress every Sunday.

I looked across the aisle and down toward the front. Patti Lynn's family pew was empty. Disappointment got on me pretty heavy. I hadn't seen her since the day I rode my bike to her house. Whenever I called from Mrs. White's telephone, nobody answered. Whenever I knocked on the door, nobody come to open it. I thought sure they'd be at church; they never missed. Mrs. Todd said her boys was always in so much mischief, they couldn't afford to miss a Sunday—but she'd been smiling when she'd said it.

I wondered if Mrs. Todd had smiled all week, or if she was ruined forever.

My mind kept flitterin' around, thinking about Patti Lynn and not concentrating on figuring out what God was teachin' me.

Finally church was over. While the organ was still playing, I heard Mamie say to Daddy, "I'm surprised to see you here."

Daddy said, just like nothing had happened, "It's Sunday."

I got up then. I wanted to get away as fast as I could, but folks was yakking in the aisle, blocking my way. I squeezed past Mrs. Frieberger, but I was still close enough to hear Mamie say, "Well"—she sounded like her regular snippy self; she didn't usually when talking to anybody but me—"I don't suppose you want to come home for dinner?"

I wanted to turn around and holler, Home is Mrs.White's house now. But I didn't dare sass across the church crowd.

I heard Daddy say, "Thanks, Mother, but Eula already put a chicken" The crowd got inching too far away for me to hear.

I stood outside the church, nervousness kickin' in my belly. At home, we was still sitting on the floor to eat, so I hoped that'd keep Daddy from inviting Mamie to eat at our house. I picked holly berries—they wouldn't be red for a while yet—off the bushes, threw them on the ground, and rolled them under my shoe until the skin rubbed off and left little, wedge-shaped seeds behind. Mamie hated it when I did that.

Daddy had been telling me things was gonna be different with Mamie now that she didn't have the responsibility of making me a good person. But I wasn't feeling in the mood to find out. My tongue was just now healin' up.

When Daddy come out, he was alone. (Thank you, baby Jesus.)

At first I thought Daddy couldn't find me. Then I saw he was looking at Sheriff Reese. He wasn't wearing his uniform, but his brown Sunday suit.

You don't go pokin' a hornets' nest. Daddy had said it plenty of times when he saw me headed for trouble. But it looked like that's just what he meant to do hisself.

I tried to get to him before he got to the sheriff, but Mrs. Jacobi stopped me, telling me how happy she was that I'd got back home safe and reminding me that trouble can't be outrun. Didn't I know that now! By the time I got to Daddy, he was shaking hands with Sheriff Reese.

Daddy asked him where things stood with Eula and the law.

I almost kicked him in the shin.

The sheriff rubbed his jaw, like he was thinking. "Didn't I get back to you on that?"

"No, sir. I hope that means things are going in Eula Littleton's favor."

Me, too. I forgot to breathe until I started to get dizzy.

"Well, we been pretty busy. But I can't see pressin' charges." He said it like Eula wasn't really worth even thinking much about, one way or the other. I took a step backward to keep myself from kickin' my own hornets' nest. I had to keep thinking, Eula's free! Then my heart got icy. Maybe not. What about baby James? I shook my head to get the clutter out of it. The sheriff was still talking. "Coroner said the man's skull was cracked all right, so her story stands. I did some checkin' around; seems that woman did the county a favor. That husband of hers couldn't keep a job 'cause he kept pickin' a fight with his betters. As far as I'm concerned, one less Negro to worry about. As for that baby . . . I won't drag a good family through the courts just to make a point to some colored woman."

I took another step backward. Don't say nothin'. Eula's free. That's all that matters.

"That's good news, sir." Daddy shook the sheriff's hand again. We walked away together.

Finally I couldn't hold it no more. "He acted like Eula wasn't worth nothin'. Why didn't you say something!"

Daddy stopped and looked down at me. "What would you have me do, Starla, argue with the man to get him to arrest her?"

"Well, no . . . but . . ."

"You and I are going to thank our lucky stars that in the state of Mississippi the life of a black man weighs less than that of a white one, that's what we'll do. Because that means Eula is safe. That's what counts right now."

I got another thought and it made my stomach turn over. "What if she packs up her grip and leaves now?"

Daddy put his hands on my shoulders. "You were just mad at me because I didn't make the sheriff see she was a person who meant something. And you're right, Eula deserves more respect. I'm glad you're learning something it took me years of working with men from all over the country to begin to understand. If Eula decides to leave, it's something we have to accept." He kissed the top of my head, then started walking again.

I followed along, feeling like the wind was blowin' two different directions in my soul.

It took a while for me to figure out the good that come from my running away and it come a little bit at a time, like learnin' arithmetic The first little bit of figuring out come when we told Eula she was free from the law, that she could leave Cayuga Springs and go wherever she wanted. Daddy didn't let a heartbeat slide by before he said she was welcome to stay with us as long as she could stand sleeping on that cot.

"Or you can have my room if you want a real bed," I said. "I don't mind sleepin' on the cot." I'd already lost one momma twice. If I lost Eula, I wasn't sure I could stand it. I wasn't even sure how I'd made it my whole life without her.

Daddy looked at me in a way that made me feel selfish. "Starla, Eula needs to be able to make a choice without you pushing her. She's already done so much for us."

I thought about how I thought I could boss Wallace just 'cause he was colored. I'm not sure I'd think that now. Eula was a person. She should be able to do whatever she wanted . . . and I really didn't feel like I had any right to be bossy about it. But I didn't want her to go.

I held my breath and waited. It was hard to be still. Then Eula gave a smile as bright as the sun. "Where you think I'm gonna go?" She looked at me. "We family; they ain't all about blood, you know. Families is people lookin' out after each other, not hidin' behind secrets." She touched the top of my head. "I'd say that you and me right down to the bone."

That had made me think of Cathy's secret and how it had wrecked Patti Lynn's family—and almost wrecked Eula's life forever, too. And then I thought about how me and Eula finding out each other's secrets had made us both better, and how we both had our own way of whistling past the graveyard. I wondered if Patti Lynn had one, too. I noticed that me and Eula didn't need ours nearly as much anymore and hoped Patti Lynn wouldn't either pretty soon.

Mrs. Todd had finally stopped hiding and was able to laugh again, but things in her house wasn't the same. Nobody was allowed to even say Cathy's name anymore; it was like she'd never been alive. And baby James, well, me and Eula talked about him a lot, made up stories of his new family and what he was doing, how much he was growing, the things he'd do as he growed up. We did that about her white baby, too, now that he wasn't a secret anymore. Course he was a boy now, so his stories was different. It made us both feel a lot better about not being able to be with them. Eula had finally decided to believe that Charles had done just what he'd said, give that baby to a family moving North.

I thought maybe talking about James and Cathy with Patti Lynn would make her less sad, but it just made her mad . . . real mad.

It took a while for me to stop trying, even though Eula said I should let Patti Lynn be if she didn't want to talk about it. Eula explained that sometimes it took time for the hurt to go away enough to be able to look at something so painful, and I needed to be there to help Patti Lynn when it did. Just like I'd helped Eula. That made me feel good, that I'd helped Eula with our talks. I think Eula was still too hurt to talk about Wallace, so we didn't.

It took a while for Patti Lynn to get over being mad about it though. But once school started up and we saw each other every day, we started getting back to our regular selves and was biking to each other's houses.

My hair started to turn red again. I looked like a sunburned zebra, so Daddy took me to a hairdresser. She got some of the black out and cut it short . . . almost boy-short. The lady called it a pixie cut and said it was gonna be real popular. Daddy said that was a good name for it. At first I didn't like it. But when I figured out how fast I could wash it and that it didn't get all knotted when I was riding my bike really fast, I got to thinking I might keep it that way.

Eula was having trouble finding steady work. Even though the sheriff had said she wasn't going to jail, the idea she'd done killed somebody hung on her like skunk spray. None of the ladies of Cayuga Springs would hire her to work inside their homes. Lucky they wasn't so worried that they thought she'd poison them—I think Mrs. White mighta had something to do with that. So Eula went back to making baked goods in our little oven, which, dinky as it was, was still way better'n that woodstove she used to use out at her place. I helped her sometimes, but we mostly bumped into each other in that tiny kitchen. Business was good enough that before long, she was looking to fold up her little cot and rent a room somewhere. Daddy had said she could use our kitchen for her baking as long as she wanted. I was glad, 'cause I'd still get to see her every day.

Then, even before Eula found an affordable room in the colored part of town, Mrs. White took a fall on her back steps and needed live-in help she couldn't afford. Now Eula was baking in Mrs. White's kitchen, helping her for room and board.

I wondered if that was part of God's plan. And if it was, was it Eula or Mrs. White who was supposed to learn a lesson from it? The more I looked at things like that, the more confused I got, so I decided to just concentrate on my own lessons.

One rainy Tuesday evening in October, after Eula had moved downstairs to take care of Mrs. White, there come a knock at our apartment door. I figured it was one of Daddy's friends since it was too dark and wet for Patti Lynn to be riding her bike over. I stayed on the floor where I was making a pot holder with the loom Mrs. White gave me. This one was red and white to match Mrs. White's kitchen wallpaper with the cherries on it. Seemed most polite to make my first one for her—even though Eula'd be the one using it.

When Daddy opened the door, I looked up. Mamie was standing there under a pink umbrella. Before Daddy could say boo, she handed him a brown bag. "I thought Starla might want these." Then she turned around to leave like she was in a big hurry.

Daddy called after her and asked her to come inside. I gritted my teeth. It'd been bad enough sitting at church in the same pew with her on Sundays; but since she didn't want to talk to me any more than I wanted to talk to her, we'd been managin' just fine. Still, I sure didn't want her inside me and Daddy's house.

Lucky she said she couldn't stay and went right on.

Daddy closed the door and handed me the rain-dotted bag. Inside was my plastic cereal bowl with the cowboy on the bottom and the checkers game. I wondered what made Mamie bring them over after all this time. I didn't think she'd been eating out of it or playing checkers all by herself. I put the bowl in the kitchen cabinet and asked Daddy if he wanted to play checkers. While we played, Daddy said now that Mamie had taken the first step in mendin' our fences, I was gonna have to get over it and start talking to her again.

I was still thinking on it.

The next evening, Mrs. White was feelin' poorly and Daddy had to work late. Me and Eula made bologna sandwiches and ate in front of the TV. I kinda liked it when it was just the two of us. Eula said Walter Cronkite doing the news made her feel like the world was more safe and in order, so that was what we were watching. I thought he needed to get rid of his mustache.

Walter Cronkite was talking about President Kennedy and the civil rights laws he was trying to get passed. Thanks to Miss Cyrena, I knew what he was talking about. It made me feel pretty grown-up.

The TV news started talking about a march in Wichita, Kansas, and others that was being planned. He reminded us of the big March on Washington that had happened in August, where 250,000 people marched peaceful-like and heard talks by Dr. Martin Luther King. Miss Cyrena had gone; she wrote us all about it. On the TV it had looked like there was nothin' but buildings and people packed like peanuts in a bag, not a speck of ground to be seen.

Walter Cronkite said there was still a long battle ahead for civil rights laws in the Congress. There'd been another sit-in at a lunch counter; this time in Warner Robins, Georgia. Some college students had got arrested, but there wasn't any fighting. They'd just come in, sit down where they wasn't supposed to, refused to leave, then got drug off to jail like they was rag dolls. That made me think of Wallace hauling me around like I wasn't a person at all. I bet them students felt a lot like that.

I looked at Eula, "You gonna go to a march? Fight for your civil rights?" Then I thought about how hard it'd been when we'd just tried to get to Nashville and felt sorry for asking.

Eula's eyes was glued on the TV, watching like she wanted to climb right inside and be with them.

"No, child, I ain't brave like them folks. 'Sides, I done all the fightin' I want to do in this lifetime."

"You are too brave!" I stopped for a second, not sure why I was all stirred up. "Maybe not in the marchin'-in-the-street way. But that's okay." It come clear to me then. Some of them college students had been white. "You don't have to fight anymore. I'm gonna do the fightin' for you."

She reached over and took my hand. "I do believe you will. Just not yet, child. Not quite yet. You need to get grown-up first."

"What if the fightin' gets all done before I'm old enough?" I really didn't want to miss my chance to fight for Eula.

Eula shook her head real slow. "Been fightin' for a hundred years, can't see it bein' over, even once the Congress signs a piece of paper killin' Jim Crow. There be plenty left to fight for."

I sat there and watched as another news story come on, but my mind was still on those people fighting for civil rights. I hoped they got what they wanted, but saved just a little bit of the fight for me.

Miss Cyrena was invited to Thanksgiving dinner. Even though our whole country was sad for our president getting shot, Mrs. White had said we still had to show thanks for our blessings and rejoice in being together.

I was glad for something to do other than be sad and watch the funeral on television and see how miserable our dead president's kids were.

Miss Cyrena got to Mrs. White's house at one o'clock. Me and Eula was happy as bees in honey to see her. Daddy shook her hand and thanked her for helping me and Eula. When she apologized for not easin' his worry while I was missing, Daddy was real nice and said he understood and that I could be a tough nut to crack. I reckoned he meant it was hard to get me to tell when I didn't want to. Miss Cyrena laughed. I think maybe her and Daddy might be friends, even though they was different kinds of bears.

Miss Cyrena had brung Eula's picture of grown-up Jesus; it had been too big to fit in Eula's grip when we'd had to run. Eula was real happy to have it back and went right away to hang it over her bed in the little room she had in Mrs. White's downstairs.

After Miss Cyrena handed over grown-up Jesus, she got in her purse and pulled out a little brown bag. She handed it over to me with a smile. "Your friend sent this to you."

"My friend?"

"The young man from the carnival. He came to my school a few days after you left and wanted me to give it to you."

"How'd he know you taught at the school?" I asked, taking the bag. It wasn't much bigger than the ones that hold penny candy.

"Everybody in town knows I teach at that school."

I unfolded the top of the bag and peeked inside. Something red and fuzzy was in there. I reached down and pulled it out.

"A troll doll!" Patti Lynn had a whole collection of trolls; we made clothes for them. I'd been hoping to get one for Christmas.

Miss Cyrena said, "He said to tell you it wasn't the same as winning a teddy bear, but he thought you'd like it. He picked this one because it had red hair and reminded him of you."

Daddy looked at the funny little doll. "It does look a little like you!"

"Daddy!" I nudged him with my elbow.

"Y'all come on now. Dinner's ready," Eula called.

All of us, except Mrs. White, who still had trouble walking, helped Eula take the food to the dining-room table. There was a turkey, sweet-potato casserole and corn-bread dressing, giblet gravy and biscuits, and a pecan pie for dessert. I'd never seen so much food at once.

Mrs. White insisted all five of us, polar bears and regular bears together, eat in her dining room off her good china. I was so used to eating with Eula that I didn't think much about it, until I saw how nervous it made her to eat with white grown-ups. But Miss Cyrena seemed just fine with it.

Mrs. White asked Daddy to give the blessing. We all held hands and bowed our heads. He asked the good Lord to continue to bless us and those who couldn't be with us today. (I thought of baby James; Daddy might have been thinking of Mamie, who'd refused to come out of spite. I was pretty sure nobody was thinking of Lulu this year.) Daddy thanked God for his bounty and for his love. Then he asked that the Lord help ease the grief of our president's family, especially his children.

"In Jesus's name, amen."

"Amen," all of our voices said together.

As I sat there, looking from one face to another, I thought, This is my family. These are the people who look out for me. The people I look after.

Sometimes in the night, when my heart gets to hurtin' over Momma, I pull out the memory of Thanksgiving dinner and it makes me feel some better.

I think that was the last piece of the good I was supposed to learn from my running away. I wasn't never gonna run off again, no matter how bad things got. But I wasn't gonna be too scared to love the folks that took the time to love me back, and I sure wasn't gonna chase them that don't. And I was gonna spend the rest of my life asking questions and looking behind everything that happened, so I could find the gifts I got tucked inside me.

Acknowledgments

If not for watching my feisty mother, Margie Zinn-Lynch, and hearing the stories of her youth, and for growing up alongside my red-headed-through-and-through sister, Sally Zinn Knopp, I wouldn't have been able portray Starla (a girl far, far from my own personality) as I have. Unbeknownst to any of us, over the years you two helped create this character.

Thanks to my family for their support and patience. To Bill for living with me when my mind remained with Starla in 1963 instead of returning to real life for dinnertime conversations. To Allison for "liking lunch" and the shopping therapy. To Reid and Melissa who each helped talk through story issues.

I'm indebted to the people who encouraged me to follow my instincts and take the risk to write a book that was a huge departure from anything I've ever written. Thanks to my fantastic agent, Jennifer Schober for believing in this book and guiding it to its final home. A huge hug of appreciation to both Wendy Wax and Karen White for their keen insight, tireless cheerleading, hours of critiquing, and multiple telephone conversations, even as you were both dealing with your own deadlines. Thanks to IndyWITTS, writing group extraordinaire.

I had to call on the help of an old classmate for details concerning the Nashville music scene in 1963. Thanks Terry (TK) Kimbrell for sharing your intimate knowledge on the subject.

And thanks to my editor, Karen Kosztolnyik, and the team at Gallery for loving this book as much as I do and for helping make it strong enough to go out in the world and stand on its own two feet.